SACRAMENTO PUBLIC LIBRARY
828 "I" Street
Sacramento, CA 95814
12/19

#2

BATTLE STATION PRIME
SAVING
FORTRESS CITY

AN UNOFFICIAL GRAPHIC NOVEL
FOR MINECRAFTERS

D0055132

CARA J. STEVENS

ILLUSTRATED BY SAM NEEDHAM

SKY PONY PRESS
New York

This book is not authorized or sponsored by
Microsoft Corp., Mojang AB, Notch
Development AB or Scholastic Inc., or any other
person or entity owning or controlling rights in the
Minecraft name, trademark, or copyrights.

Copyright © 2019 by Hollan Publishing, Inc.

Minecraft® is a registered trademark of Notch Development AB.

The Minecraft game is copyright © Mojang AB.

This book is not authorized or sponsored by Microsoft Corp., Mojang AB, Notch Development AB or Scholastic Inc., or any other person or entity owning or controlling rights in the Minecraft name, trademark, or copyrights.

All rights reserved. No part of this book may be reproduced in any manner without the express written consent of the publisher, except in the case of brief excerpts in critical reviews or articles. All inquiries should be addressed to Sky Pony Press, 307 West 36th Street, 11th Floor, New York, NY 10018.

Sky Pony Press books may be purchased in bulk at special discounts for sales promotion, corporate gifts, fund-raising, or educational purposes. Special editions can also be created to specifications. For details, contact the Special Sales Department, Sky Pony Press, 307 West 36th Street, 11th Floor, New York, NY 10018 or info@ skyhorsepublishing.com.

Sky Pony® is a registered trademark of Skyhorse Publishing, Inc.®, a Delaware corporation.

Minecraft® is a registered trademark of Notch Development AB.
The Minecraft game is copyright © Mojang AB.

Visit our website at www.skyponypress.com.

10 9 8 7 6 5 4 3 2 1

Library of Congress Cataloging-in- Publication Data is available on file.

Cover design by Brian Peterson
Cover and interior art by Sam Needham

Print ISBN: 978-1-5107-4137-9
Ebook ISBN: 978-1-5107-4142-3

Printed in the United States of America

#2

BATTLE STATION PRIME
SAVING
FORTRESS CITY

MEET THE CHARACTERS

NAME: Pell

Problem-solver who wants everyone to get along.

NAME: Logan

Expert builder and programmer.

NAME: Maddy

Logan's genius younger sister.

NAME: Uncle Colin

Pell's uncle, who is part of the resistance.

NAME: Ned

A homesteader in a prison jumpsuit.

NAME: Zoe

Ace warrior and part-time griefer.

NAME: Brooklyn

Frenemy of the Fortress City kids.

NAME: Cloud

Secret potion-master who longs to return to the sea.

NAME: Mr James

The leader of Battle Station Prime.

INTRODUCTION

Fortress City was designed to be the perfect city, where everyone could live in peace without fear of being attacked by hostile mobs. In reality, it is a terrible place to live if you have no money or power. Pell, Logan, and Maddy were saved from that unfortunate life, and were brought to a rural outpost by Pell's Uncle Colin. They were recruited to become part of a rebel army sworn to make things right. When we last left our three young heroes, they were roughing it in the wild, doing farm chores, mining, enchanting, and battling hostile mobs. They had just defeated the evil Mr. Jones and his men, who were planning to blow up Fortress City from the inside. Little do they know that Mr. Jones had already planted the seed of Fortress City's destruction and it is up to them to save the city they had sworn to take down.

We resume our story at the outpost called Homestead, where Pell, Logan, and Maddy are finally getting used to their new peaceful life.

CHAPTER 1

HOMESTEAD
SWEET HOME

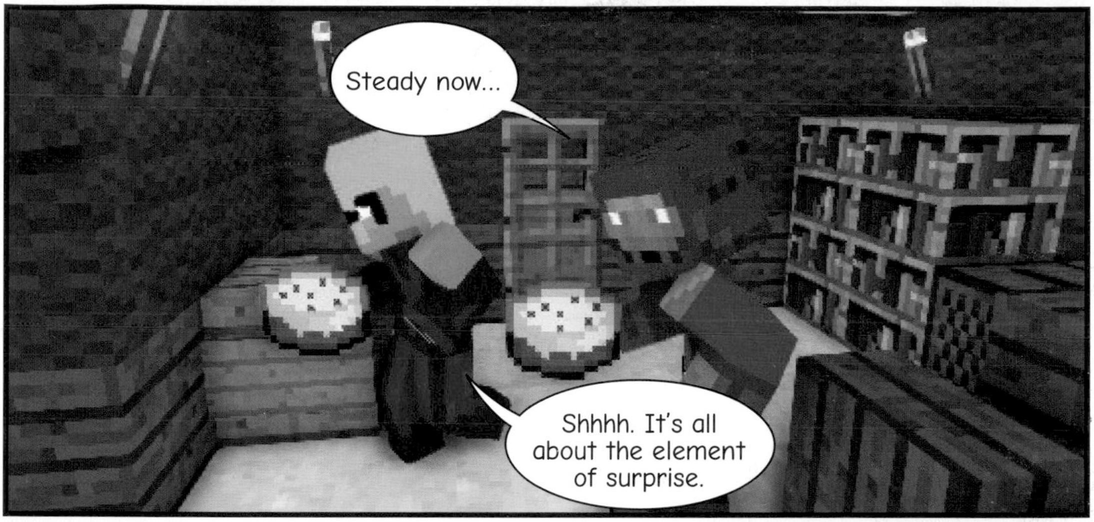

Steady now...
Shhhh. It's all about the element of surprise.

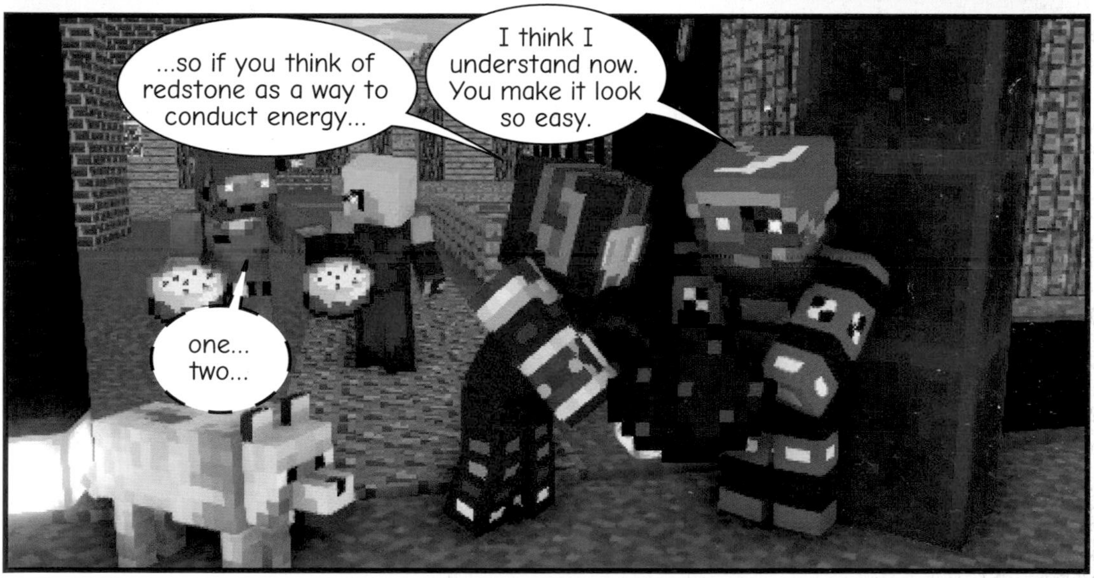

...so if you think of redstone as a way to conduct energy...
I think I understand now. You make it look so easy.
one... two...

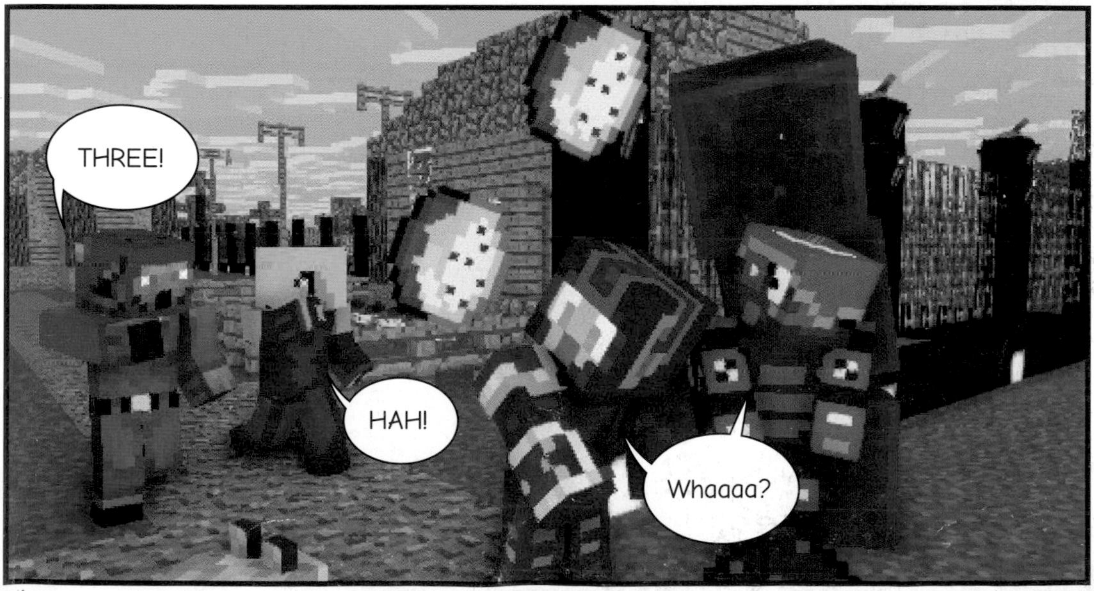

THREE!
HAH!
Whaaaa?

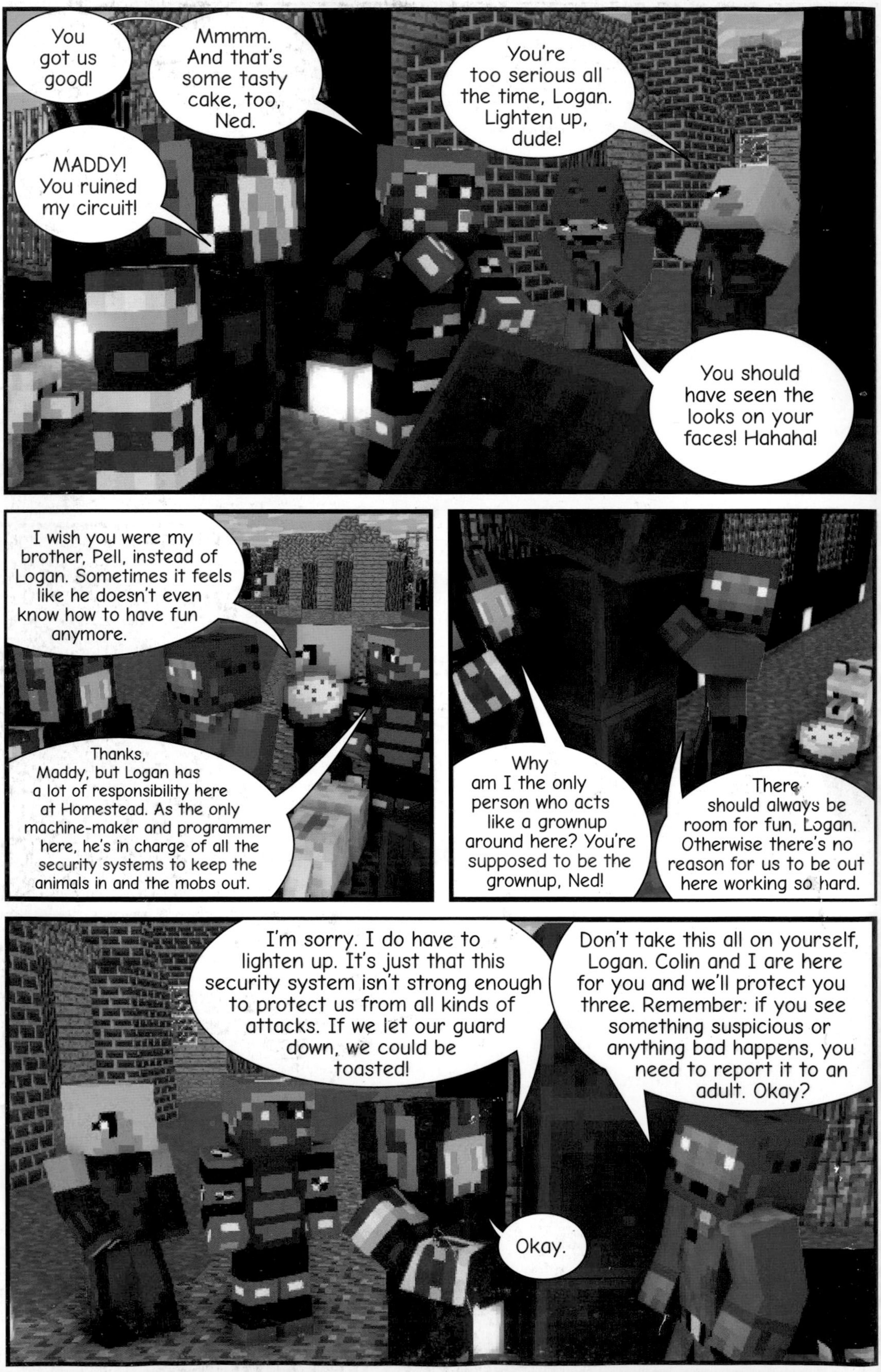

You got us good!
Mmmm. And that's some tasty cake, too, Ned.
MADDY! You ruined my circuit!
You're too serious all the time, Logan. Lighten up, dude!
You should have seen the looks on your faces! Hahaha!
I wish you were my brother, Pell, instead of Logan. Sometimes it feels like he doesn't even know how to have fun anymore.
Thanks, Maddy, but Logan has a lot of responsibility here at Homestead. As the only machine-maker and programmer here, he's in charge of all the security systems to keep the animals in and the mobs out.
Why am I the only person who acts like a grownup around here? You're supposed to be the grownup, Ned!
There should always be room for fun, Logan. Otherwise there's no reason for us to be out here working so hard.
I'm sorry. I do have to lighten up. It's just that this security system isn't strong enough to protect us from all kinds of attacks. If we let our guard down, we could be toasted!
Don't take this all on yourself, Logan. Colin and I are here for you and we'll protect you three. Remember: if you see something suspicious or anything bad happens, you need to report it to an adult. Okay?
Okay.

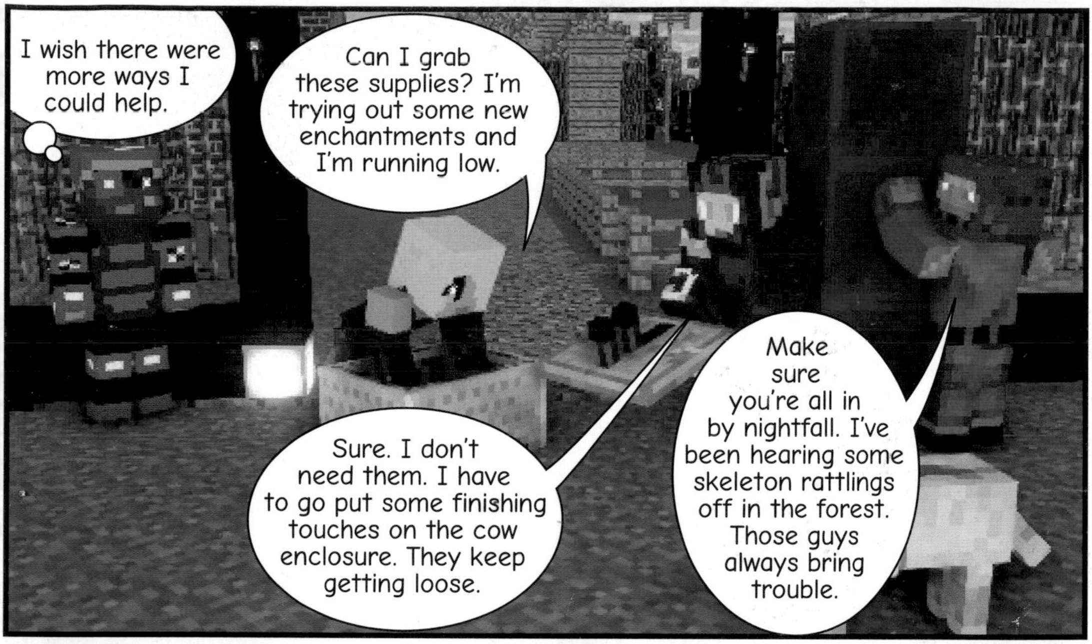
I wish there were more ways I could help.
Can I grab these supplies? I'm trying out some new enchantments and I'm running low.
Sure. I don't need them. I have to go put some finishing touches on the cow enclosure. They keep getting loose.
Make sure you're all in by nightfall. I've been hearing some skeleton rattlings off in the forest. Those guys always bring trouble.

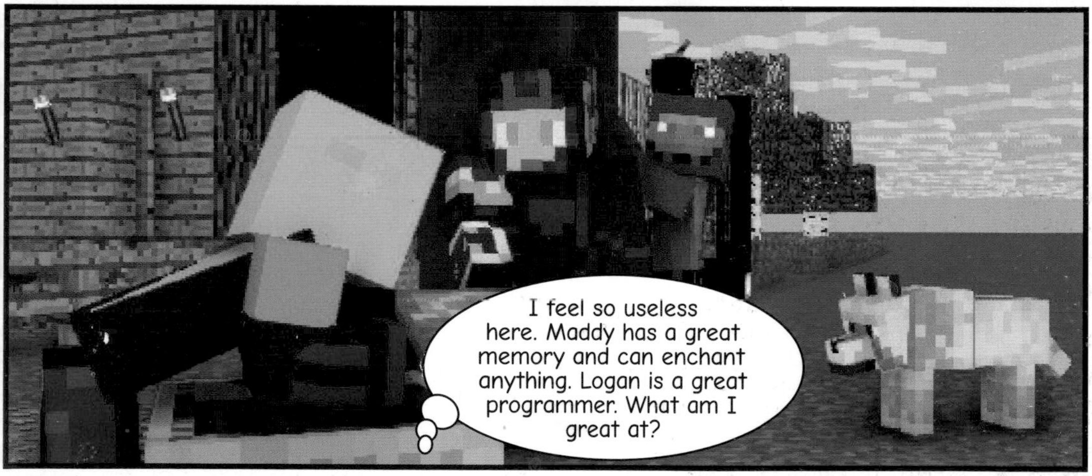
I feel so useless here. Maddy has a great memory and can enchant anything. Logan is a great programmer. What am I great at?

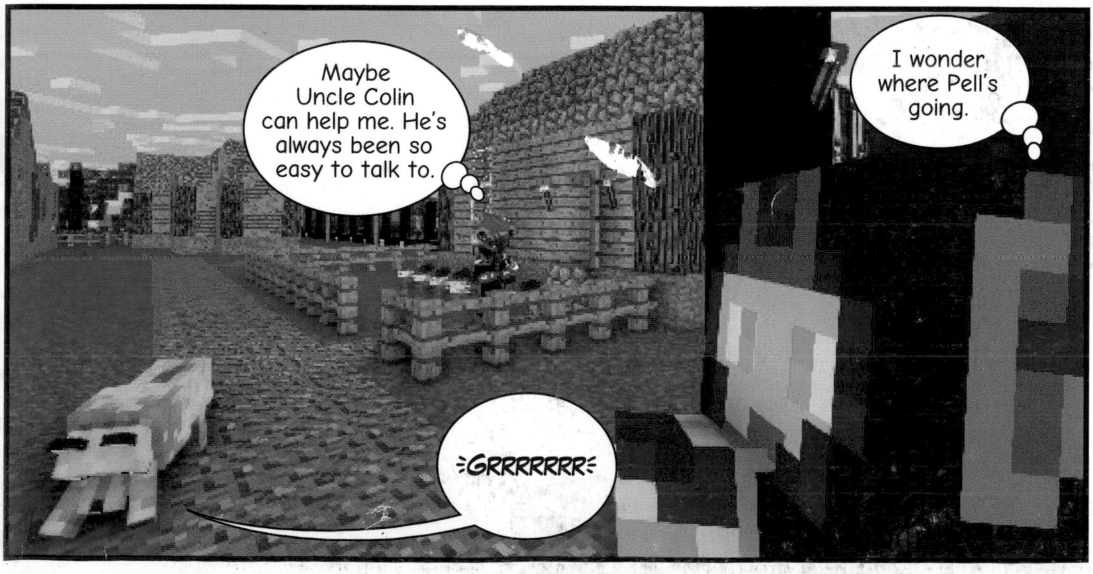
Maybe Uncle Colin can help me. He's always been so easy to talk to.
I wonder where Pell's going.
GRRRRRRR

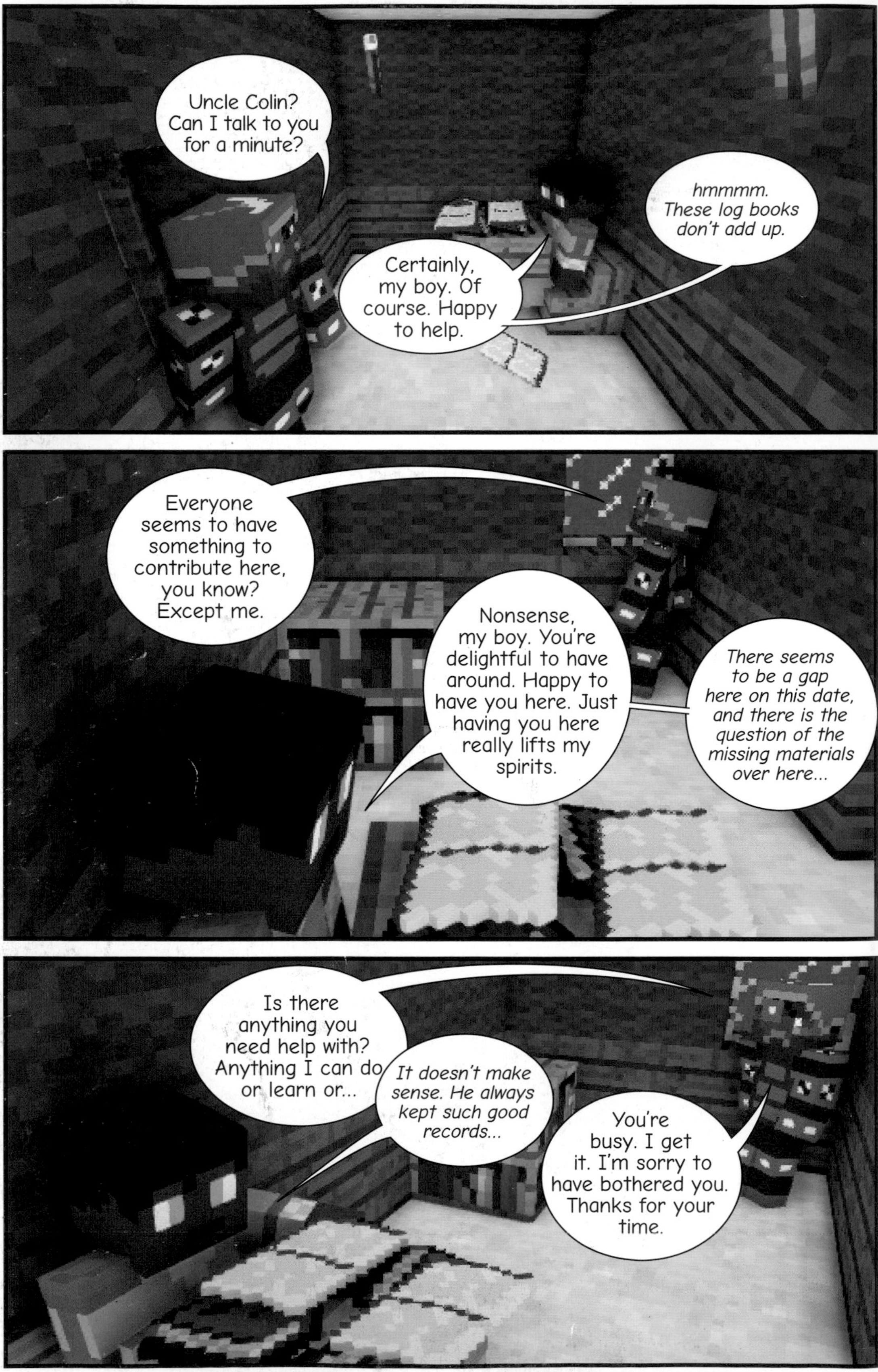
Uncle Colin? Can I talk to you for a minute?
hmmmm. These log books don't add up.
Certainly, my boy. Of course. Happy to help.
Everyone seems to have something to contribute here, you know? Except me.
Nonsense, my boy. You're delightful to have around. Happy to have you here. Just having you here really lifts my spirits.
There seems to be a gap here on this date, and there is the question of the missing materials over here...
Is there anything you need help with? Anything I can do or learn or...
It doesn't make sense. He always kept such good records...
You're busy. I get it. I'm sorry to have bothered you. Thanks for your time.

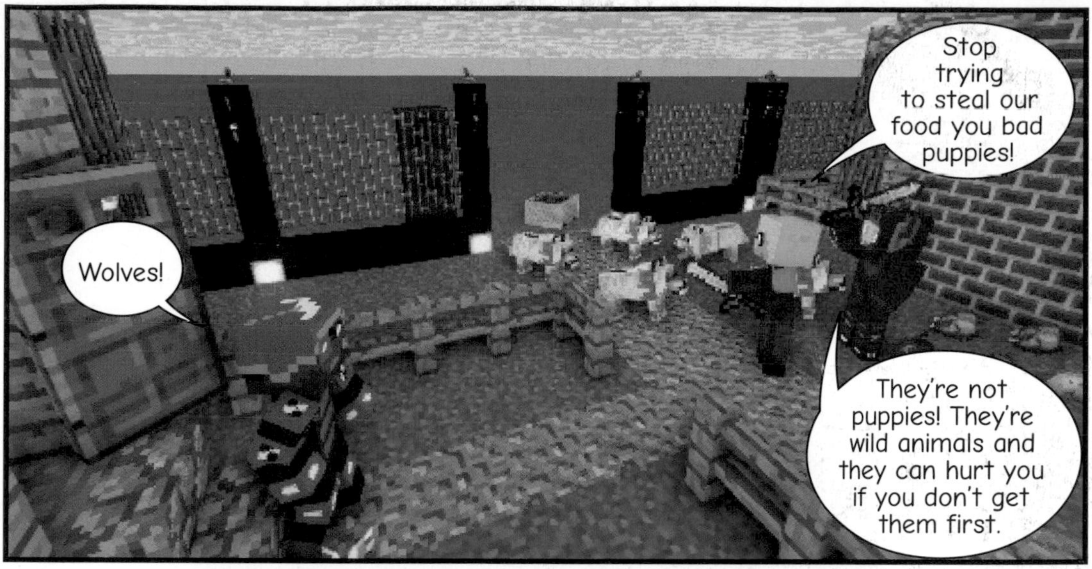
Wolves!
Stop trying to steal our food you bad puppies!
They're not puppies! They're wild animals and they can hurt you if you don't get them first.

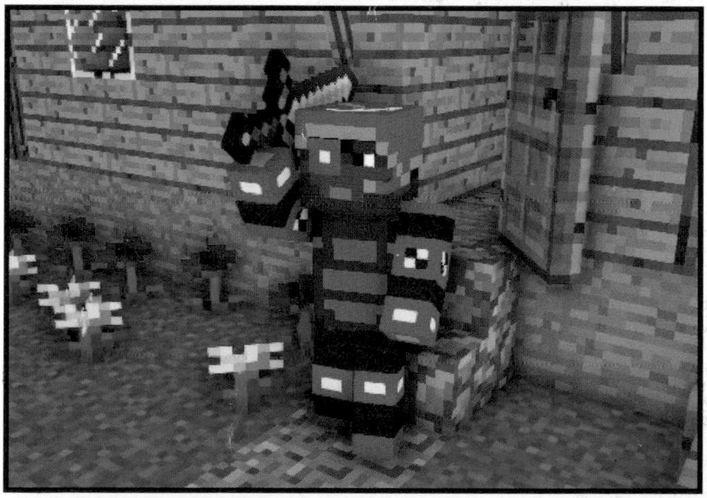

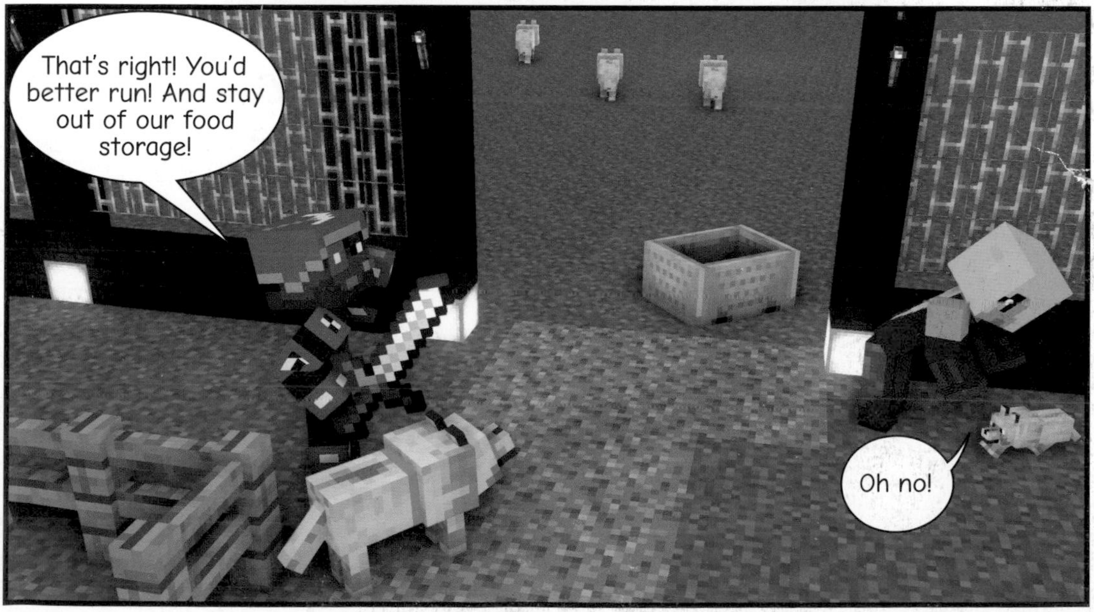
That's right! You'd better run! And stay out of our food storage!
Oh no!

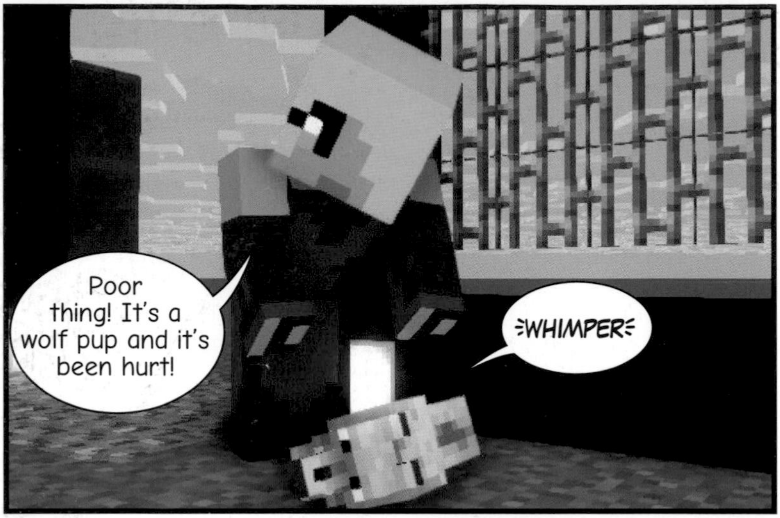
Poor thing! It's a wolf pup and it's been hurt!
WHIMPER

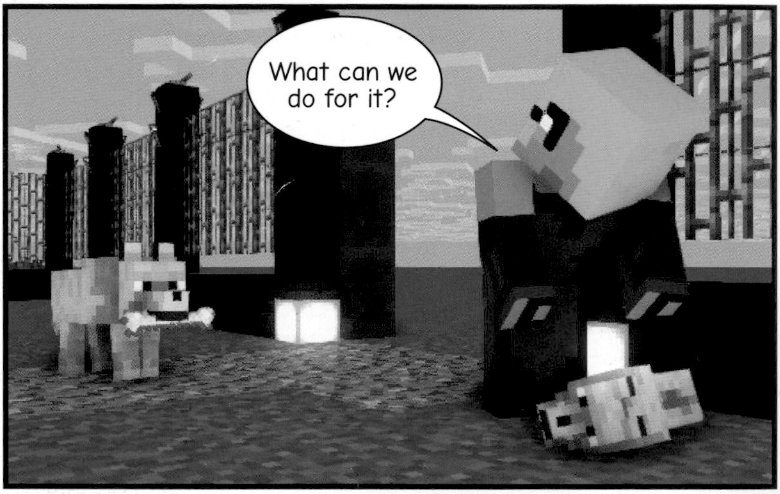
What can we do for it?

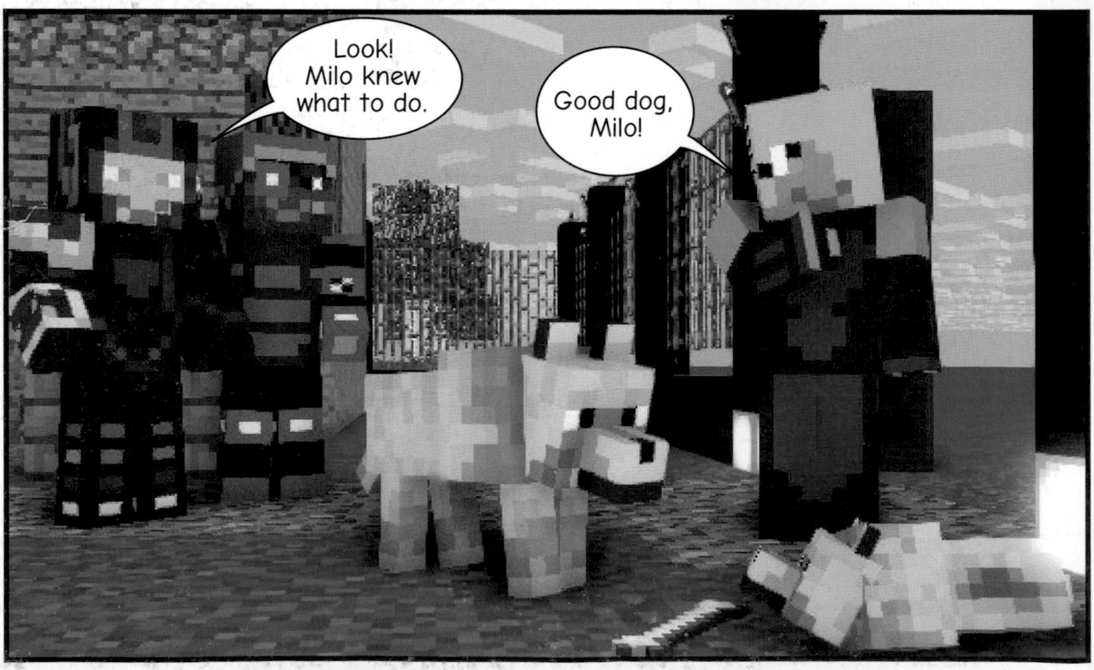
Look! Milo knew what to do.
Good dog, Milo!

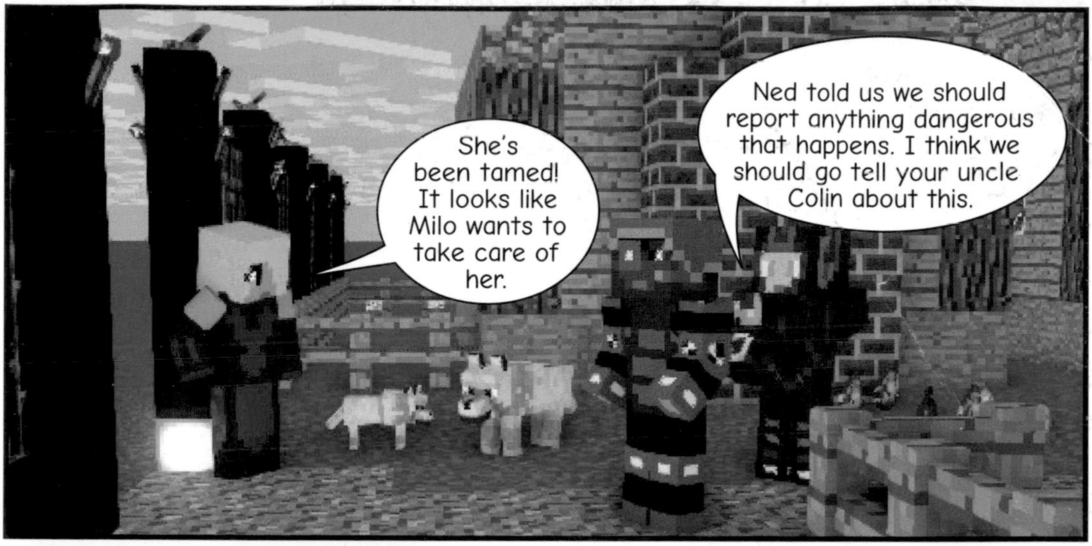
She's been tamed! It looks like Milo wants to take care of her.
Ned told us we should report anything dangerous that happens. I think we should go tell your uncle Colin about this.

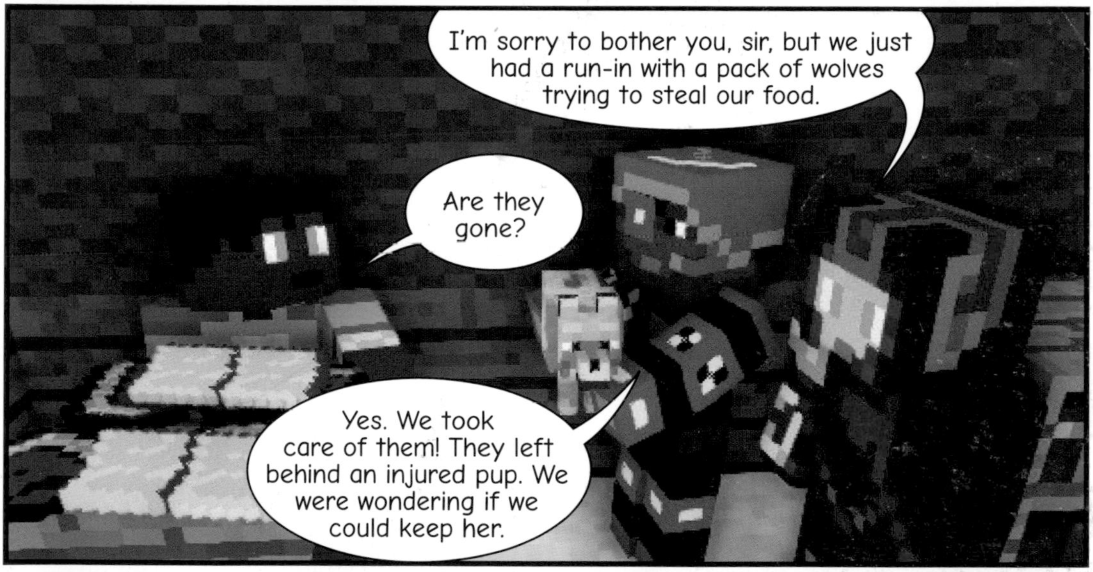
I'm sorry to bother you, sir, but we just had a run-in with a pack of wolves trying to steal our food.
Are they gone?
Yes. We took care of them! They left behind an injured pup. We were wondering if we could keep her.

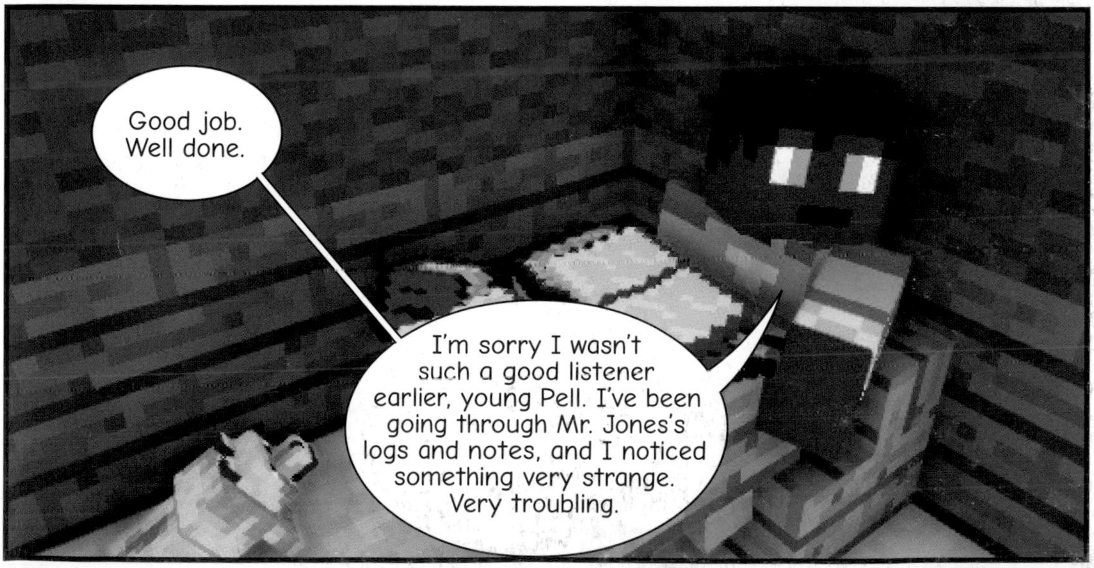
Good job. Well done.
I'm sorry I wasn't such a good listener earlier, young Pell. I've been going through Mr. Jones's logs and notes, and I noticed something very strange. Very troubling.

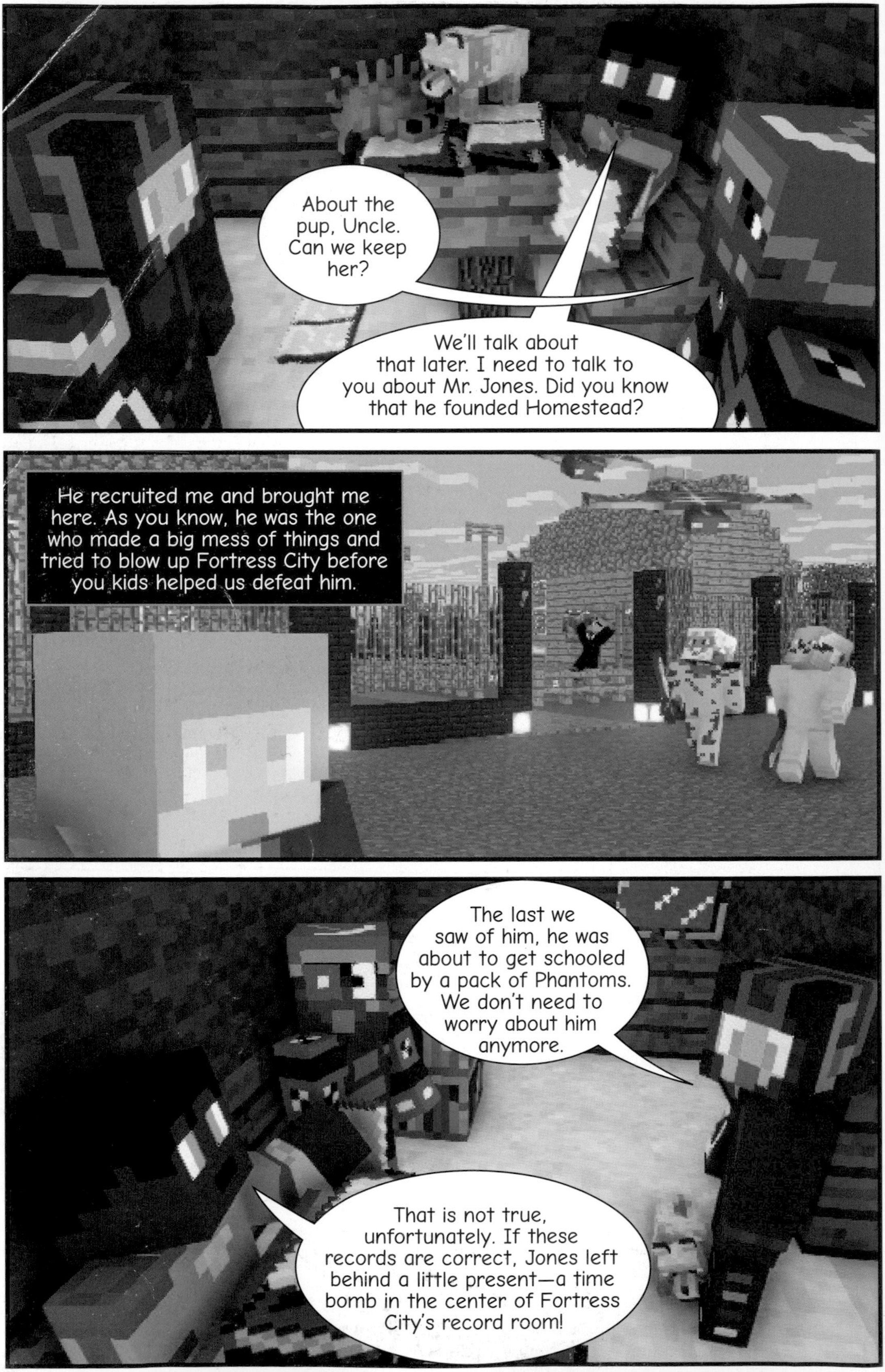
About the pup, Uncle. Can we keep her?
We'll talk about that later. I need to talk to you about Mr. Jones. Did you know that he founded Homestead?
He recruited me and brought me here. As you know, he was the one who made a big mess of things and tried to blow up Fortress City before you kids helped us defeat him.
The last we saw of him, he was about to get schooled by a pack of Phantoms. We don't need to worry about him anymore.
That is not true, unfortunately. If these records are correct, Jones left behind a little present—a time bomb in the center of Fortress City's record room!

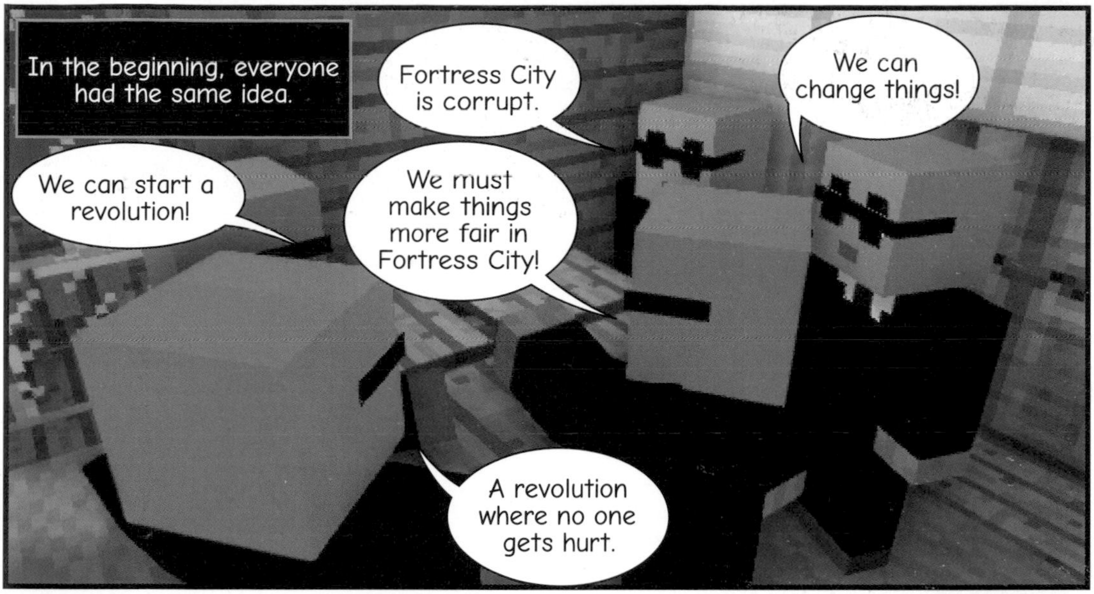
In the beginning, everyone had the same idea.
Fortress City is corrupt.
We can change things!
We can start a revolution!
We must make things more fair in Fortress City!
A revolution where no one gets hurt.

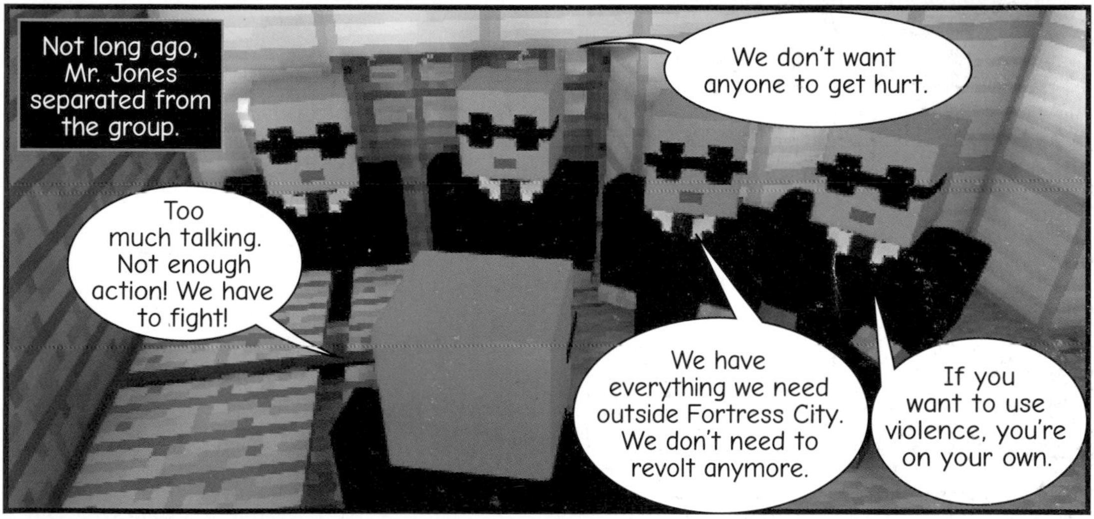
Not long ago, Mr. Jones separated from the group.
We don't want anyone to get hurt.
Too much talking. Not enough action! We have to fight!
We have everything we need outside Fortress City. We don't need to revolt anymore.
If you want to use violence, you're on your own.

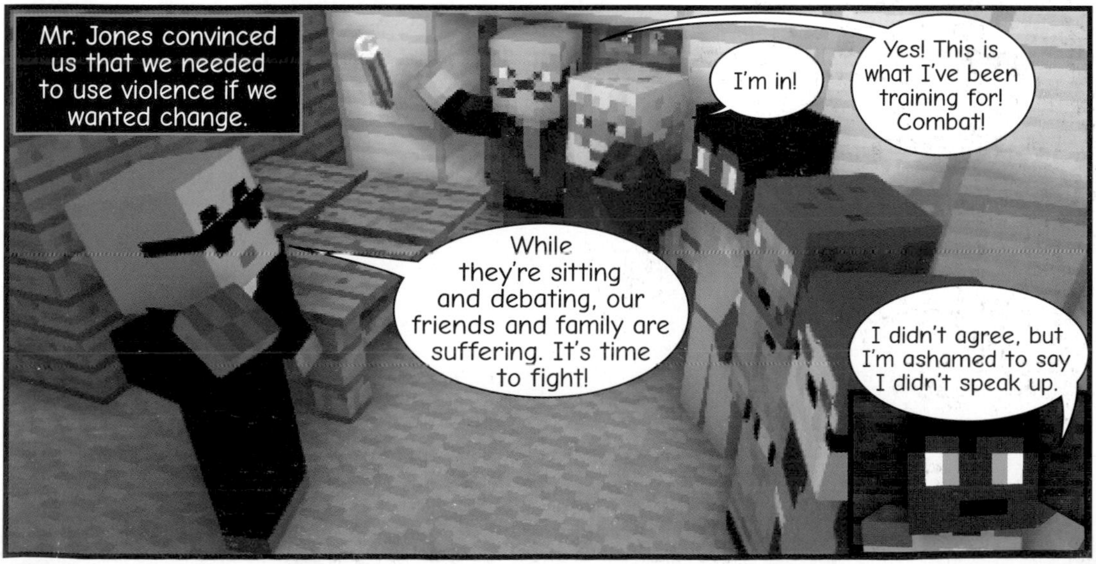
Mr. Jones convinced us that we needed to use violence if we wanted change.
I'm in!
Yes! This is what I've been training for! Combat!
While they're sitting and debating, our friends and family are suffering. It's time to fight!
I didn't agree, but I'm ashamed to say I didn't speak up.

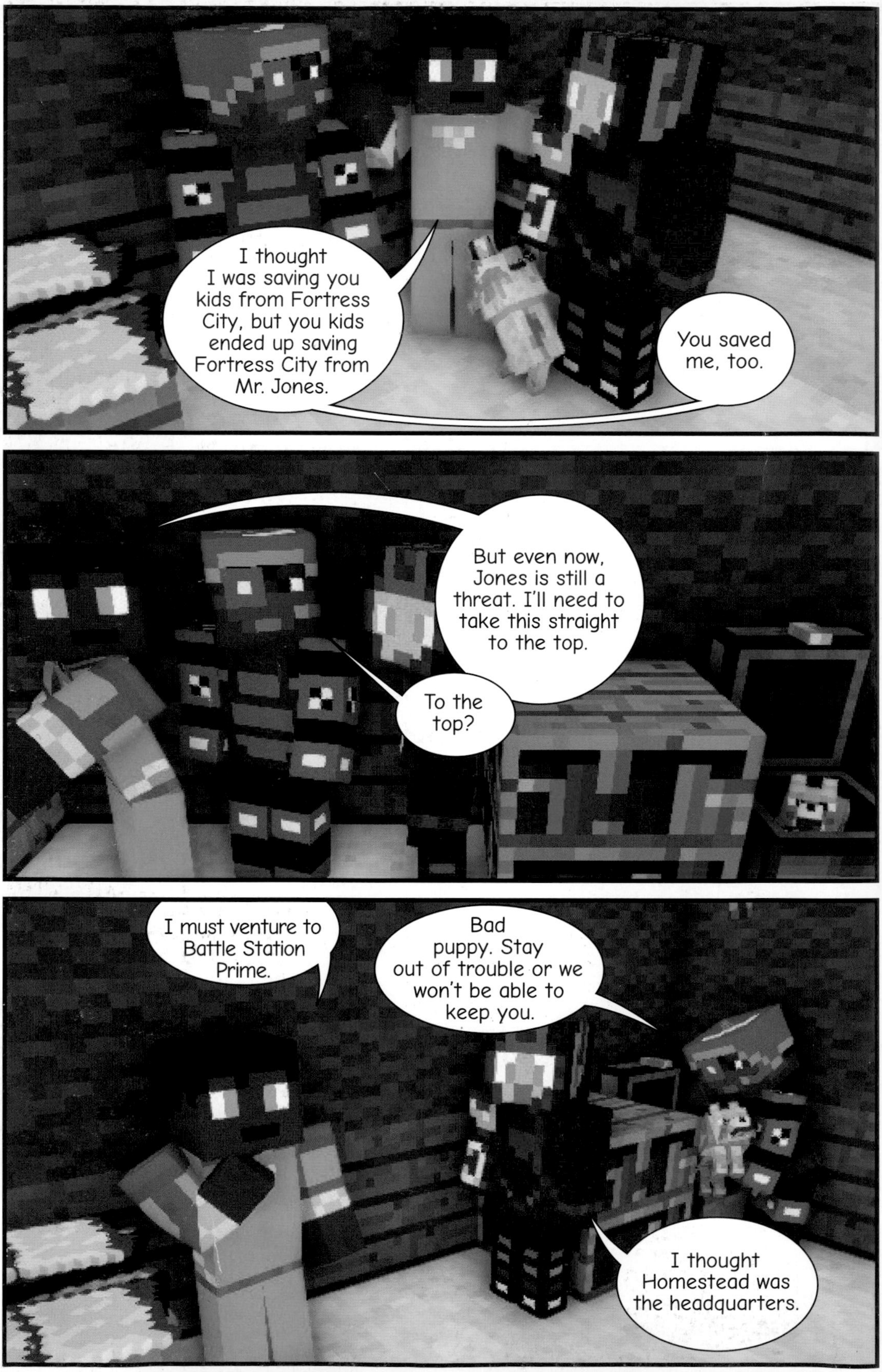
I thought I was saving you kids from Fortress City, but you kids ended up saving Fortress City from Mr. Jones.
You saved me, too.
But even now, Jones is still a threat. I'll need to take this straight to the top.
To the top?
I must venture to Battle Station Prime.
Bad puppy. Stay out of trouble or we won't be able to keep you.
I thought Homestead was the headquarters.

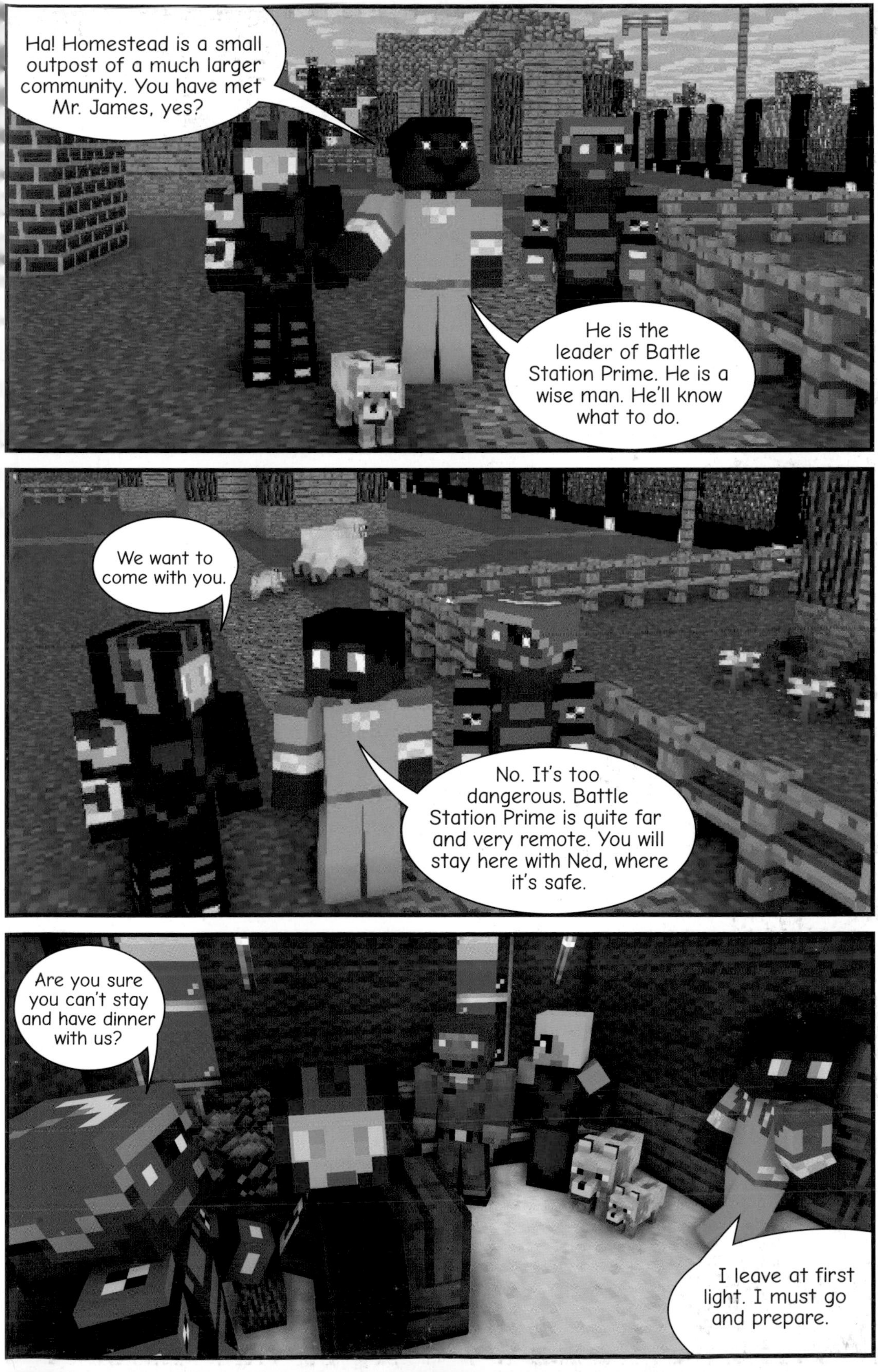
Ha! Homestead is a small outpost of a much larger community. You have met Mr. James, yes?
He is the leader of Battle Station Prime. He is a wise man. He'll know what to do.
We want to come with you.
No. It's too dangerous. Battle Station Prime is quite far and very remote. You will stay here with Ned, where it's safe.
Are you sure you can't stay and have dinner with us?
I leave at first light. I must go and prepare.

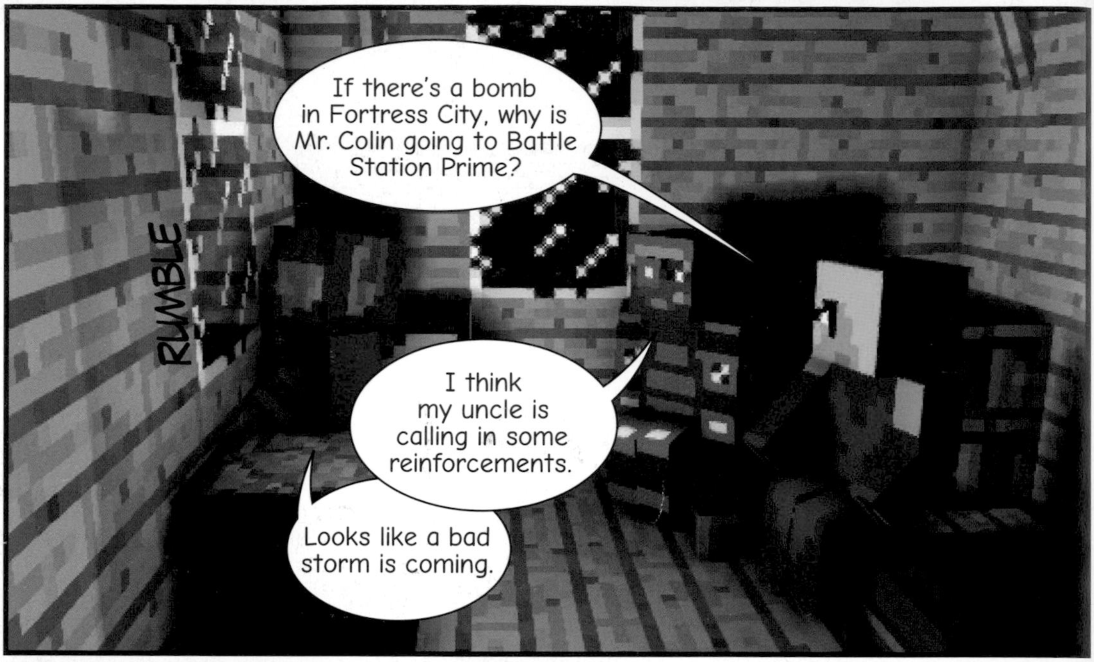
If there's a bomb in Fortress City, why is Mr. Colin going to Battle Station Prime?
I think my uncle is calling in some reinforcements.
Looks like a bad storm is coming.
RUMBLE

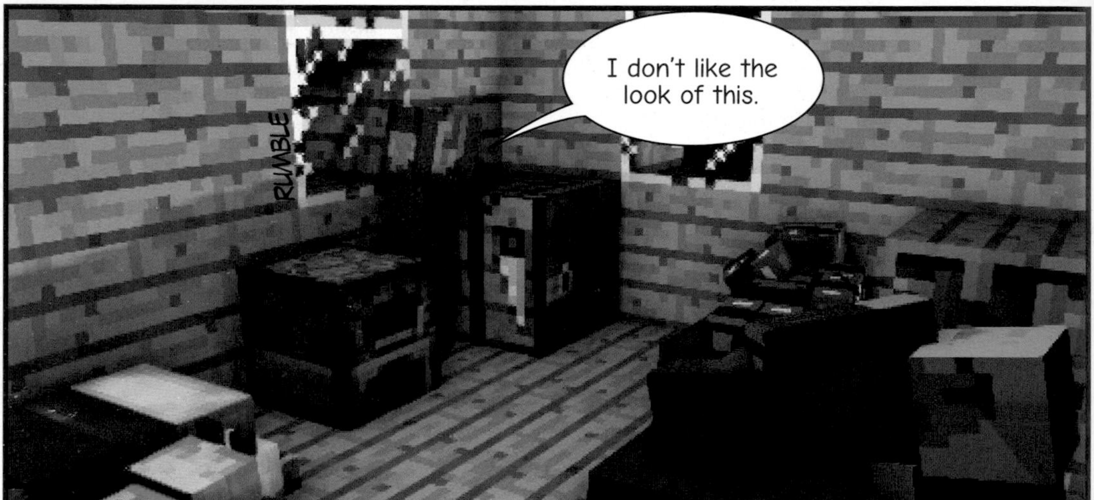
I don't like the look of this.
RUMBLE

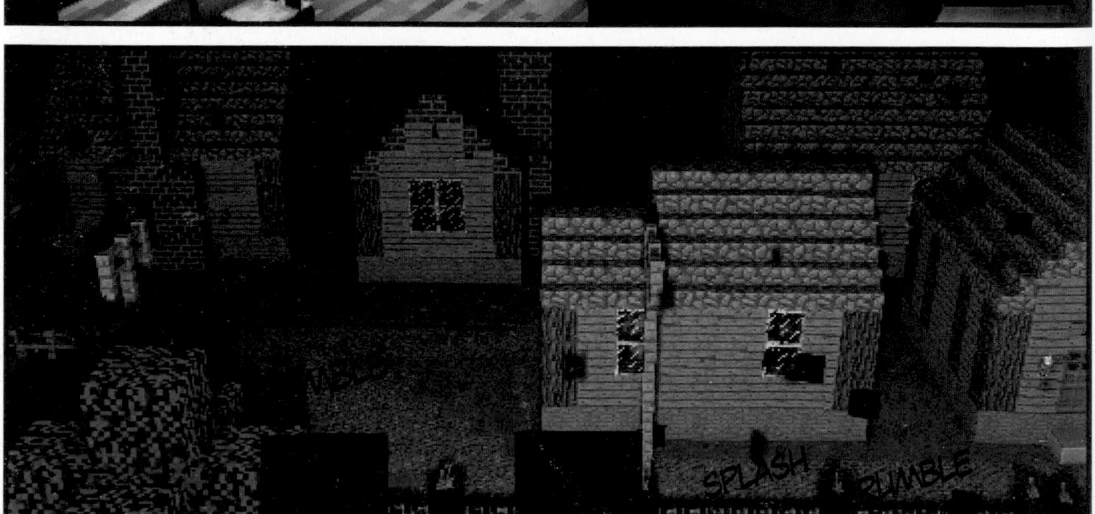
SPLASH
RUMBLE

CHAPTER 2

DISASTER

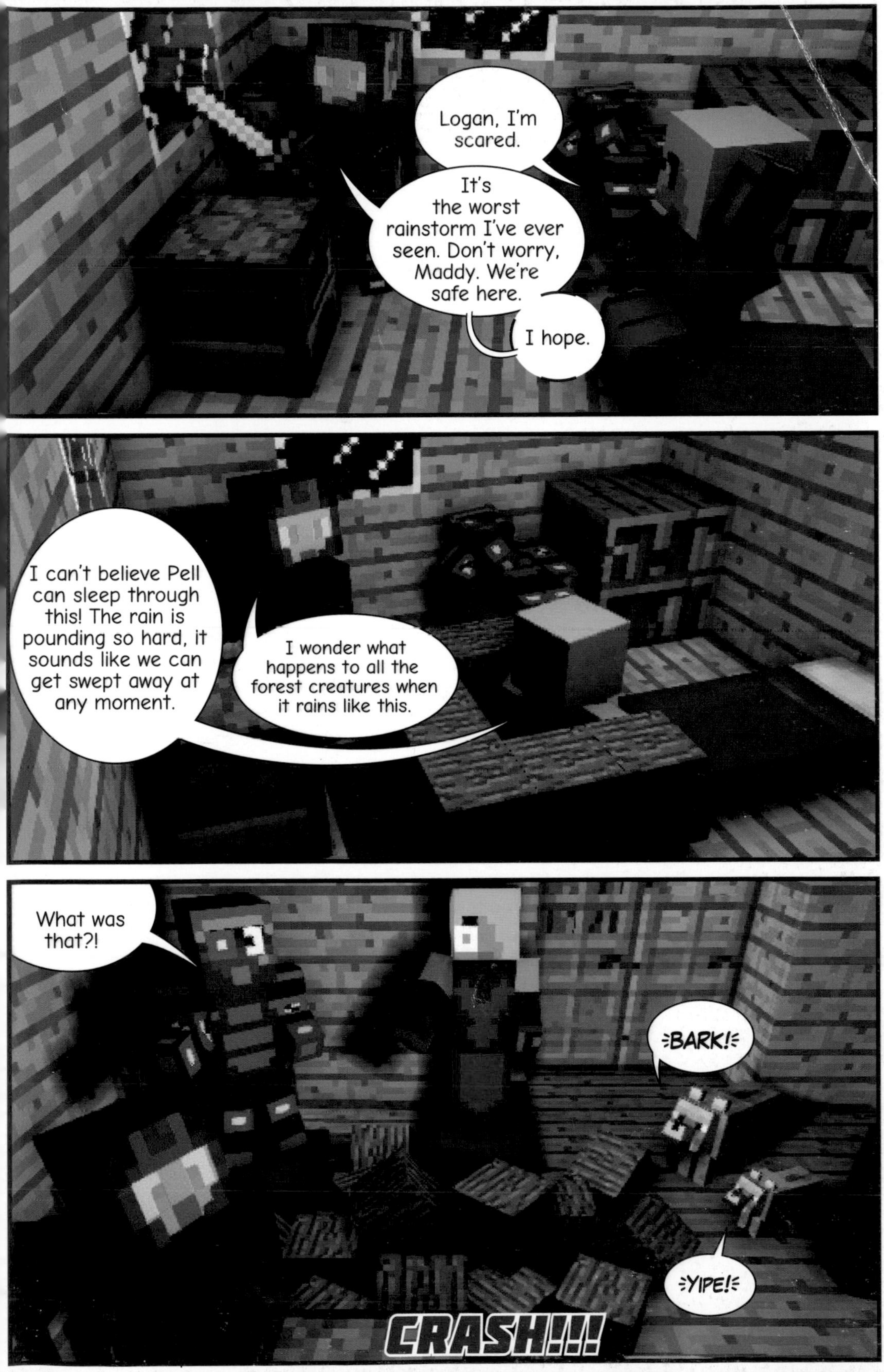
Logan, I'm scared.
It's the worst rainstorm I've ever seen. Don't worry, Maddy. We're safe here.
I hope.
I can't believe Pell can sleep through this! The rain is pounding so hard, it sounds like we can get swept away at any moment.
I wonder what happens to all the forest creatures when it rains like this.
What was that?!
BARK!
YIPE!
CRASH!!!

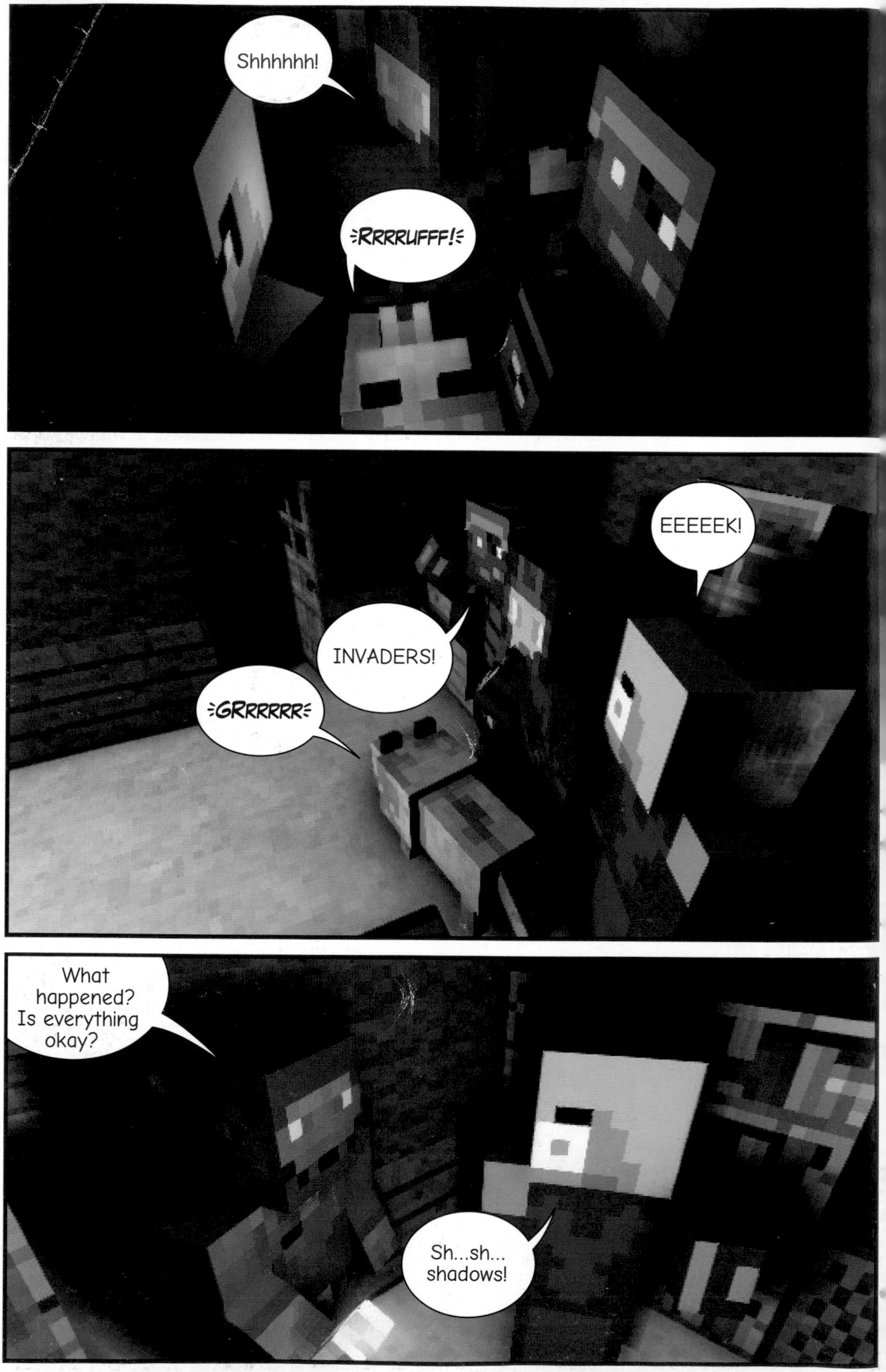
Shhhhhh!
RRRRUFFF!
EEEEEK!
INVADERS!
GRRRRRR
What happened? Is everything okay?
Sh...sh... shadows!

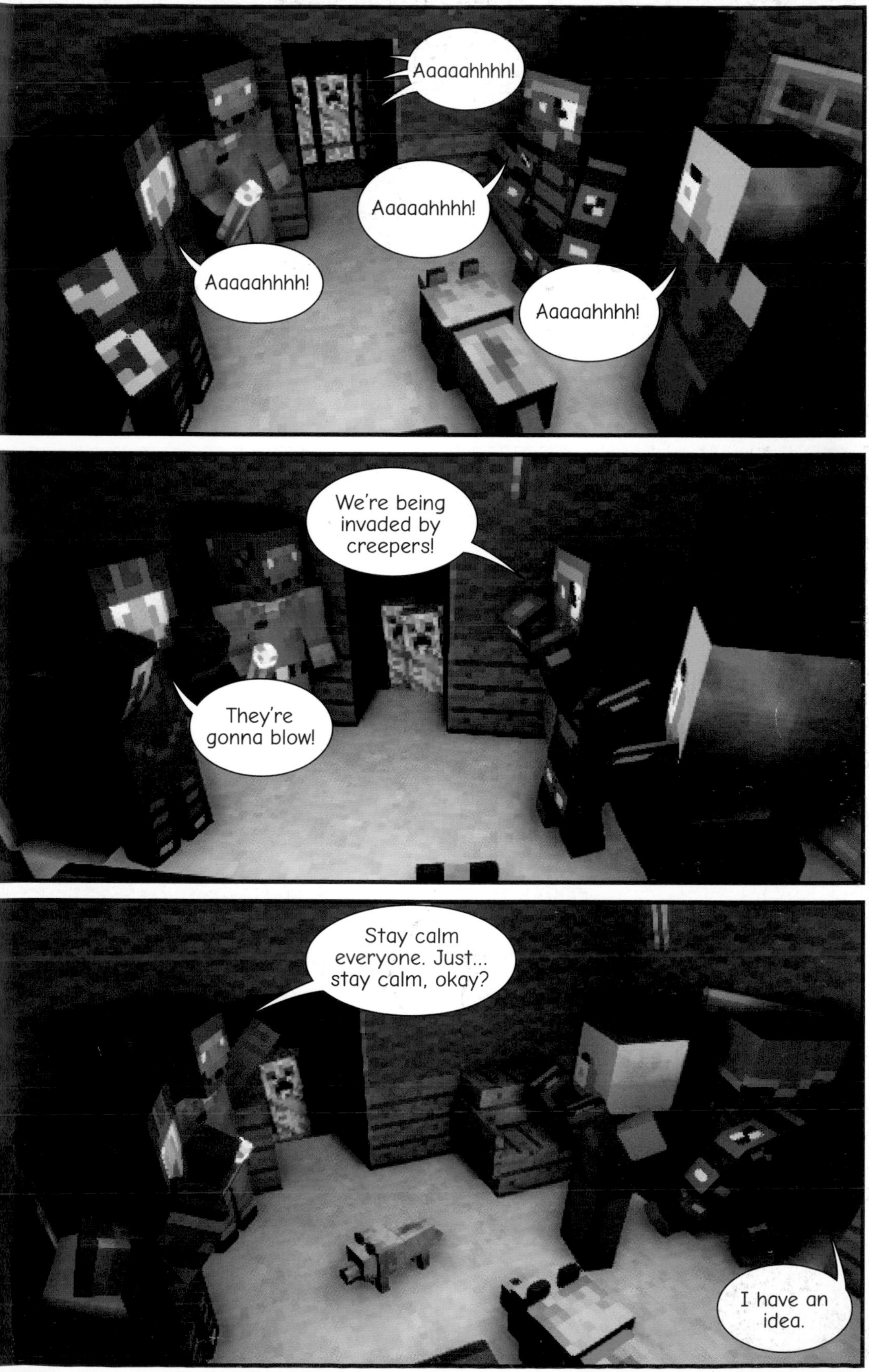
Aaaaahhhh!
Aaaaahhhh!
Aaaaahhhh!
Aaaaahhhh!
We're being invaded by creepers!
They're gonna blow!
Stay calm everyone. Just... stay calm, okay?
I have an idea.

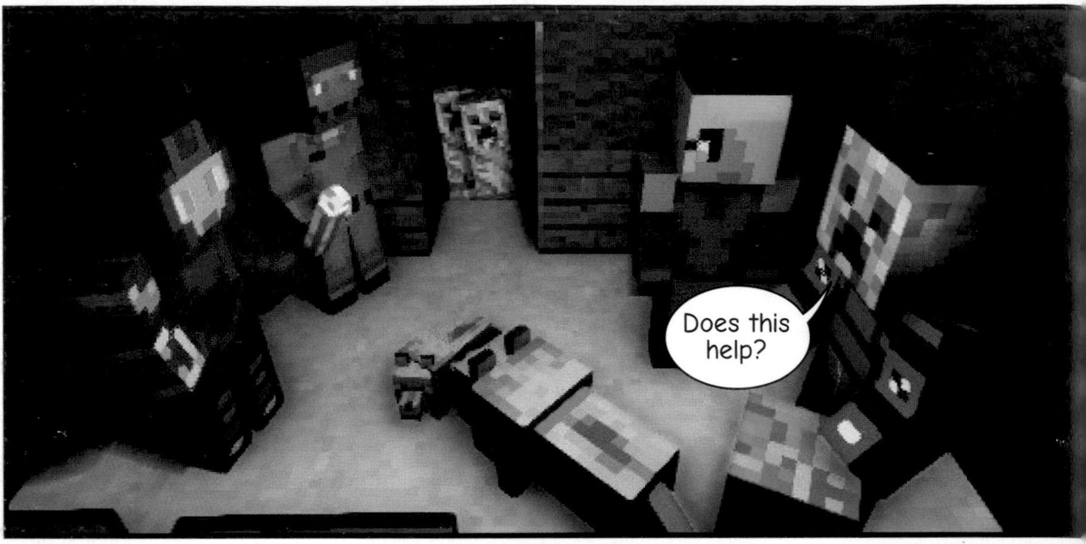
Does this help?

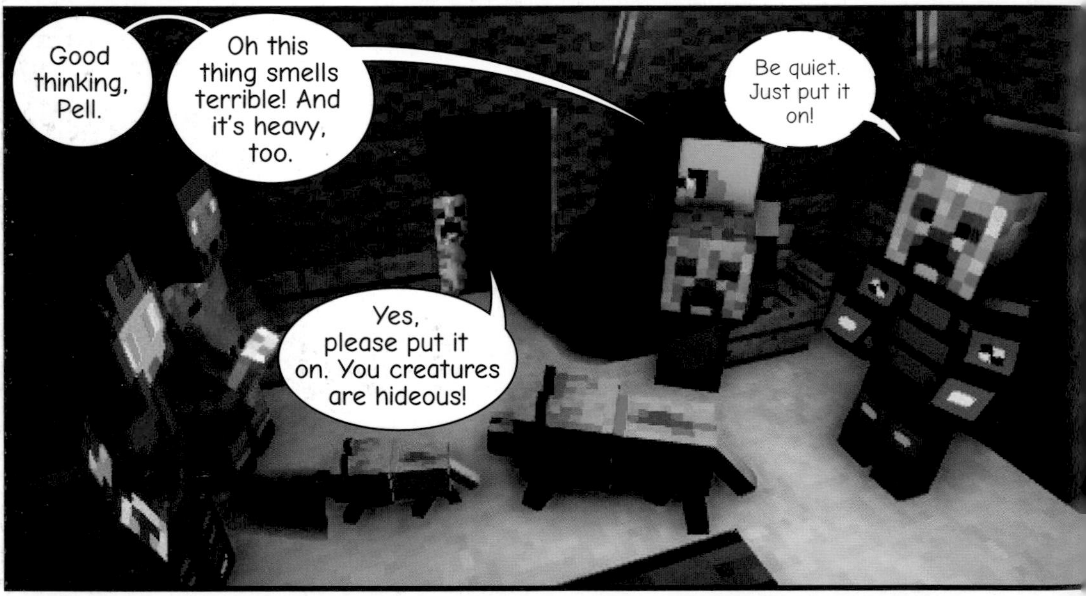
Good thinking, Pell.
Oh this thing smells terrible! And it's heavy, too.
Be quiet. Just put it on!
Yes, please put it on. You creatures are hideous!

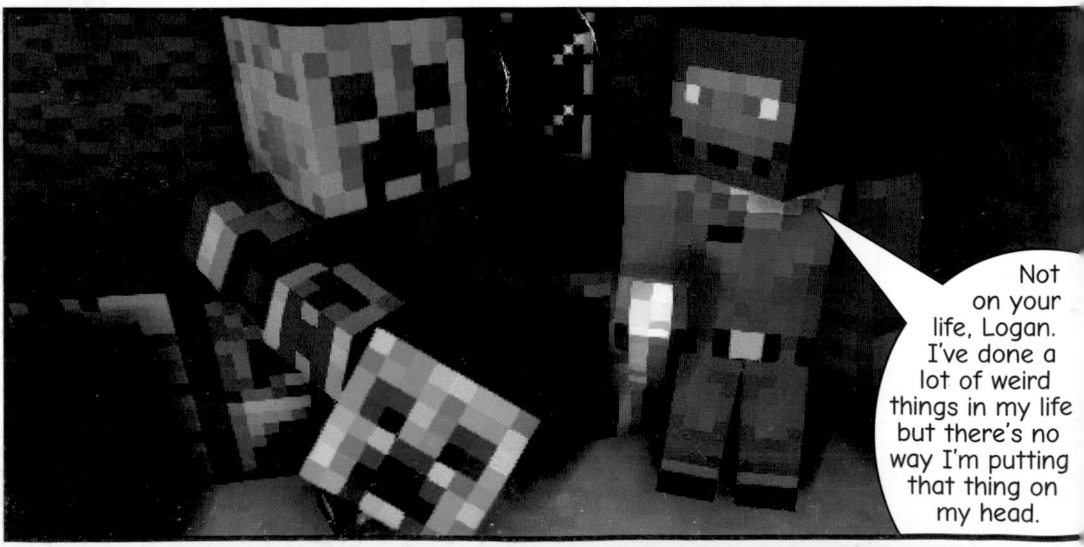
Not on your life, Logan. I've done a lot of weird things in my life but there's no way I'm putting that thing on my head.

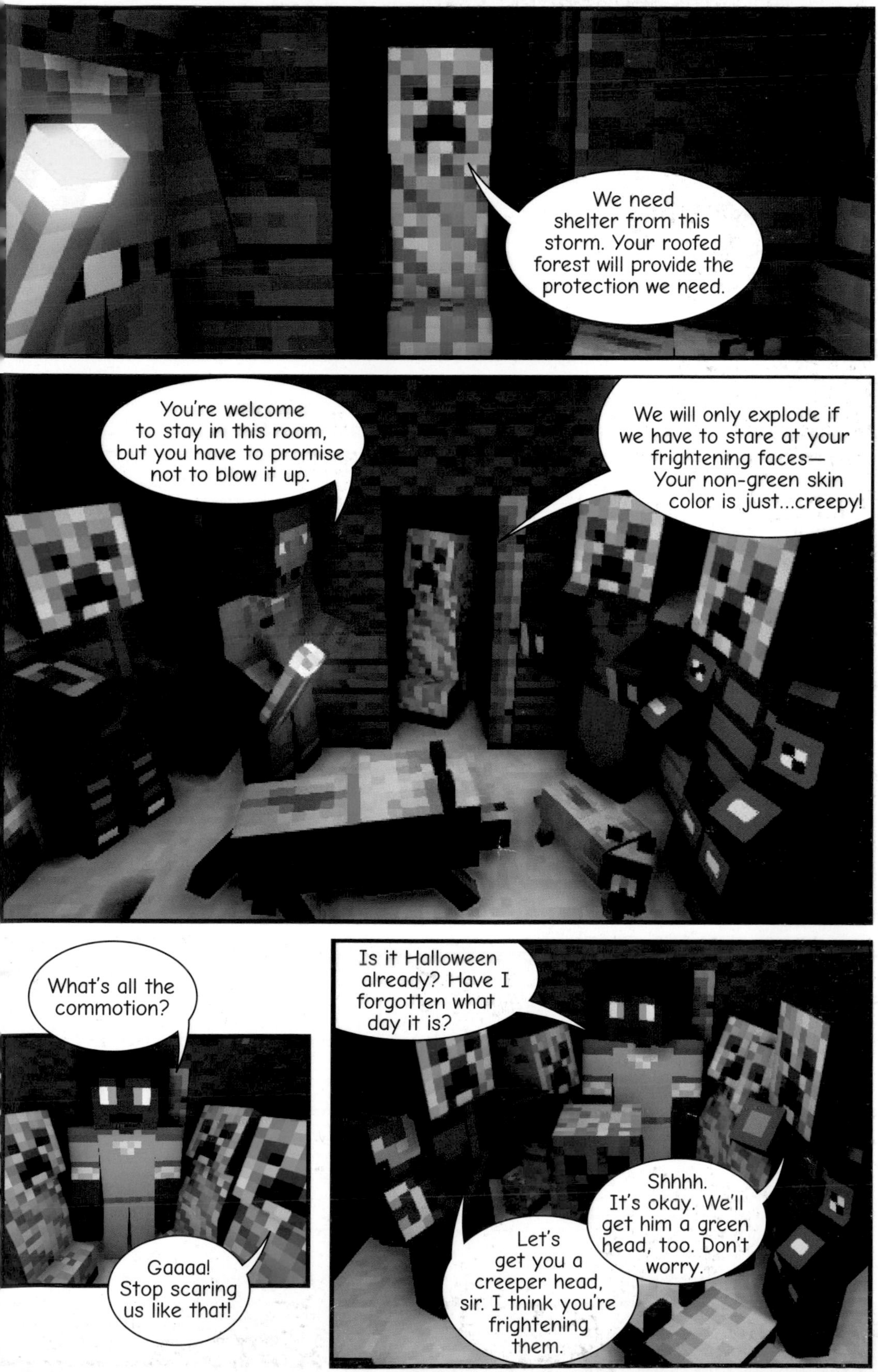
We need shelter from this storm. Your roofed forest will provide the protection we need.
You're welcome to stay in this room, but you have to promise not to blow it up.
We will only explode if we have to stare at your frightening faces— Your non-green skin color is just...creepy!
What's all the commotion?
Gaaaa! Stop scaring us like that!
Is it Halloween already? Have I forgotten what day it is?
Let's get you a creeper head, sir. I think you're frightening them.
Shhhh. It's okay. We'll get him a green head, too. Don't worry.

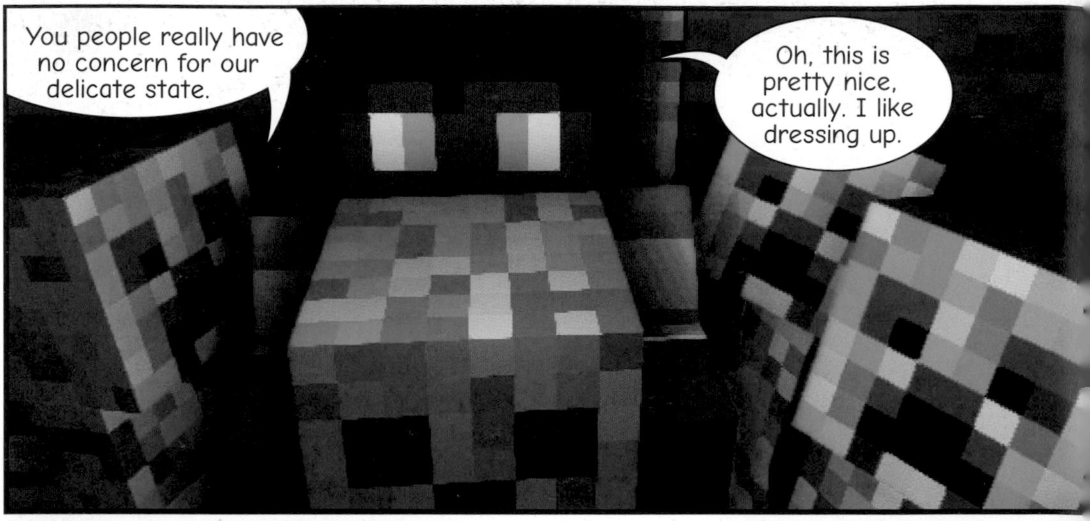
You people really have no concern for our delicate state.
Oh, this is pretty nice, actually. I like dressing up.

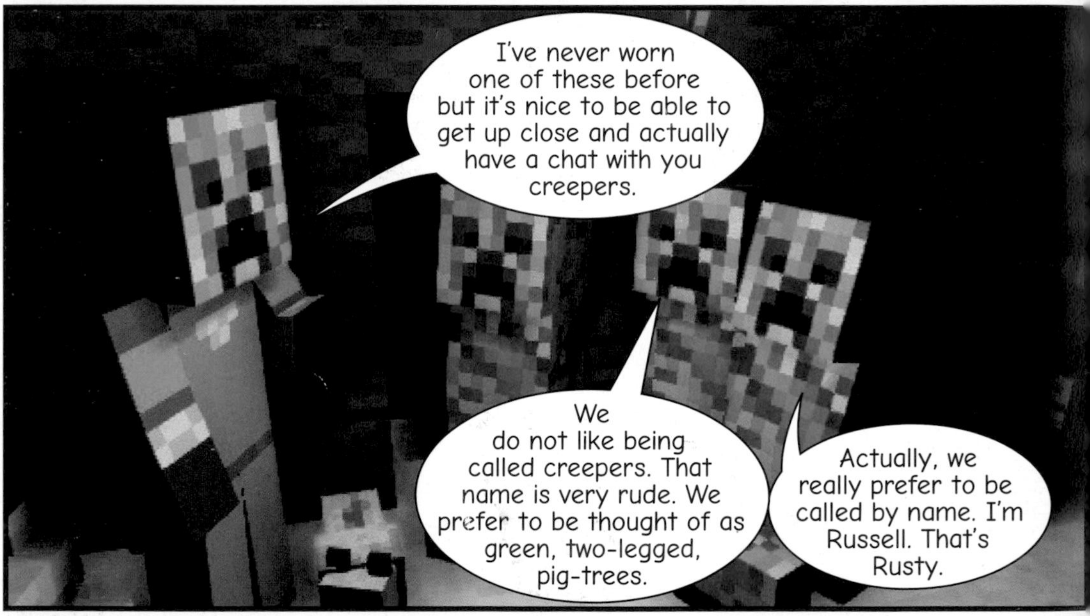
I've never worn one of these before but it's nice to be able to get up close and actually have a chat with you creepers.
We do not like being called creepers. That name is very rude. We prefer to be thought of as green, two-legged, pig-trees.
Actually, we really prefer to be called by name. I'm Russell. That's Rusty.

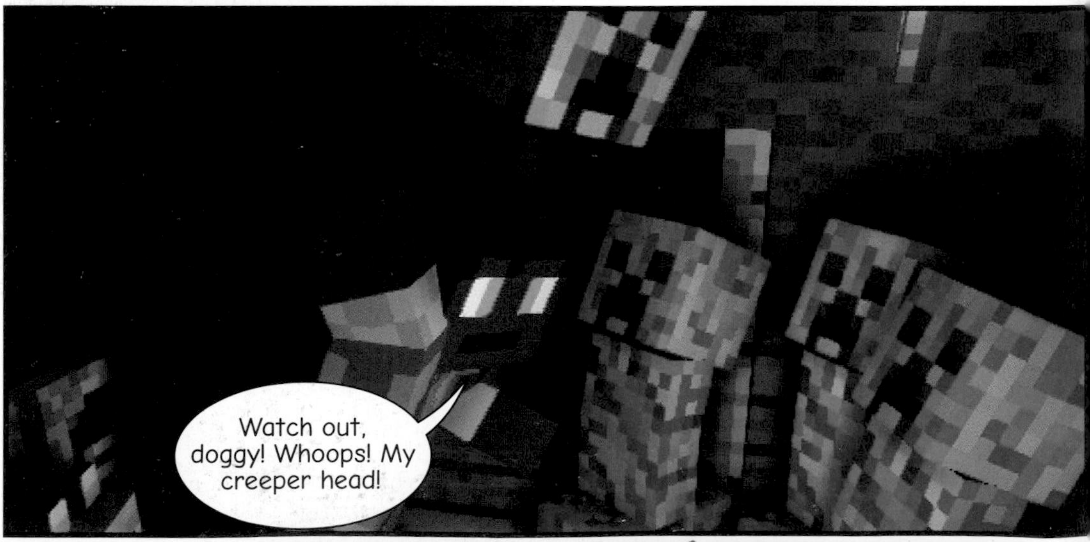
Watch out, doggy! Whoops! My creeper head!

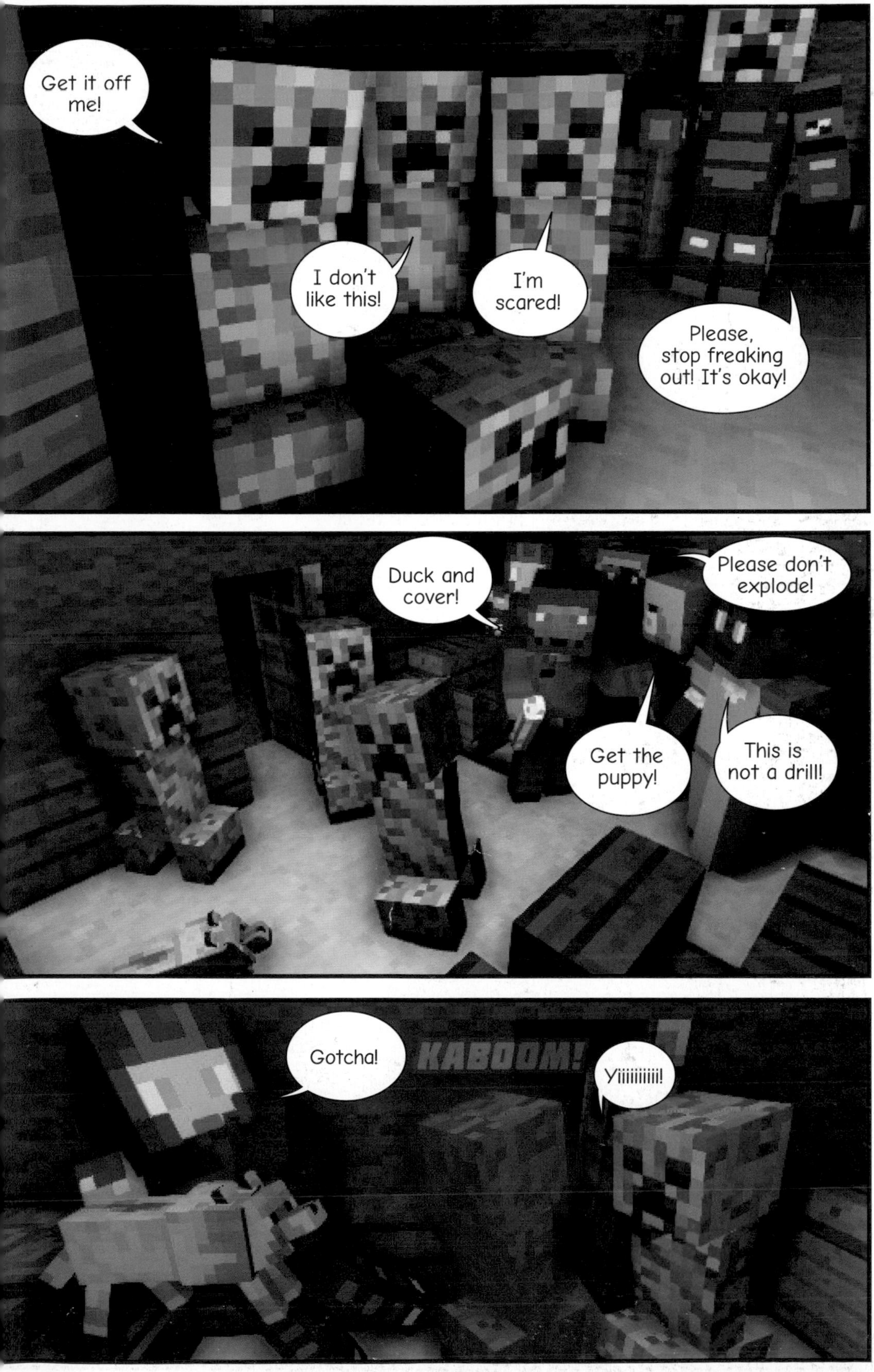
Get it off me!
I don't like this!
I'm scared!
Please, stop freaking out! It's okay!
Duck and cover!
Please don't explode!
Get the puppy!
This is not a drill!
Gotcha!
KABOOM!
Yiiiiiiiiiii!

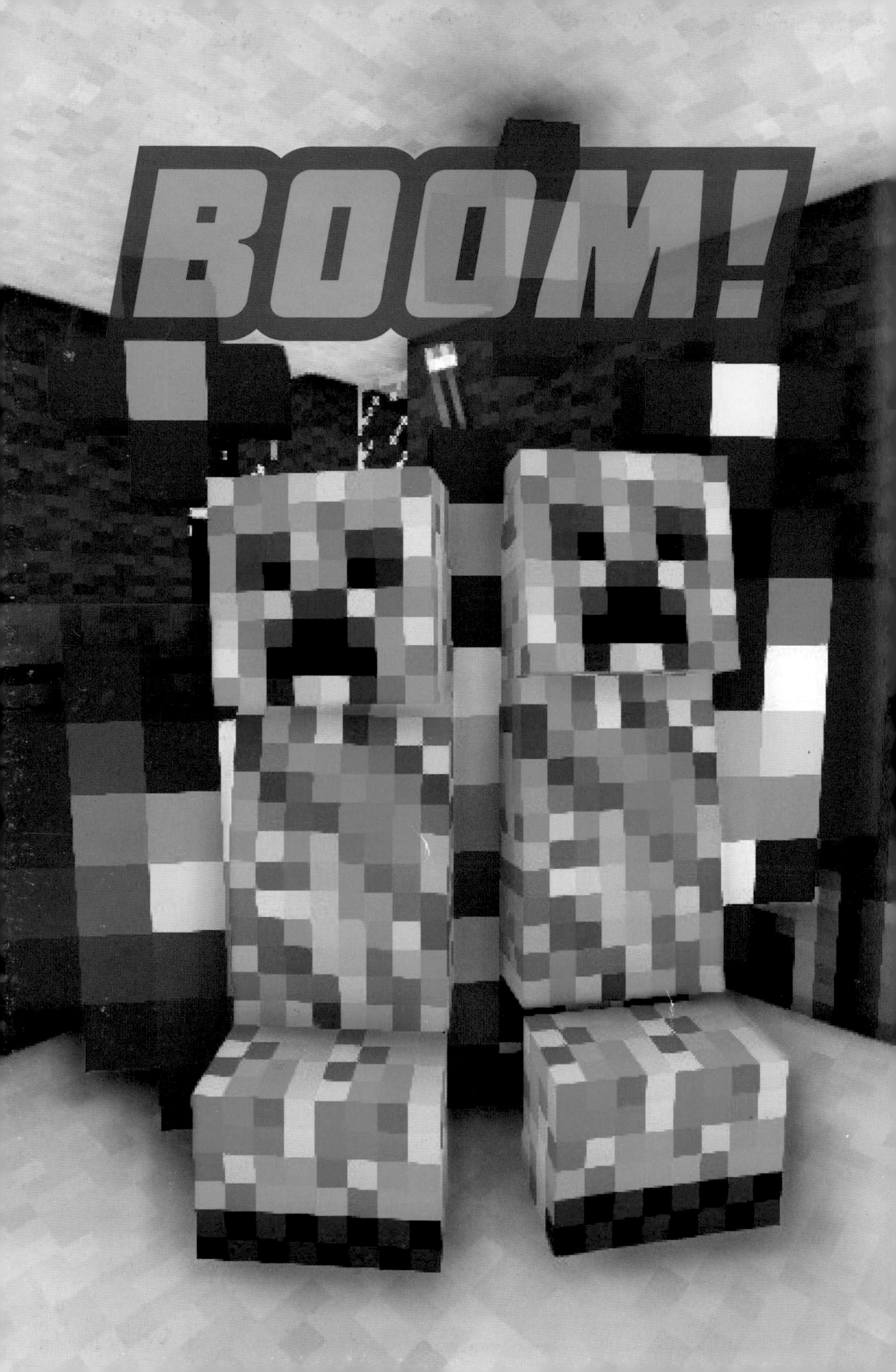
BOOM!

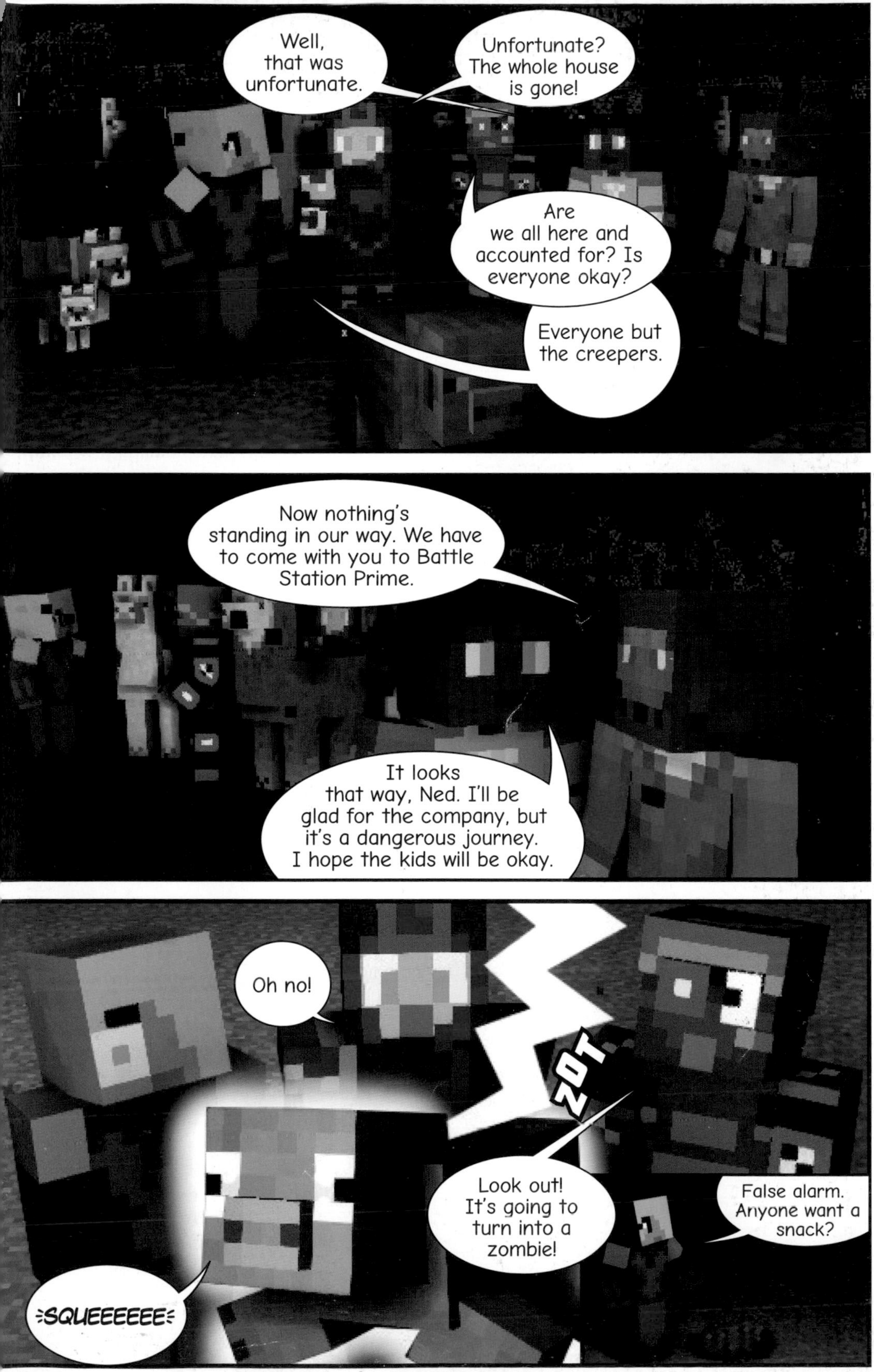
Well, that was unfortunate.
Unfortunate? The whole house is gone!
Are we all here and accounted for? Is everyone okay?
Everyone but the creepers.
Now nothing's standing in our way. We have to come with you to Battle Station Prime.
It looks that way, Ned. I'll be glad for the company, but it's a dangerous journey. I hope the kids will be okay.
Oh no!
ZOT
Look out! It's going to turn into a zombie!
False alarm. Anyone want a snack?
SQUEEEEEE

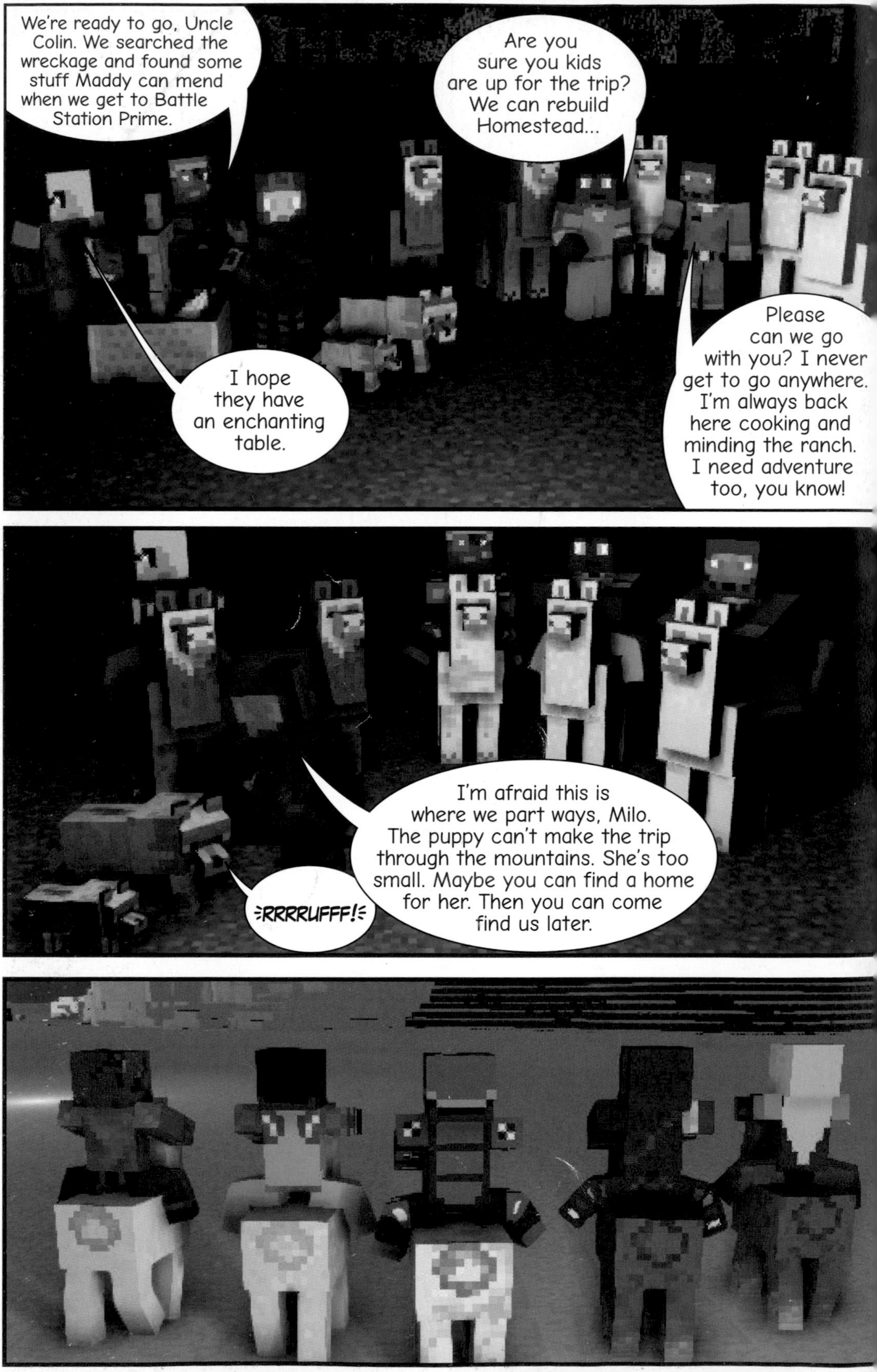
We're ready to go, Uncle Colin. We searched the wreckage and found some stuff Maddy can mend when we get to Battle Station Prime.
Are you sure you kids are up for the trip? We can rebuild Homestead...
I hope they have an enchanting table.
Please can we go with you? I never get to go anywhere. I'm always back here cooking and minding the ranch. I need adventure too, you know!
I'm afraid this is where we part ways, Milo. The puppy can't make the trip through the mountains. She's too small. Maybe you can find a home for her. Then you can come find us later.
RRRRUFFF!

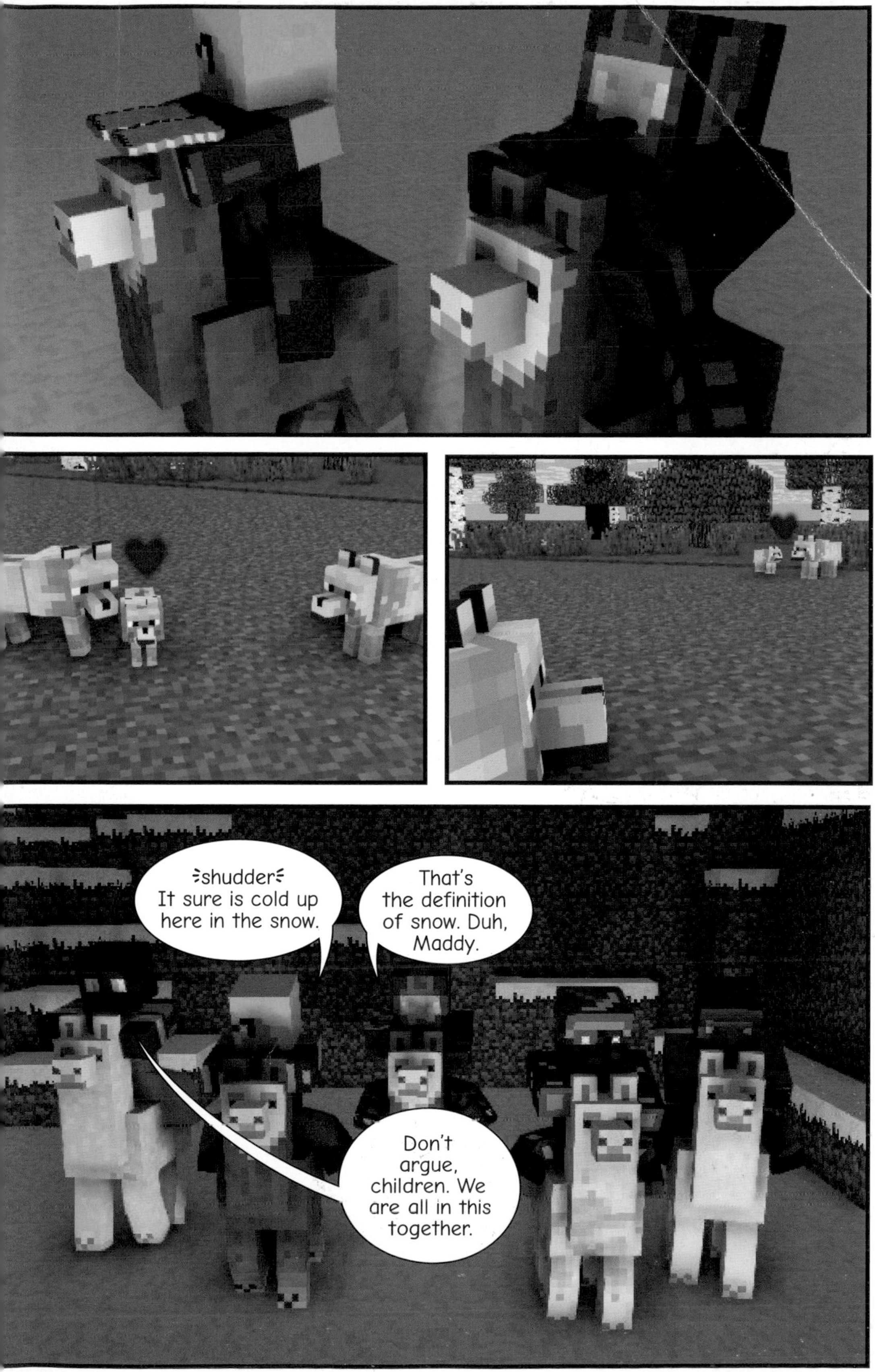
shudder It sure is cold up here in the snow.
That's the definition of snow. Duh, Maddy.
Don't argue, children. We are all in this together.

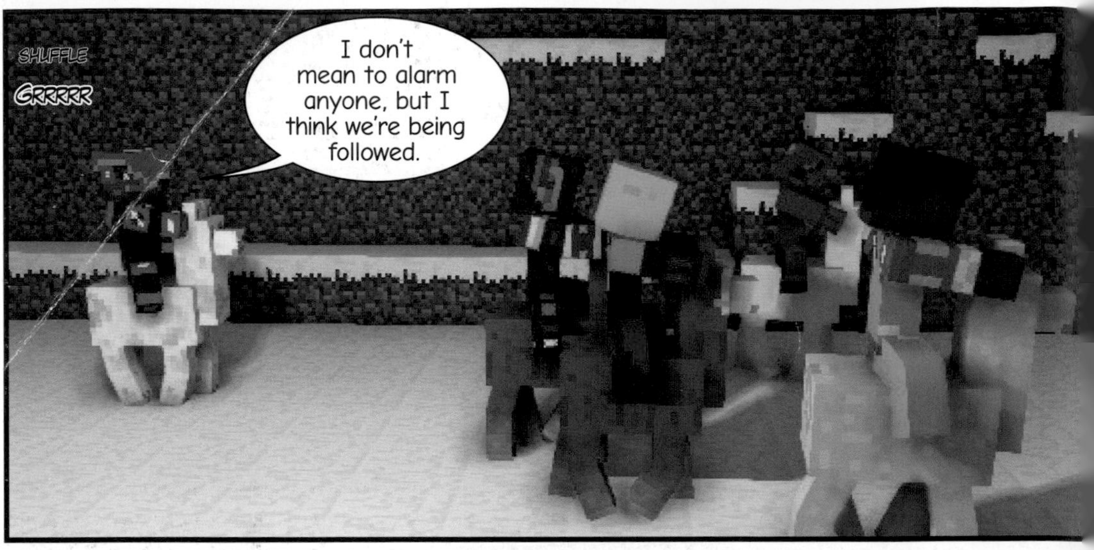
SHUFFLE
GRRRRR
I don't mean to alarm anyone, but I think we're being followed.

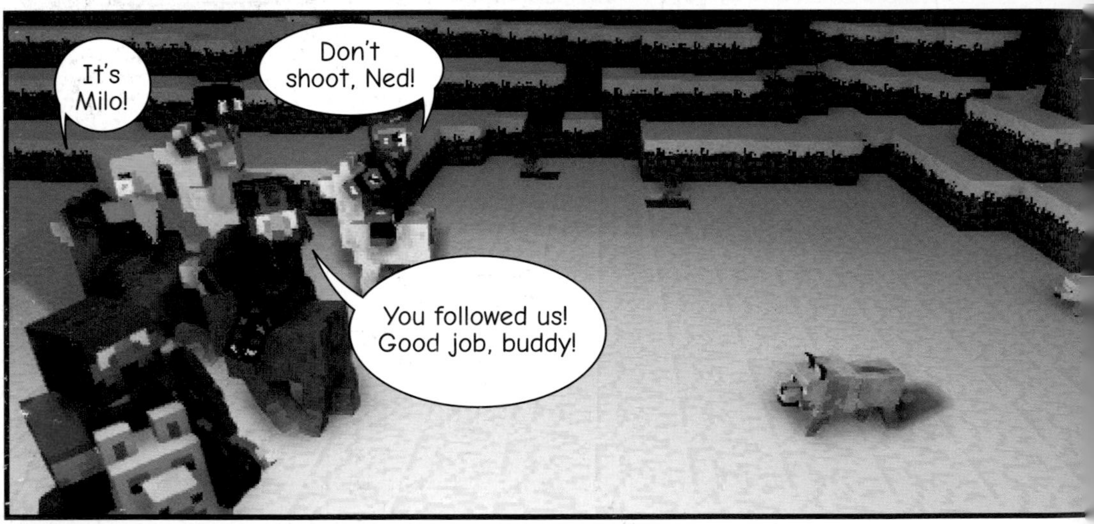
It's Milo!
Don't shoot, Ned!
You followed us! Good job, buddy!

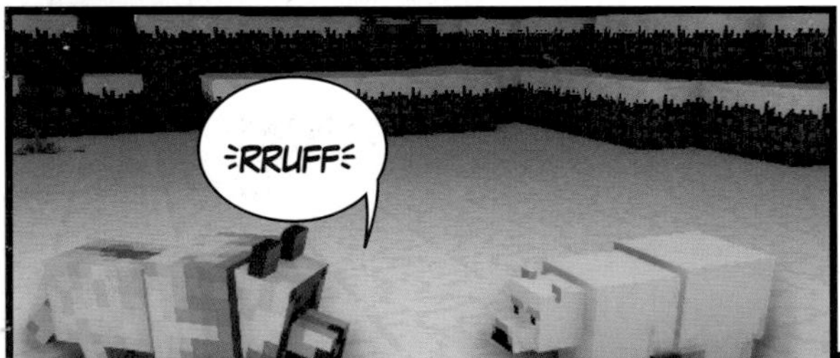
RRUFF
GRRRRROWL

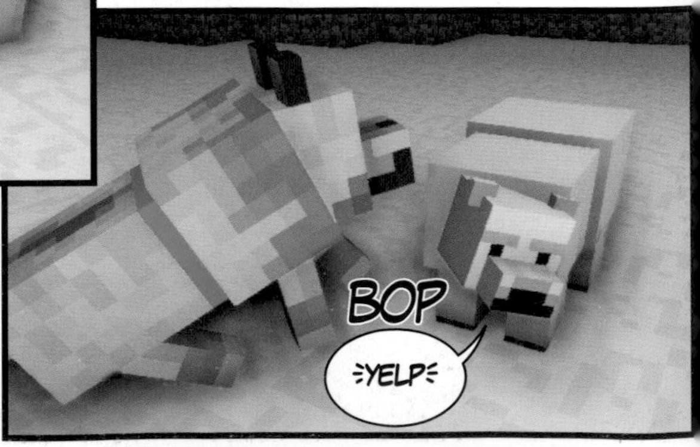
BOP
YELP

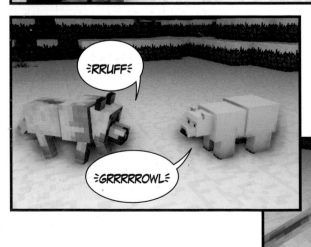

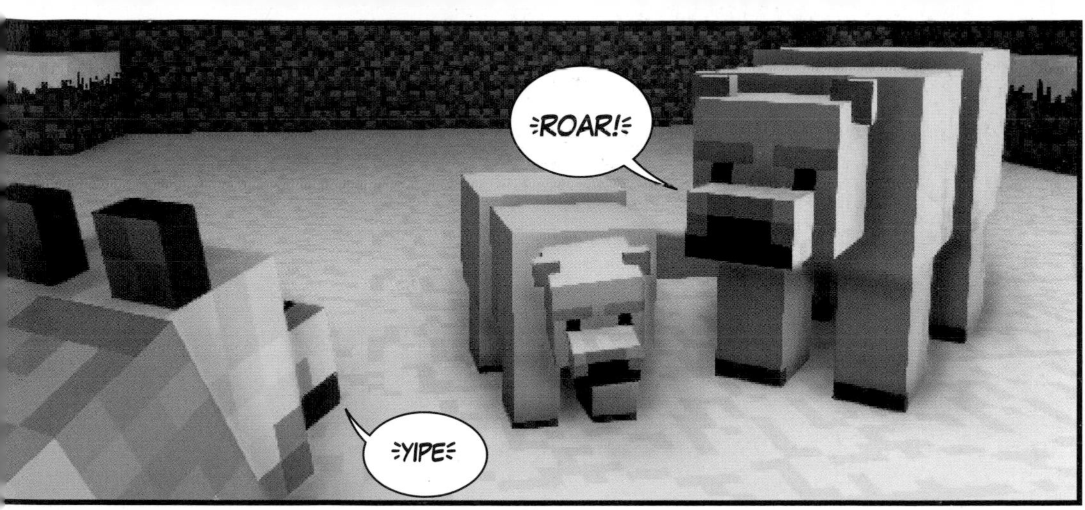
ROAR!
YIPE

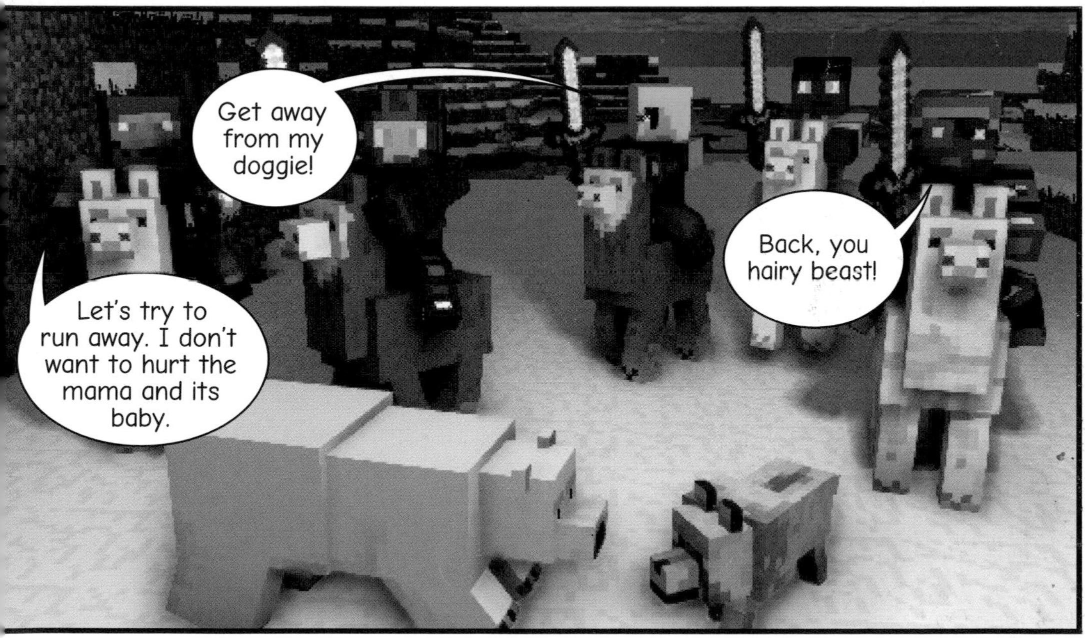
Get away from my doggie!
Back, you hairy beast!
Let's try to run away. I don't want to hurt the mama and its baby.

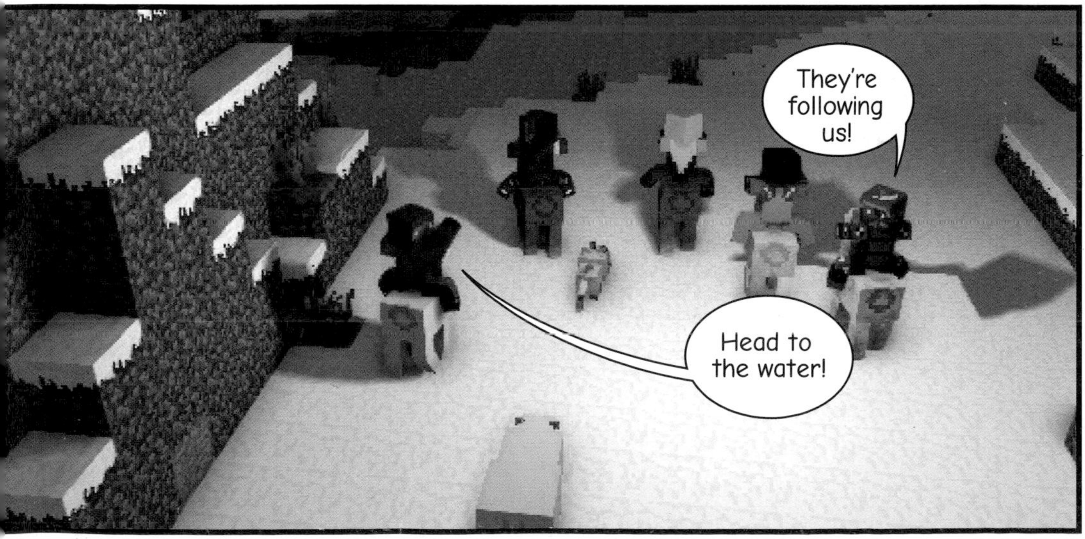
They're following us!
Head to the water!

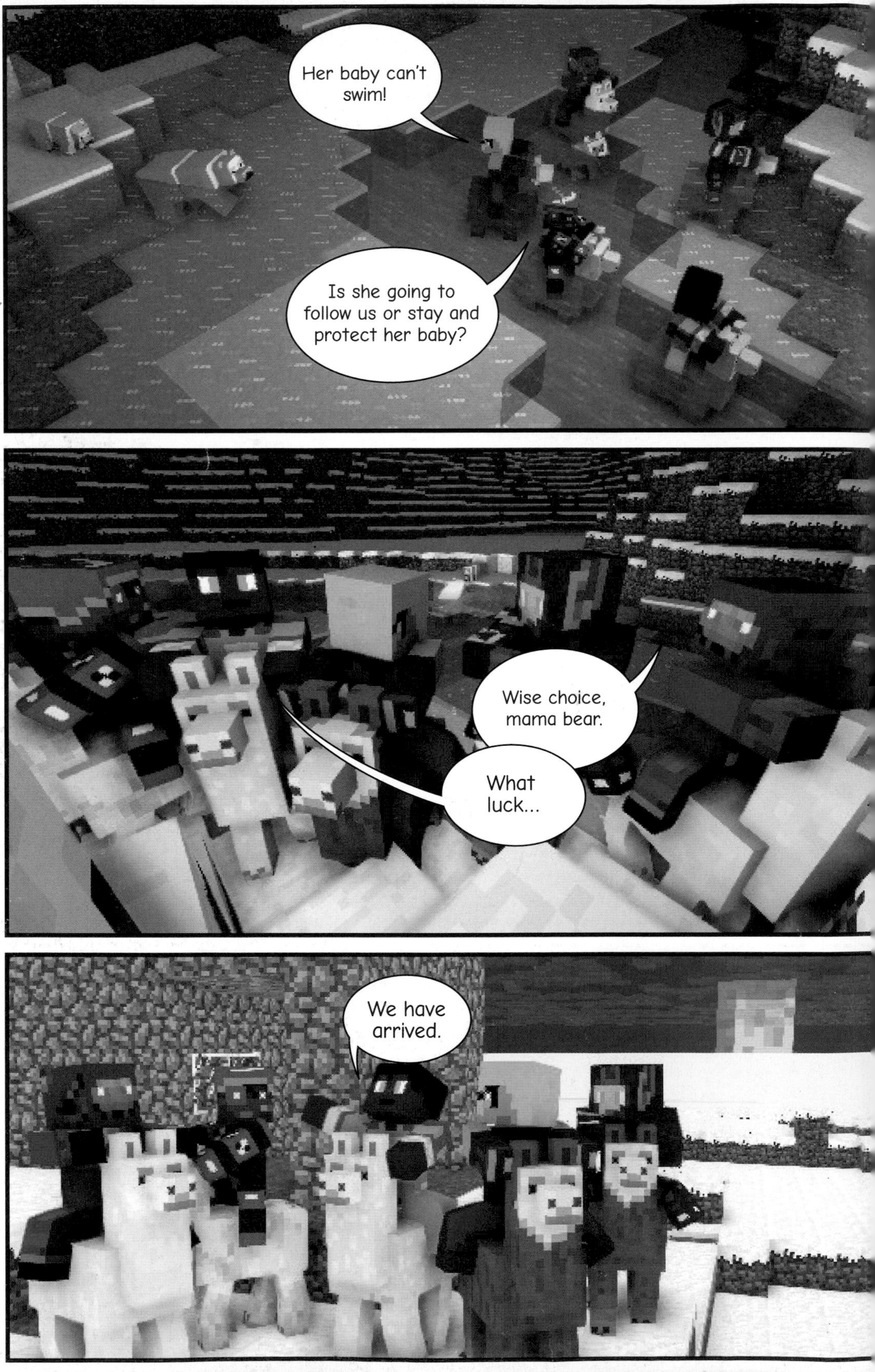
Her baby can't swim!
Is she going to follow us or stay and protect her baby?
Wise choice, mama bear.
What luck...
We have arrived.

CHAPTER 3

FRENEMIES

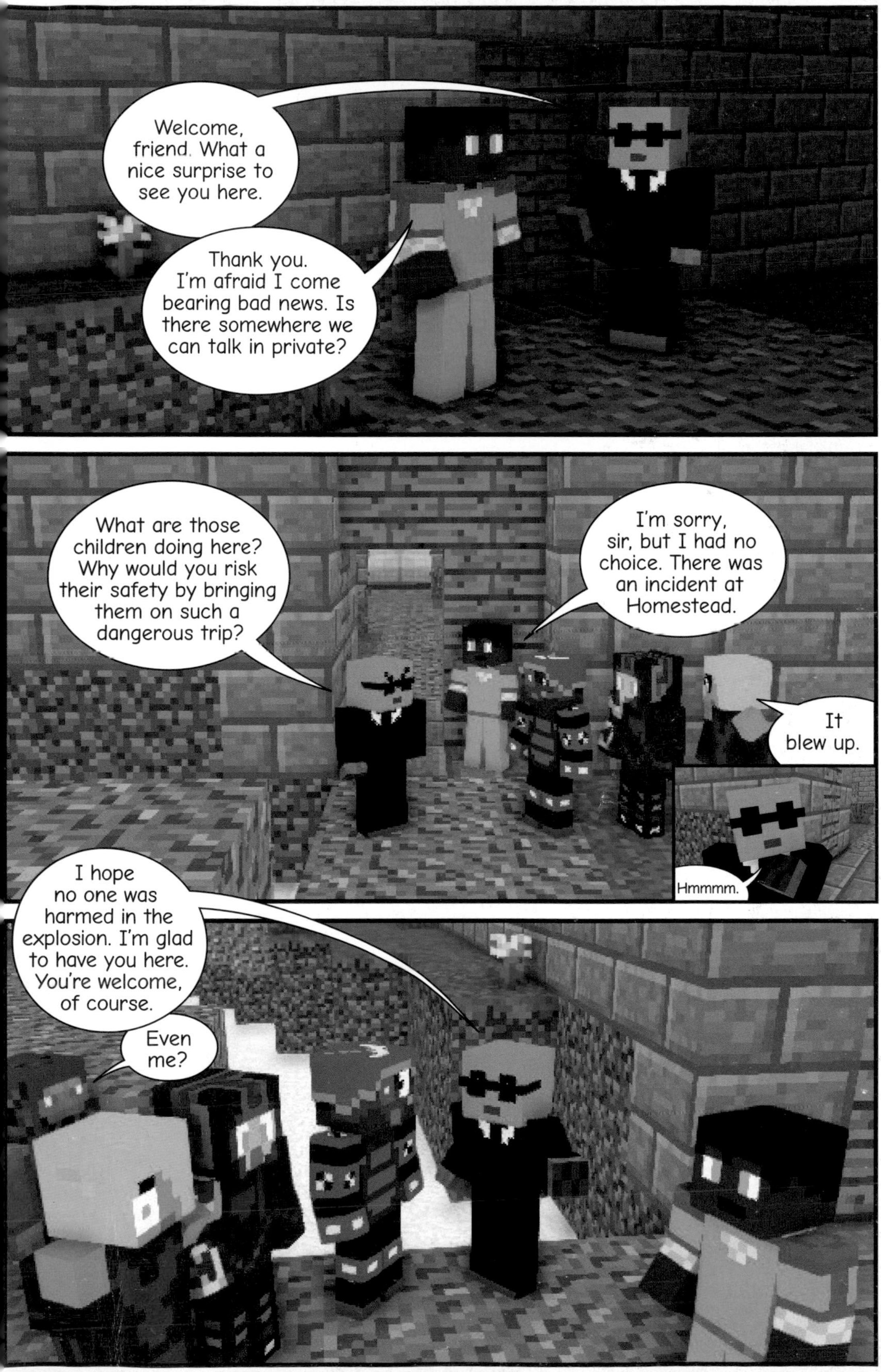
Welcome, friend. What a nice surprise to see you here.
Thank you. I'm afraid I come bearing bad news. Is there somewhere we can talk in private?
What are those children doing here? Why would you risk their safety by bringing them on such a dangerous trip?
I'm sorry, sir, but I had no choice. There was an incident at Homestead.
It blew up.
Hmmmm.
I hope no one was harmed in the explosion. I'm glad to have you here. You're welcome, of course.
Even me?

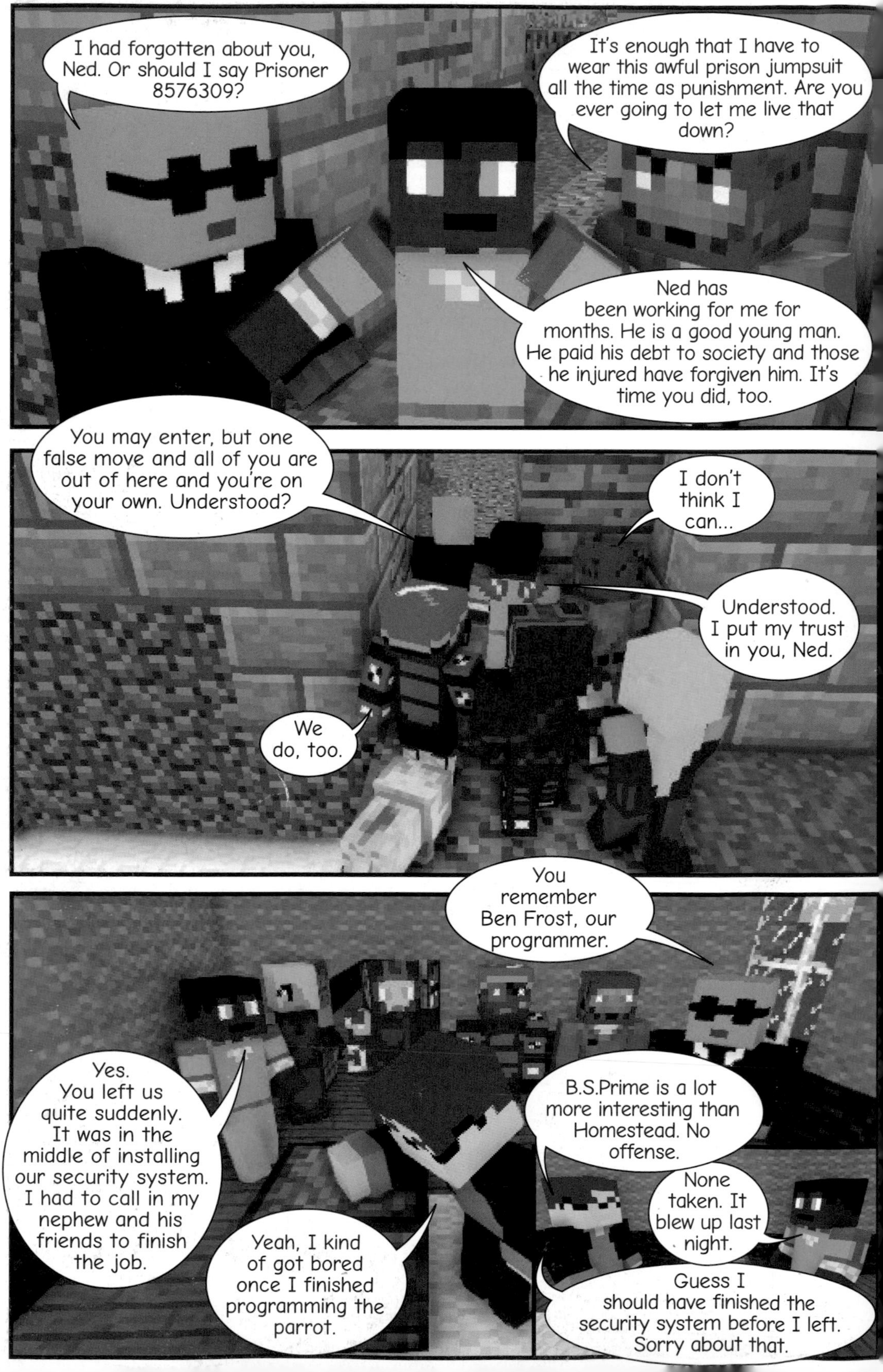
I had forgotten about you, Ned. Or should I say Prisoner 8576309?
It's enough that I have to wear this awful prison jumpsuit all the time as punishment. Are you ever going to let me live that down?
Ned has been working for me for months. He is a good young man. He paid his debt to society and those he injured have forgiven him. It's time you did, too.
You may enter, but one false move and all of you are out of here and you're on your own. Understood?
I don't think I can...
Understood. I put my trust in you, Ned.
We do, too.
You remember Ben Frost, our programmer.
Yes. You left us quite suddenly. It was in the middle of installing our security system. I had to call in my nephew and his friends to finish the job.
Yeah, I kind of got bored once I finished programming the parrot.
B.S.Prime is a lot more interesting than Homestead. No offense.
None taken. It blew up last night.
Guess I should have finished the security system before I left. Sorry about that.

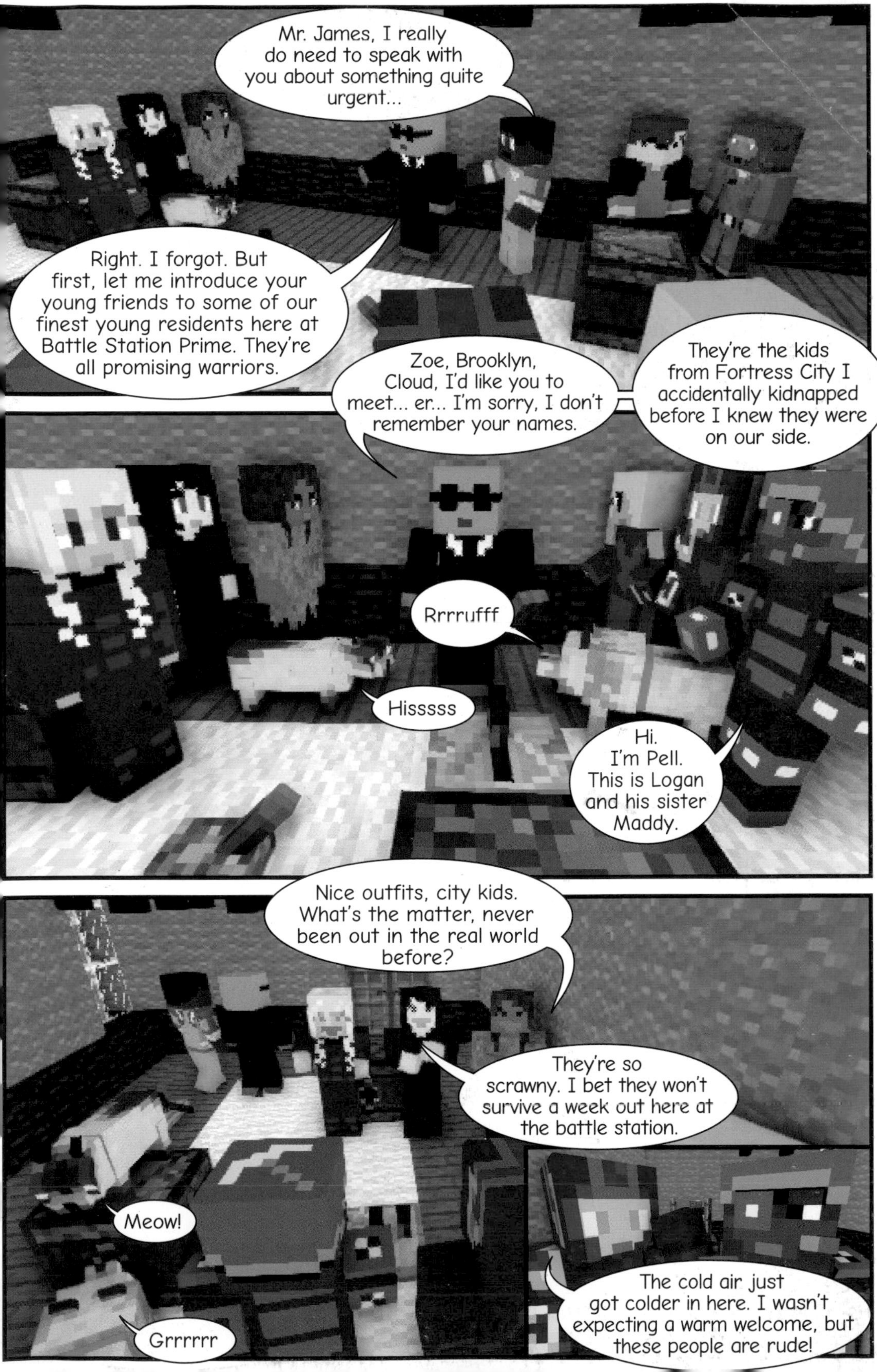
Mr. James, I really do need to speak with you about something quite urgent...
Right. I forgot. But first, let me introduce your young friends to some of our finest young residents here at Battle Station Prime. They're all promising warriors.
Zoe, Brooklyn, Cloud, I'd like you to meet... er... I'm sorry, I don't remember your names.
They're the kids from Fortress City I accidentally kidnapped before I knew they were on our side.
Rrrrufff
Hissssss
Hi. I'm Pell. This is Logan and his sister Maddy.
Nice outfits, city kids. What's the matter, never been out in the real world before?
They're so scrawny. I bet they won't survive a week out here at the battle station.
Meow!
Grrrrrr
The cold air just got colder in here. I wasn't expecting a warm welcome, but these people are rude!

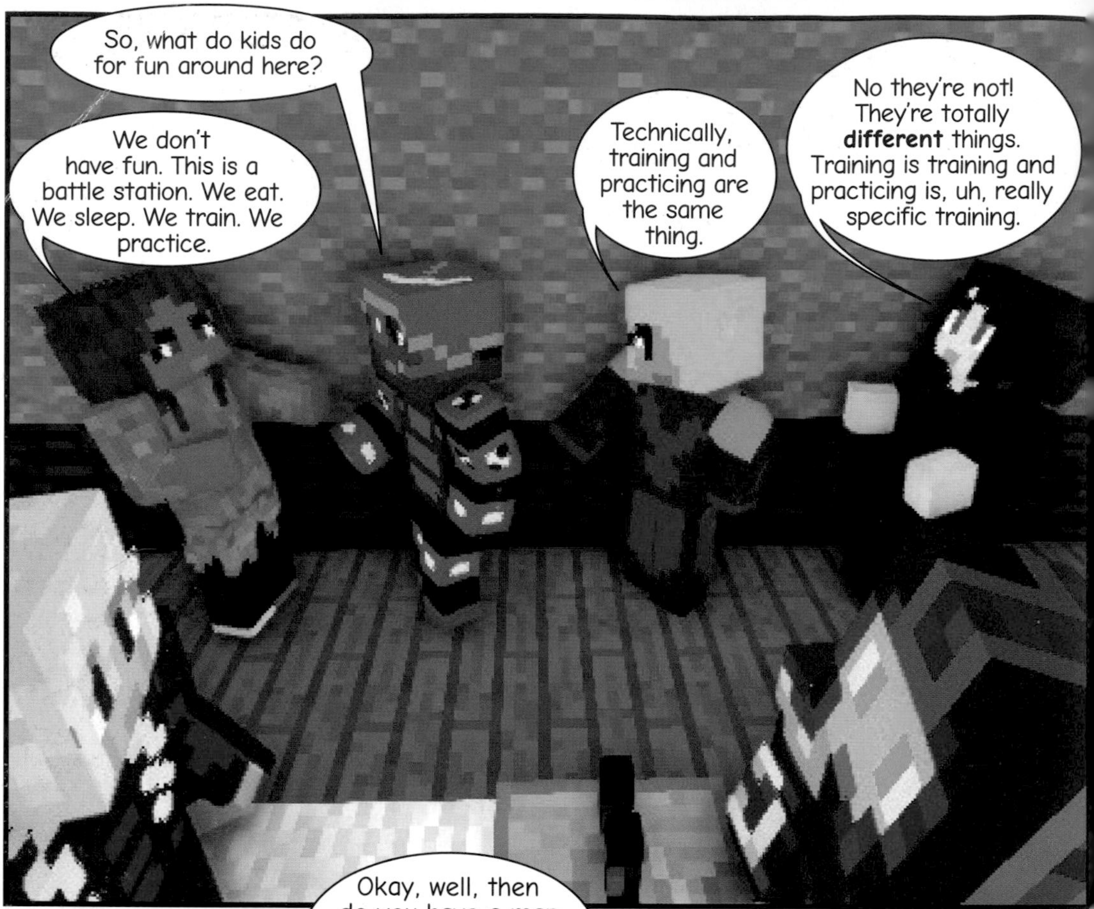
So, what do kids do for fun around here?
We don't have fun. This is a battle station. We eat. We sleep. We train. We practice.
Technically, training and practicing are the same thing.
No they're not! They're totally **different** things. Training is training and practicing is, uh, really specific training.

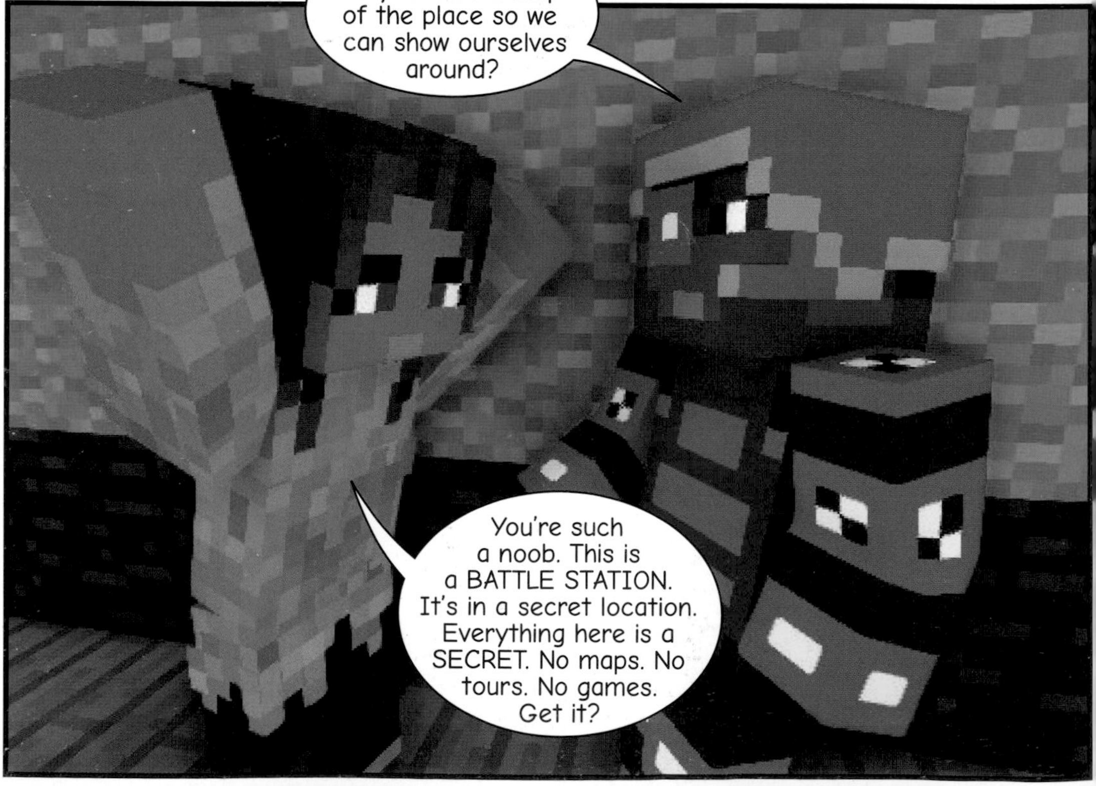
Okay, well, then do you have a map of the place so we can show ourselves around?
You're such a noob. This is a BATTLE STATION. It's in a secret location. Everything here is a SECRET. No maps. No tours. No games. Get it?

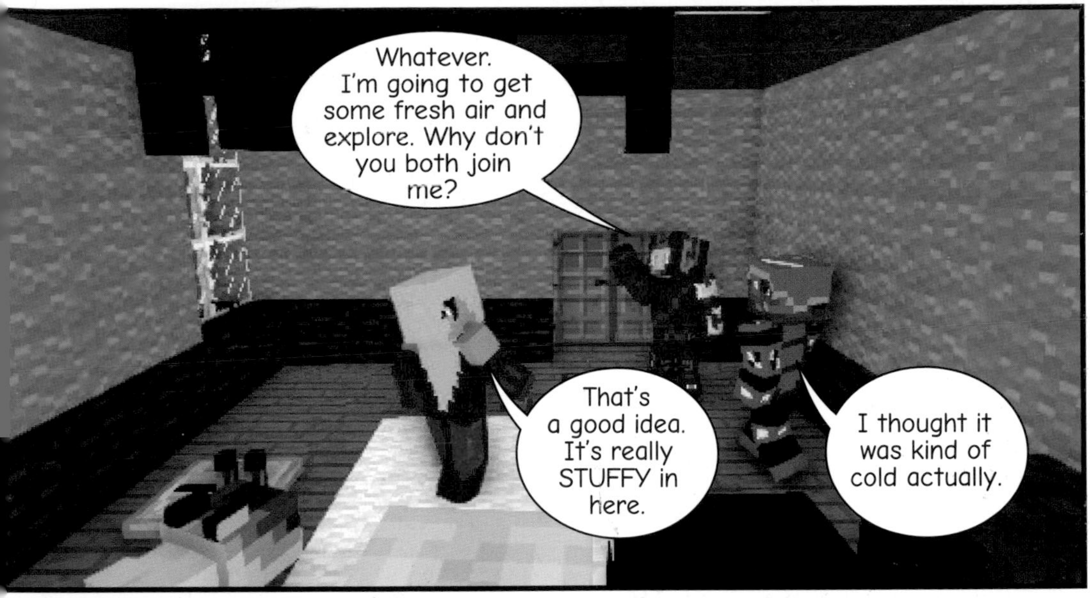
Whatever. I'm going to get some fresh air and explore. Why don't you both join me?
That's a good idea. It's really STUFFY in here.
I thought it was kind of cold actually.

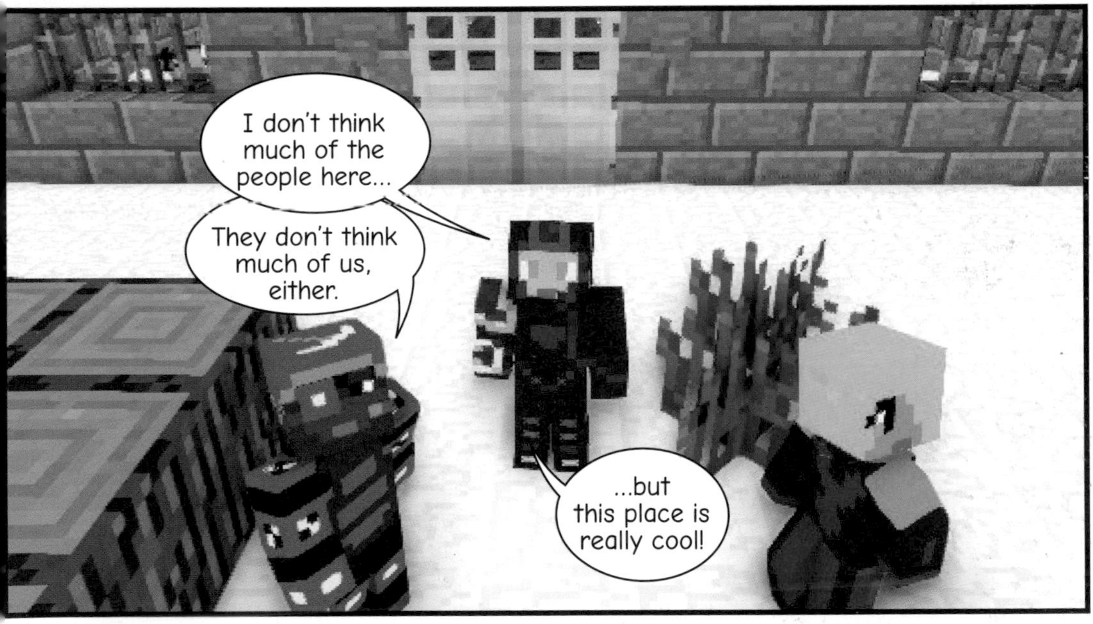
I don't think much of the people here...
They don't think much of us, either.
...but this place is really cool!

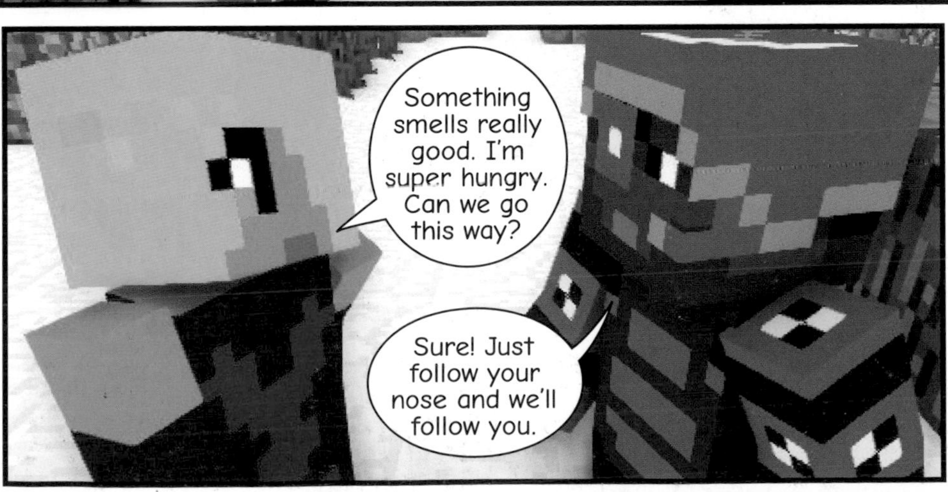
Something smells really good. I'm super hungry. Can we go this way?
Sure! Just follow your nose and we'll follow you.

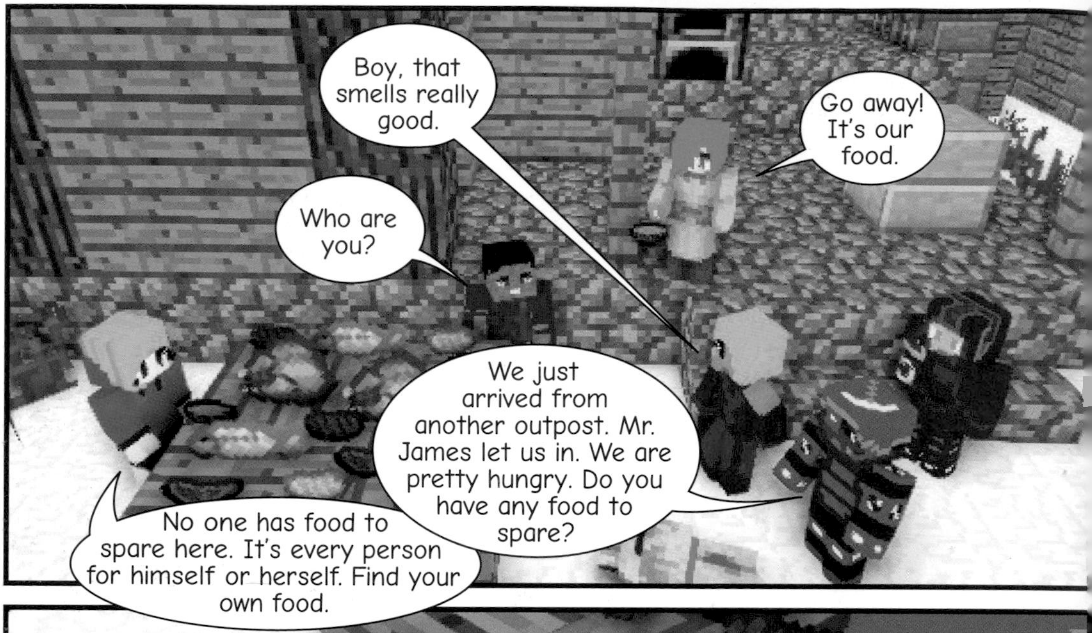
Boy, that smells really good.
Go away! It's our food.
Who are you?
We just arrived from another outpost. Mr. James let us in. We are pretty hungry. Do you have any food to spare?
No one has food to spare here. It's every person for himself or herself. Find your own food.

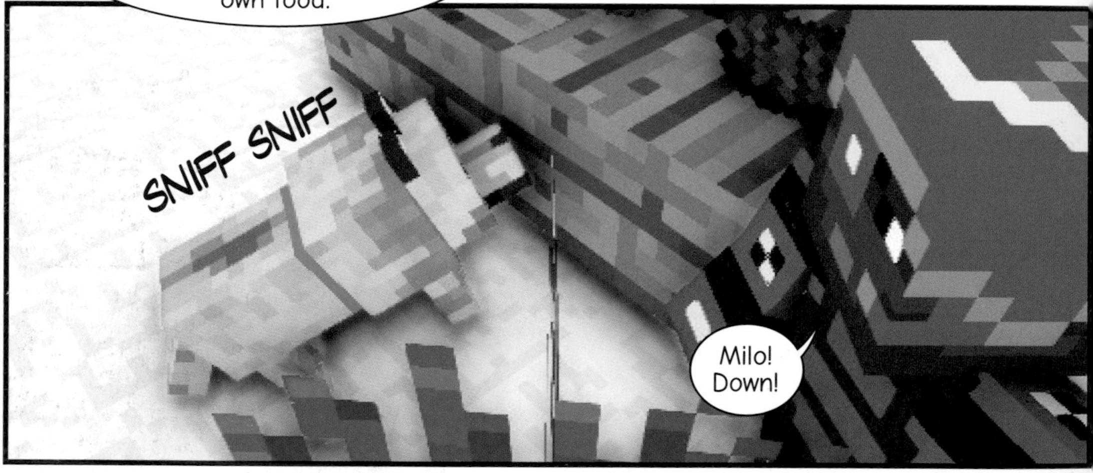
SNIFF SNIFF
Milo! Down!

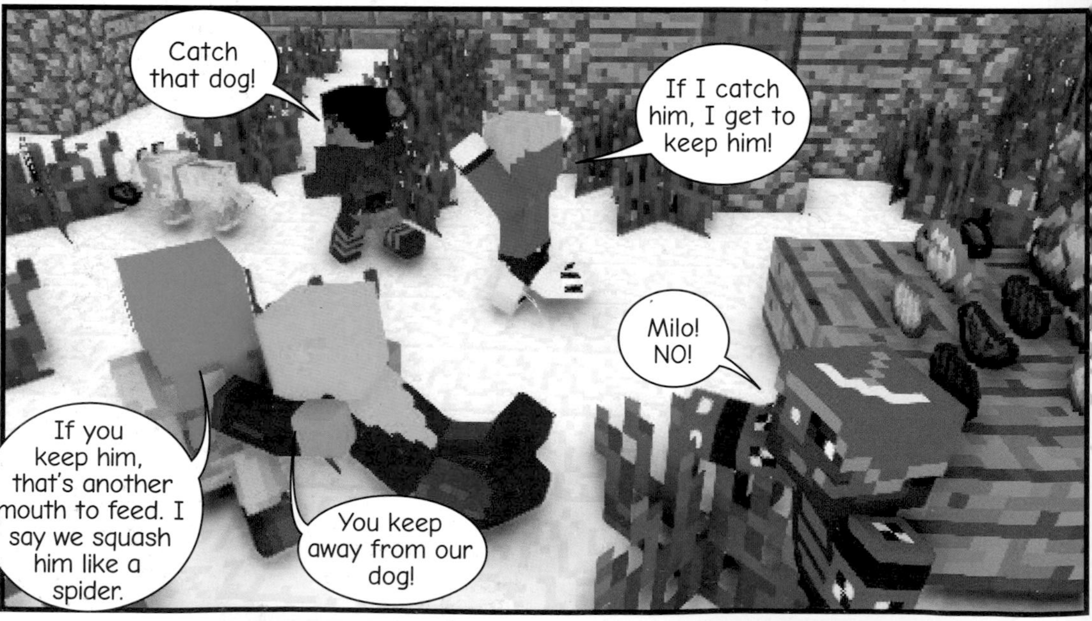
Catch that dog!
If I catch him, I get to keep him!
Milo! NO!
If you keep him, that's another mouth to feed. I say we squash him like a spider.
You keep away from our dog!

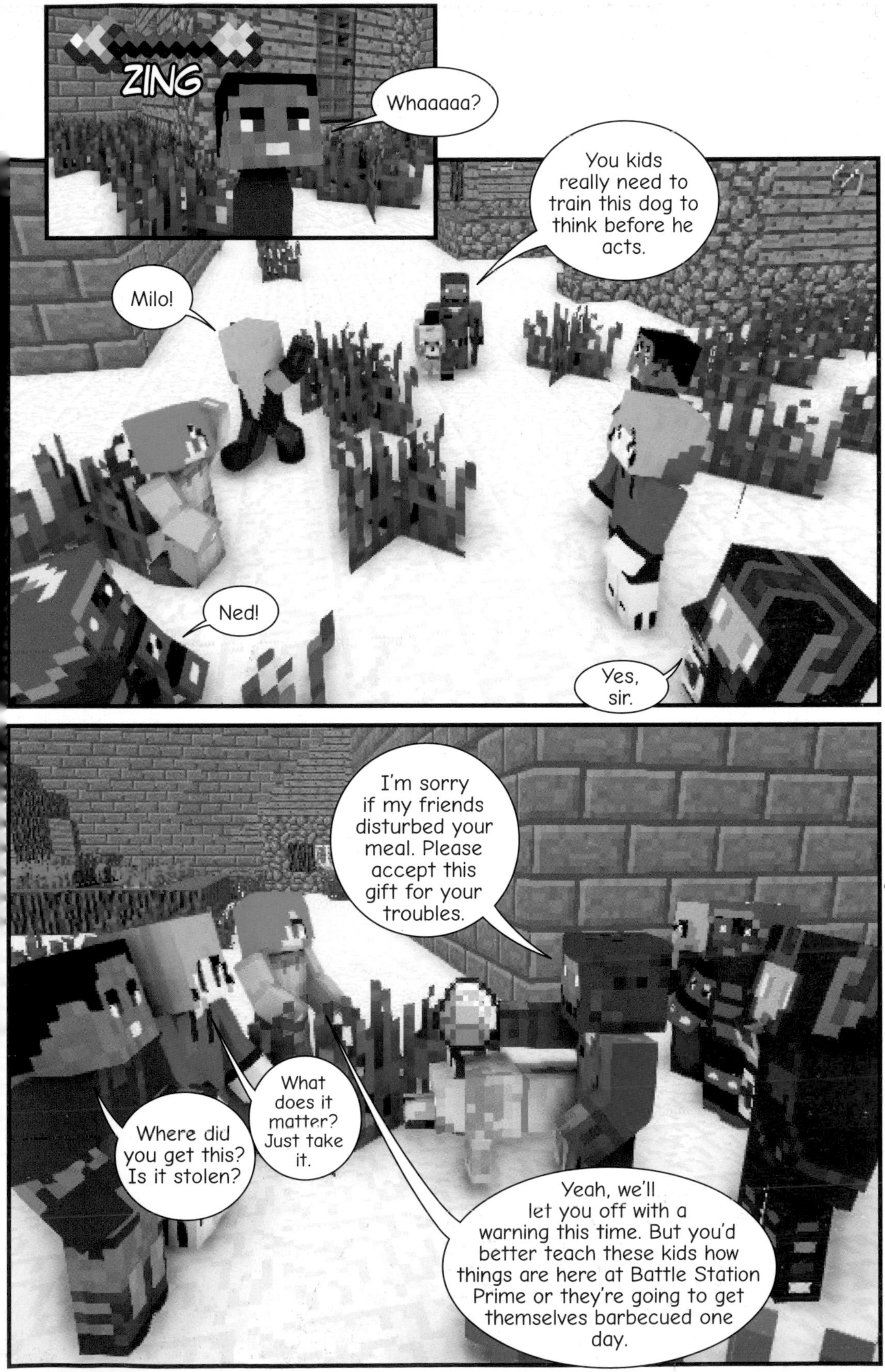
ZING
Whaaaaa?
You kids really need to train this dog to think before he acts.
Milo!
Ned!
Yes, sir.
I'm sorry if my friends disturbed your meal. Please accept this gift for your troubles.
What does it matter? Just take it.
Where did you get this? Is it stolen?
Yeah, we'll let you off with a warning this time. But you'd better teach these kids how things are here at Battle Station Prime or they're going to get themselves barbecued one day.

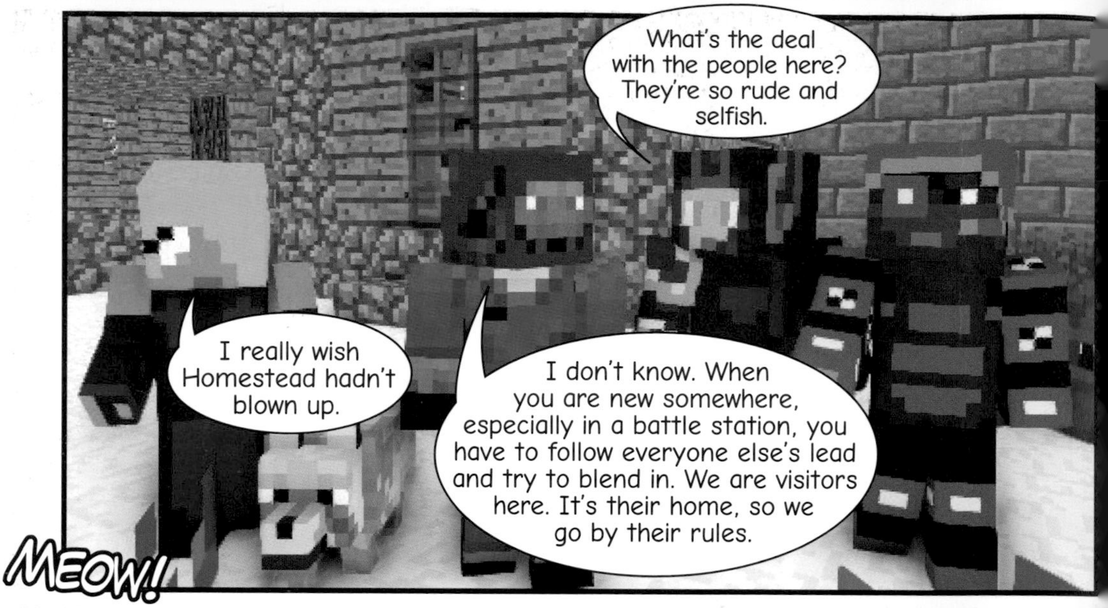
What's the deal with the people here? They're so rude and selfish.
I really wish Homestead hadn't blown up.
I don't know. When you are new somewhere, especially in a battle station, you have to follow everyone else's lead and try to blend in. We are visitors here. It's their home, so we go by their rules.
MEOW!
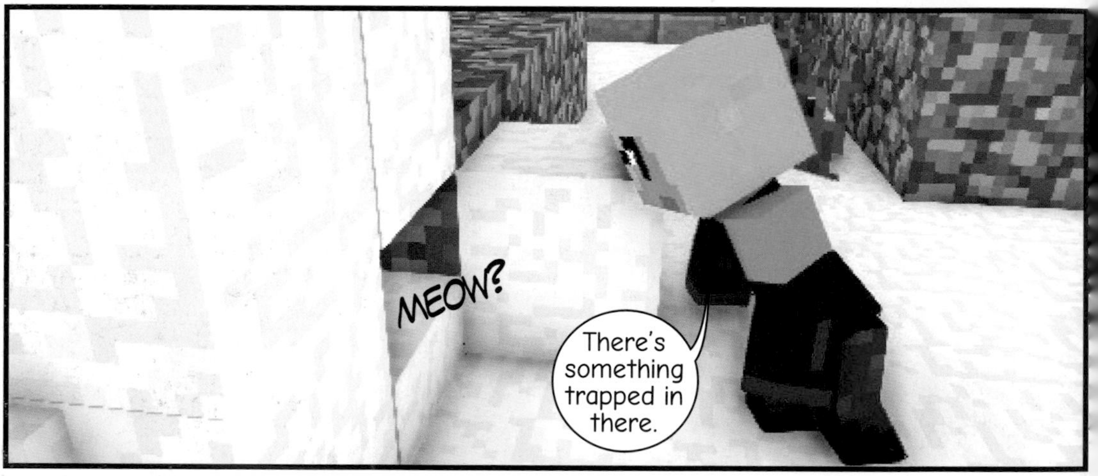
MEOW?
There's something trapped in there.
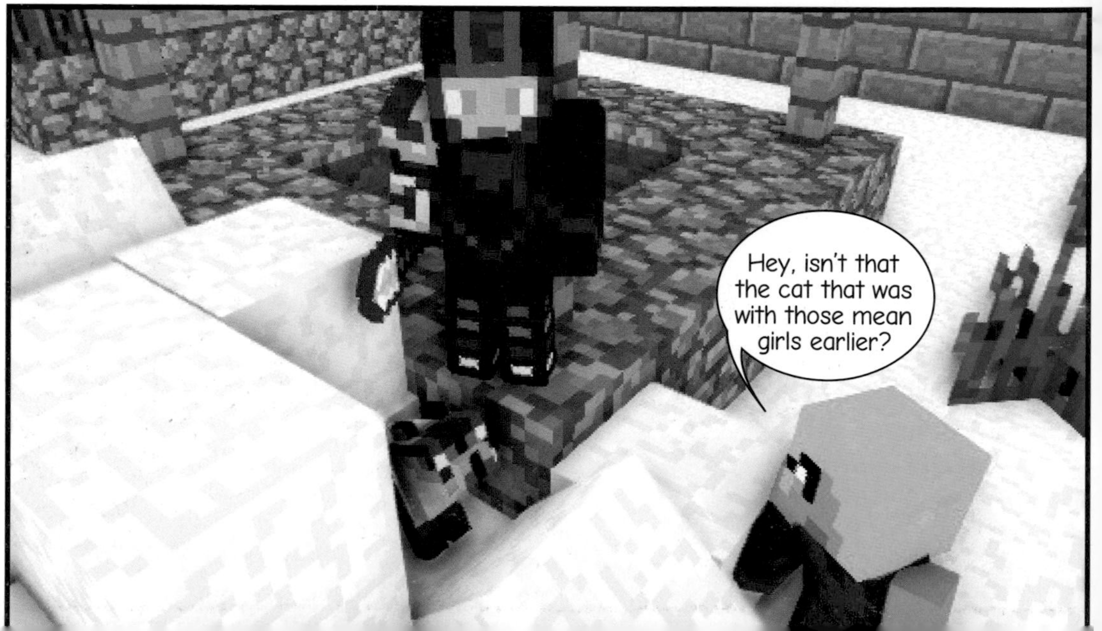
Hey, isn't that the cat that was with those mean girls earlier?

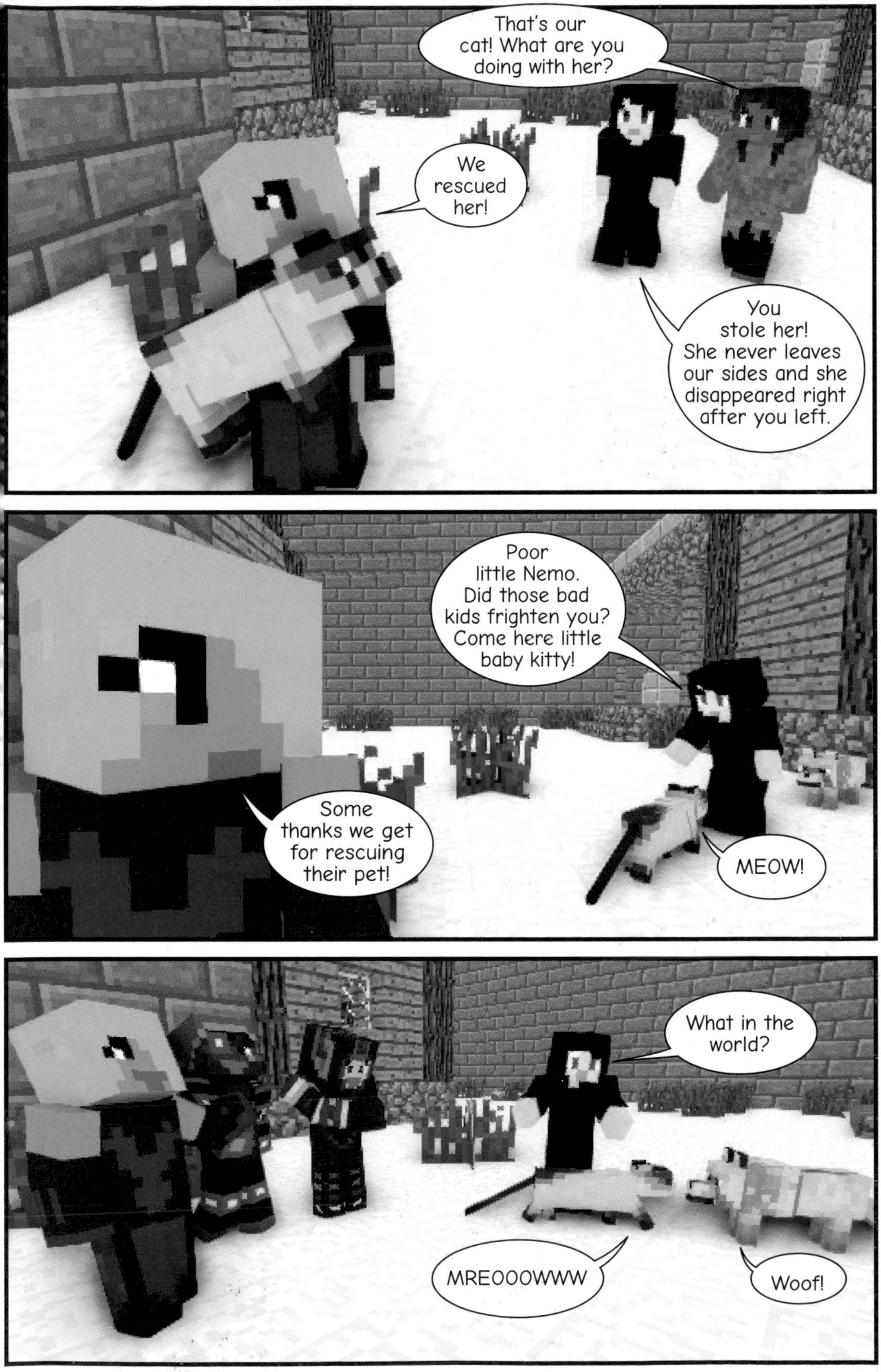
That's our cat! What are you doing with her?
We rescued her!
You stole her! She never leaves our sides and she disappeared right after you left.
Poor little Nemo. Did those bad kids frighten you? Come here little baby kitty!
Some thanks we get for rescuing their pet!
MEOW!
What in the world?
MREOOOWWW
Woof!

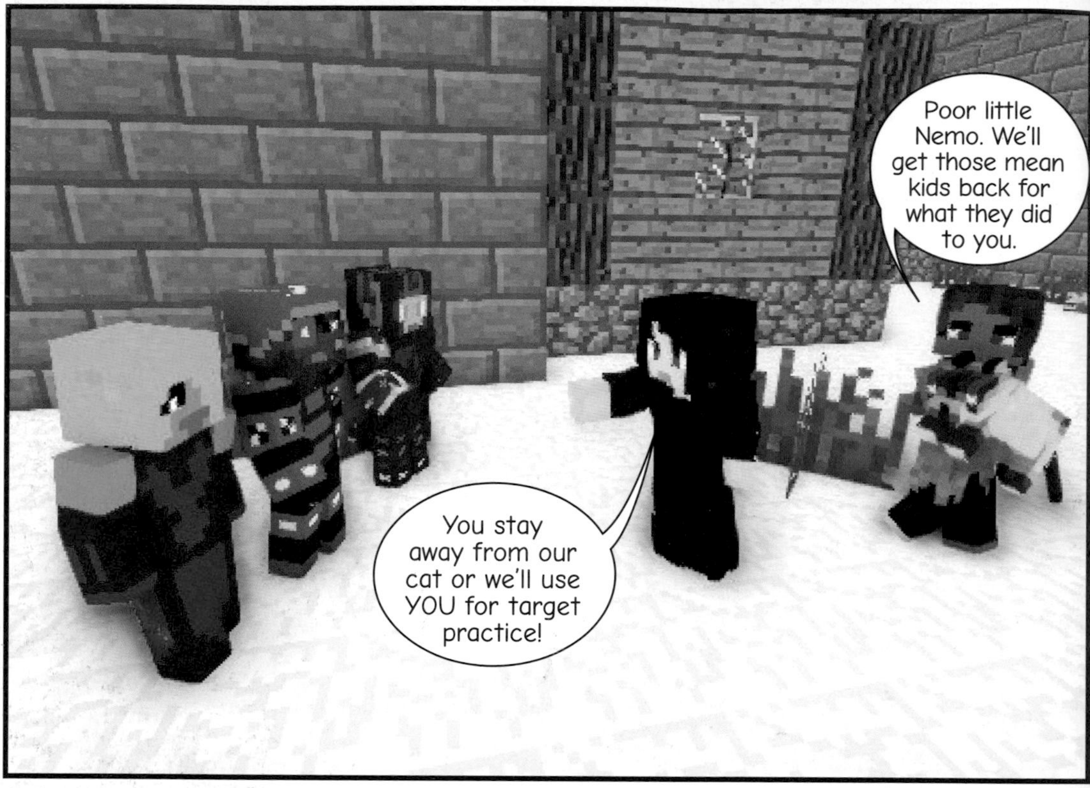
Poor little Nemo. We'll get those mean kids back for what they did to you.
You stay away from our cat or we'll use YOU for target practice!

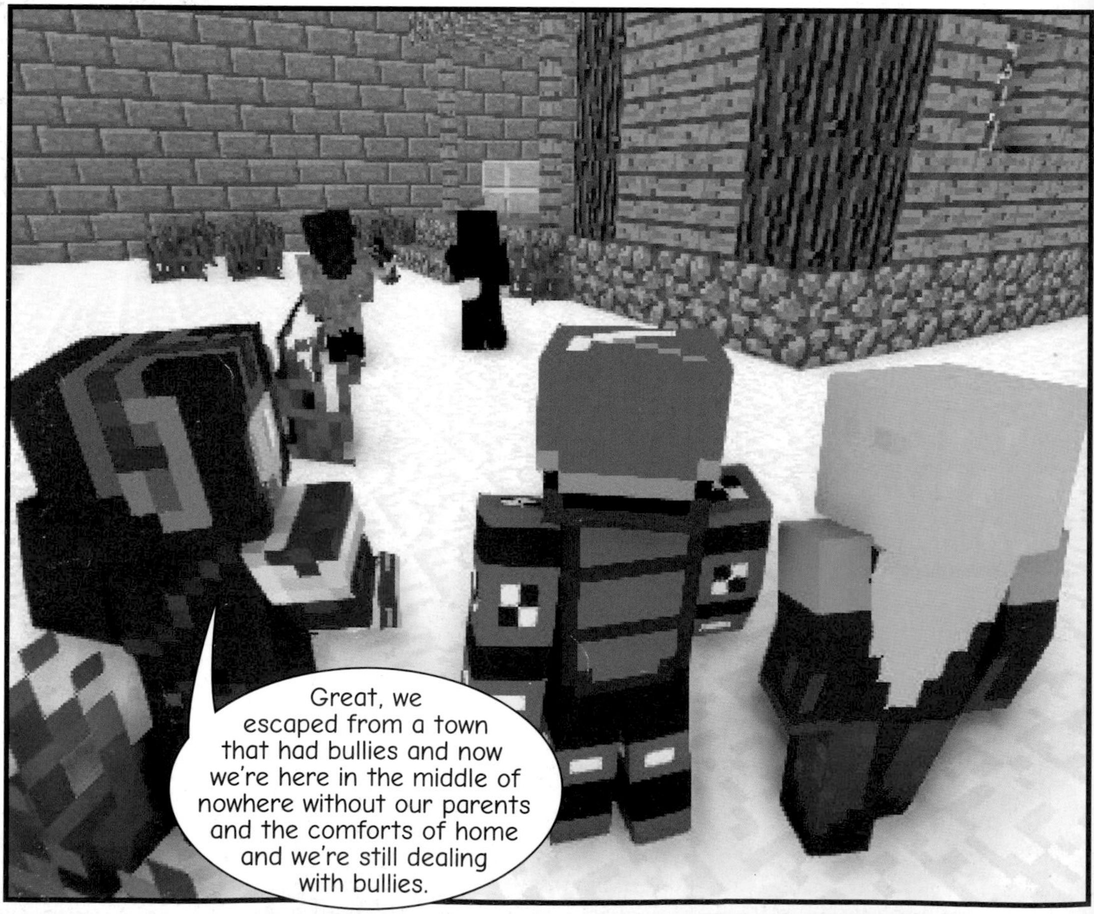
Great, we escaped from a town that had bullies and now we're here in the middle of nowhere without our parents and the comforts of home and we're still dealing with bullies.

CHAPTER 4

GRIEFING WAR

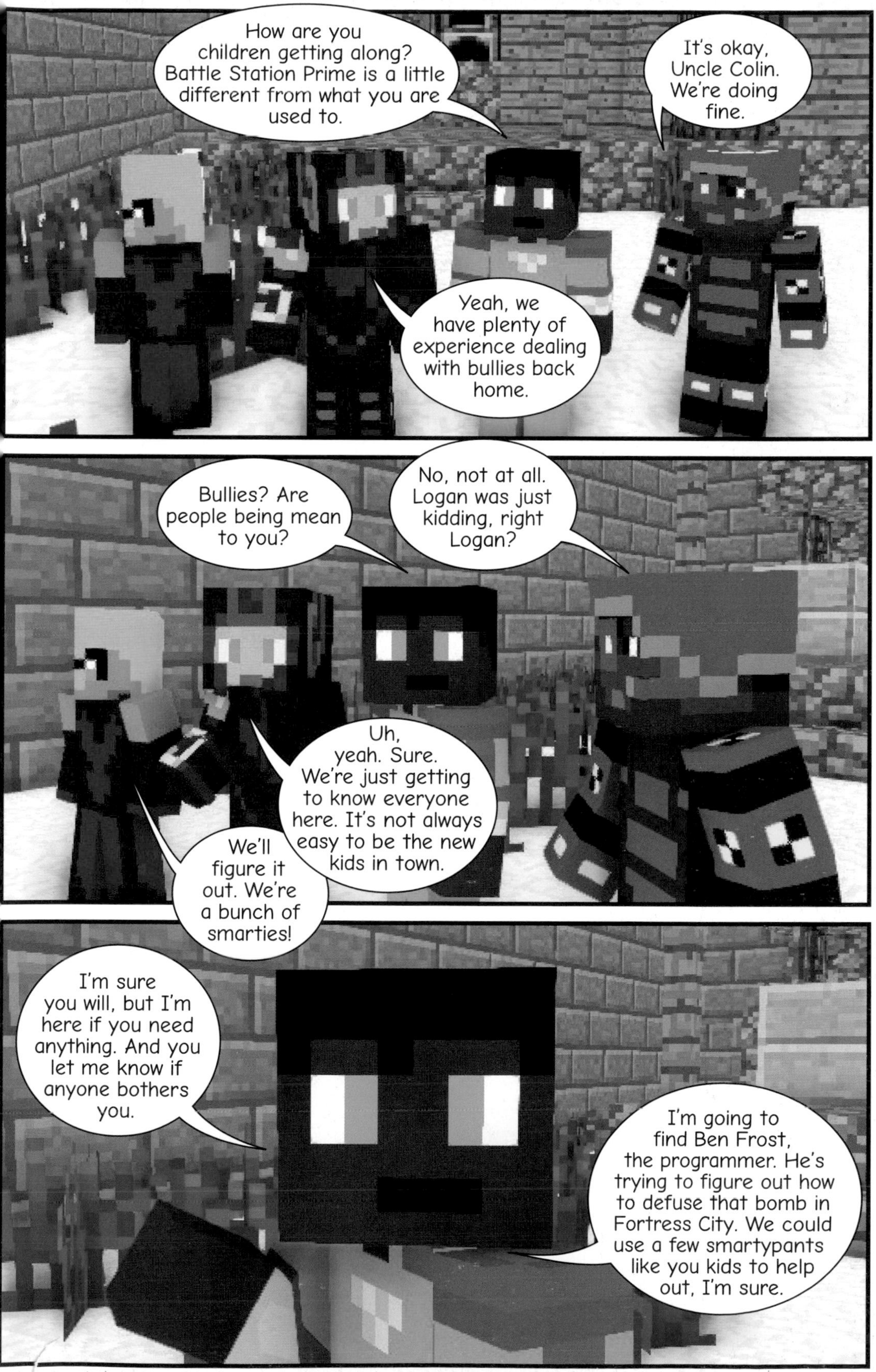
How are you children getting along? Battle Station Prime is a little different from what you are used to.
It's okay, Uncle Colin. We're doing fine.
Yeah, we have plenty of experience dealing with bullies back home.
Bullies? Are people being mean to you?
No, not at all. Logan was just kidding, right Logan?
Uh, yeah. Sure. We're just getting to know everyone here. It's not always easy to be the new kids in town.
We'll figure it out. We're a bunch of smarties!
I'm sure you will, but I'm here if you need anything. And you let me know if anyone bothers you.
I'm going to find Ben Frost, the programmer. He's trying to figure out how to defuse that bomb in Fortress City. We could use a few smartypants like you kids to help out, I'm sure.

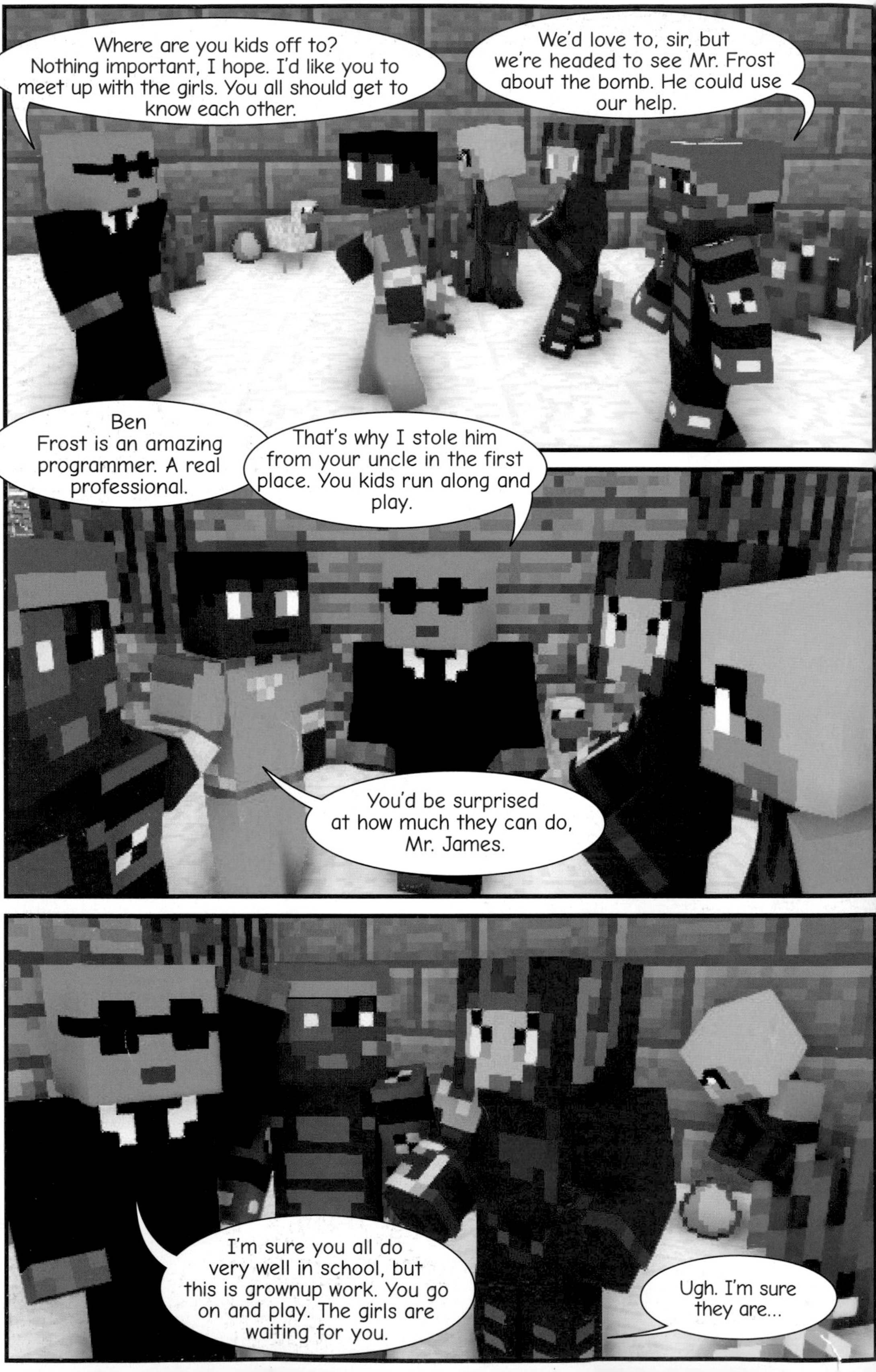
Where are you kids off to? Nothing important, I hope. I'd like you to meet up with the girls. You all should get to know each other.
We'd love to, sir, but we're headed to see Mr. Frost about the bomb. He could use our help.
Ben Frost is an amazing programmer. A real professional.
That's why I stole him from your uncle in the first place. You kids run along and play.
You'd be surprised at how much they can do, Mr. James.
I'm sure you all do very well in school, but this is grownup work. You go on and play. The girls are waiting for you.
Ugh. I'm sure they are...

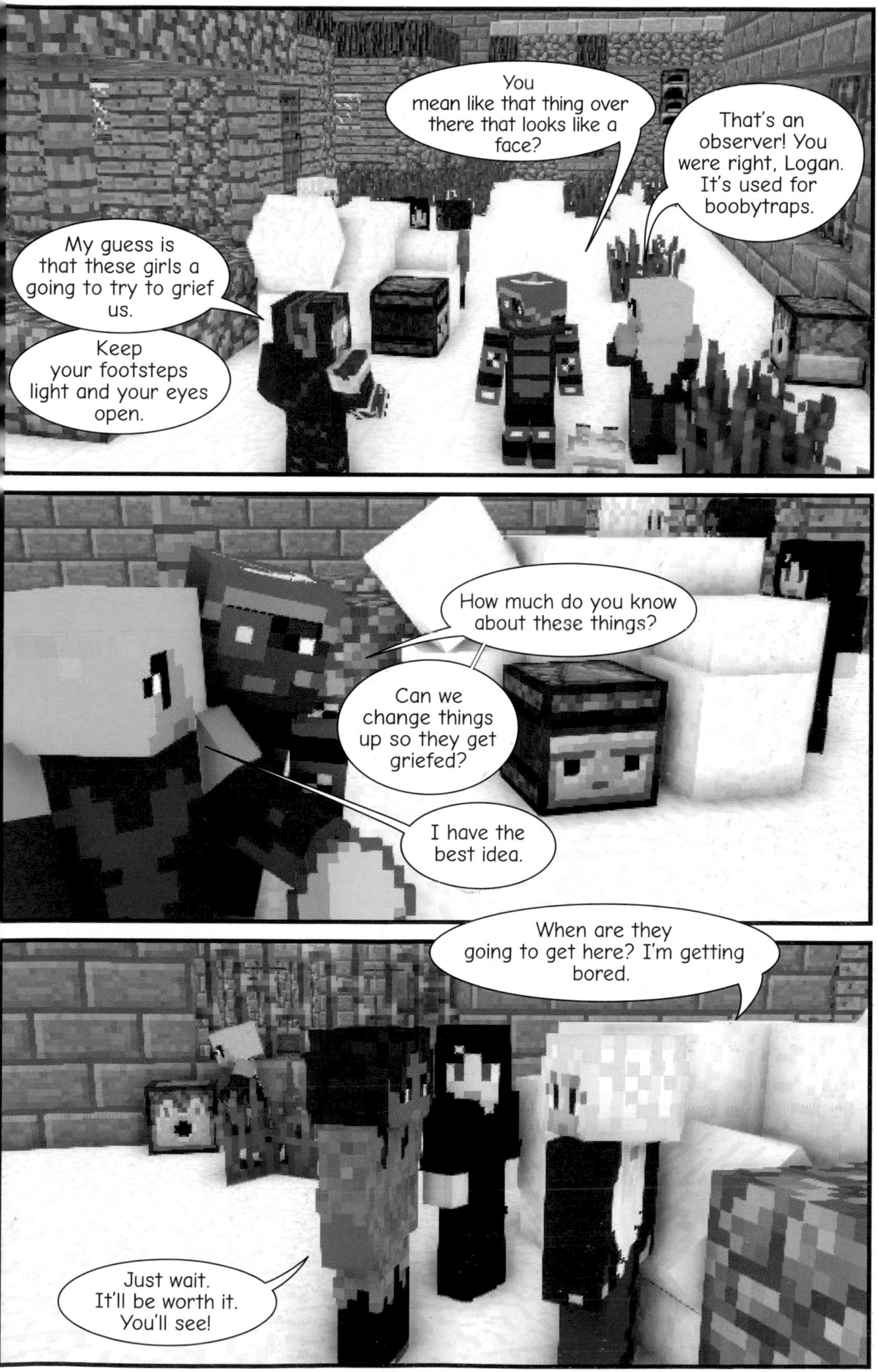
My guess is that these girls a going to try to grief us.
Keep your footsteps light and your eyes open.
You mean like that thing over there that looks like a face?
That's an observer! You were right, Logan. It's used for boobytraps.
How much do you know about these things?
Can we change things up so they get griefed?
I have the best idea.
When are they going to get here? I'm getting bored.
Just wait. It'll be worth it. You'll see!

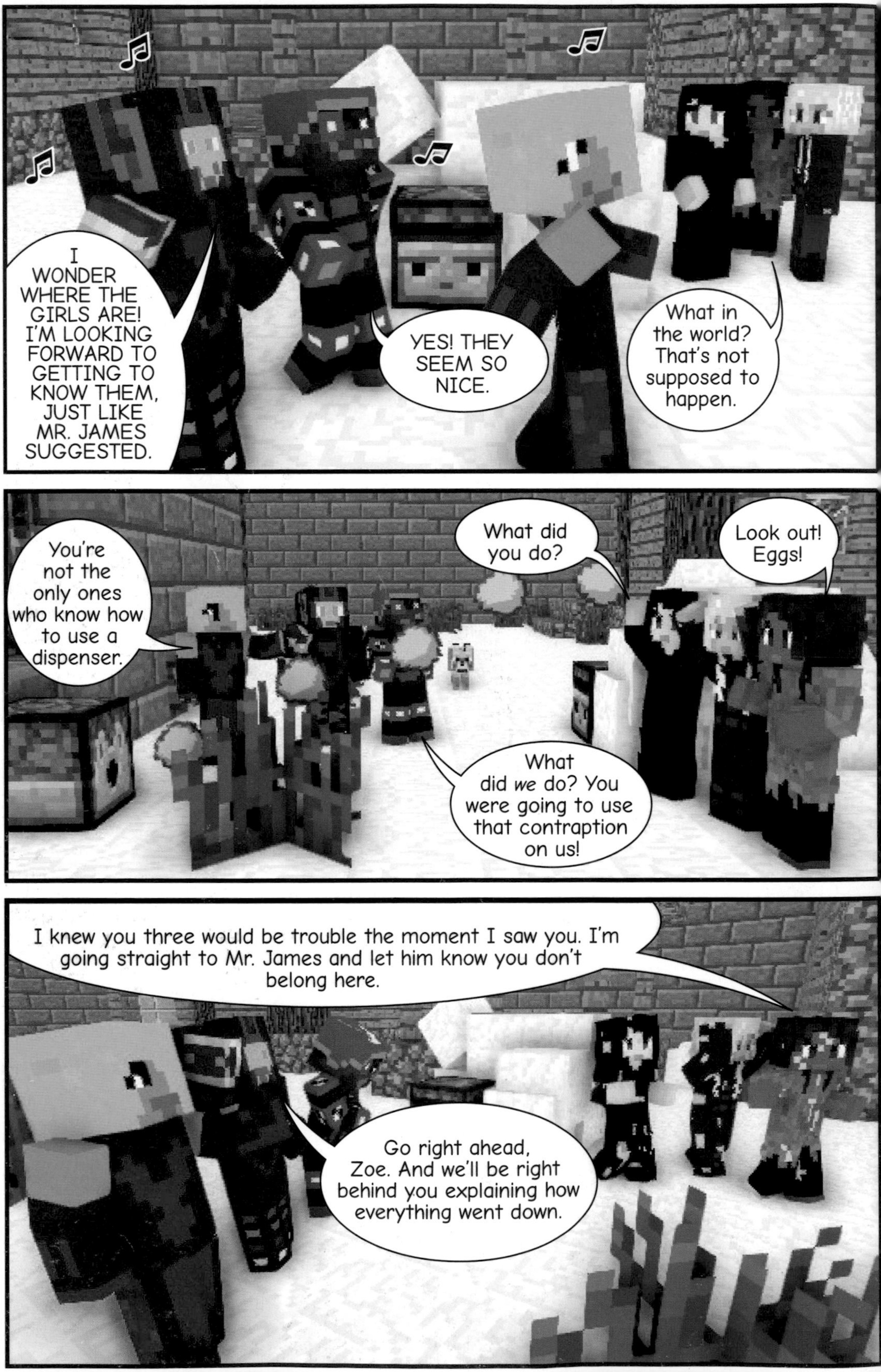
I WONDER WHERE THE GIRLS ARE! I'M LOOKING FORWARD TO GETTING TO KNOW THEM, JUST LIKE MR. JAMES SUGGESTED.
YES! THEY SEEM SO NICE.
What in the world? That's not supposed to happen.
You're not the only ones who know how to use a dispenser.
What did you do?
Look out! Eggs!
What did *we* do? You were going to use that contraption on us!
I knew you three would be trouble the moment I saw you. I'm going straight to Mr. James and let him know you don't belong here.
Go right ahead, Zoe. And we'll be right behind you explaining how everything went down.

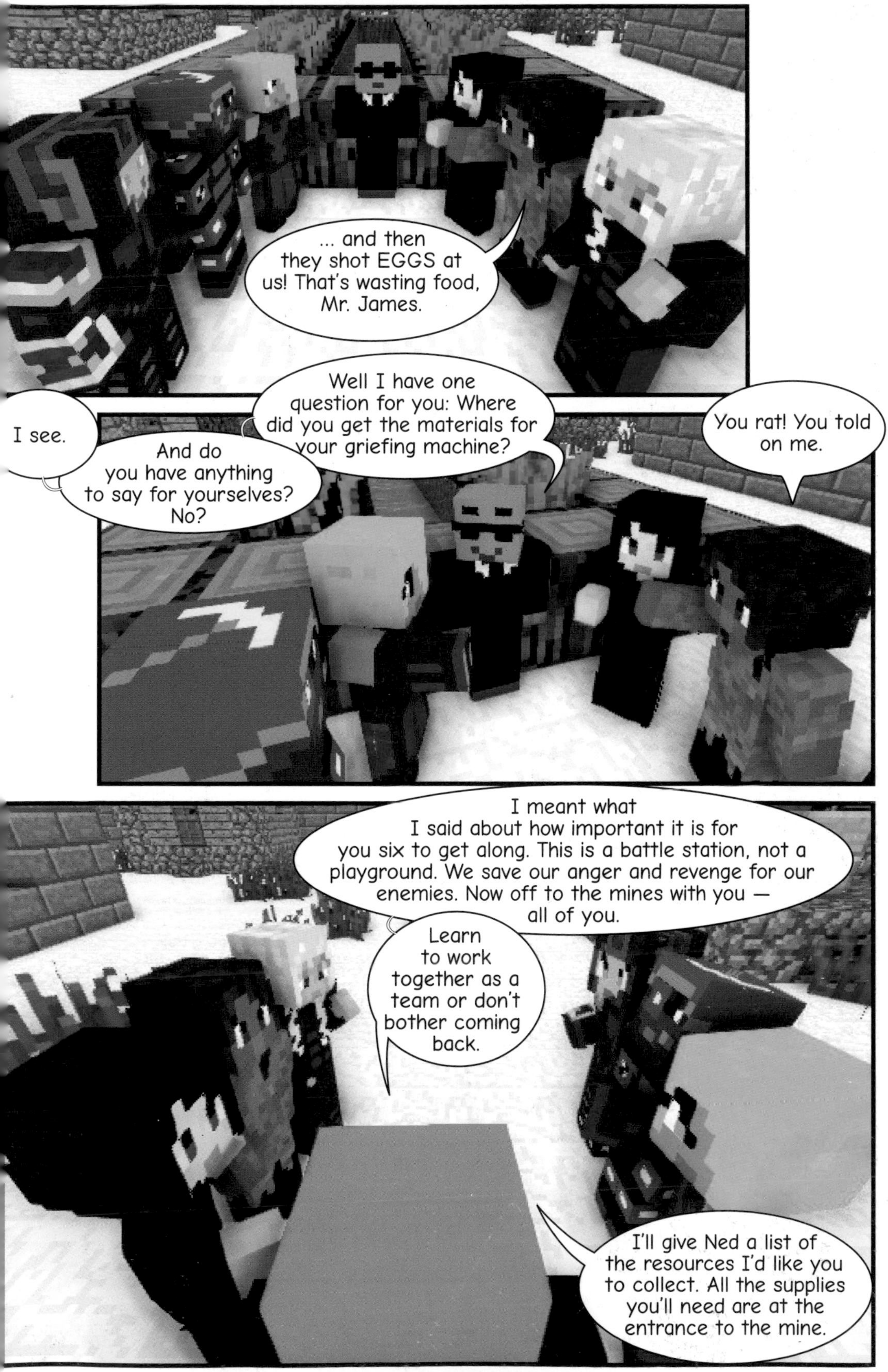
... and then they shot EGGS at us! That's wasting food, Mr. James.
I see.
And do you have anything to say for yourselves? No?
Well I have one question for you: Where did you get the materials for your griefing machine?
You rat! You told on me.
I meant what I said about how important it is for you six to get along. This is a battle station, not a playground. We save our anger and revenge for our enemies. Now off to the mines with you — all of you.
Learn to work together as a team or don't bother coming back.
I'll give Ned a list of the resources I'd like you to collect. All the supplies you'll need are at the entrance to the mine.

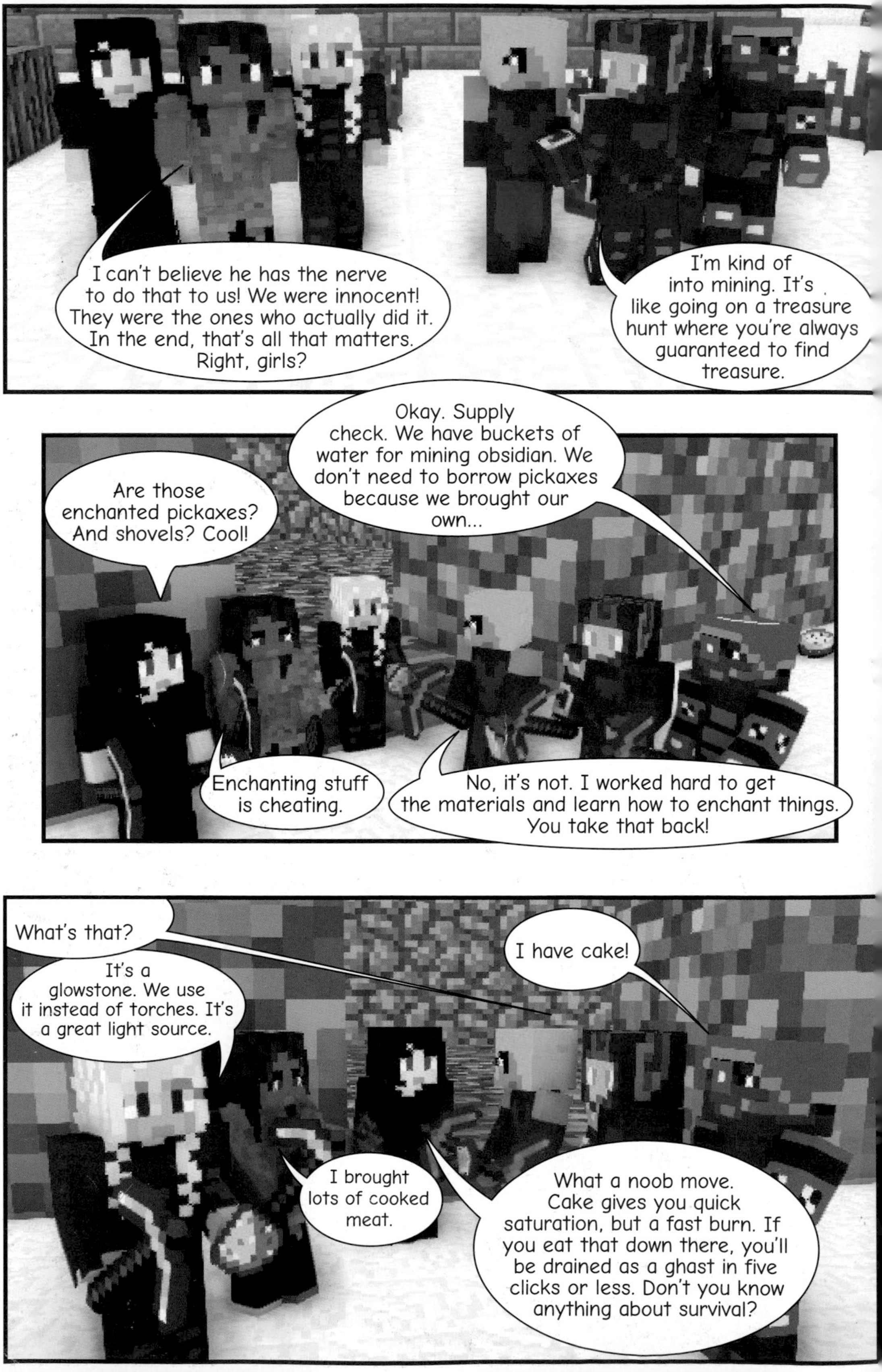

I can't believe he has the nerve to do that to us! We were innocent! They were the ones who actually did it. In the end, that's all that matters. Right, girls?
I'm kind of into mining. It's like going on a treasure hunt where you're always guaranteed to find treasure.
Okay. Supply check. We have buckets of water for mining obsidian. We don't need to borrow pickaxes because we brought our own...
Are those enchanted pickaxes? And shovels? Cool!
Enchanting stuff is cheating.
No, it's not. I worked hard to get the materials and learn how to enchant things. You take that back!
What's that?
It's a glowstone. We use it instead of torches. It's a great light source.
I have cake!
I brought lots of cooked meat.
What a noob move. Cake gives you quick saturation, but a fast burn. If you eat that down there, you'll be drained as a ghast in five clicks or less. Don't you know anything about survival?

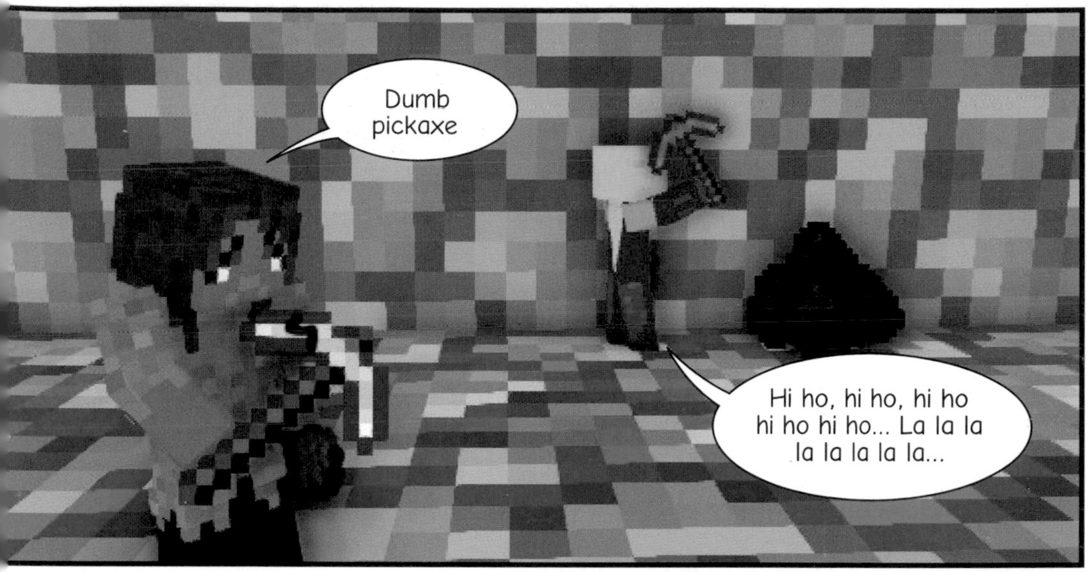
Dumb pickaxe
Hi ho, hi ho, hi ho hi ho hi ho... La la la la la la la la...

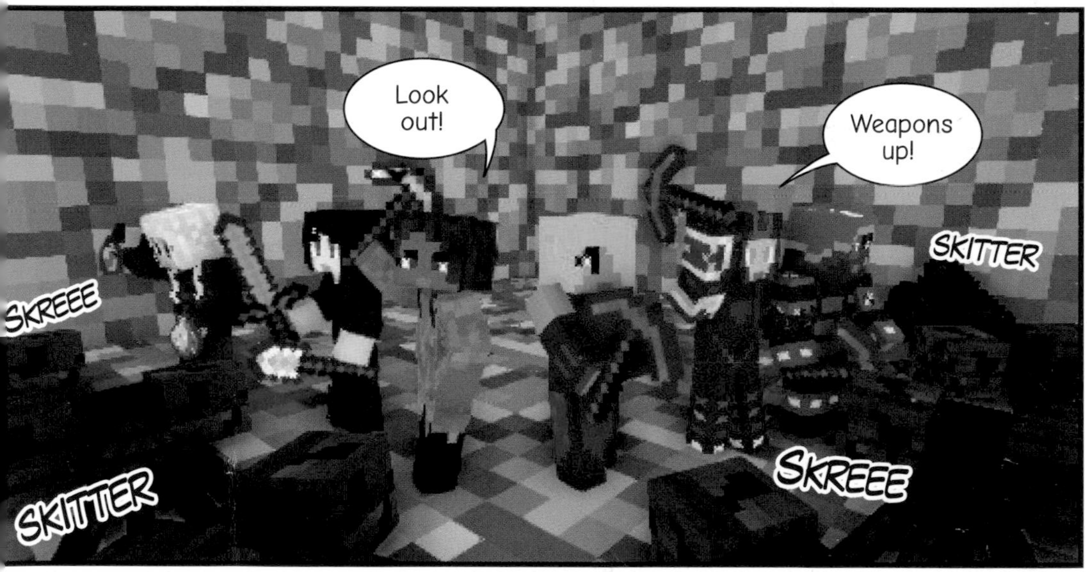
Look out!
Weapons up!
SKREEE
SKITTER
SKITTER
SKREEE

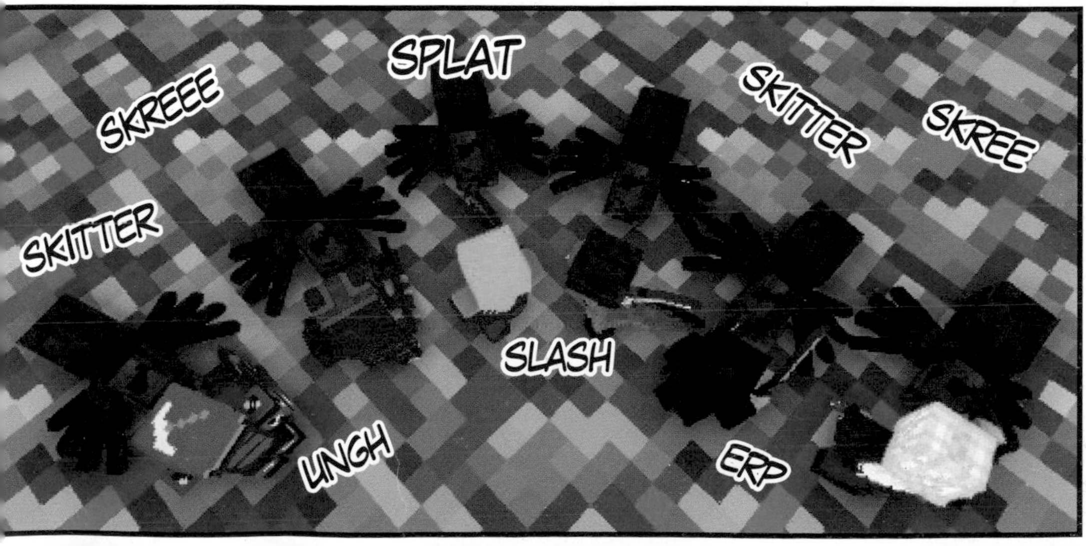
SPLAT
SKREEE
SKITTER
SKREE
SKITTER
SLASH
UNGH
ERP

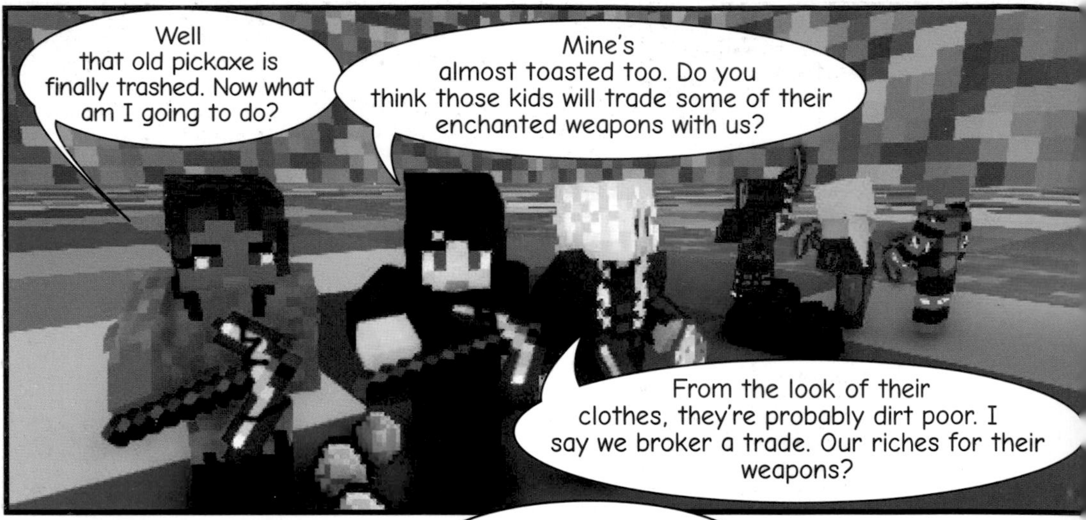
Well that old pickaxe is finally trashed. Now what am I going to do?
Mine's almost toasted too. Do you think those kids will trade some of their enchanted weapons with us?
From the look of their clothes, they're probably dirt poor. I say we broker a trade. Our riches for their weapons?

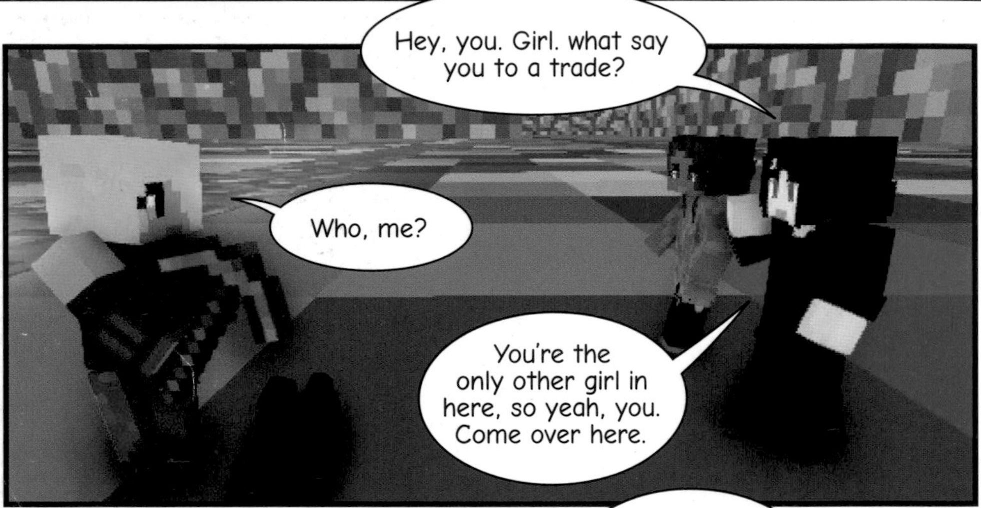
Hey, you. Girl. what say you to a trade?
Who, me?
You're the only other girl in here, so yeah, you. Come over here.

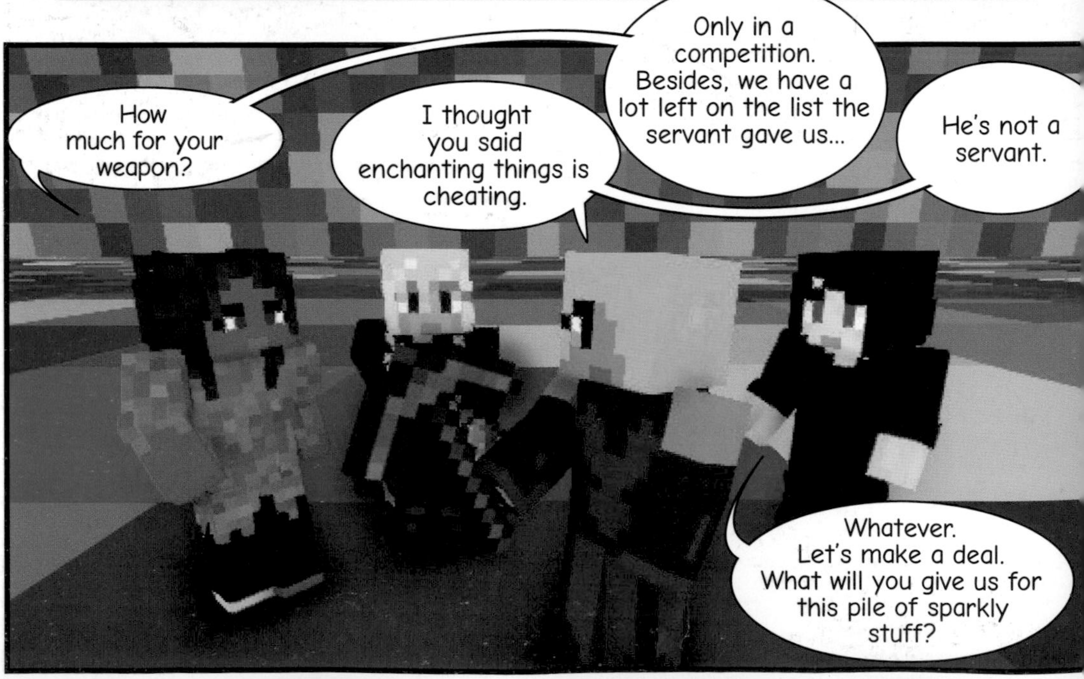
How much for your weapon?
I thought you said enchanting things is cheating.
Only in a competition. Besides, we have a lot left on the list the servant gave us...
He's not a servant.
Whatever. Let's make a deal. What will you give us for this pile of sparkly stuff?

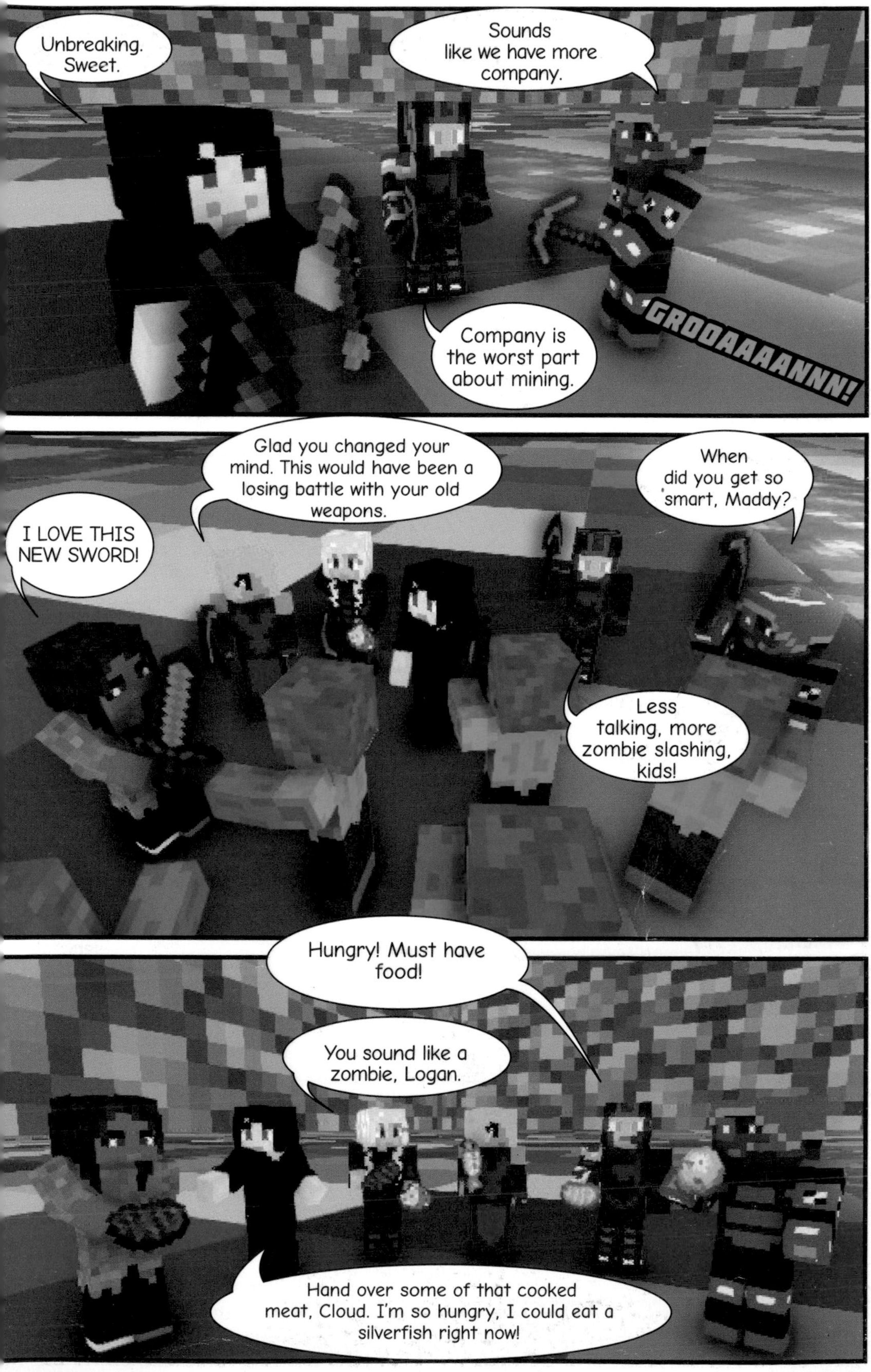
Unbreaking. Sweet.
Sounds like we have more company.
Company is the worst part about mining.
GROOAAAANNN!
I LOVE THIS NEW SWORD!
Glad you changed your mind. This would have been a losing battle with your old weapons.
When did you get so smart, Maddy?
Less talking, more zombie slashing, kids!
Hungry! Must have food!
You sound like a zombie, Logan.
Hand over some of that cooked meat, Cloud. I'm so hungry, I could eat a silverfish right now!

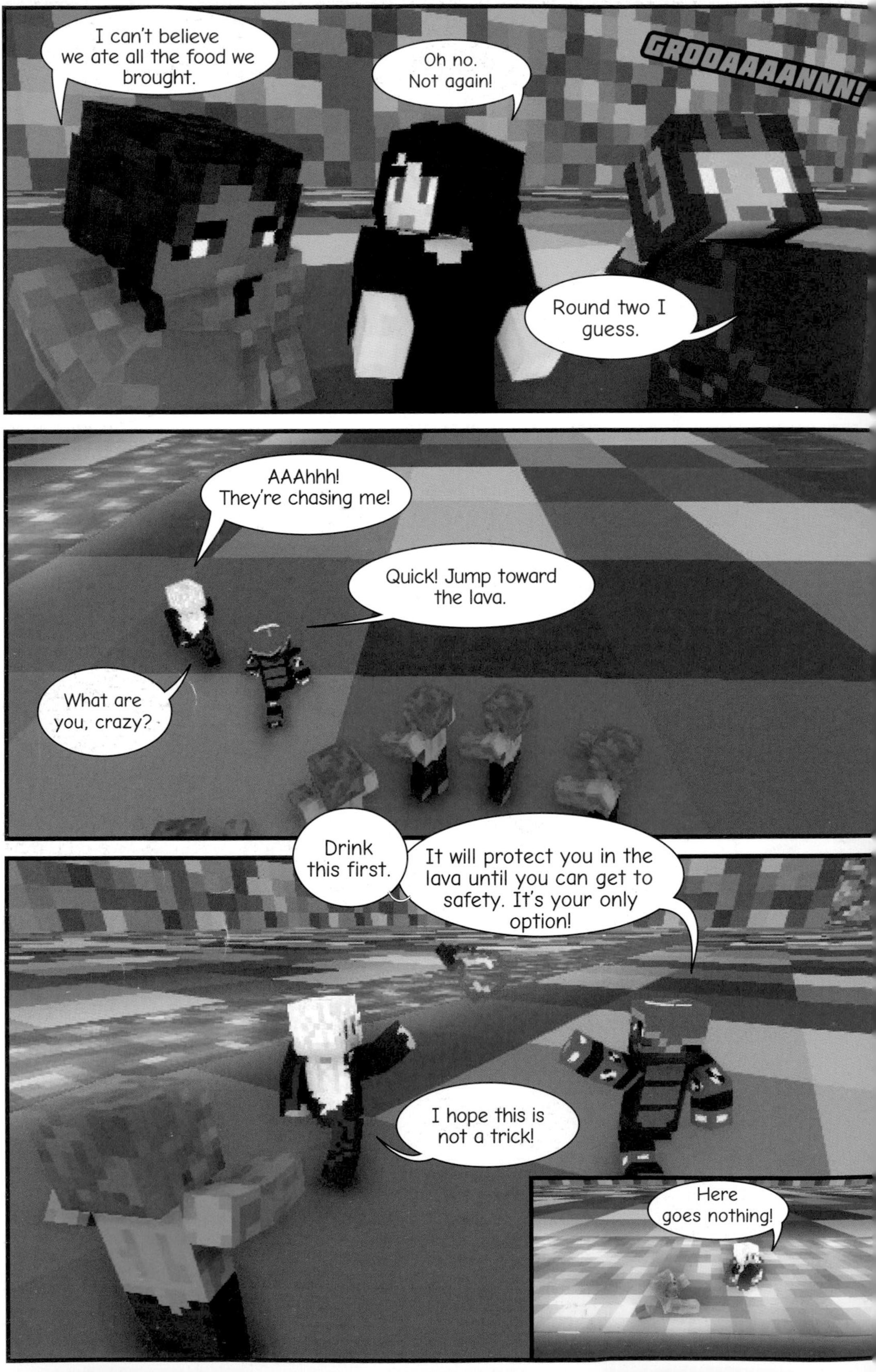
I can't believe we ate all the food we brought.
Oh no. Not again!
GROOAAAANNN!
Round two I guess.
AAAhhh! They're chasing me!
Quick! Jump toward the lava.
What are you, crazy?
Drink this first.
It will protect you in the lava until you can get to safety. It's your only option!
I hope this is not a trick!
Here goes nothing!

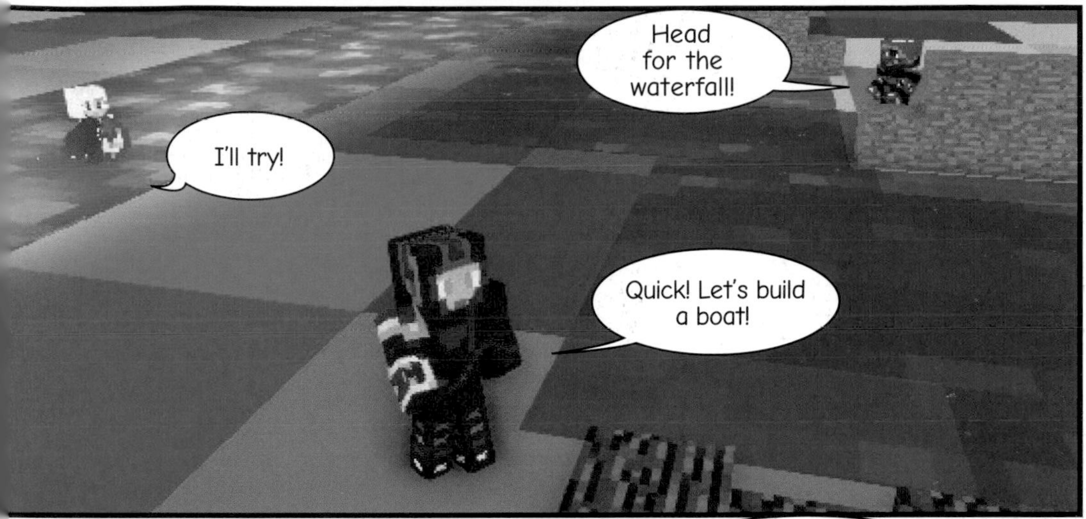
Head for the waterfall!
I'll try!
Quick! Let's build a boat!

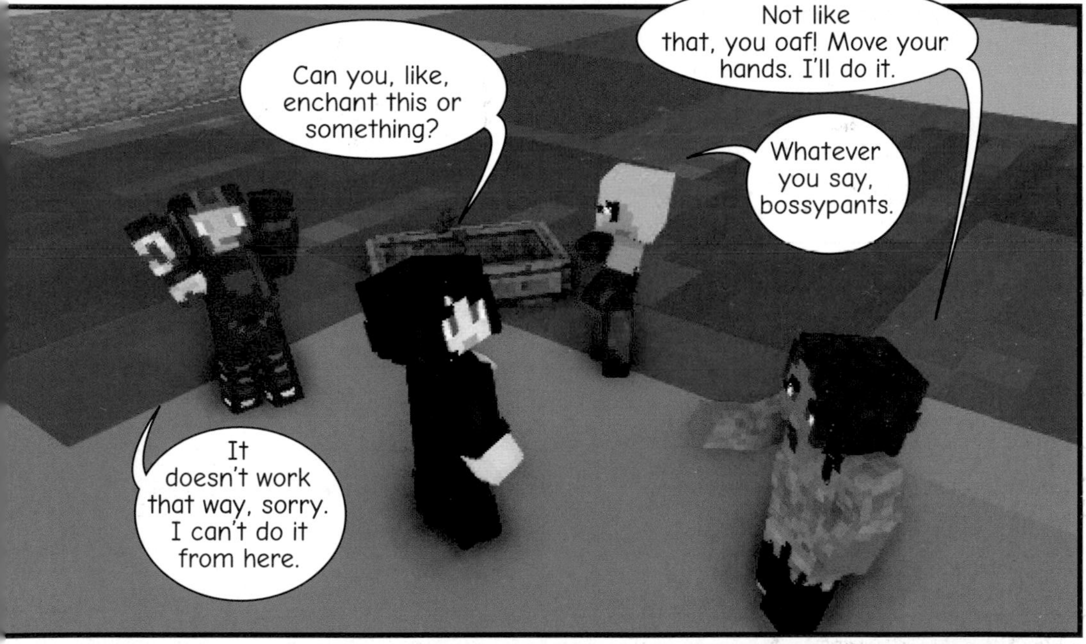
Not like that, you oaf! Move your hands. I'll do it.
Can you, like, enchant this or something?
Whatever you say, bossypants.
It doesn't work that way, sorry. I can't do it from here.

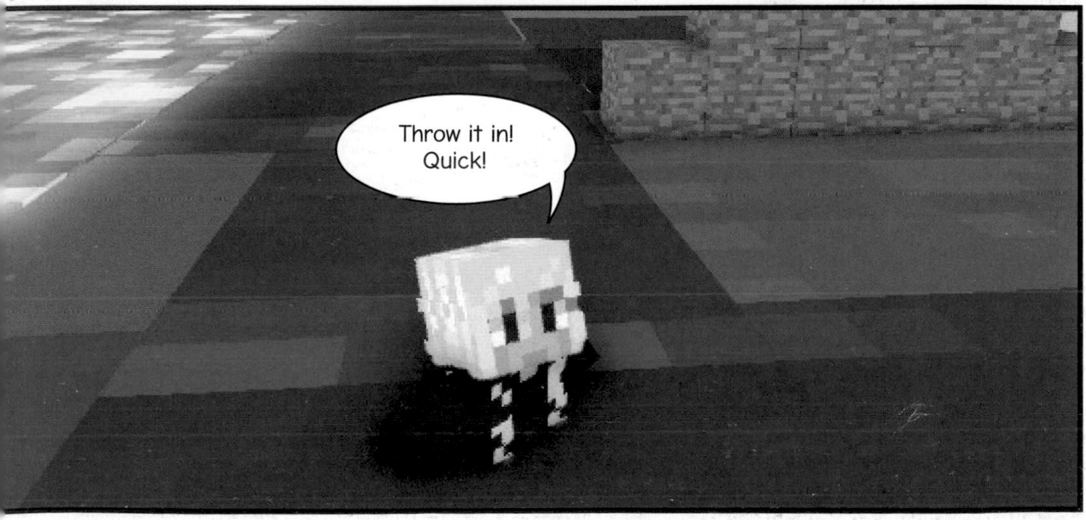
Throw it in! Quick!

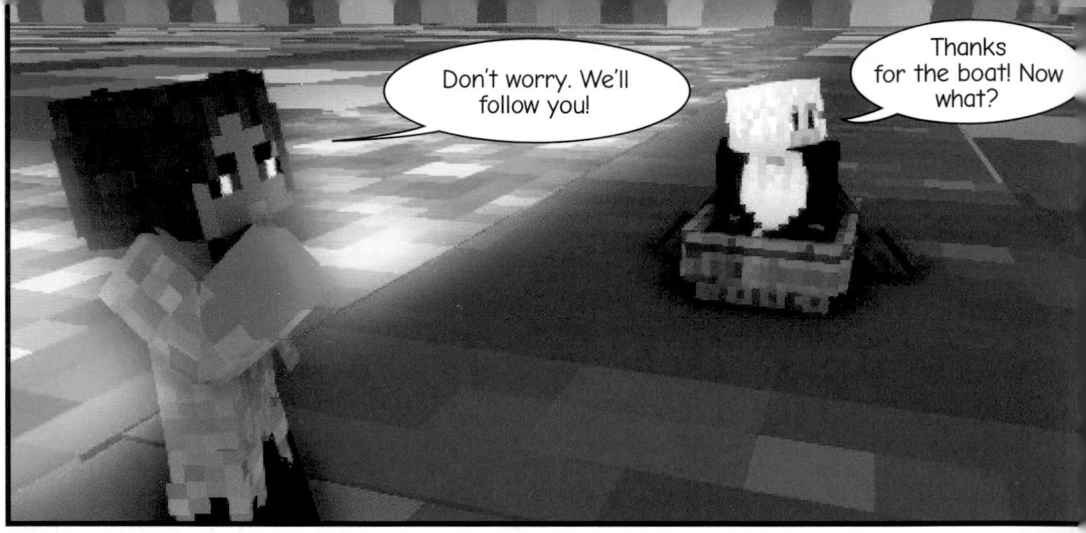
Thanks for the boat! Now what?
Don't worry. We'll follow you!

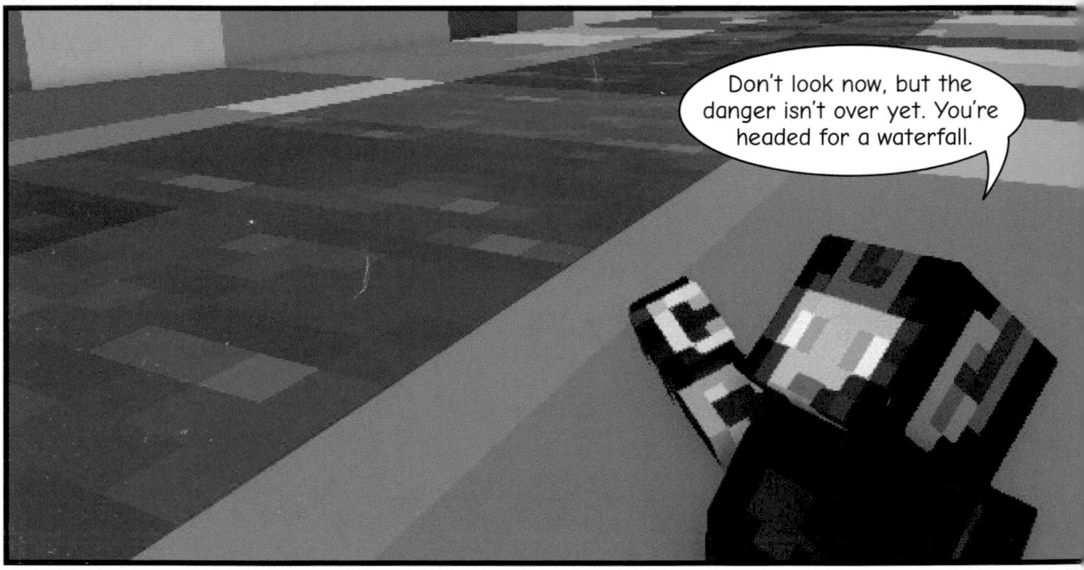
Don't look now, but the danger isn't over yet. You're headed for a waterfall.

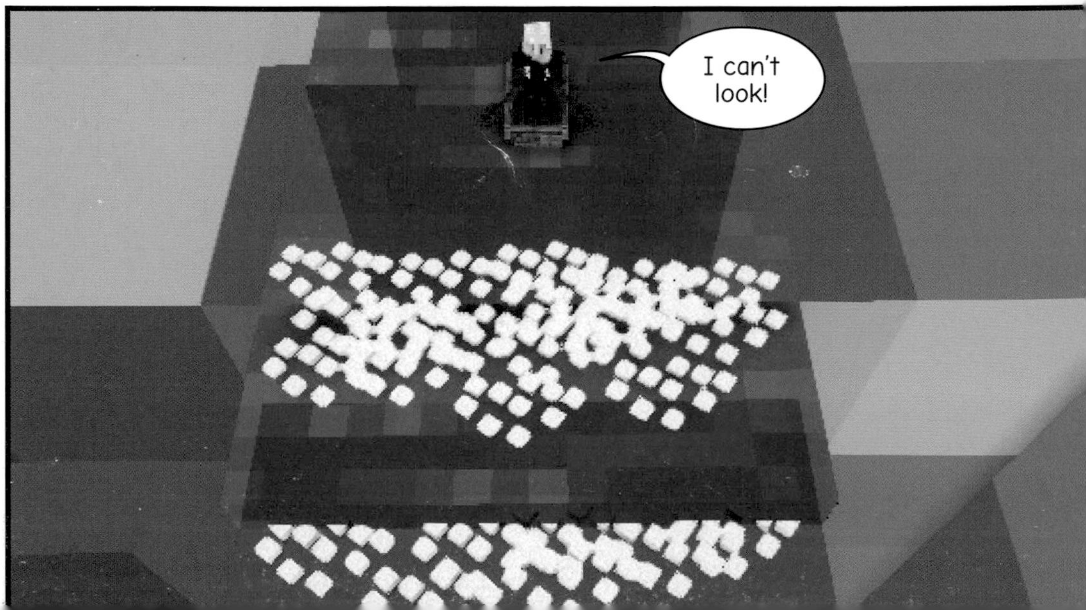
I can't look!

CHAPTER 5

LOST

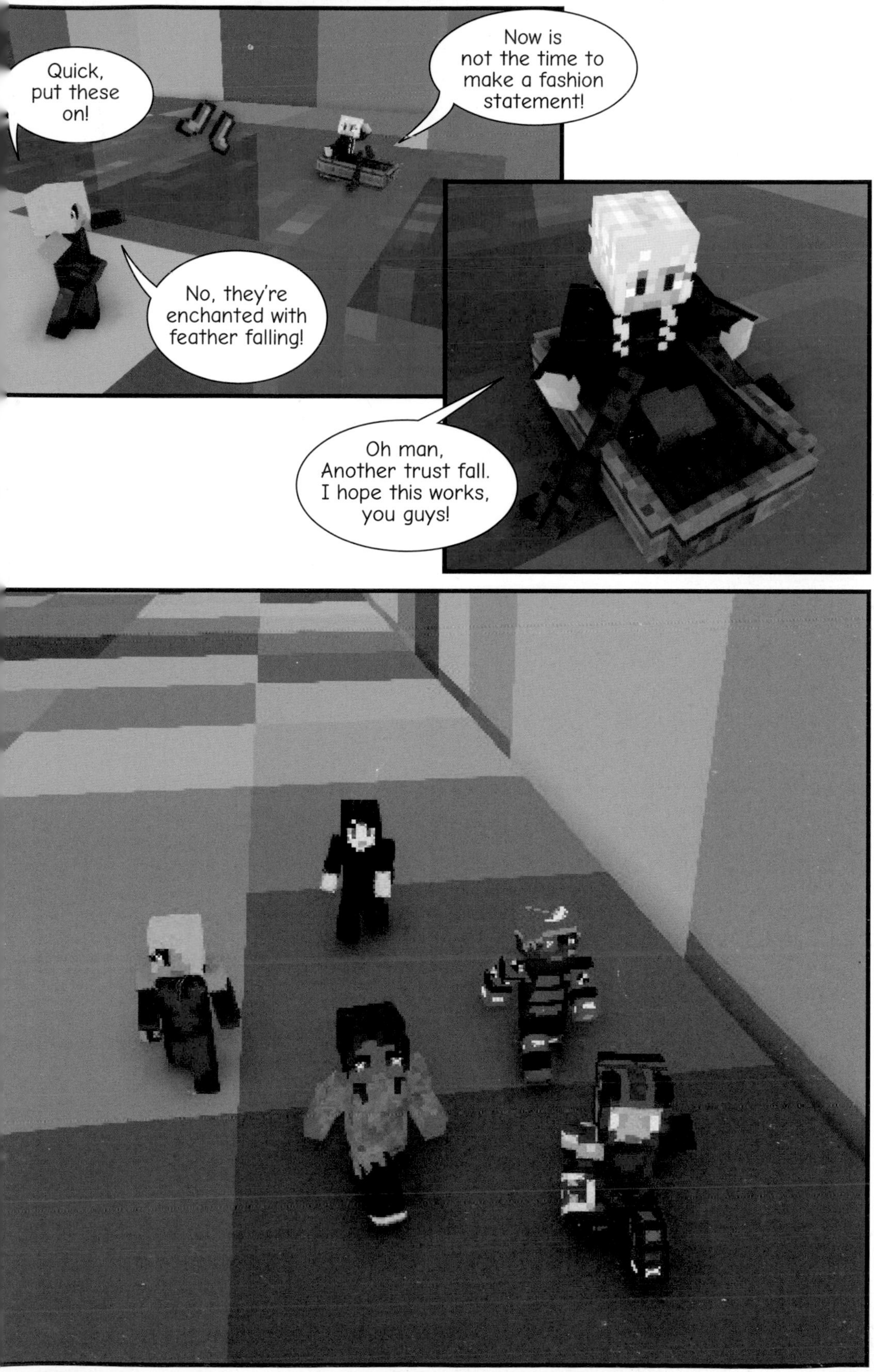
Quick, put these on!
Now is not the time to make a fashion statement!
No, they're enchanted with feather falling!
Oh man, Another trust fall. I hope this works, you guys!

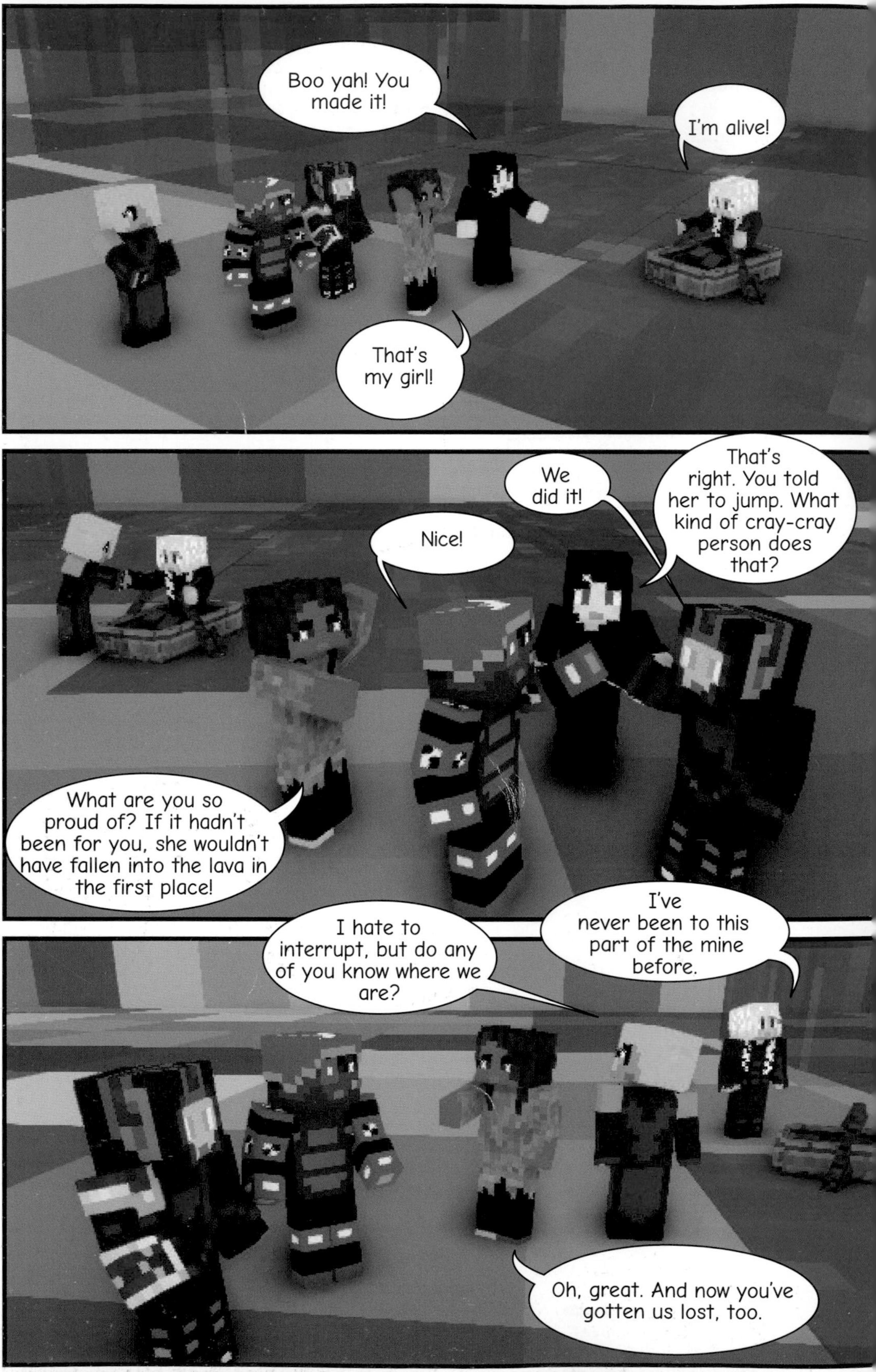

Boo yah! You made it!
I'm alive!
That's my girl!
We did it!
That's right. You told her to jump. What kind of cray-cray person does that?
Nice!
What are you so proud of? If it hadn't been for you, she wouldn't have fallen into the lava in the first place!
I hate to interrupt, but do any of you know where we are?
I've never been to this part of the mine before.
Oh, great. And now you've gotten us lost, too.

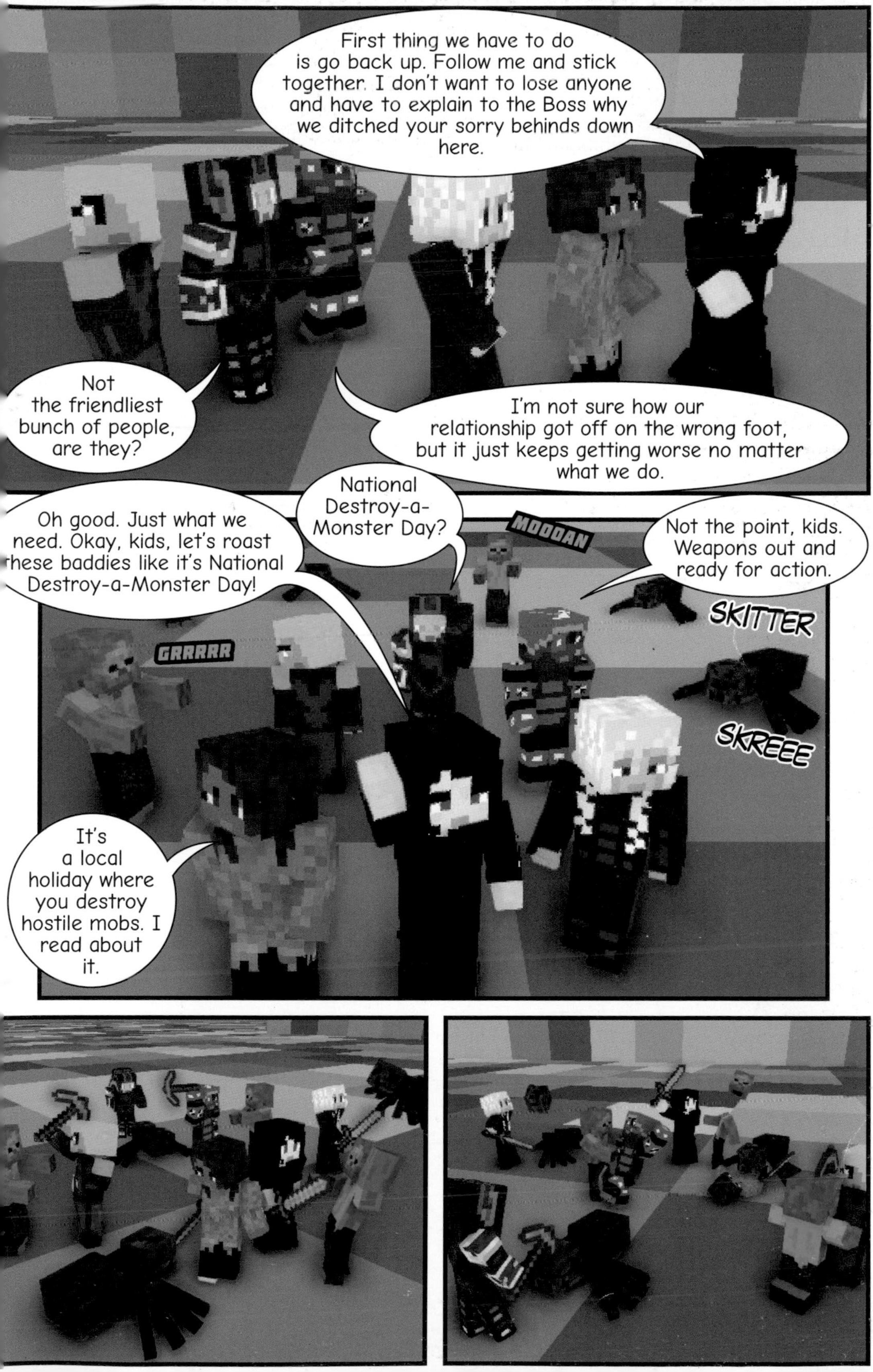
First thing we have to do is go back up. Follow me and stick together. I don't want to lose anyone and have to explain to the Boss why we ditched your sorry behinds down here.
Not the friendliest bunch of people, are they?
I'm not sure how our relationship got off on the wrong foot, but it just keeps getting worse no matter what we do.
Oh good. Just what we need. Okay, kids, let's roast these baddies like it's National Destroy-a-Monster Day!
National Destroy-a-Monster Day?
MOOOAN
Not the point, kids. Weapons out and ready for action.
SKITTER
GRRRRR
SKREEE
It's a local holiday where you destroy hostile mobs. I read about it.

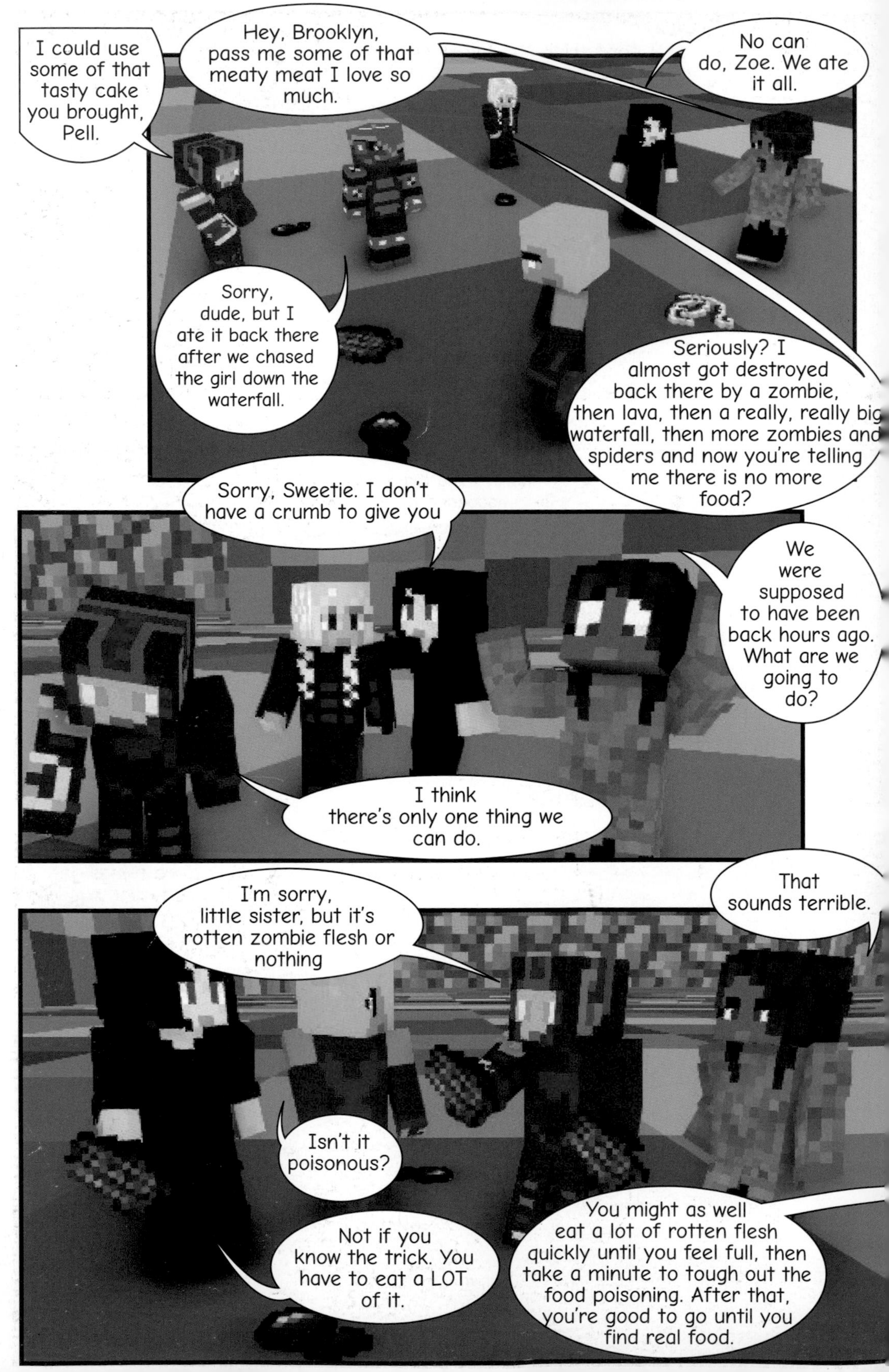
I could use some of that tasty cake you brought, Pell.
Hey, Brooklyn, pass me some of that meaty meat I love so much.
No can do, Zoe. We ate it all.
Sorry, dude, but I ate it back there after we chased the girl down the waterfall.
Seriously? I almost got destroyed back there by a zombie, then lava, then a really, really big waterfall, then more zombies and spiders and now you're telling me there is no more food?
Sorry, Sweetie. I don't have a crumb to give you
We were supposed to have been back hours ago. What are we going to do?
I think there's only one thing we can do.
I'm sorry, little sister, but it's rotten zombie flesh or nothing
That sounds terrible.
Isn't it poisonous?
Not if you know the trick. You have to eat a LOT of it.
You might as well eat a lot of rotten flesh quickly until you feel full, then take a minute to tough out the food poisoning. After that, you're good to go until you find real food.

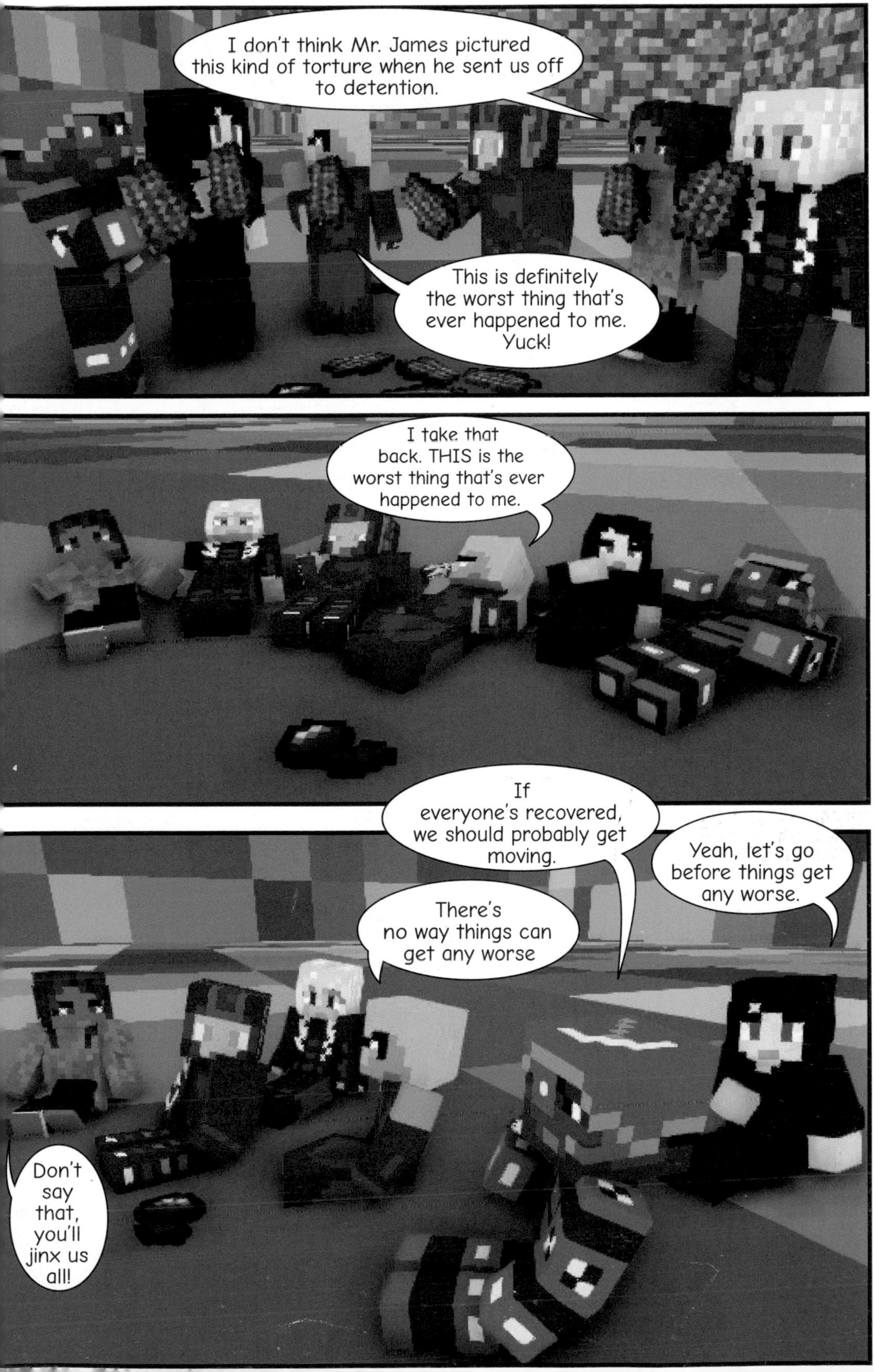
I don't think Mr. James pictured this kind of torture when he sent us off to detention.
This is definitely the worst thing that's ever happened to me. Yuck!
I take that back. THIS is the worst thing that's ever happened to me.
If everyone's recovered, we should probably get moving.
Yeah, let's go before things get any worse.
There's no way things can get any worse
Don't say that, you'll jinx us all!

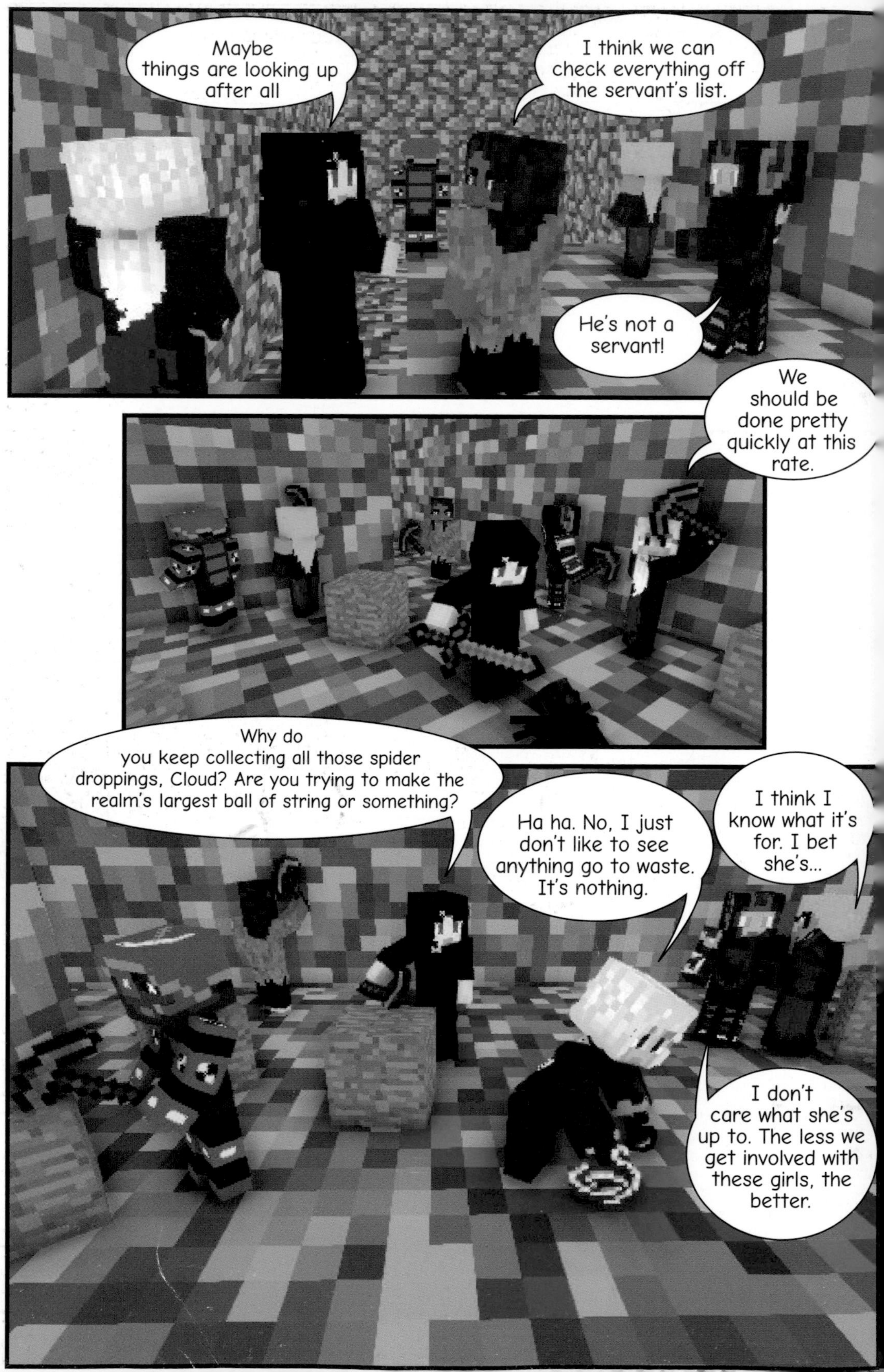
Maybe things are looking up after all
I think we can check everything off the servant's list.
He's not a servant!
We should be done pretty quickly at this rate.
Why do you keep collecting all those spider droppings, Cloud? Are you trying to make the realm's largest ball of string or something?
Ha ha. No, I just don't like to see anything go to waste. It's nothing.
I think I know what it's for. I bet she's...
I don't care what she's up to. The less we get involved with these girls, the better.

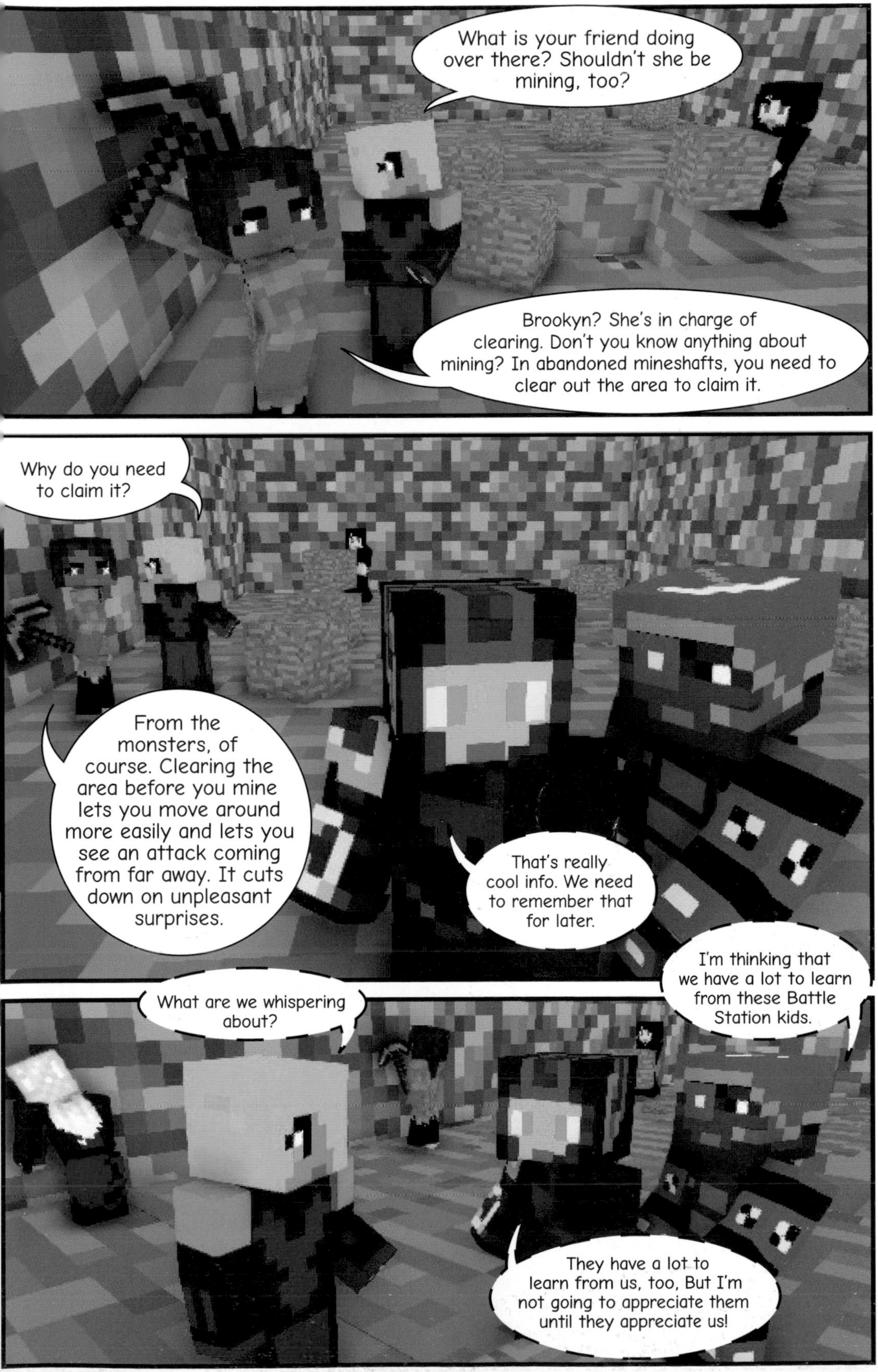
What is your friend doing over there? Shouldn't she be mining, too?
Brookyn? She's in charge of clearing. Don't you know anything about mining? In abandoned mineshafts, you need to clear out the area to claim it.
Why do you need to claim it?
From the monsters, of course. Clearing the area before you mine lets you move around more easily and lets you see an attack coming from far away. It cuts down on unpleasant surprises.
That's really cool info. We need to remember that for later.
I'm thinking that we have a lot to learn from these Battle Station kids.
What are we whispering about?
They have a lot to learn from us, too, But I'm not going to appreciate them until they appreciate us!

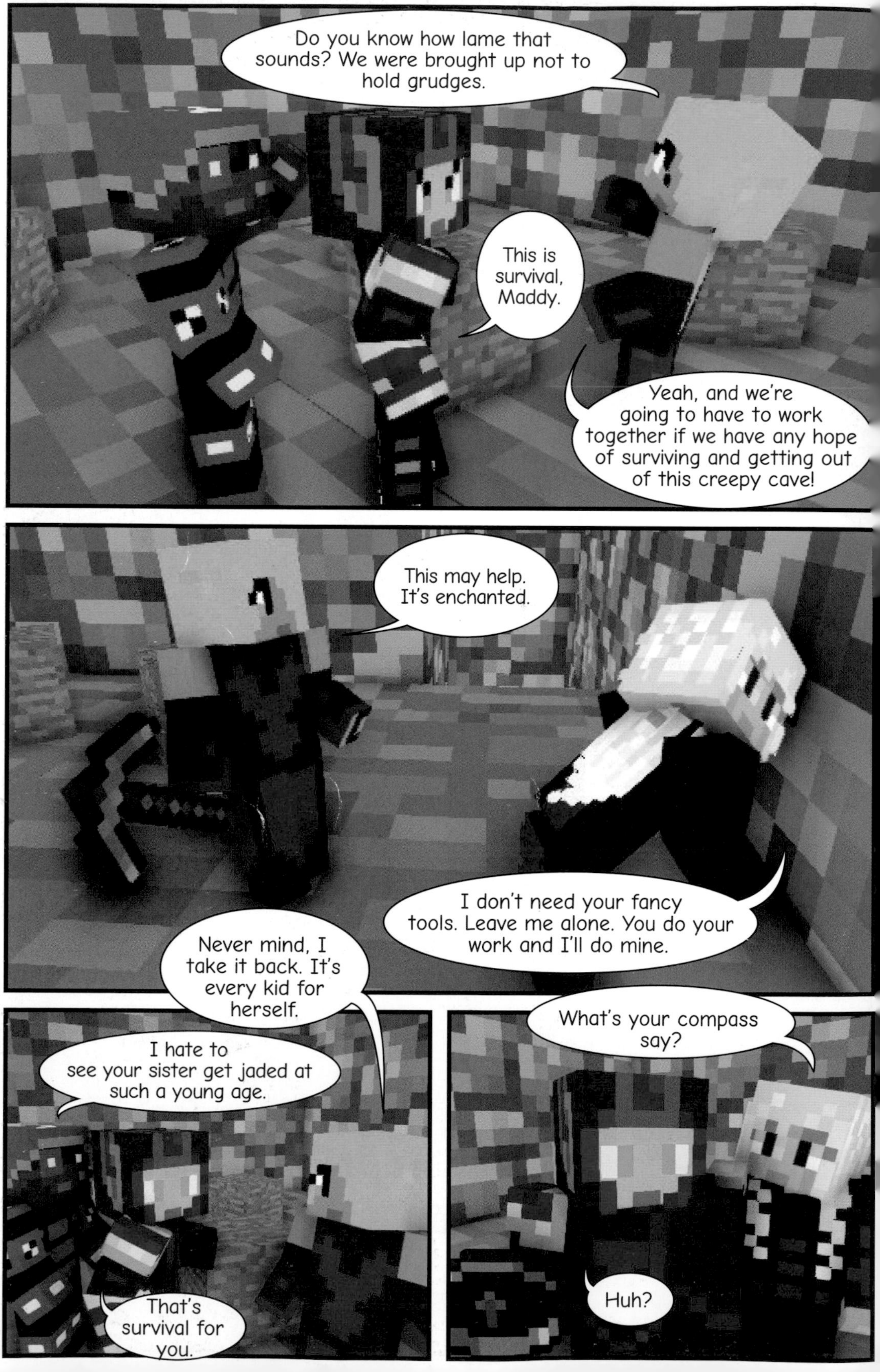
Do you know how lame that sounds? We were brought up not to hold grudges.
This is survival, Maddy.
Yeah, and we're going to have to work together if we have any hope of surviving and getting out of this creepy cave!
This may help. It's enchanted.
I don't need your fancy tools. Leave me alone. You do your work and I'll do mine.
Never mind, I take it back. It's every kid for herself.
I hate to see your sister get jaded at such a young age.
That's survival for you.
What's your compass say?
Huh?

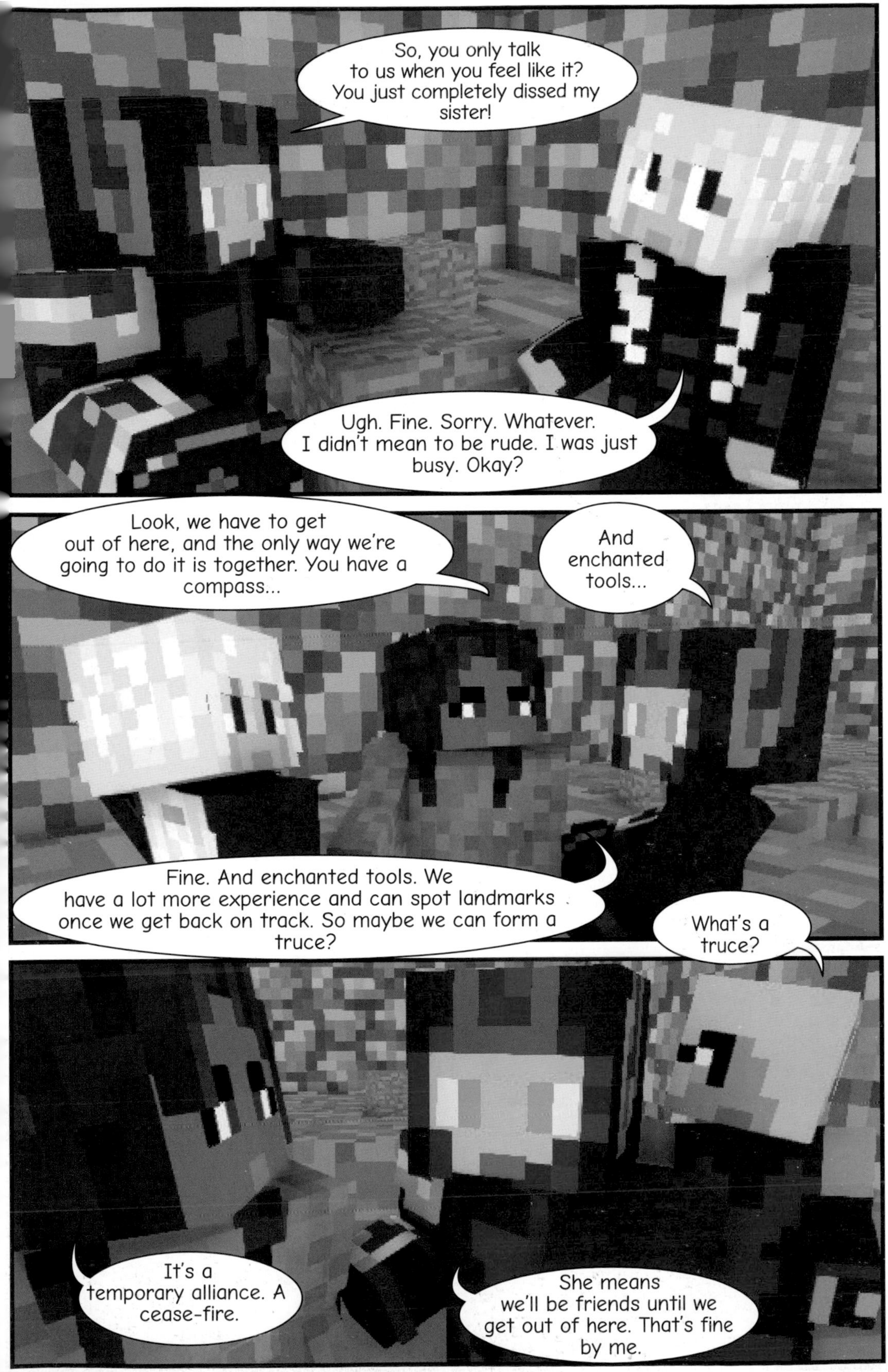
So, you only talk to us when you feel like it? You just completely dissed my sister!
Ugh. Fine. Sorry. Whatever. I didn't mean to be rude. I was just busy. Okay?
Look, we have to get out of here, and the only way we're going to do it is together. You have a compass...
And enchanted tools...
Fine. And enchanted tools. We have a lot more experience and can spot landmarks once we get back on track. So maybe we can form a truce?
What's a truce?
It's a temporary alliance. A cease-fire.
She means we'll be friends until we get out of here. That's fine by me.

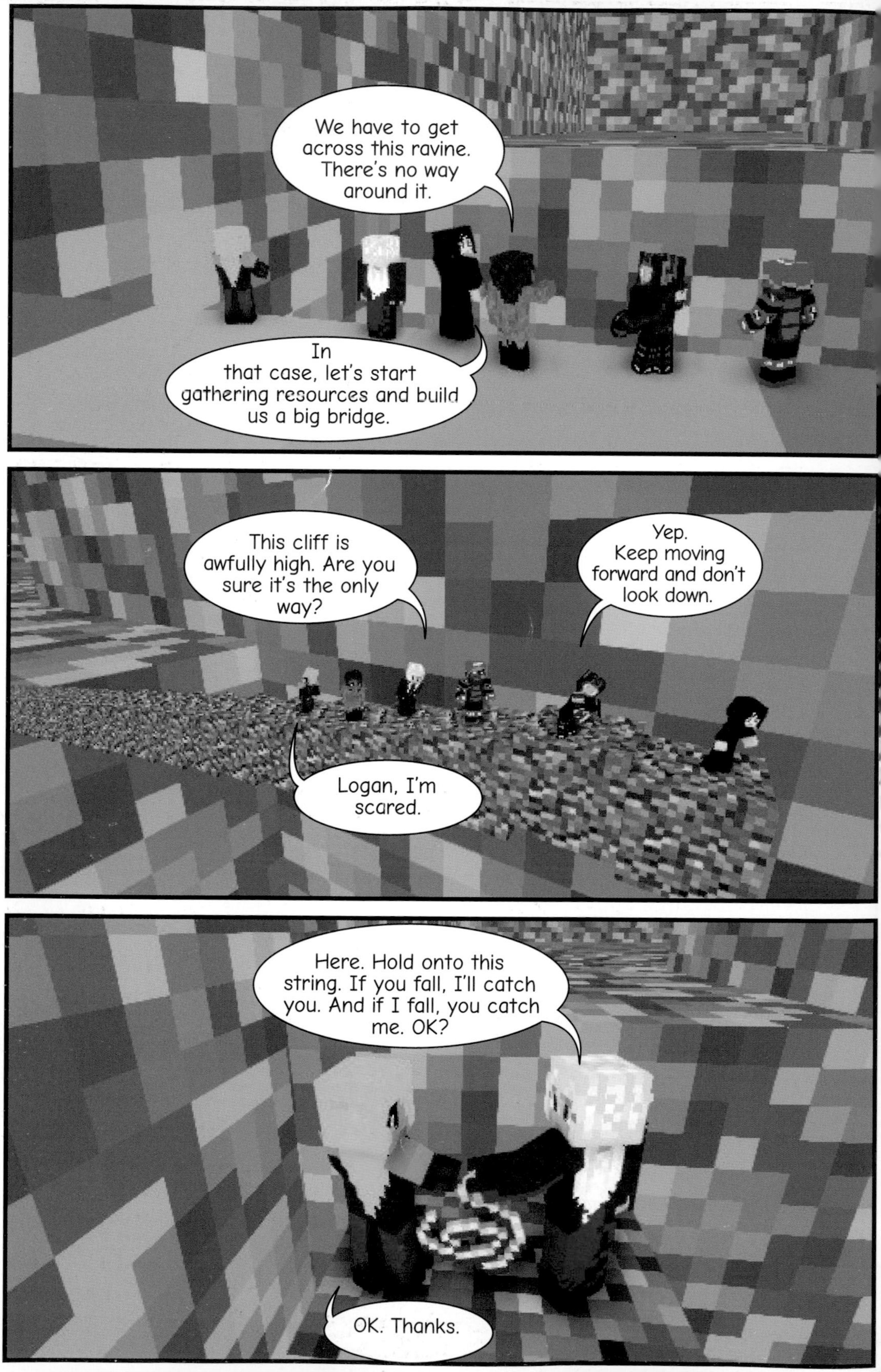
We have to get across this ravine. There's no way around it.
In that case, let's start gathering resources and build us a big bridge.
This cliff is awfully high. Are you sure it's the only way?
Yep. Keep moving forward and don't look down.
Logan, I'm scared.
Here. Hold onto this string. If you fall, I'll catch you. And if I fall, you catch me. OK?
OK. Thanks.

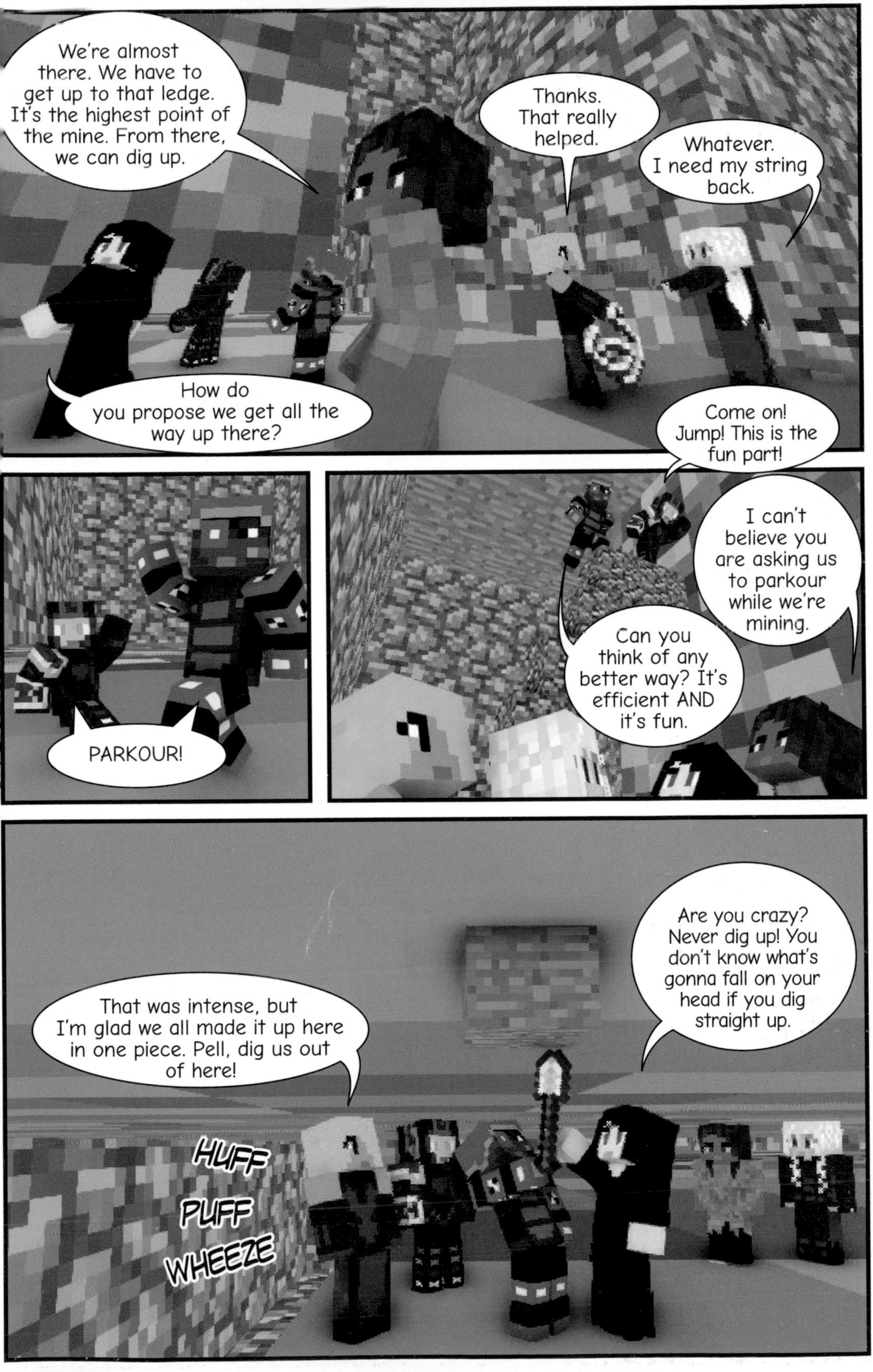
We're almost there. We have to get up to that ledge. It's the highest point of the mine. From there, we can dig up.
Thanks. That really helped.
Whatever. I need my string back.
How do you propose we get all the way up there?
Come on! Jump! This is the fun part!
PARKOUR!
I can't believe you are asking us to parkour while we're mining.
Can you think of any better way? It's efficient AND it's fun.
That was intense, but I'm glad we all made it up here in one piece. Pell, dig us out of here!
Are you crazy? Never dig up! You don't know what's gonna fall on your head if you dig straight up.
HUFF
PUFF
WHEEZE

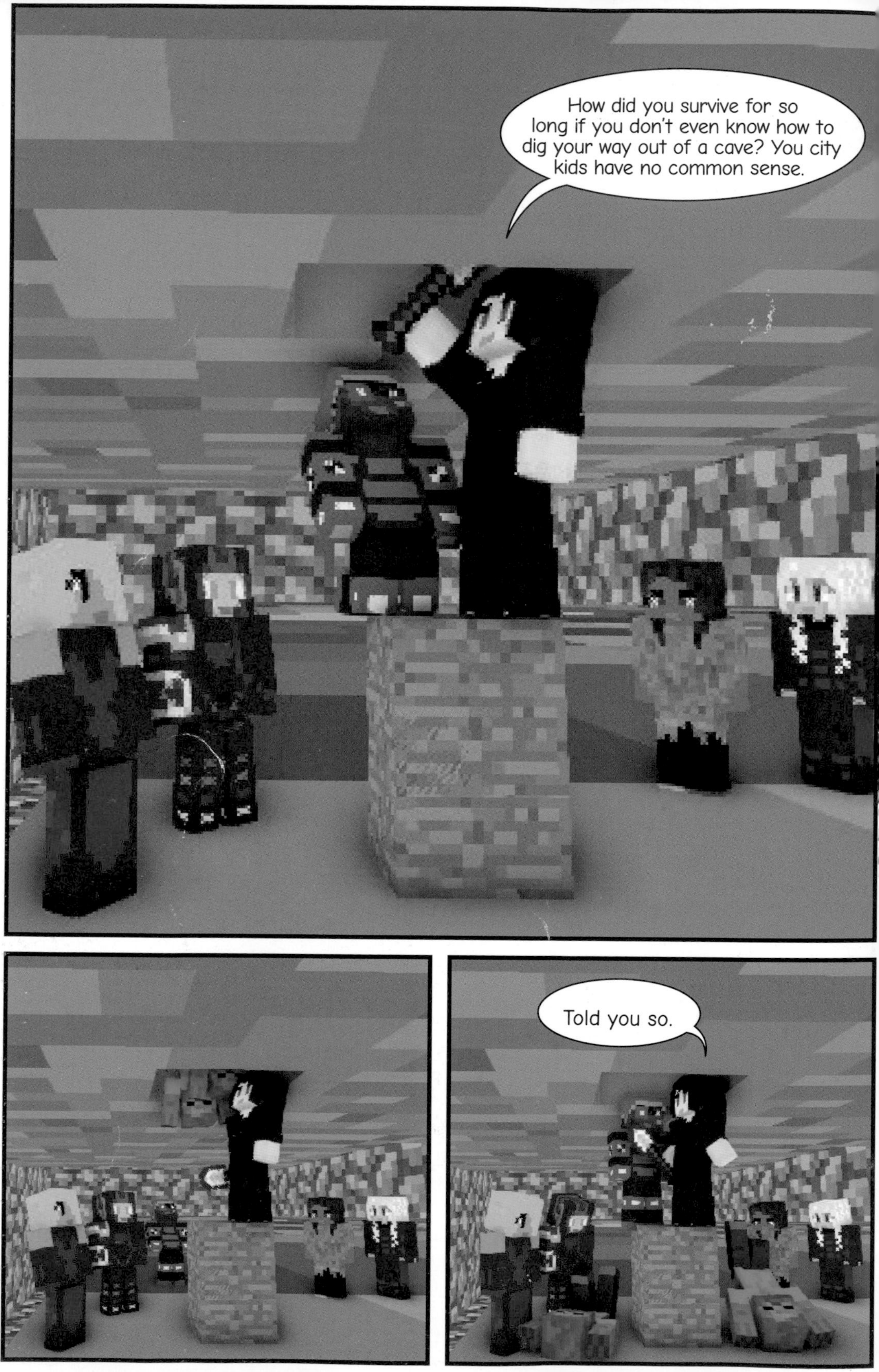
How did you survive for so long if you don't even know how to dig your way out of a cave? You city kids have no common sense.
Told you so.

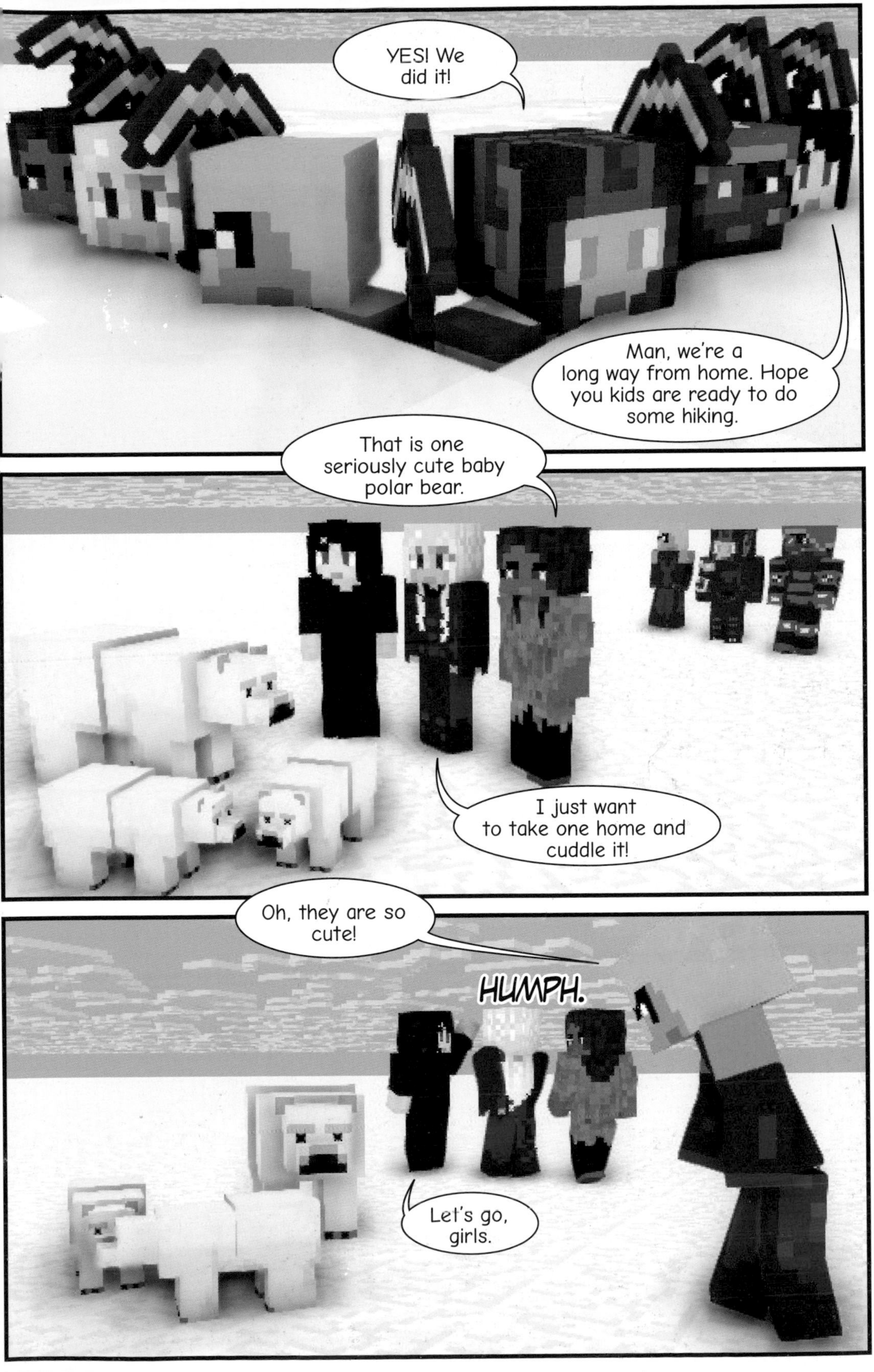
YES! We did it!
Man, we're a long way from home. Hope you kids are ready to do some hiking.
That is one seriously cute baby polar bear.
I just want to take one home and cuddle it!
Oh, they are so cute!
HUMPH.
Let's go, girls.

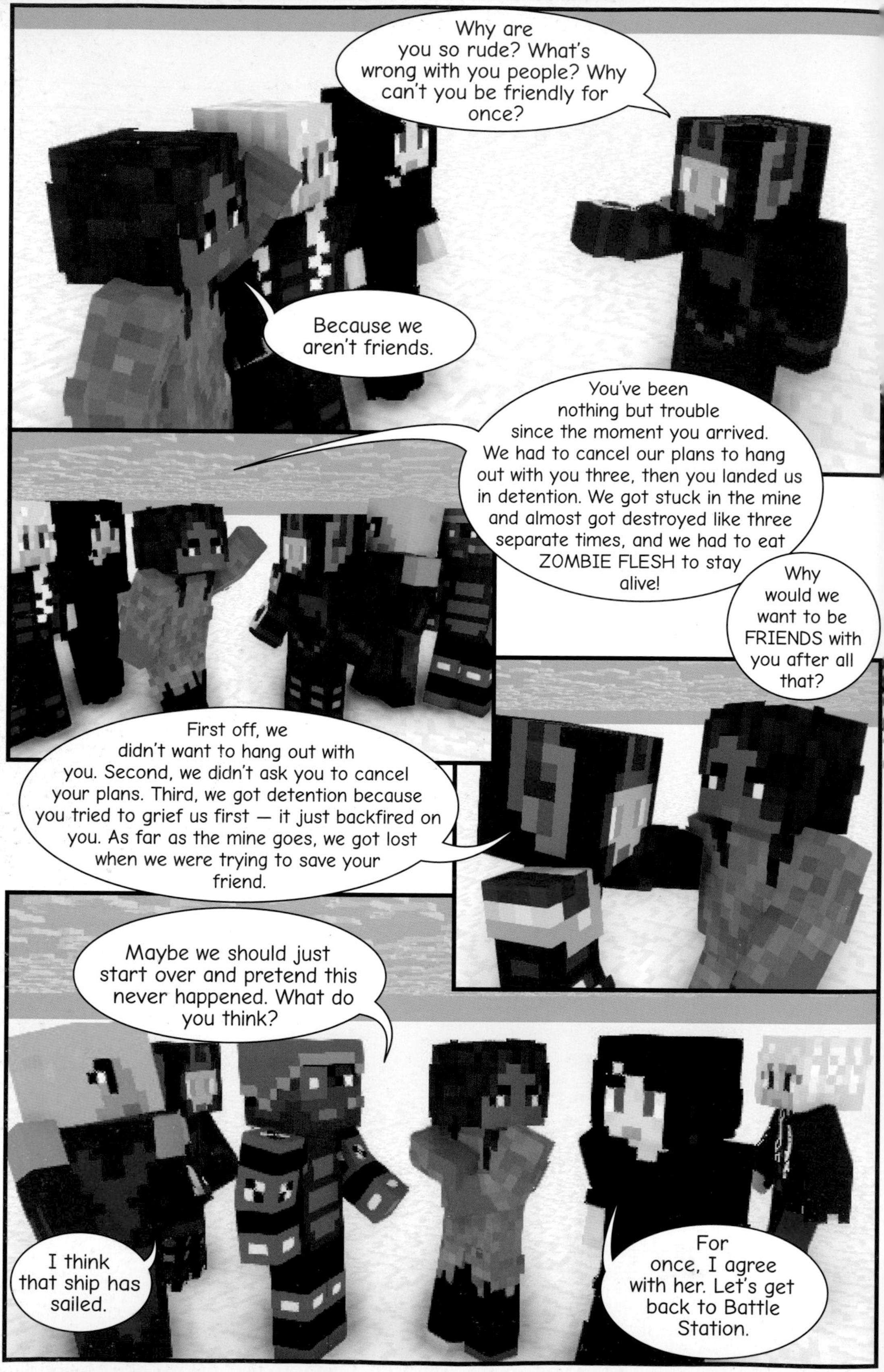

Why are you so rude? What's wrong with you people? Why can't you be friendly for once?
Because we aren't friends.
You've been nothing but trouble since the moment you arrived. We had to cancel our plans to hang out with you three, then you landed us in detention. We got stuck in the mine and almost got destroyed like three separate times, and we had to eat ZOMBIE FLESH to stay alive!
Why would we want to be FRIENDS with you after all that?
First off, we didn't want to hang out with you. Second, we didn't ask you to cancel your plans. Third, we got detention because you tried to grief us first — it just backfired on you. As far as the mine goes, we got lost when we were trying to save your friend.
Maybe we should just start over and pretend this never happened. What do you think?
I think that ship has sailed.
For once, I agree with her. Let's get back to Battle Station.

CHAPTER 6

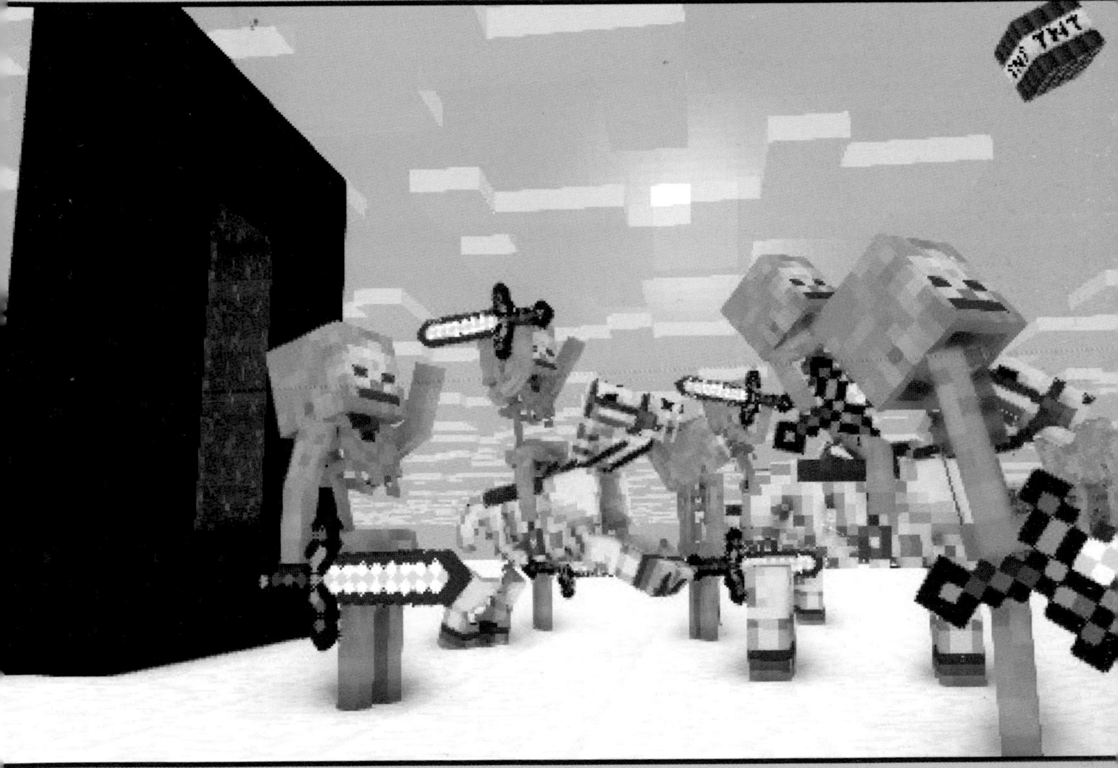
TNT TNT

RED ALERT

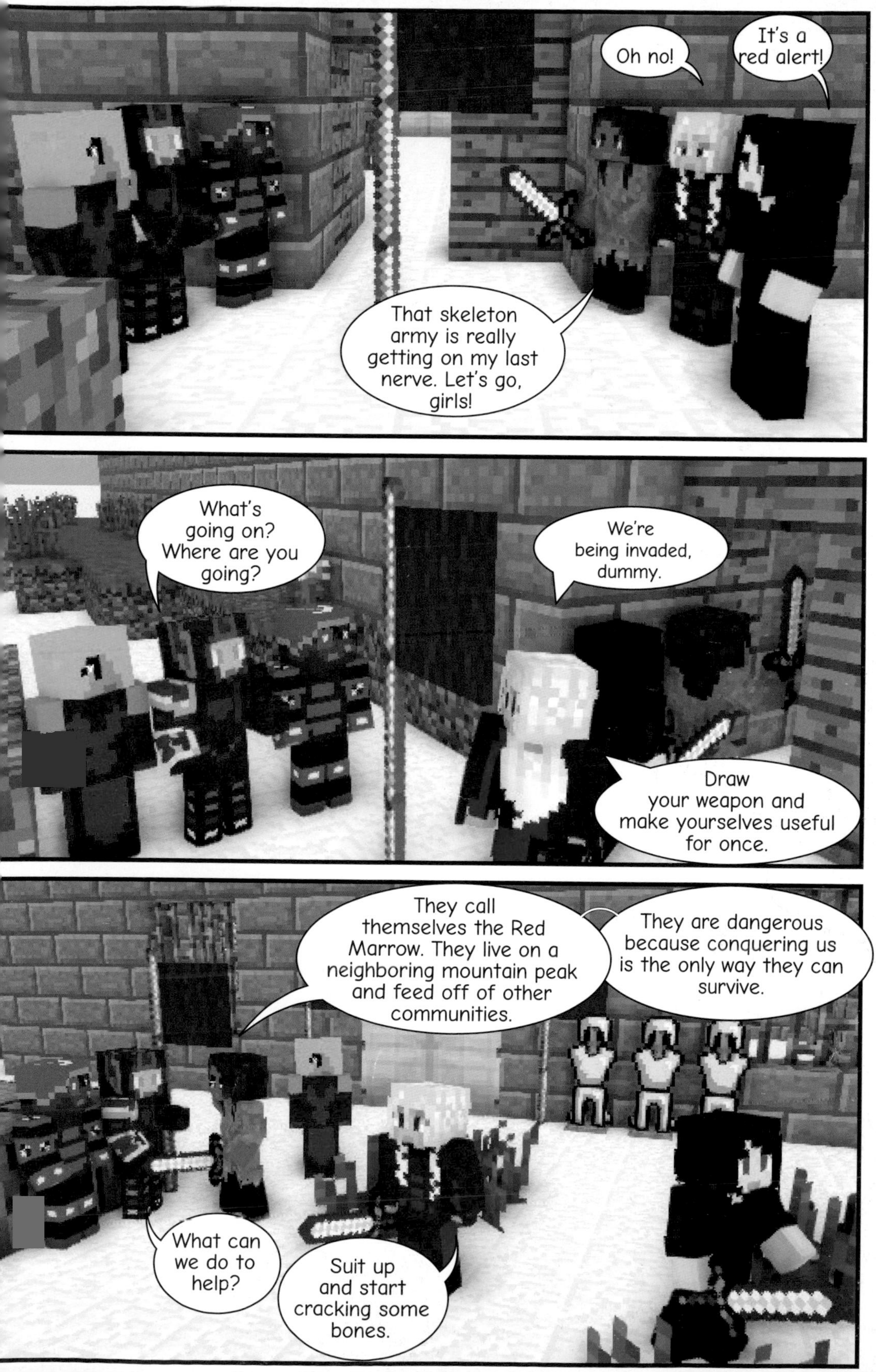
Oh no!
It's a red alert!
That skeleton army is really getting on my last nerve. Let's go, girls!
What's going on? Where are you going?
We're being invaded, dummy.
Draw your weapon and make yourselves useful for once.
They call themselves the Red Marrow. They live on a neighboring mountain peak and feed off of other communities.
They are dangerous because conquering us is the only way they can survive.
What can we do to help?
Suit up and start cracking some bones.

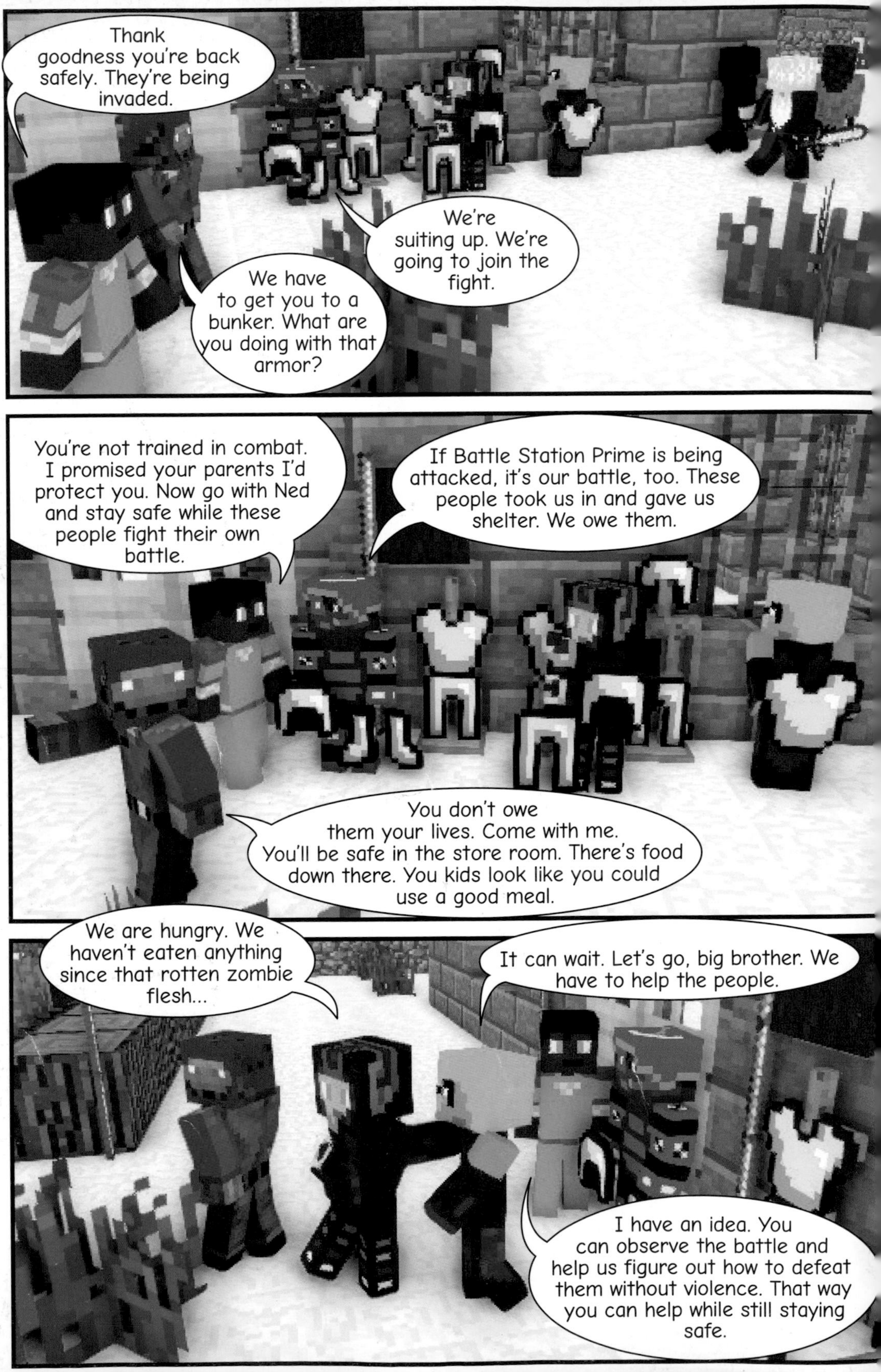
Thank goodness you're back safely. They're being invaded.
We have to get you to a bunker. What are you doing with that armor?
We're suiting up. We're going to join the fight.
You're not trained in combat. I promised your parents I'd protect you. Now go with Ned and stay safe while these people fight their own battle.
If Battle Station Prime is being attacked, it's our battle, too. These people took us in and gave us shelter. We owe them.
You don't owe them your lives. Come with me. You'll be safe in the store room. There's food down there. You kids look like you could use a good meal.
We are hungry. We haven't eaten anything since that rotten zombie flesh...
It can wait. Let's go, big brother. We have to help the people.
I have an idea. You can observe the battle and help us figure out how to defeat them without violence. That way you can help while still staying safe.

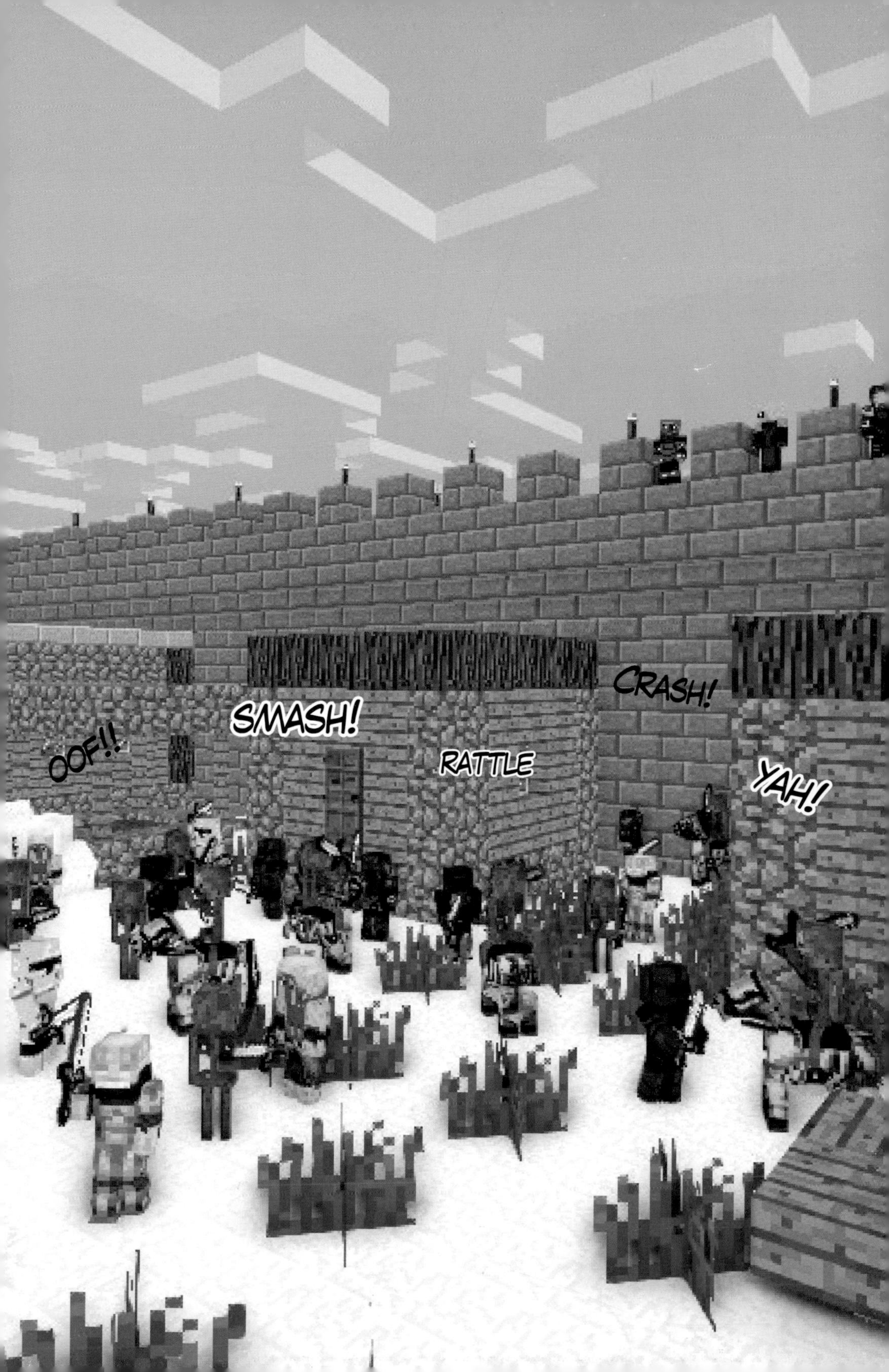
OOF!!
SMASH!
RATTLE
CRASH!
YAH!

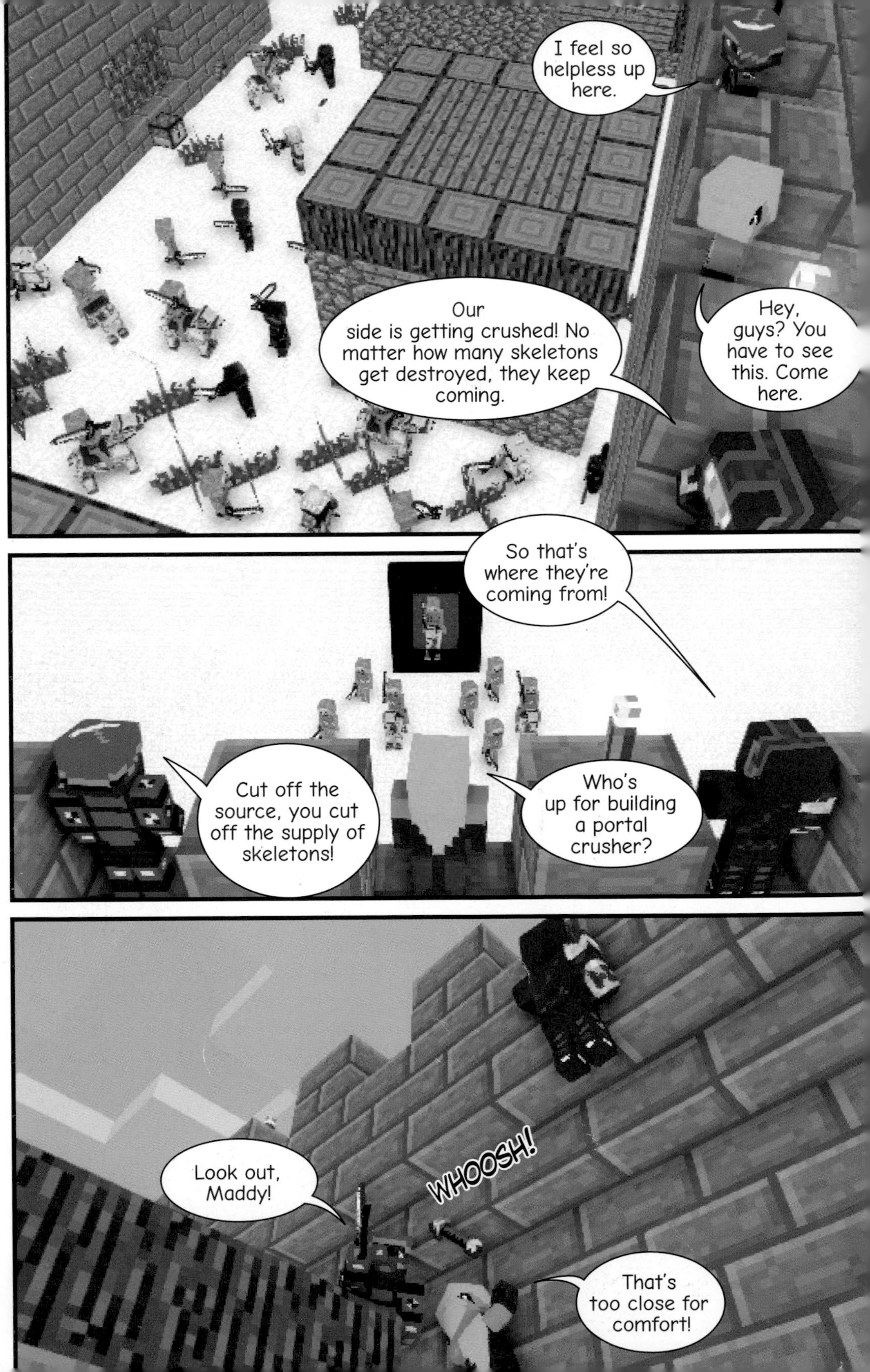
I feel so helpless up here.
Our side is getting crushed! No matter how many skeletons get destroyed, they keep coming.
Hey, guys? You have to see this. Come here.
So that's where they're coming from!
Cut off the source, you cut off the supply of skeletons!
Who's up for building a portal crusher?
Look out, Maddy!
WHOOSH!
That's too close for comfort!

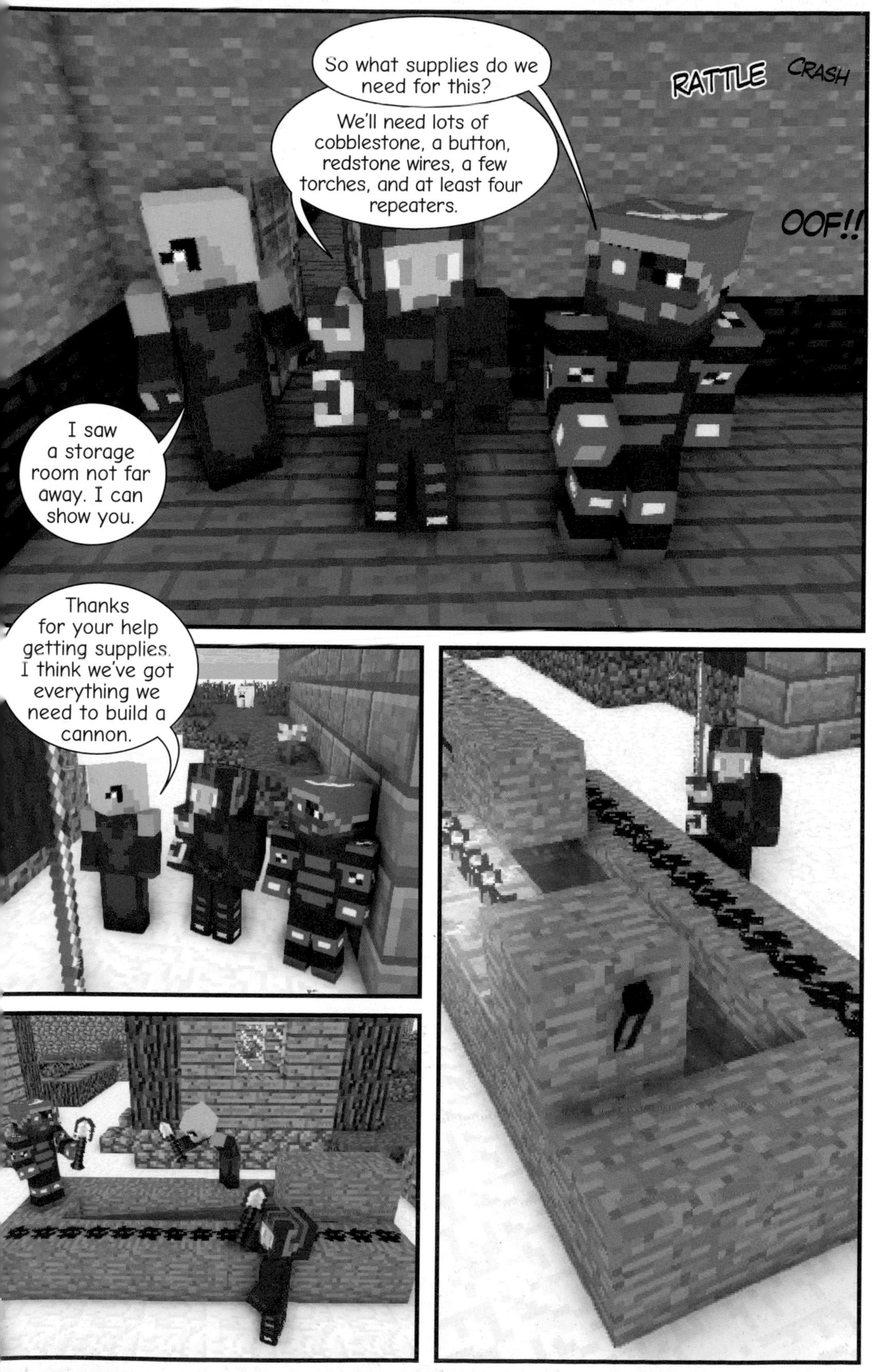
So what supplies do we need for this?
We'll need lots of cobblestone, a button, redstone wires, a few torches, and at least four repeaters.
RATTLE
CRASH
OOF!!
I saw a storage room not far away. I can show you.
Thanks for your help getting supplies. I think we've got everything we need to build a cannon.

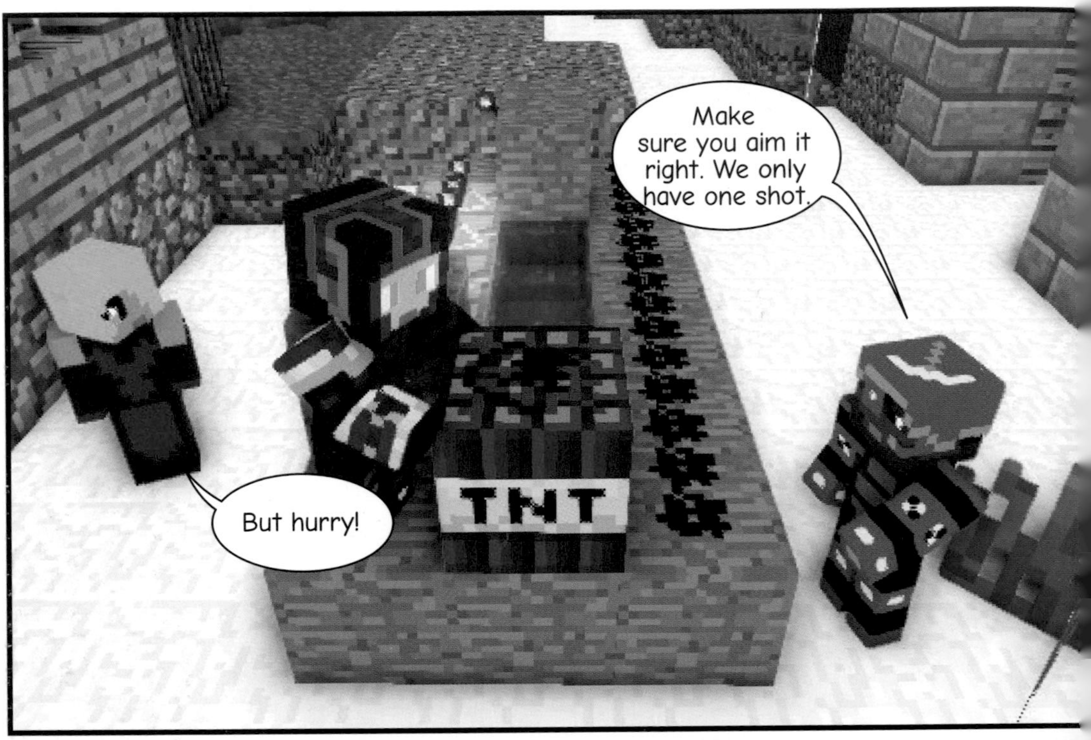
Make sure you aim it right. We only have one shot.
But hurry!
TNT

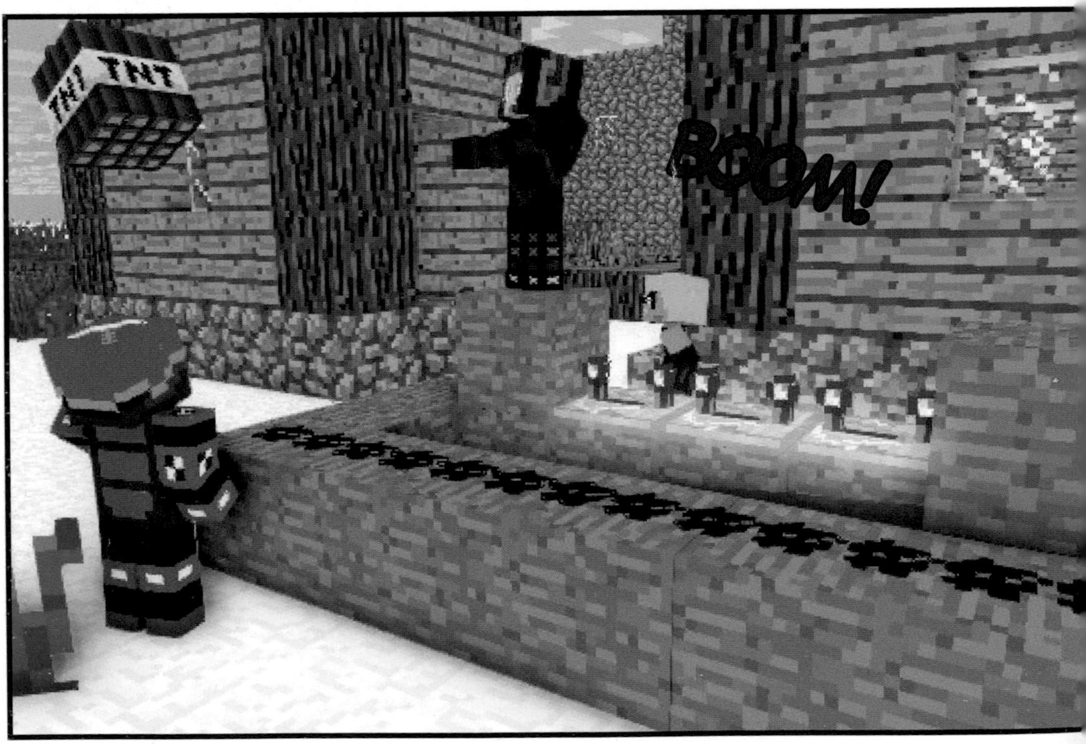
TNT
TNT
BOOM!

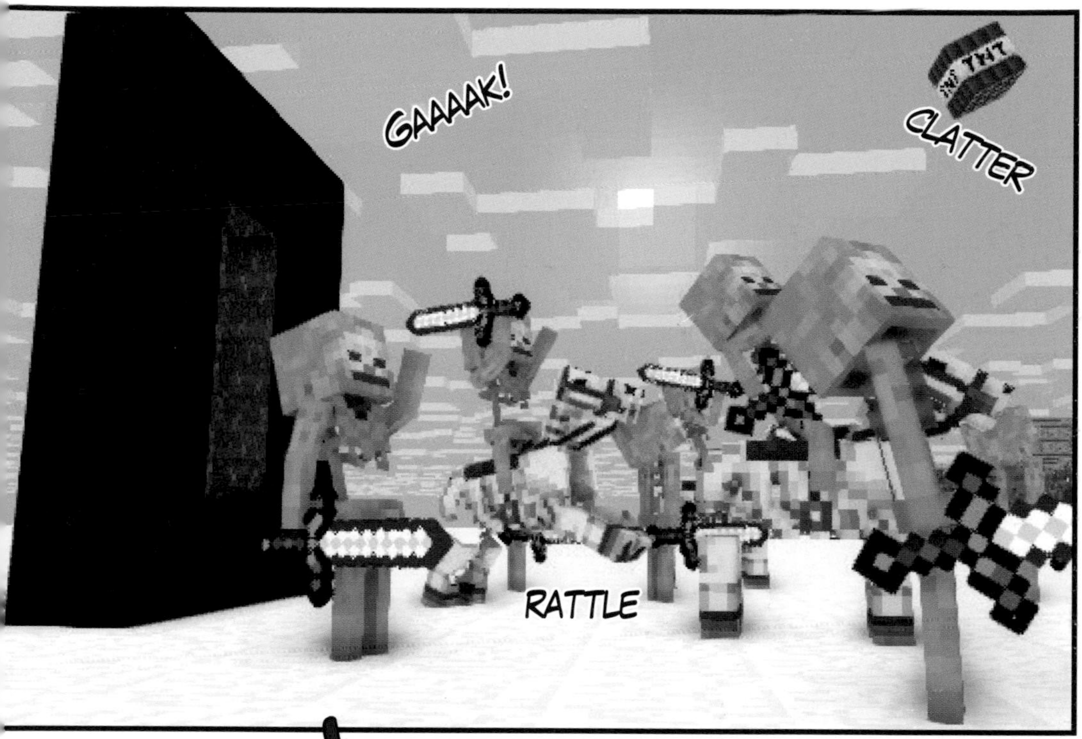
GAAAAK!
TNT
CLATTER
RATTLE

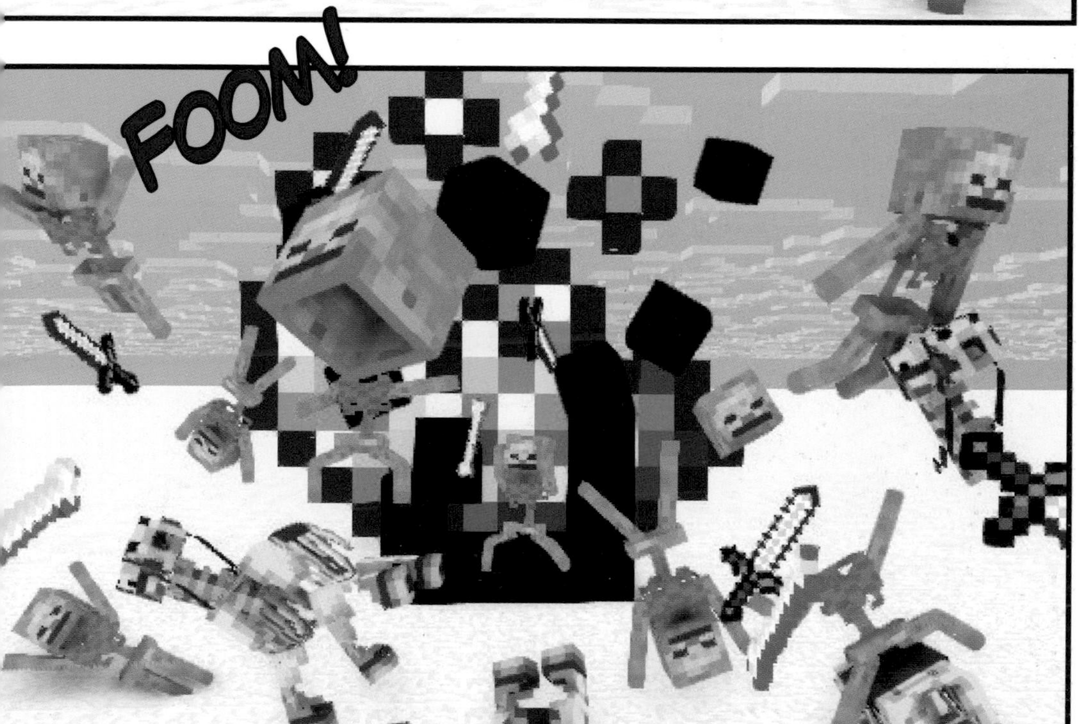
FOOM!

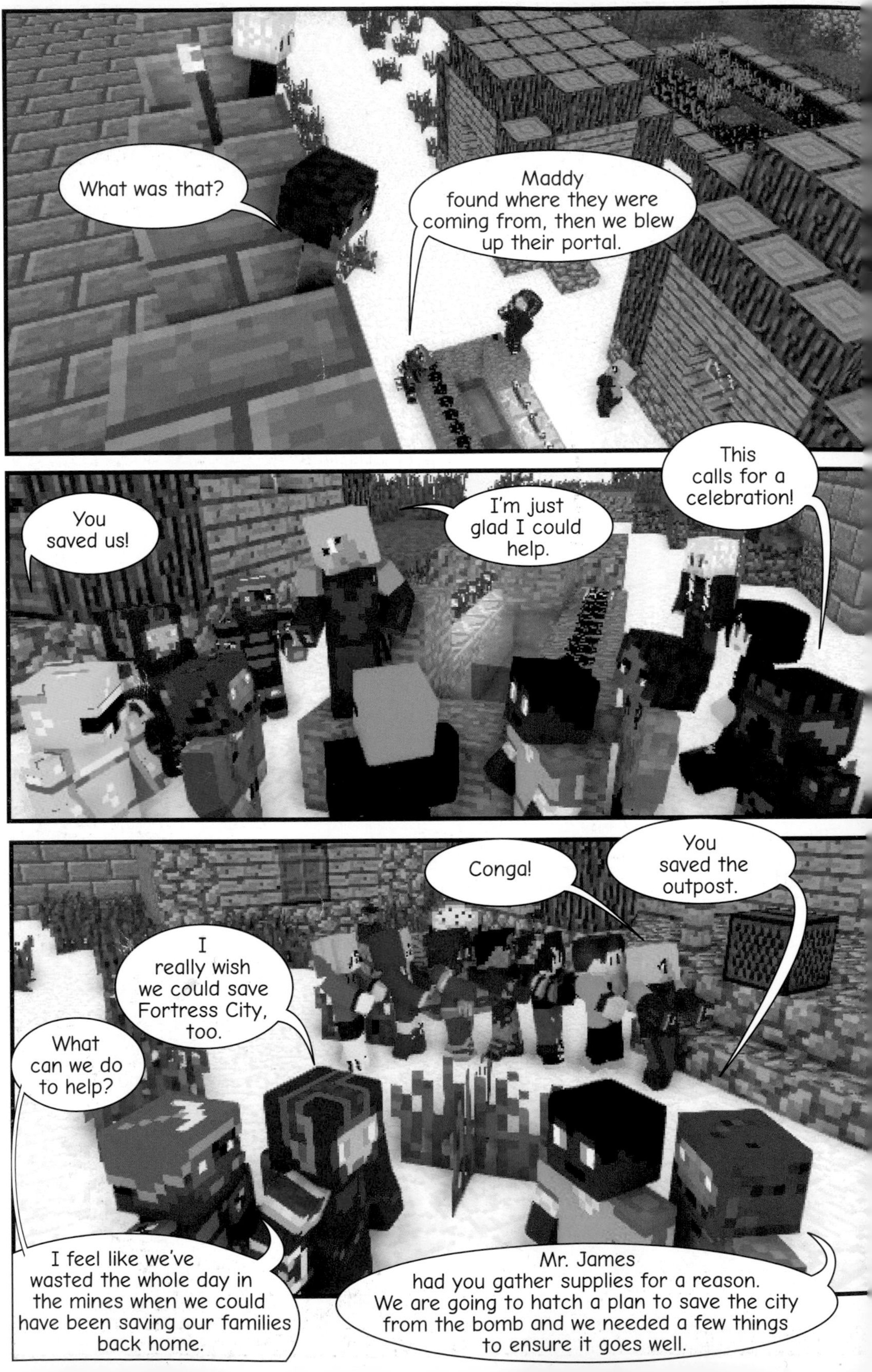
What was that?
Maddy found where they were coming from, then we blew up their portal.
You saved us!
I'm just glad I could help.
This calls for a celebration!
Conga!
You saved the outpost.
I really wish we could save Fortress City, too.
What can we do to help?
I feel like we've wasted the whole day in the mines when we could have been saving our families back home.
Mr. James had you gather supplies for a reason. We are going to hatch a plan to save the city from the bomb and we needed a few things to ensure it goes well.

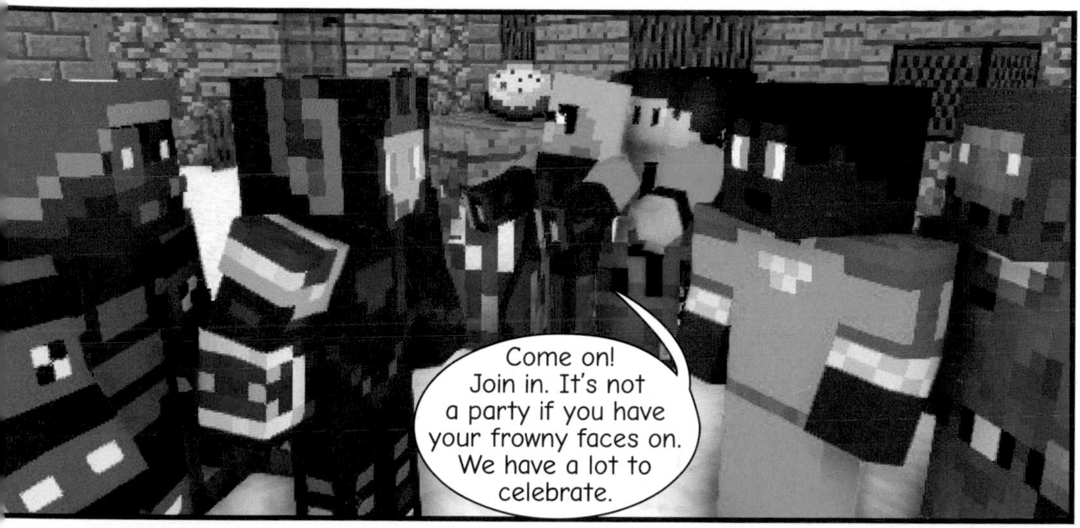
Come on! Join in. It's not a party if you have your frowny faces on. We have a lot to celebrate.

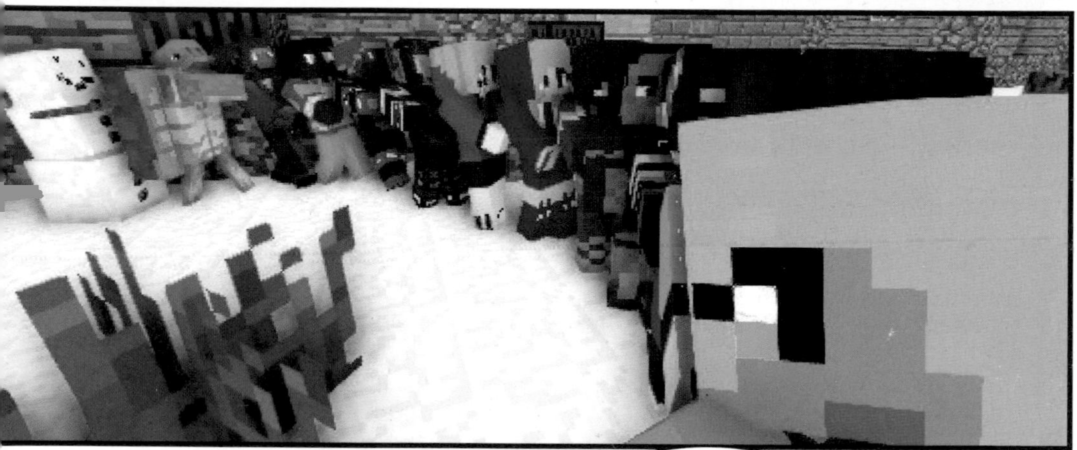

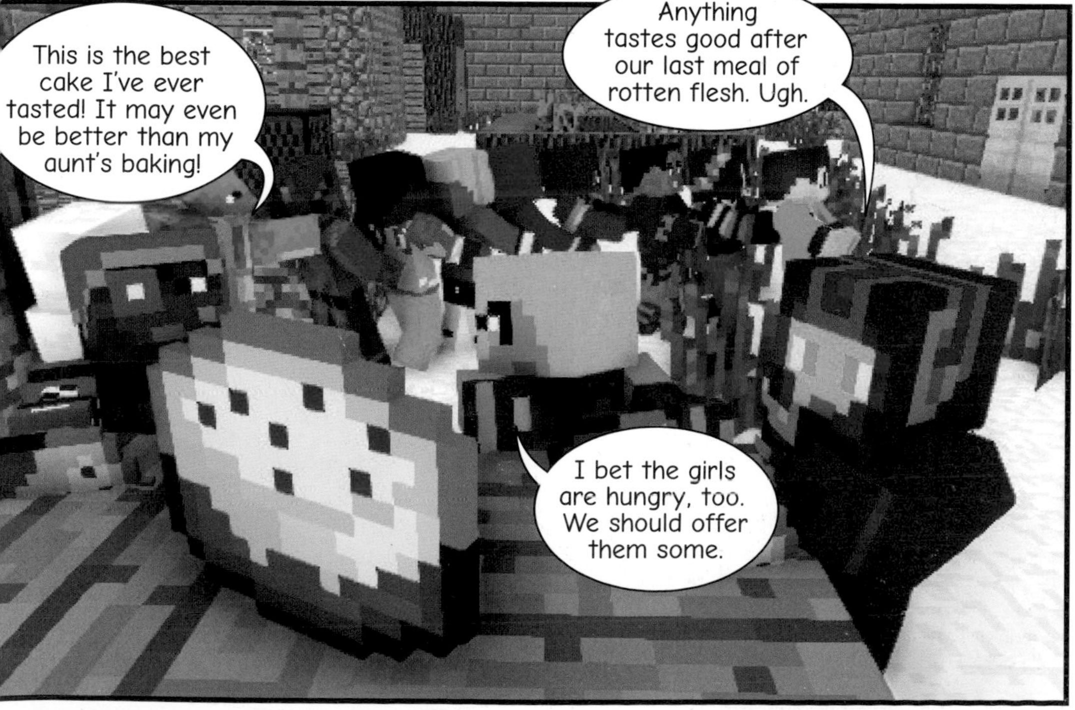
This is the best cake I've ever tasted! It may even be better than my aunt's baking!
Anything tastes good after our last meal of rotten flesh. Ugh.
I bet the girls are hungry, too. We should offer them some.

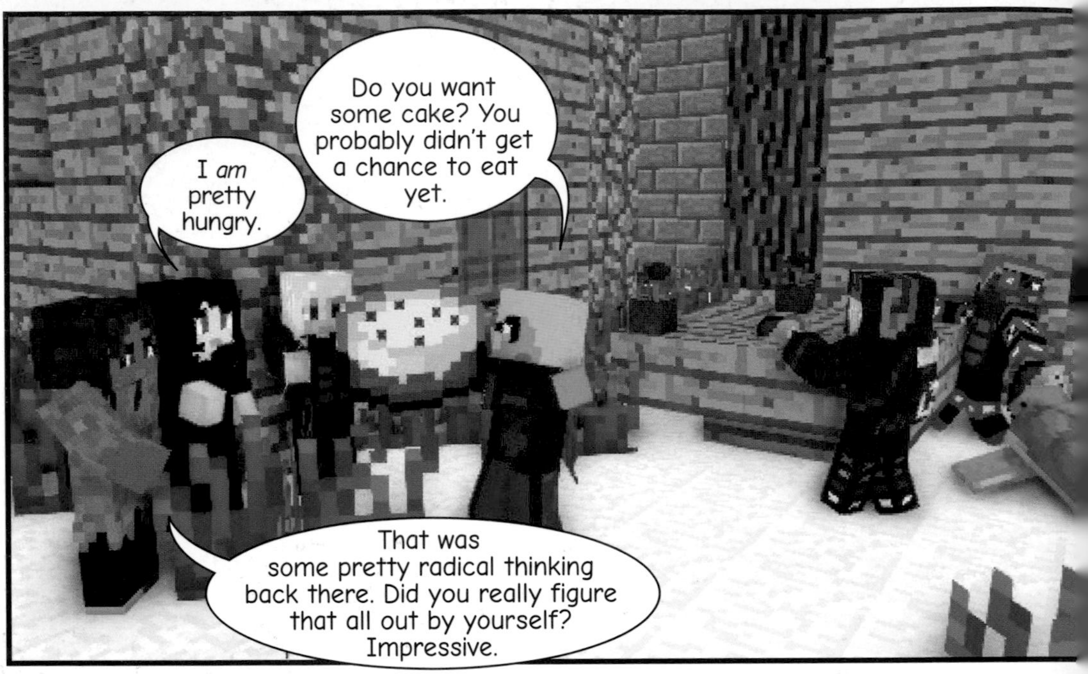
I *am* pretty hungry.
Do you want some cake? You probably didn't get a chance to eat yet.
That was some pretty radical thinking back there. Did you really figure that all out by yourself? Impressive.

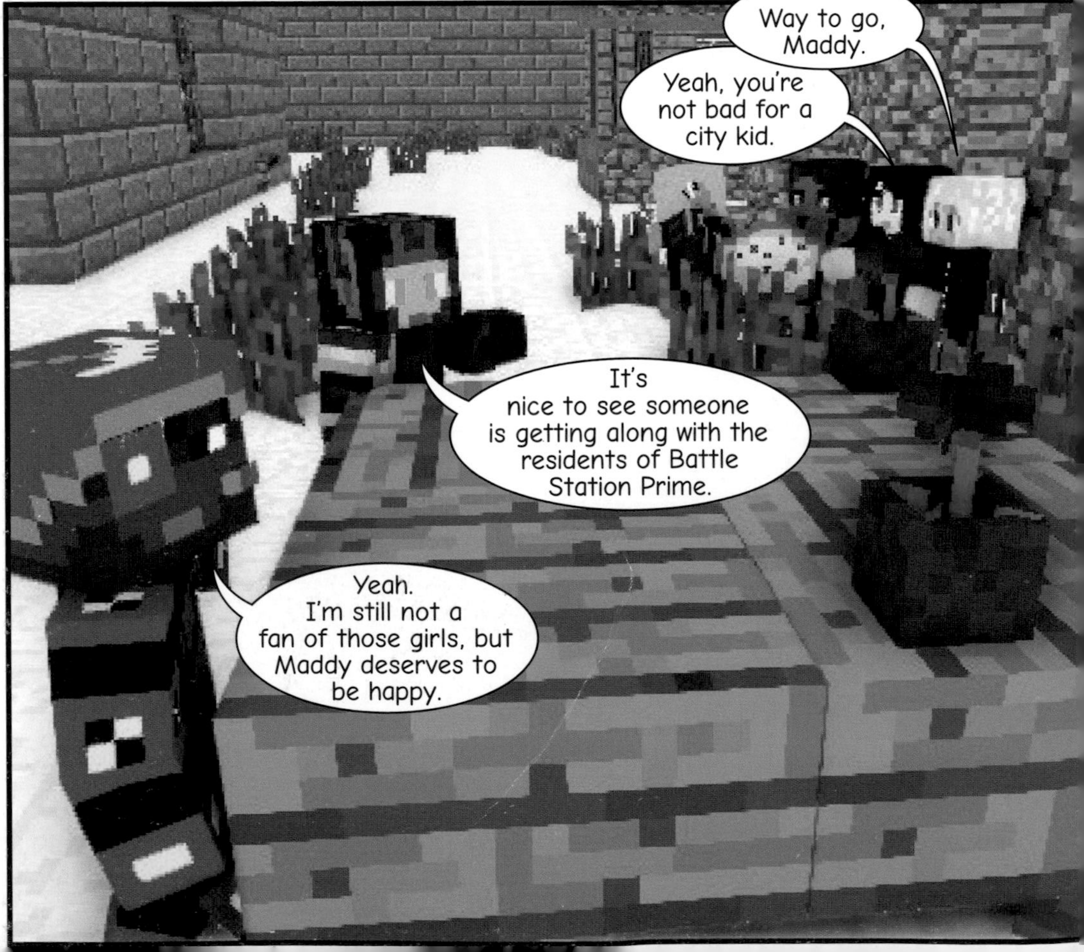
Way to go, Maddy.
Yeah, you're not bad for a city kid.
It's nice to see someone is getting along with the residents of Battle Station Prime.
Yeah. I'm still not a fan of those girls, but Maddy deserves to be happy.

CHAPTER 7

A NEW PLAN

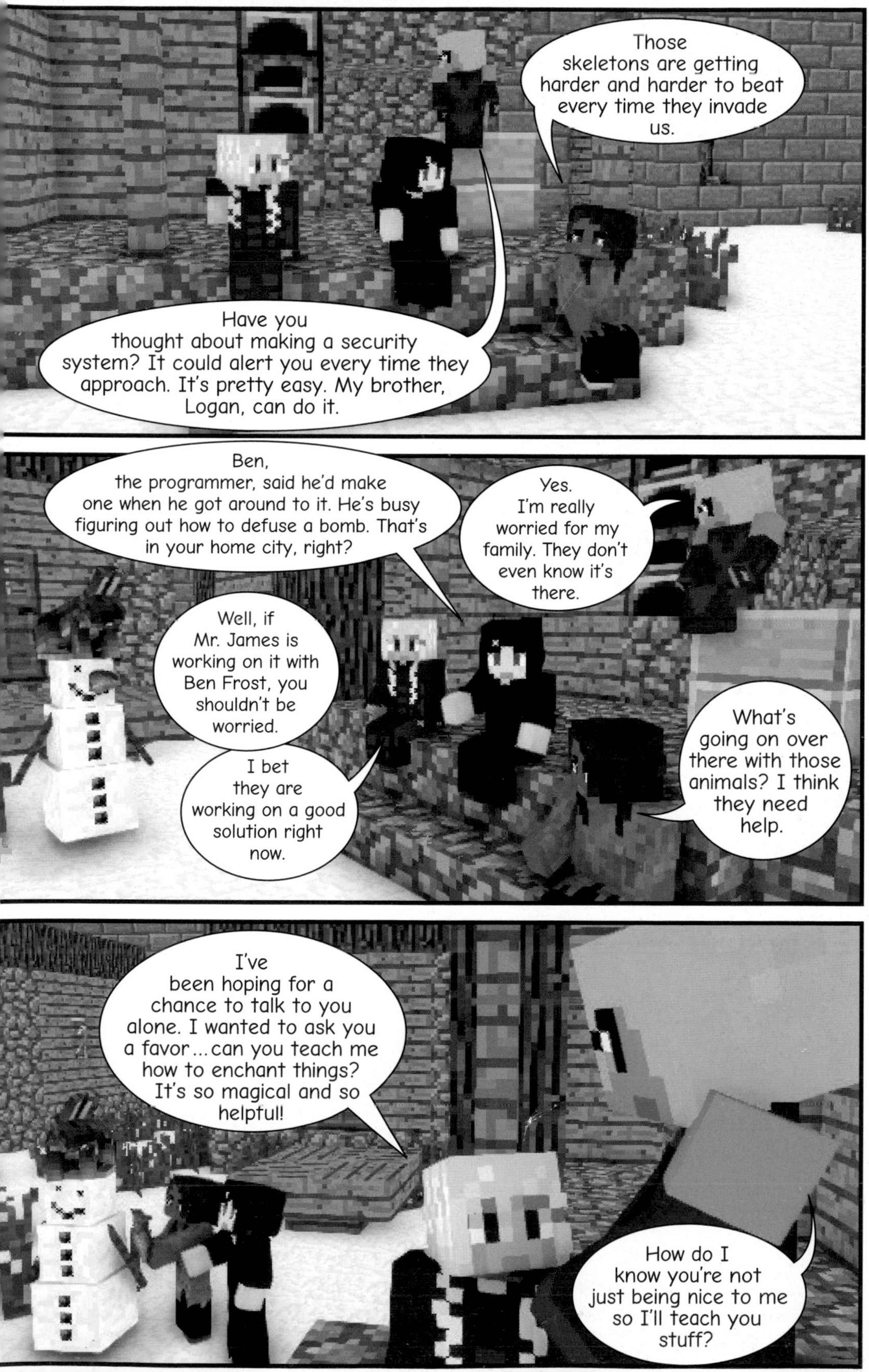
Those skeletons are getting harder and harder to beat every time they invade us.
Have you thought about making a security system? It could alert you every time they approach. It's pretty easy. My brother, Logan, can do it.
Ben, the programmer, said he'd make one when he got around to it. He's busy figuring out how to defuse a bomb. That's in your home city, right?
Yes. I'm really worried for my family. They don't even know it's there.
Well, if Mr. James is working on it with Ben Frost, you shouldn't be worried.
I bet they are working on a good solution right now.
What's going on over there with those animals? I think they need help.
I've been hoping for a chance to talk to you alone. I wanted to ask you a favor...can you teach me how to enchant things? It's so magical and so helpful!
How do I know you're not just being nice to me so I'll teach you stuff?

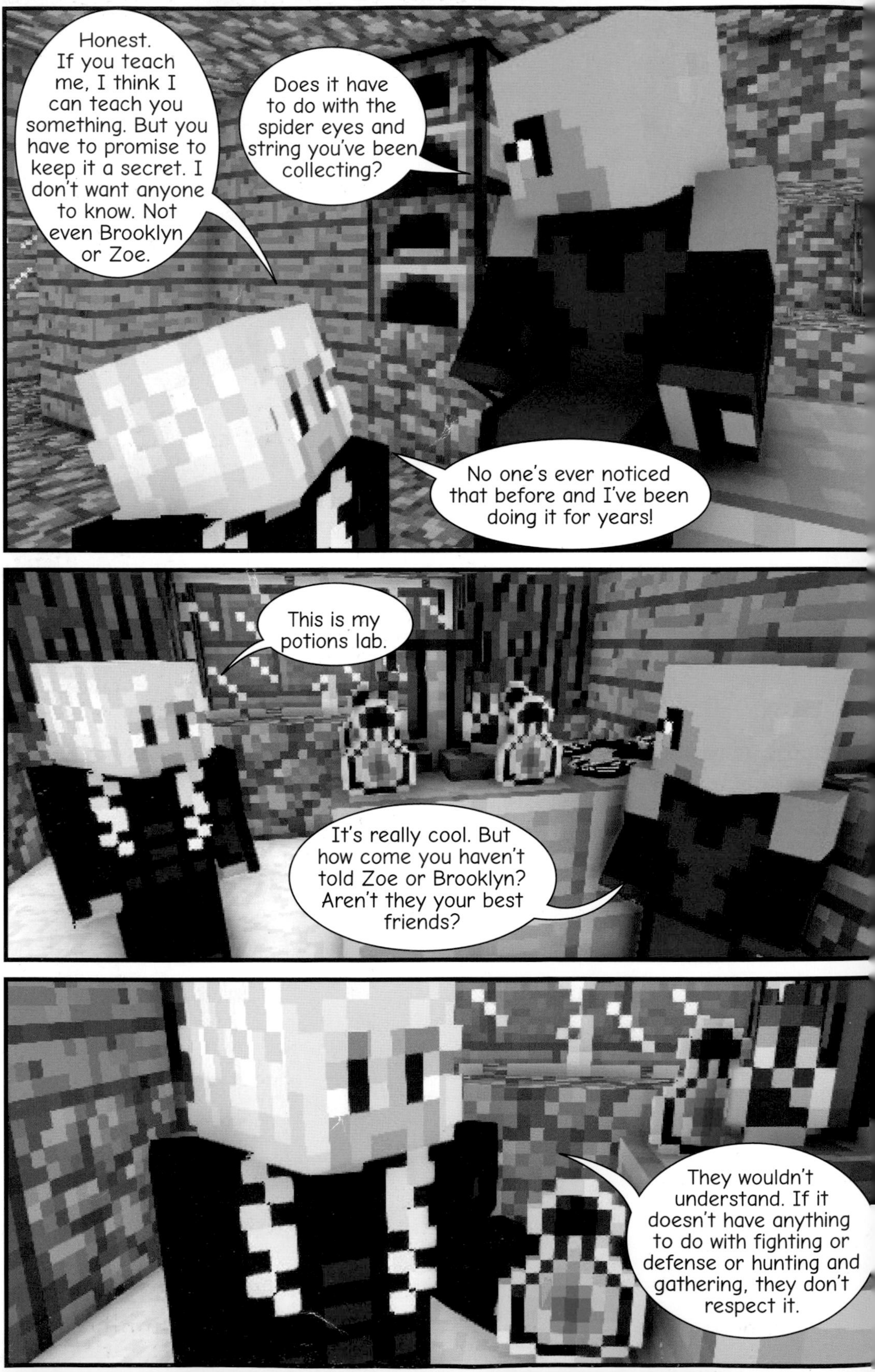

Honest. If you teach me, I think I can teach you something. But you have to promise to keep it a secret. I don't want anyone to know. Not even Brooklyn or Zoe.
Does it have to do with the spider eyes and string you've been collecting?
No one's ever noticed that before and I've been doing it for years!
This is my potions lab.
It's really cool. But how come you haven't told Zoe or Brooklyn? Aren't they your best friends?
They wouldn't understand. If it doesn't have anything to do with fighting or defense or hunting and gathering, they don't respect it.

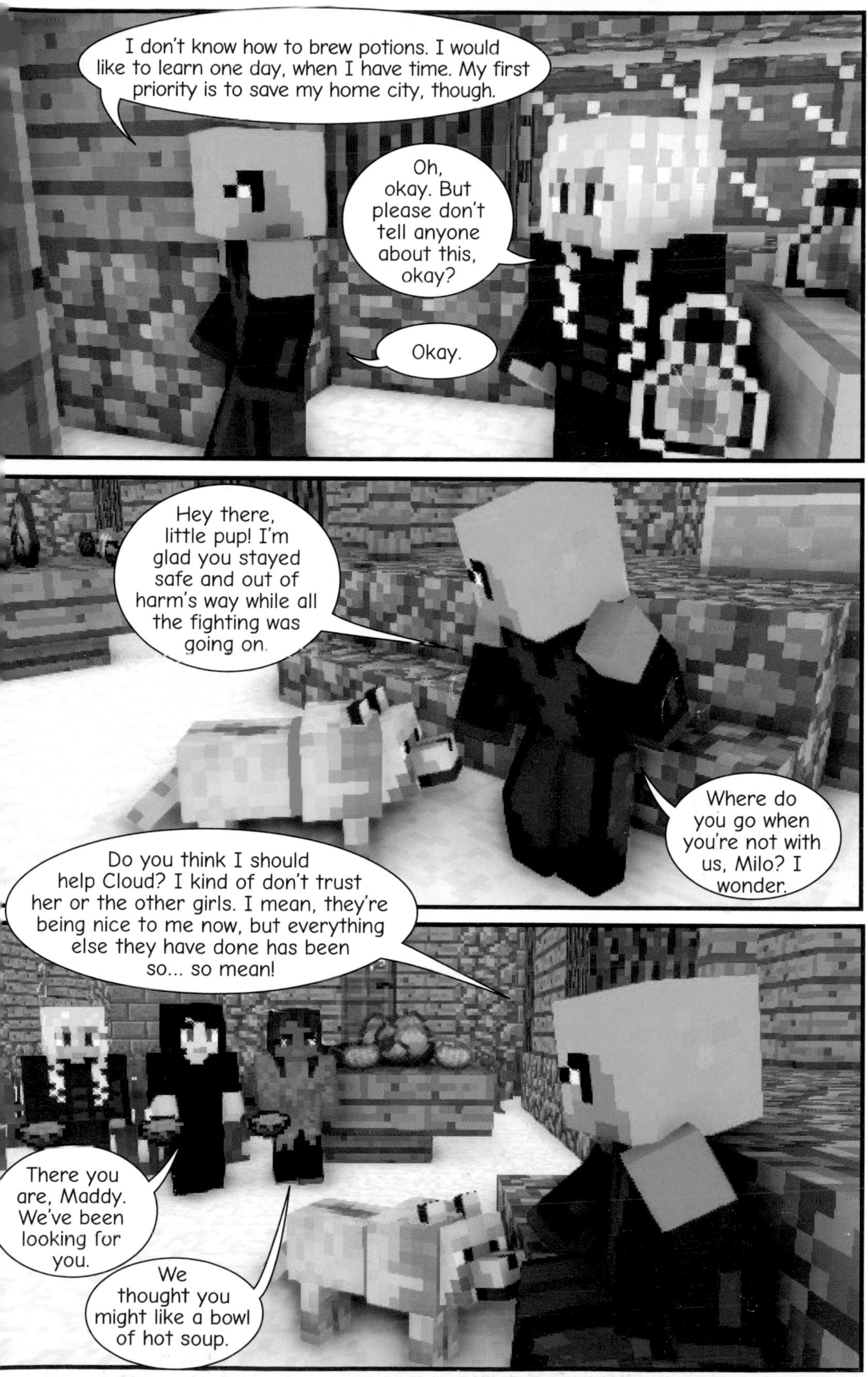

I don't know how to brew potions. I would like to learn one day, when I have time. My first priority is to save my home city, though.
Oh, okay. But please don't tell anyone about this, okay?
Okay.
Hey there, little pup! I'm glad you stayed safe and out of harm's way while all the fighting was going on.
Where do you go when you're not with us, Milo? I wonder.
Do you think I should help Cloud? I kind of don't trust her or the other girls. I mean, they're being nice to me now, but everything else they have done has been so... so mean!
There you are, Maddy. We've been looking for you.
We thought you might like a bowl of hot soup.

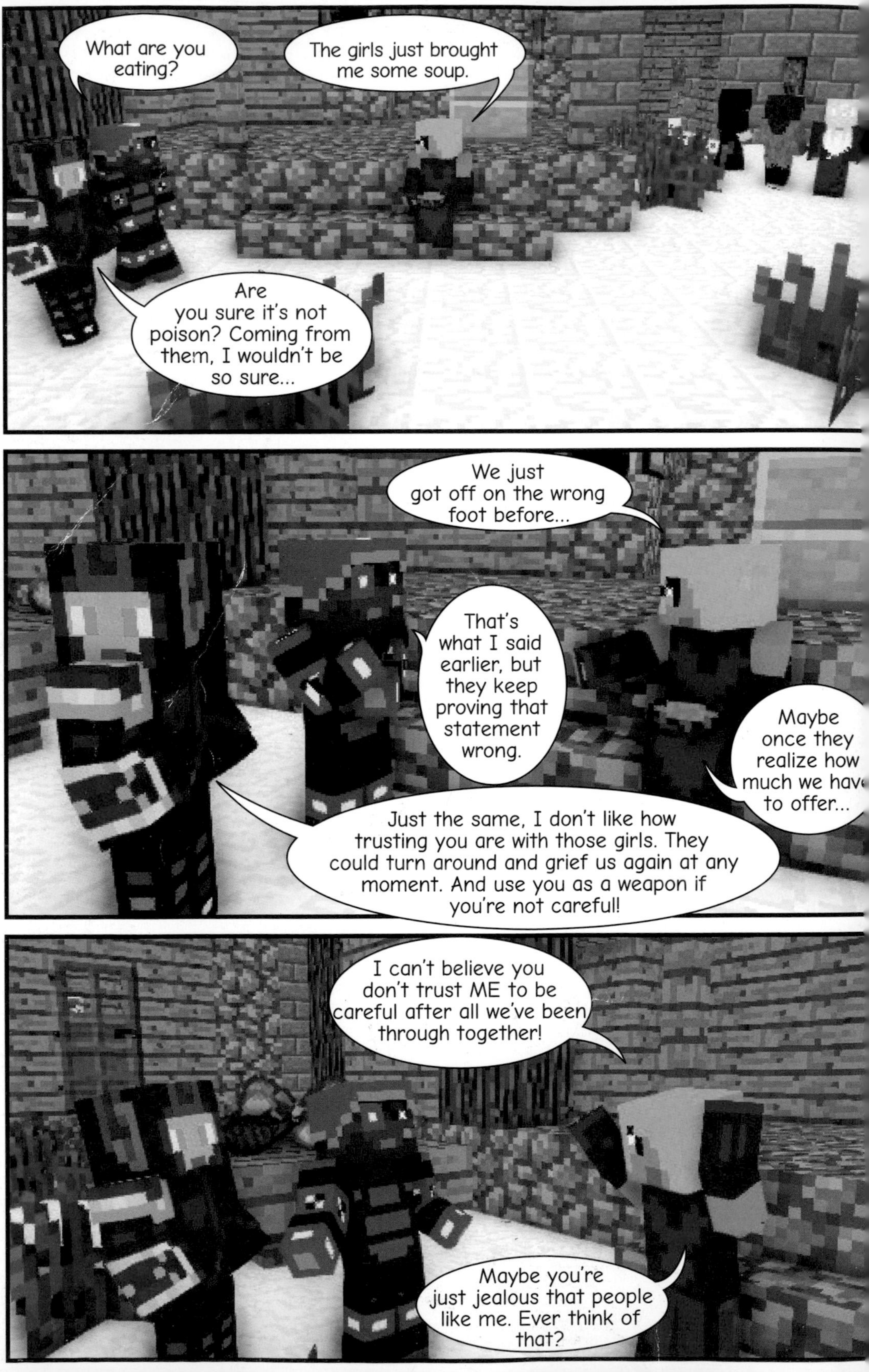
What are you eating?
The girls just brought me some soup.
Are you sure it's not poison? Coming from them, I wouldn't be so sure...
We just got off on the wrong foot before...
That's what I said earlier, but they keep proving that statement wrong.
Maybe once they realize how much we have to offer...
Just the same, I don't like how trusting you are with those girls. They could turn around and grief us again at any moment. And use you as a weapon if you're not careful!
I can't believe you don't trust ME to be careful after all we've been through together!
Maybe you're just jealous that people like me. Ever think of that?

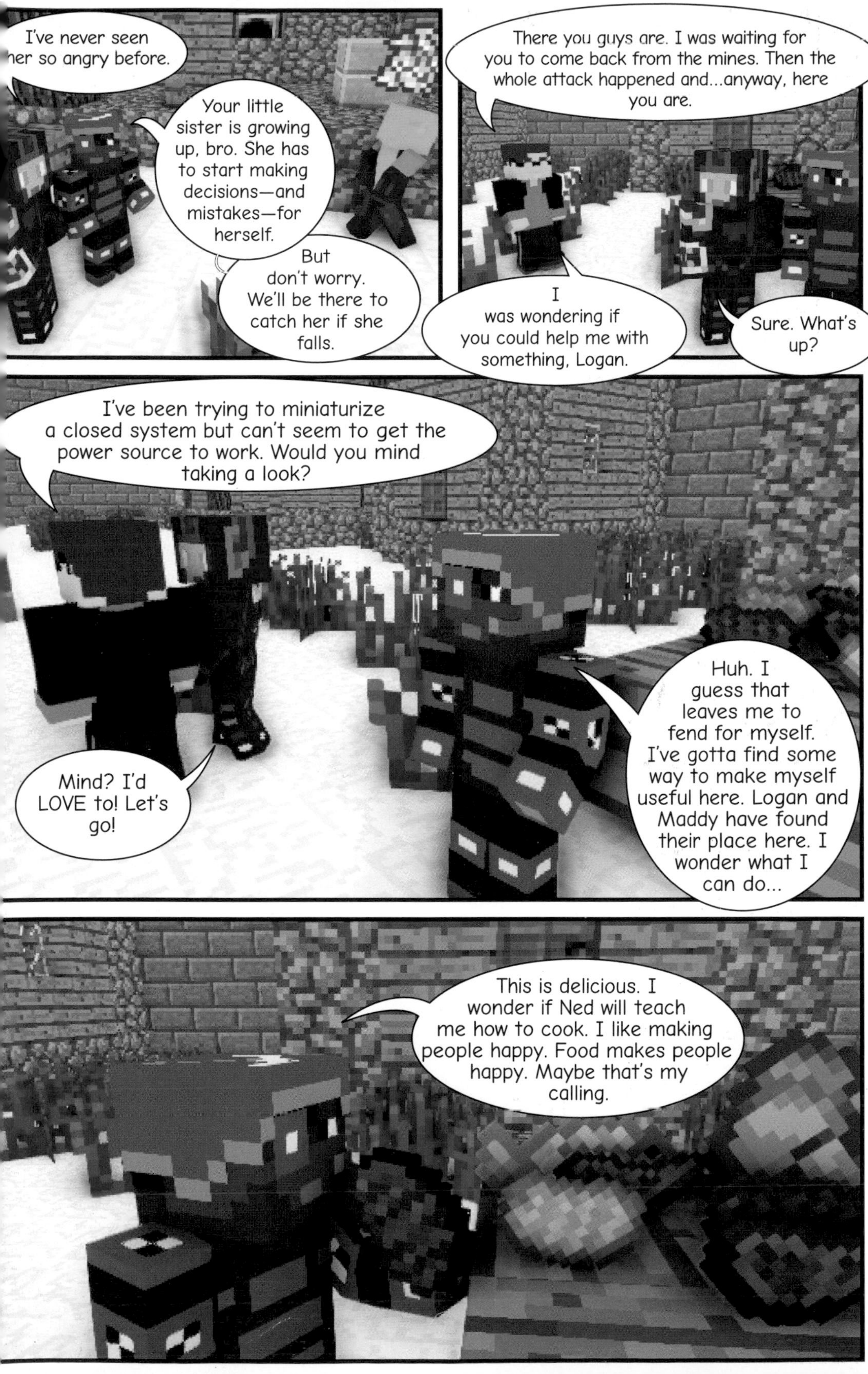
I've never seen her so angry before.
Your little sister is growing up, bro. She has to start making decisions—and mistakes—for herself.
But don't worry. We'll be there to catch her if she falls.
There you guys are. I was waiting for you to come back from the mines. Then the whole attack happened and...anyway, here you are.
I was wondering if you could help me with something, Logan.
Sure. What's up?
I've been trying to miniaturize a closed system but can't seem to get the power source to work. Would you mind taking a look?
Mind? I'd LOVE to! Let's go!
Huh. I guess that leaves me to fend for myself. I've gotta find some way to make myself useful here. Logan and Maddy have found their place here. I wonder what I can do...
This is delicious. I wonder if Ned will teach me how to cook. I like making people happy. Food makes people happy. Maybe that's my calling.

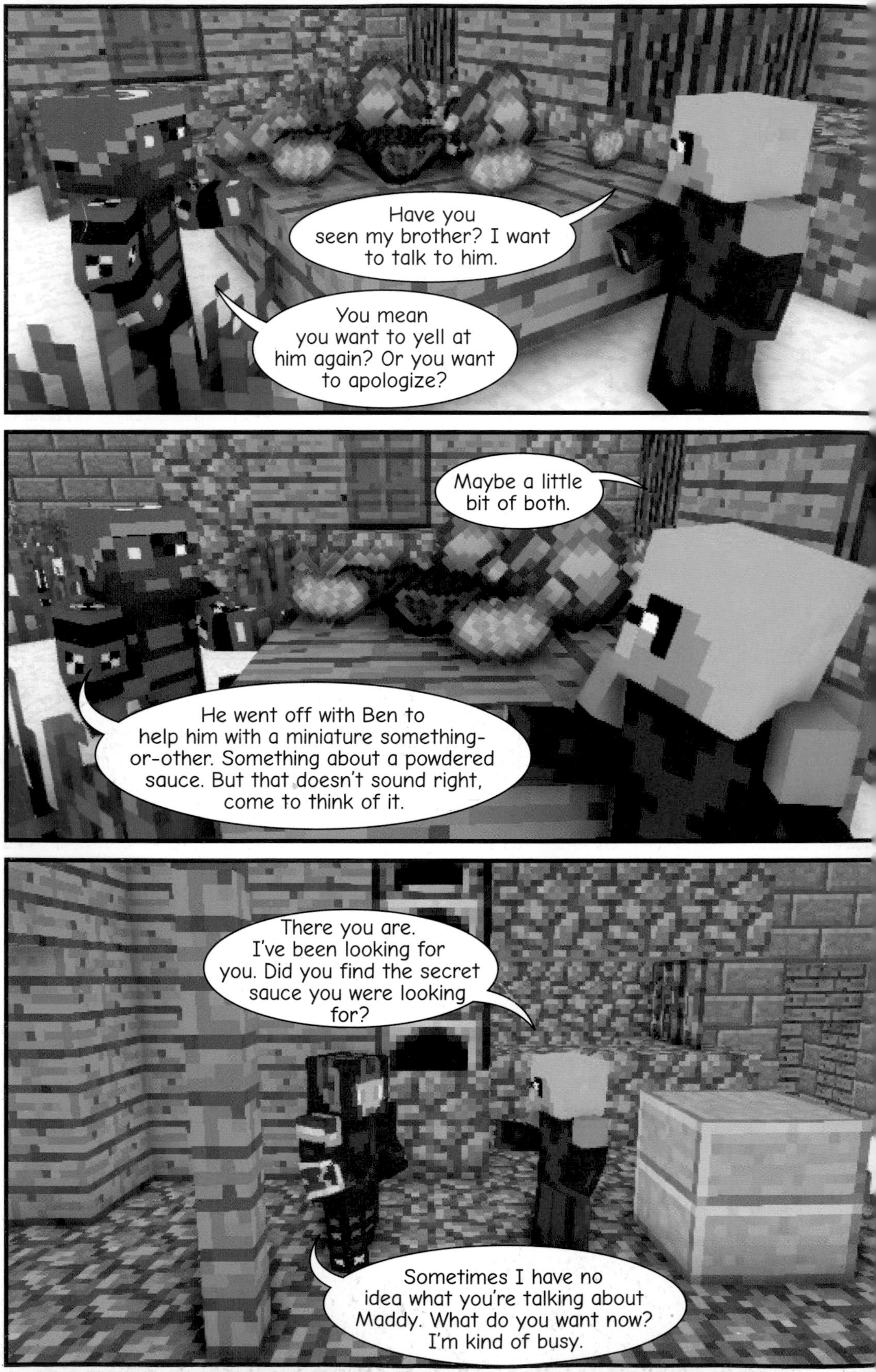
Have you seen my brother? I want to talk to him.
You mean you want to yell at him again? Or you want to apologize?
Maybe a little bit of both.
He went off with Ben to help him with a miniature something-or-other. Something about a powdered sauce. But that doesn't sound right, come to think of it.
There you are. I've been looking for you. Did you find the secret sauce you were looking for?
Sometimes I have no idea what you're talking about Maddy. What do you want now? I'm kind of busy.

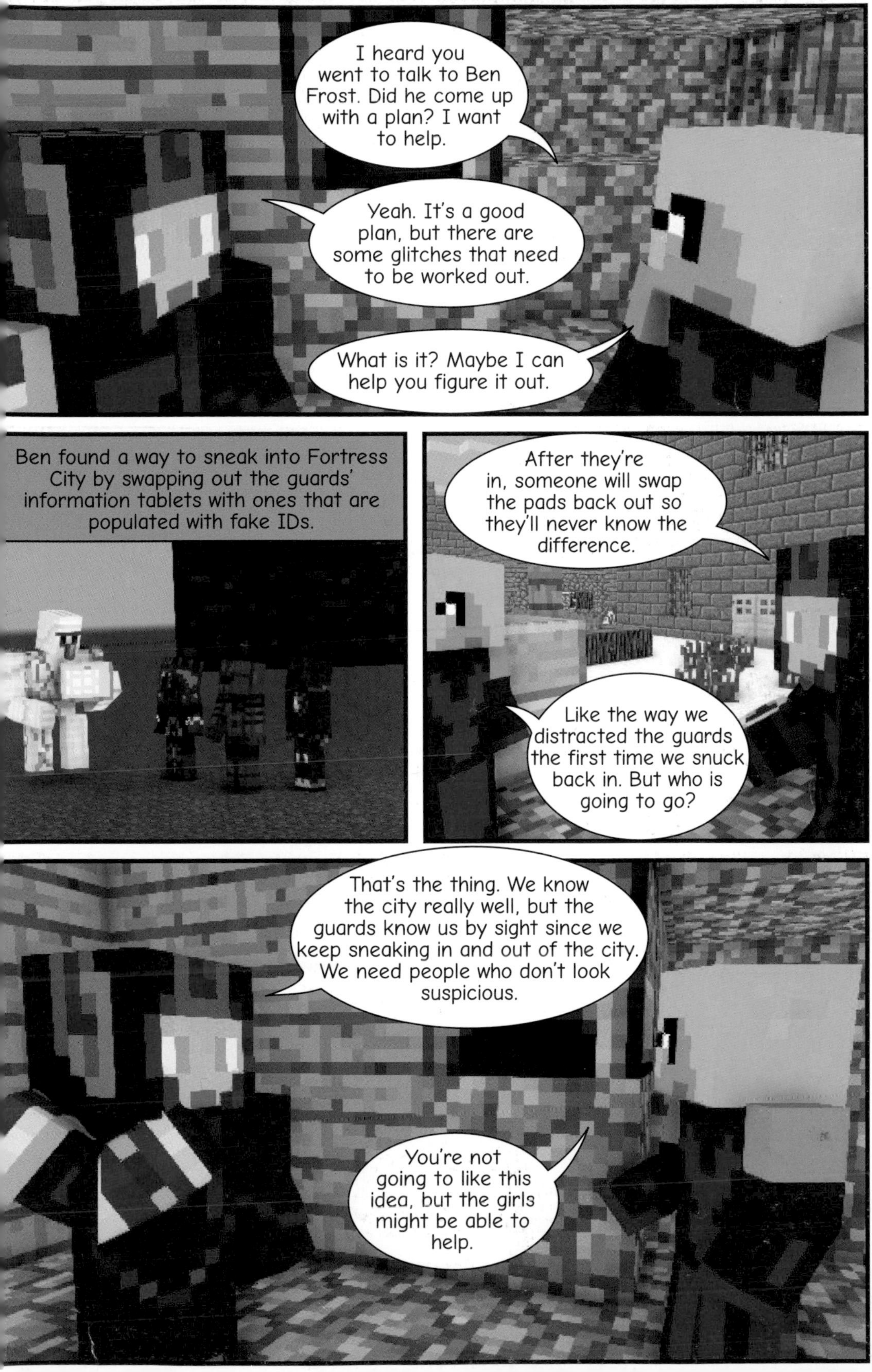
I heard you went to talk to Ben Frost. Did he come up with a plan? I want to help.
Yeah. It's a good plan, but there are some glitches that need to be worked out.
What is it? Maybe I can help you figure it out.
Ben found a way to sneak into Fortress City by swapping out the guards' information tablets with ones that are populated with fake IDs.
After they're in, someone will swap the pads back out so they'll never know the difference.
Like the way we distracted the guards the first time we snuck back in. But who is going to go?
That's the thing. We know the city really well, but the guards know us by sight since we keep sneaking in and out of the city. We need people who don't look suspicious.
You're not going to like this idea, but the girls might be able to help.

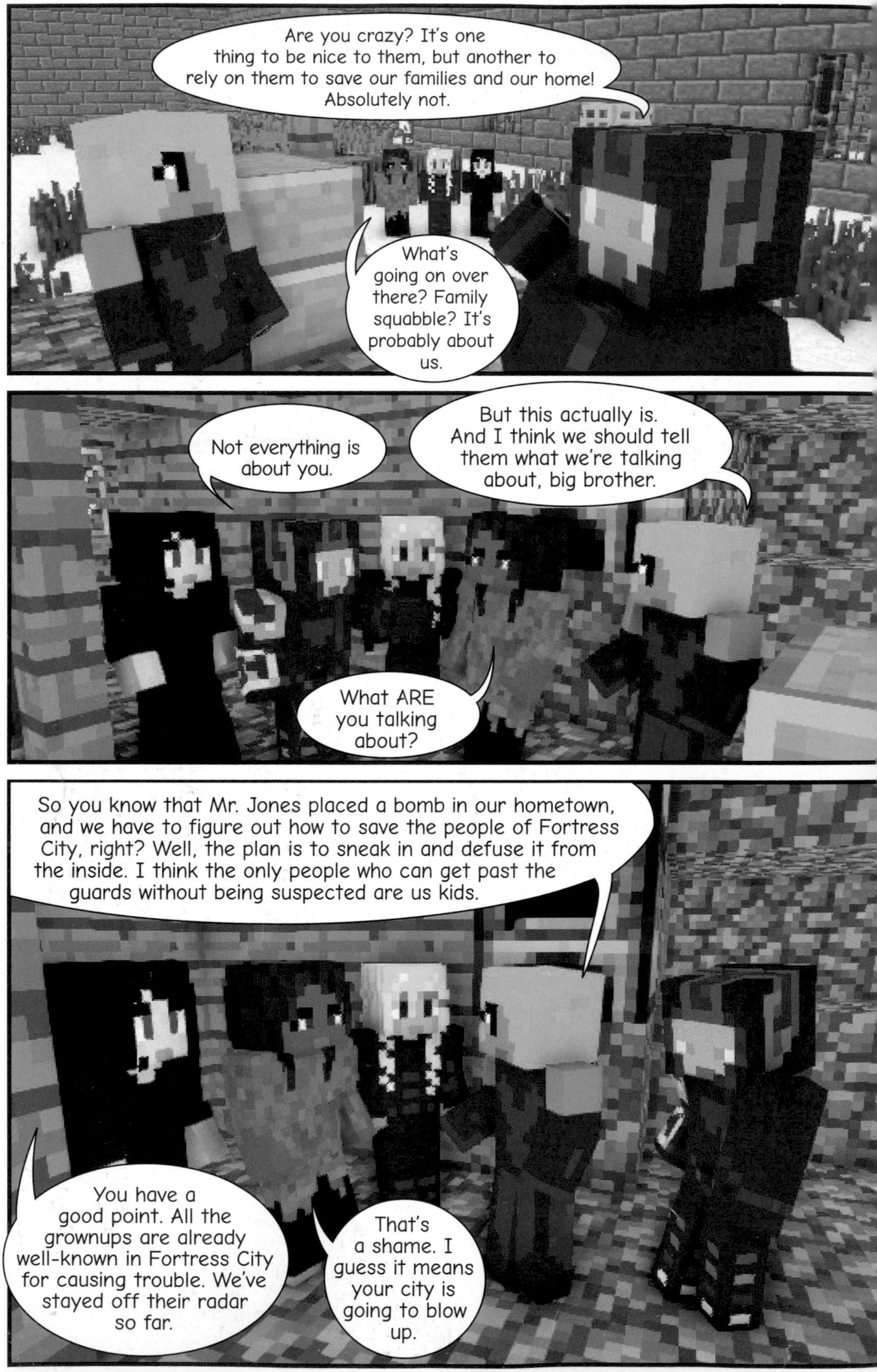
Are you crazy? It's one thing to be nice to them, but another to rely on them to save our families and our home! Absolutely not.
What's going on over there? Family squabble? It's probably about us.
Not everything is about you.
But this actually is. And I think we should tell them what we're talking about, big brother.
What ARE you talking about?
So you know that Mr. Jones placed a bomb in our hometown, and we have to figure out how to save the people of Fortress City, right? Well, the plan is to sneak in and defuse it from the inside. I think the only people who can get past the guards without being suspected are us kids.
You have a good point. All the grownups are already well-known in Fortress City for causing trouble. We've stayed off their radar so far.
That's a shame. I guess it means your city is going to blow up.

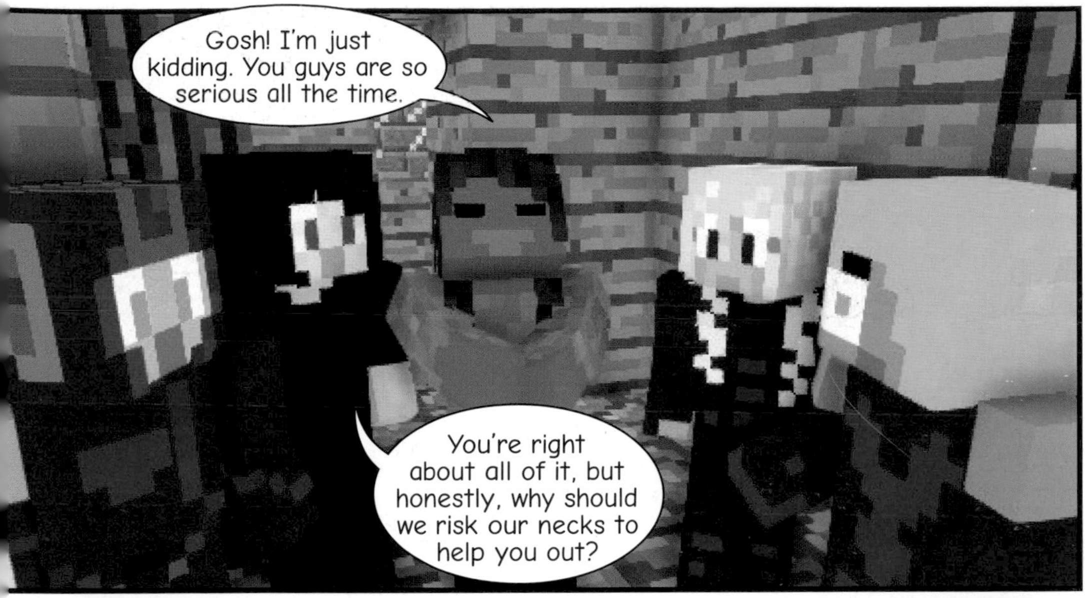
Gosh! I'm just kidding. You guys are so serious all the time.
You're right about all of it, but honestly, why should we risk our necks to help you out?

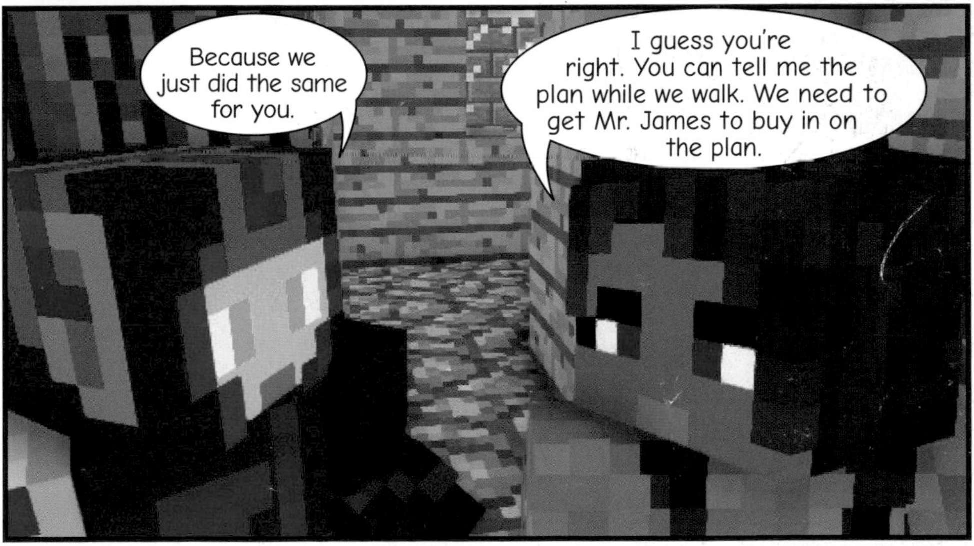
Because we just did the same for you.
I guess you're right. You can tell me the plan while we walk. We need to get Mr. James to buy in on the plan.

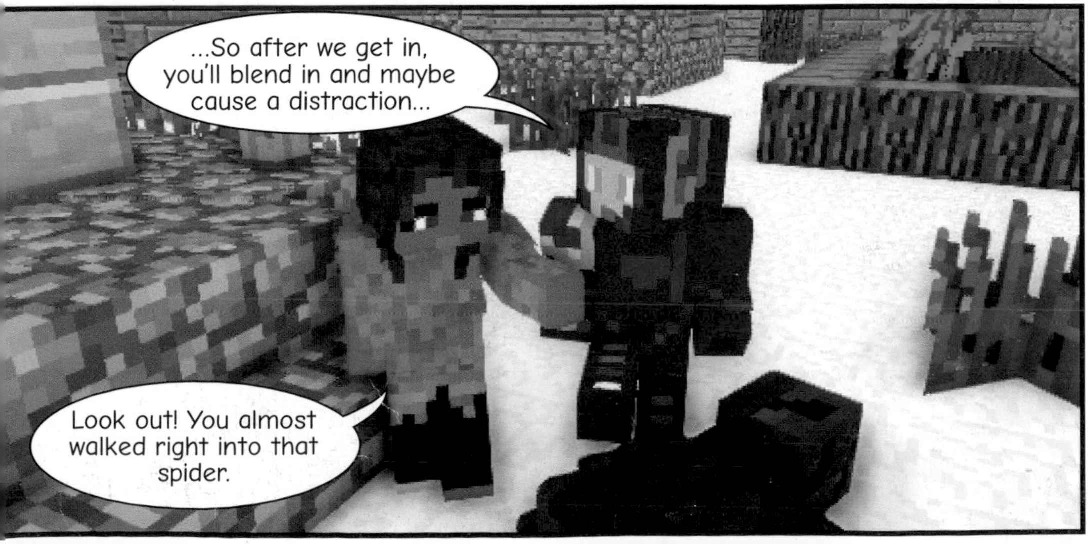
...So after we get in, you'll blend in and maybe cause a distraction...
Look out! You almost walked right into that spider.

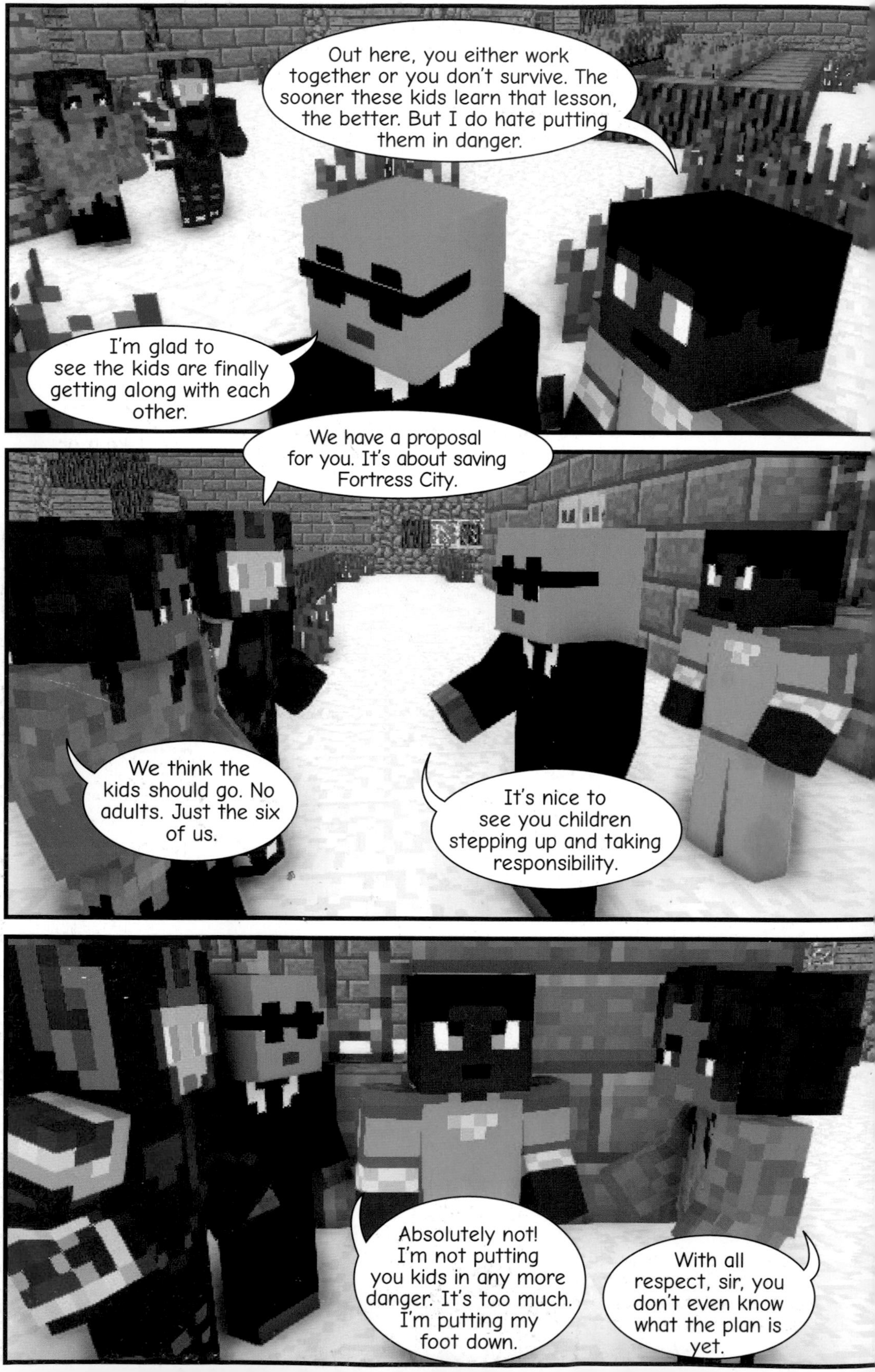

Out here, you either work together or you don't survive. The sooner these kids learn that lesson, the better. But I do hate putting them in danger.
I'm glad to see the kids are finally getting along with each other.
We have a proposal for you. It's about saving Fortress City.
We think the kids should go. No adults. Just the six of us.
It's nice to see you children stepping up and taking responsibility.
Absolutely not! I'm not putting you kids in any more danger. It's too much. I'm putting my foot down.
With all respect, sir, you don't even know what the plan is yet.

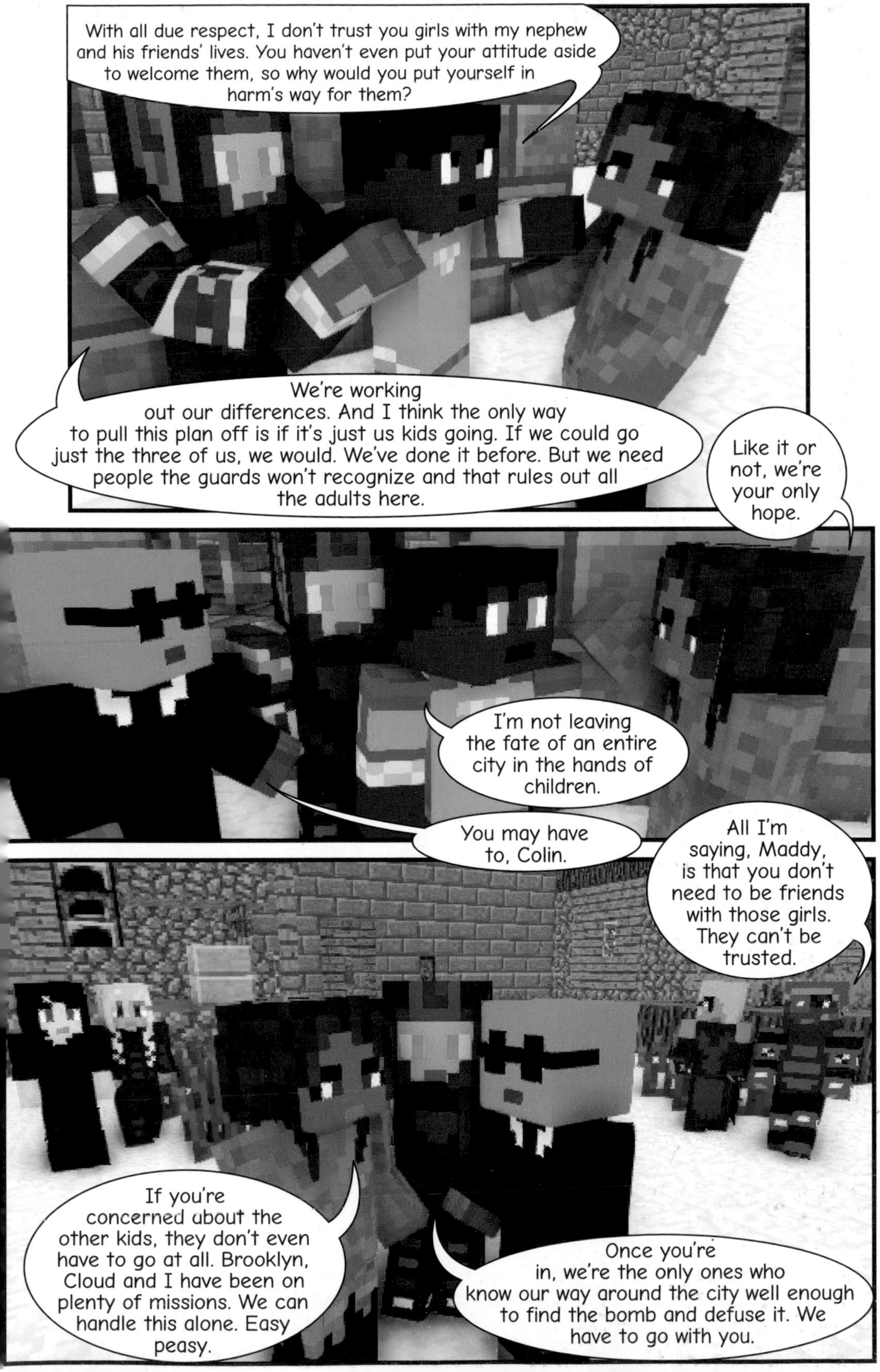

With all due respect, I don't trust you girls with my nephew and his friends' lives. You haven't even put your attitude aside to welcome them, so why would you put yourself in harm's way for them?
We're working out our differences. And I think the only way to pull this plan off is if it's just us kids going. If we could go just the three of us, we would. We've done it before. But we need people the guards won't recognize and that rules out all the adults here.
Like it or not, we're your only hope.
I'm not leaving the fate of an entire city in the hands of children.
You may have to, Colin.
All I'm saying, Maddy, is that you don't need to be friends with those girls. They can't be trusted.
If you're concerned about the other kids, they don't even have to go at all. Brooklyn, Cloud and I have been on plenty of missions. We can handle this alone. Easy peasy.
Once you're in, we're the only ones who know our way around the city well enough to find the bomb and defuse it. We have to go with you.

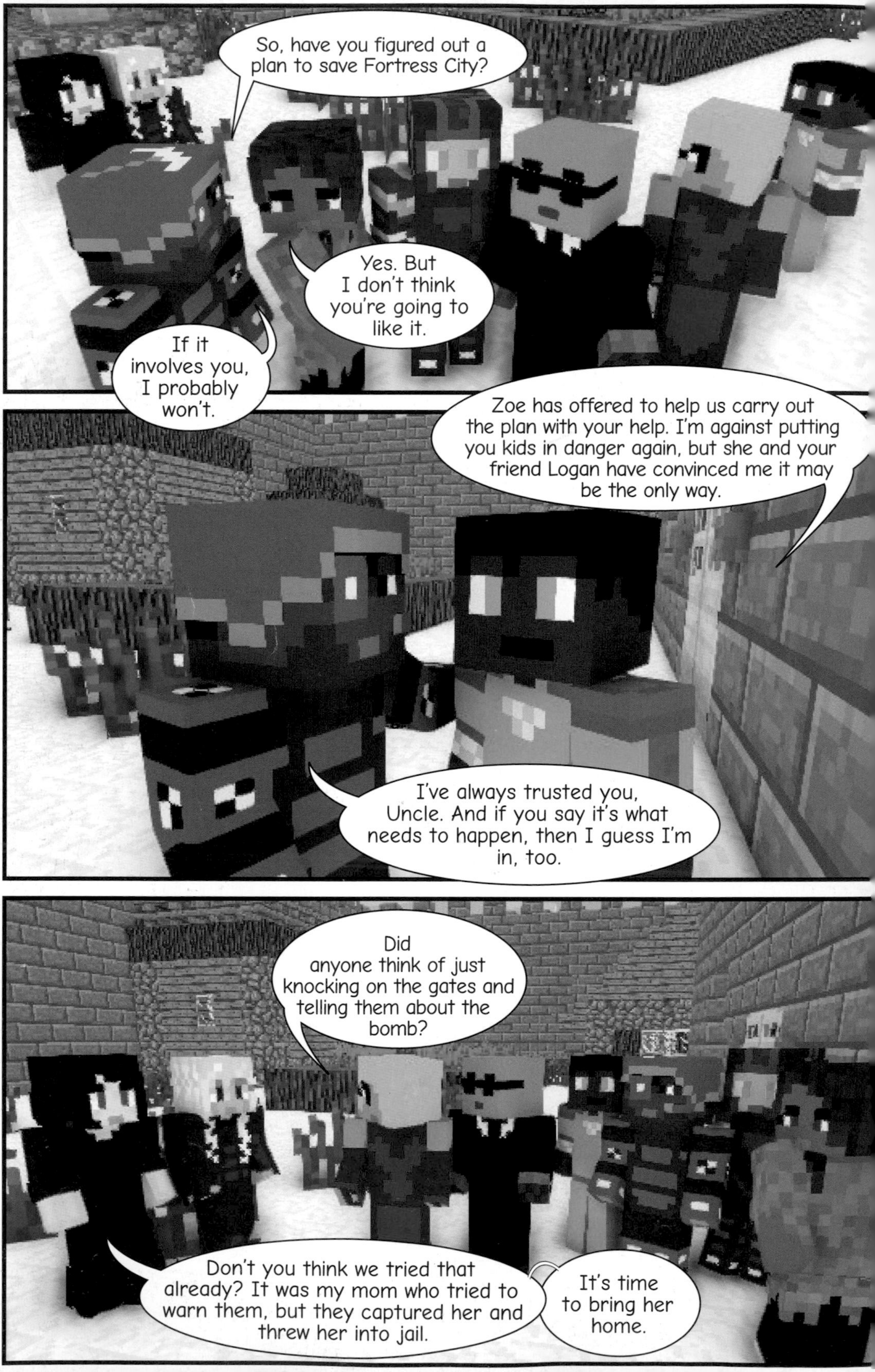
So, have you figured out a plan to save Fortress City?
Yes. But I don't think you're going to like it.
If it involves you, I probably won't.
Zoe has offered to help us carry out the plan with your help. I'm against putting you kids in danger again, but she and your friend Logan have convinced me it may be the only way.
I've always trusted you, Uncle. And if you say it's what needs to happen, then I guess I'm in, too.
Did anyone think of just knocking on the gates and telling them about the bomb?
Don't you think we tried that already? It was my mom who tried to warn them, but they captured her and threw her into jail.
It's time to bring her home.

CHAPTER 8

THE JOURNEY

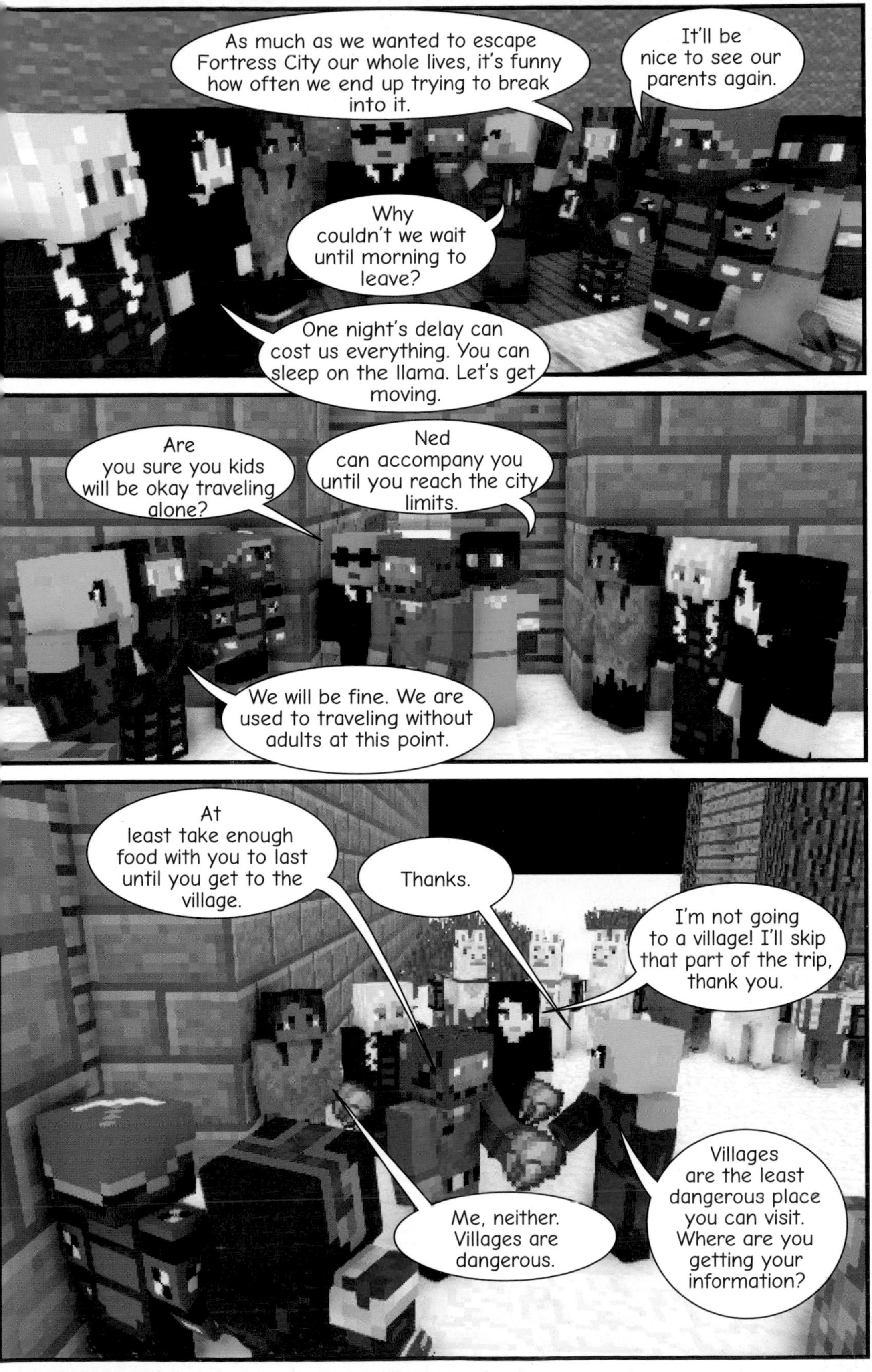
As much as we wanted to escape Fortress City our whole lives, it's funny how often we end up trying to break into it.
It'll be nice to see our parents again.
Why couldn't we wait until morning to leave?
One night's delay can cost us everything. You can sleep on the llama. Let's get moving.
Are you sure you kids will be okay traveling alone?
Ned can accompany you until you reach the city limits.
We will be fine. We are used to traveling without adults at this point.
At least take enough food with you to last until you get to the village.
Thanks.
I'm not going to a village! I'll skip that part of the trip, thank you.
Me, neither. Villages are dangerous.
Villages are the least dangerous place you can visit. Where are you getting your information?

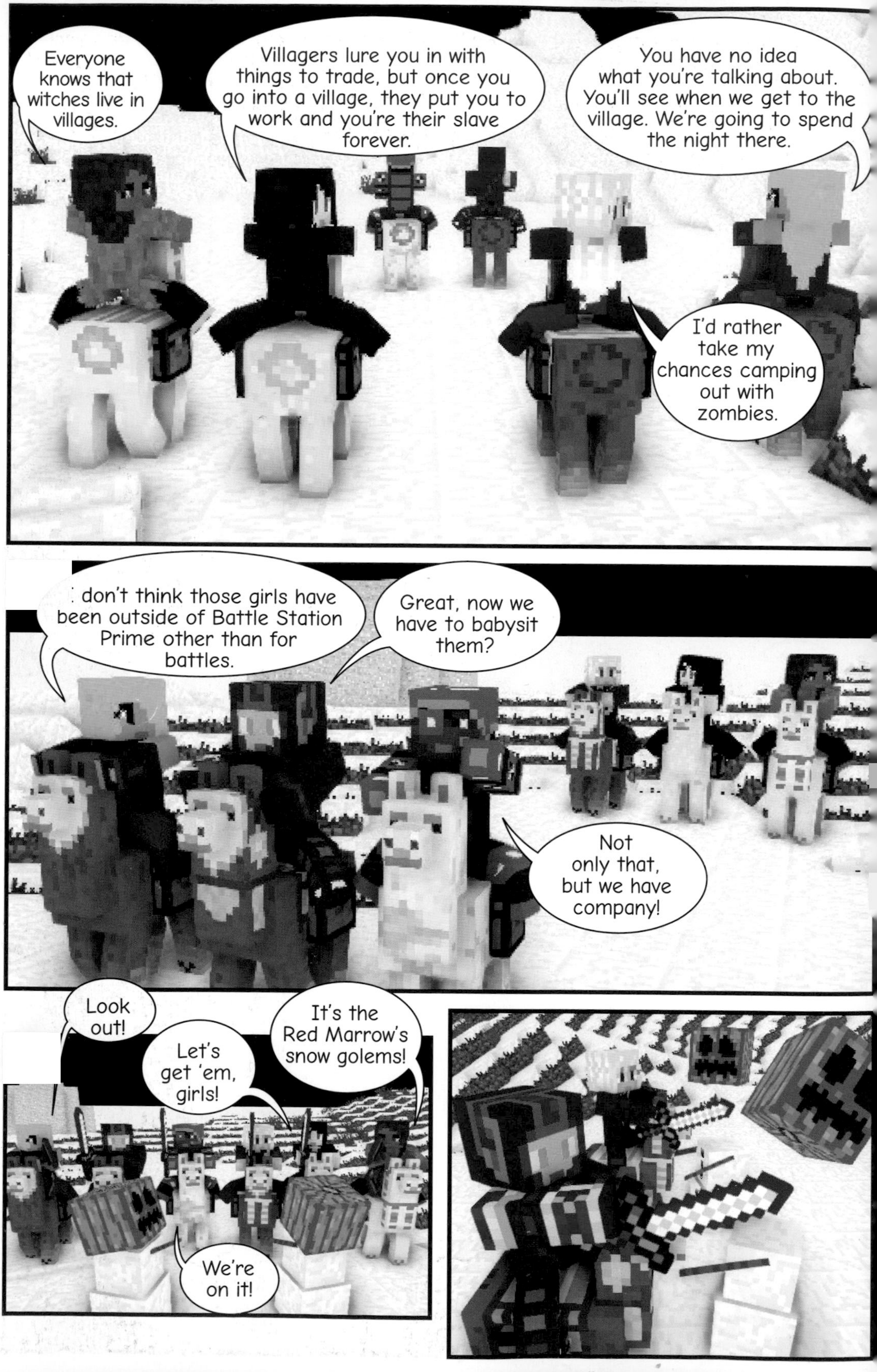
Everyone knows that witches live in villages.
Villagers lure you in with things to trade, but once you go into a village, they put you to work and you're their slave forever.
You have no idea what you're talking about. You'll see when we get to the village. We're going to spend the night there.
I'd rather take my chances camping out with zombies.
I don't think those girls have been outside of Battle Station Prime other than for battles.
Great, now we have to babysit them?
Not only that, but we have company!
Look out!
Let's get 'em, girls!
It's the Red Marrow's snow golems!
We're on it!

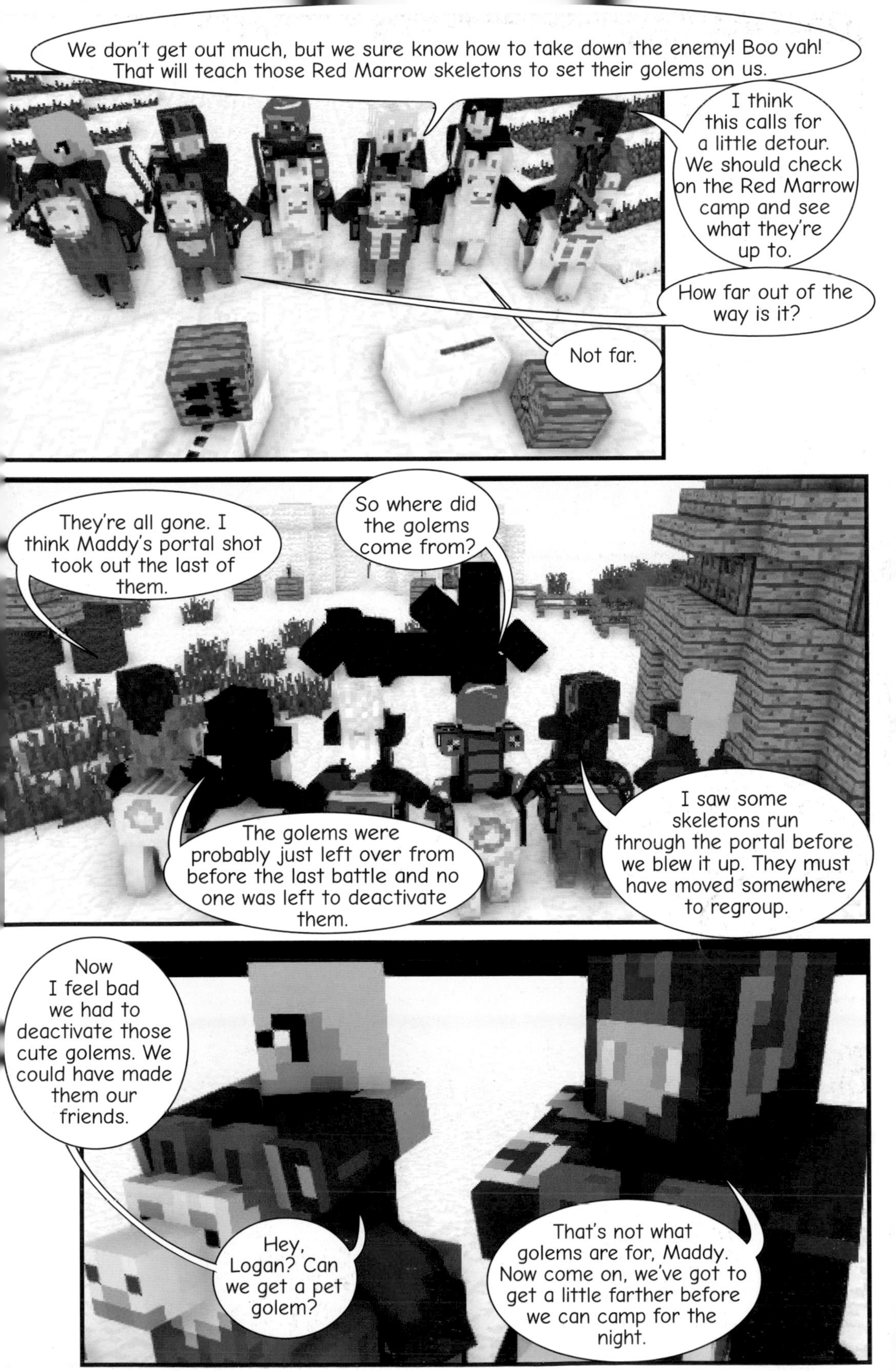
We don't get out much, but we sure know how to take down the enemy! Boo yah! That will teach those Red Marrow skeletons to set their golems on us.
I think this calls for a little detour. We should check on the Red Marrow camp and see what they're up to.
How far out of the way is it?
Not far.
They're all gone. I think Maddy's portal shot took out the last of them.
So where did the golems come from?
The golems were probably just left over from before the last battle and no one was left to deactivate them.
I saw some skeletons run through the portal before we blew it up. They must have moved somewhere to regroup.
Now I feel bad we had to deactivate those cute golems. We could have made them our friends.
Hey, Logan? Can we get a pet golem?
That's not what golems are for, Maddy. Now come on, we've got to get a little farther before we can camp for the night.

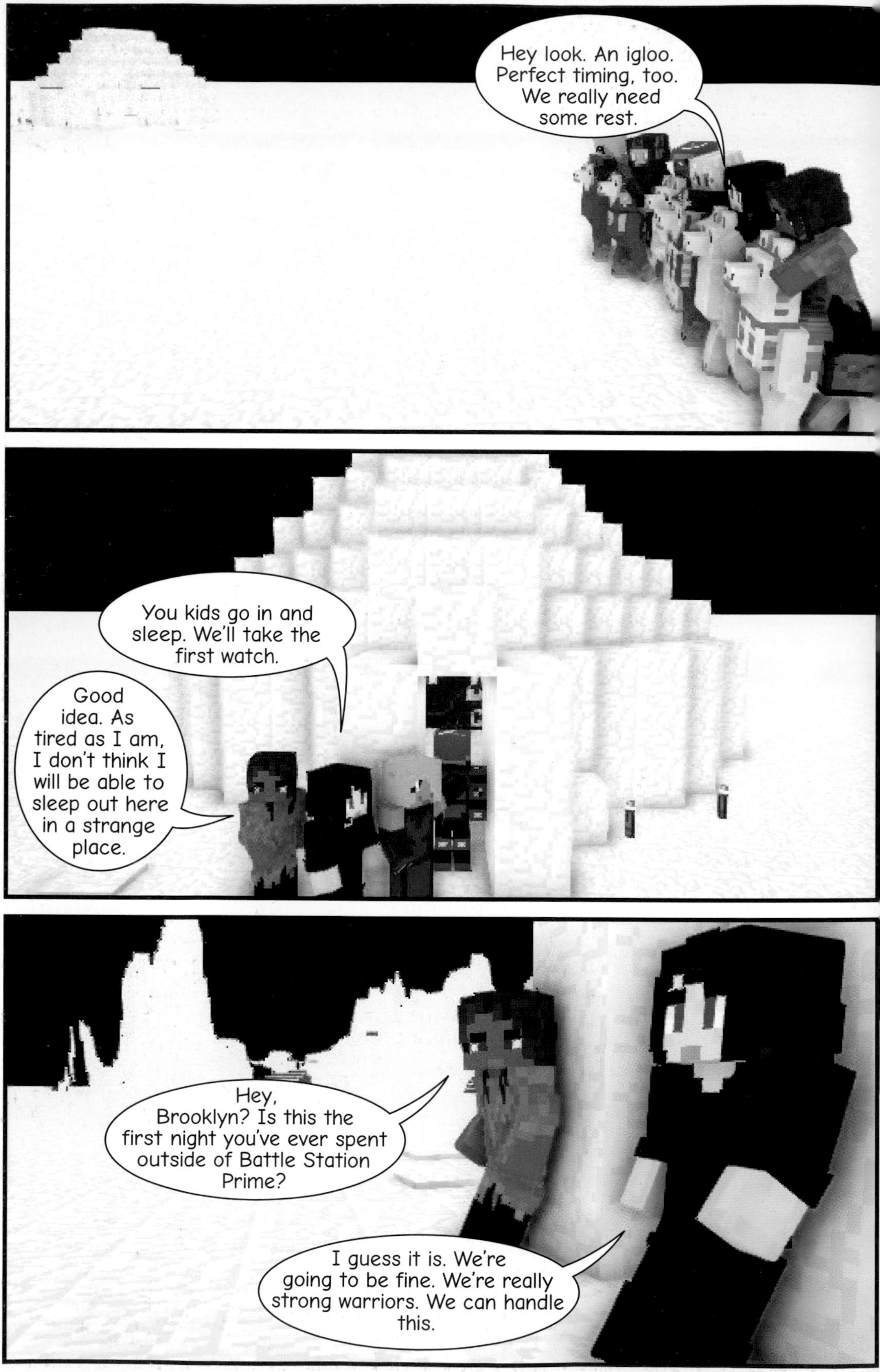
Hey look. An igloo. Perfect timing, too. We really need some rest.
You kids go in and sleep. We'll take the first watch.
Good idea. As tired as I am, I don't think I will be able to sleep out here in a strange place.
Hey, Brooklyn? Is this the first night you've ever spent outside of Battle Station Prime?
I guess it is. We're going to be fine. We're really strong warriors. We can handle this.

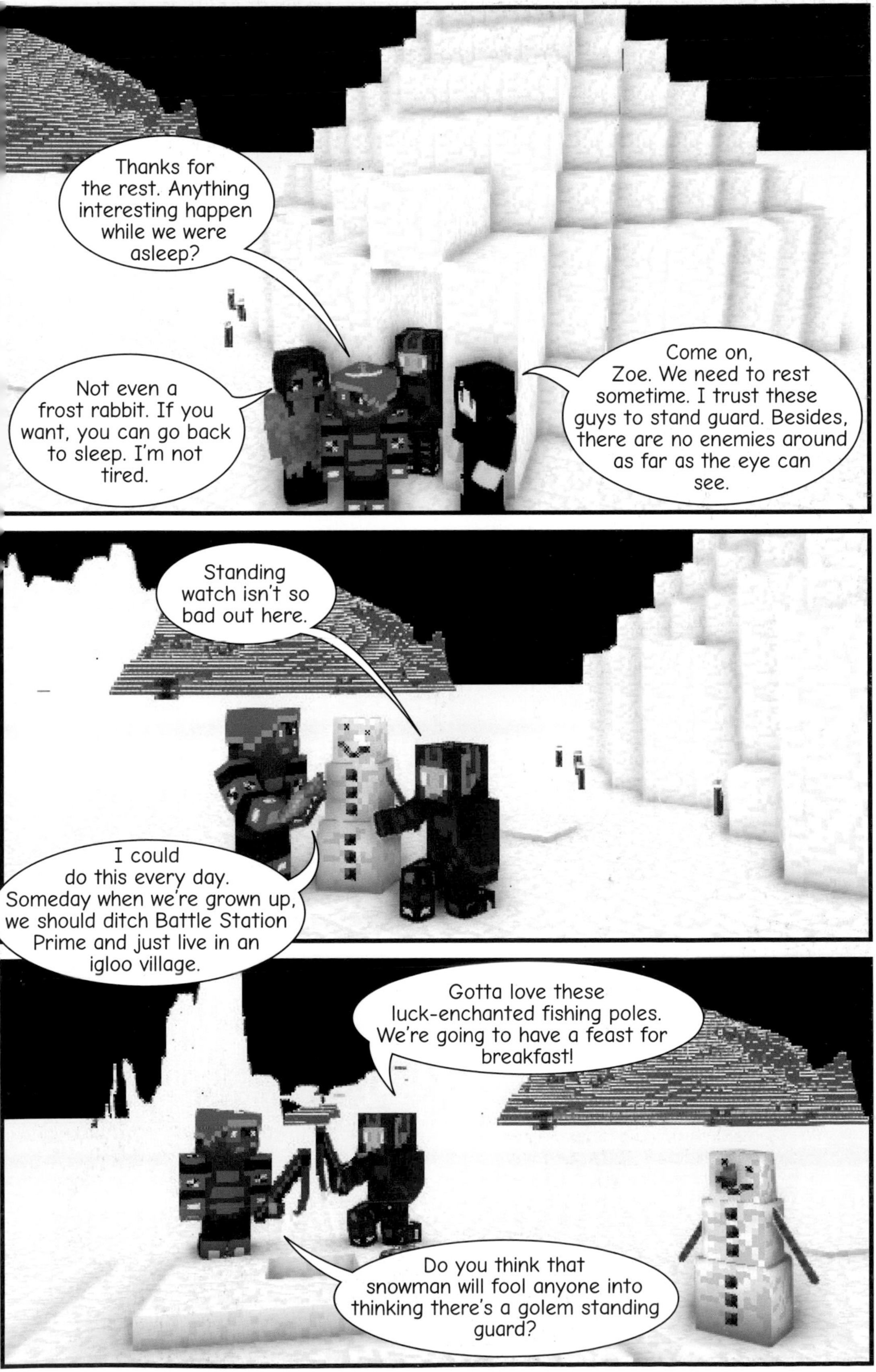
Thanks for the rest. Anything interesting happen while we were asleep?
Not even a frost rabbit. If you want, you can go back to sleep. I'm not tired.
Come on, Zoe. We need to rest sometime. I trust these guys to stand guard. Besides, there are no enemies around as far as the eye can see.
Standing watch isn't so bad out here.
I could do this every day. Someday when we're grown up, we should ditch Battle Station Prime and just live in an igloo village.
Gotta love these luck-enchanted fishing poles. We're going to have a feast for breakfast!
Do you think that snowman will fool anyone into thinking there's a golem standing guard?

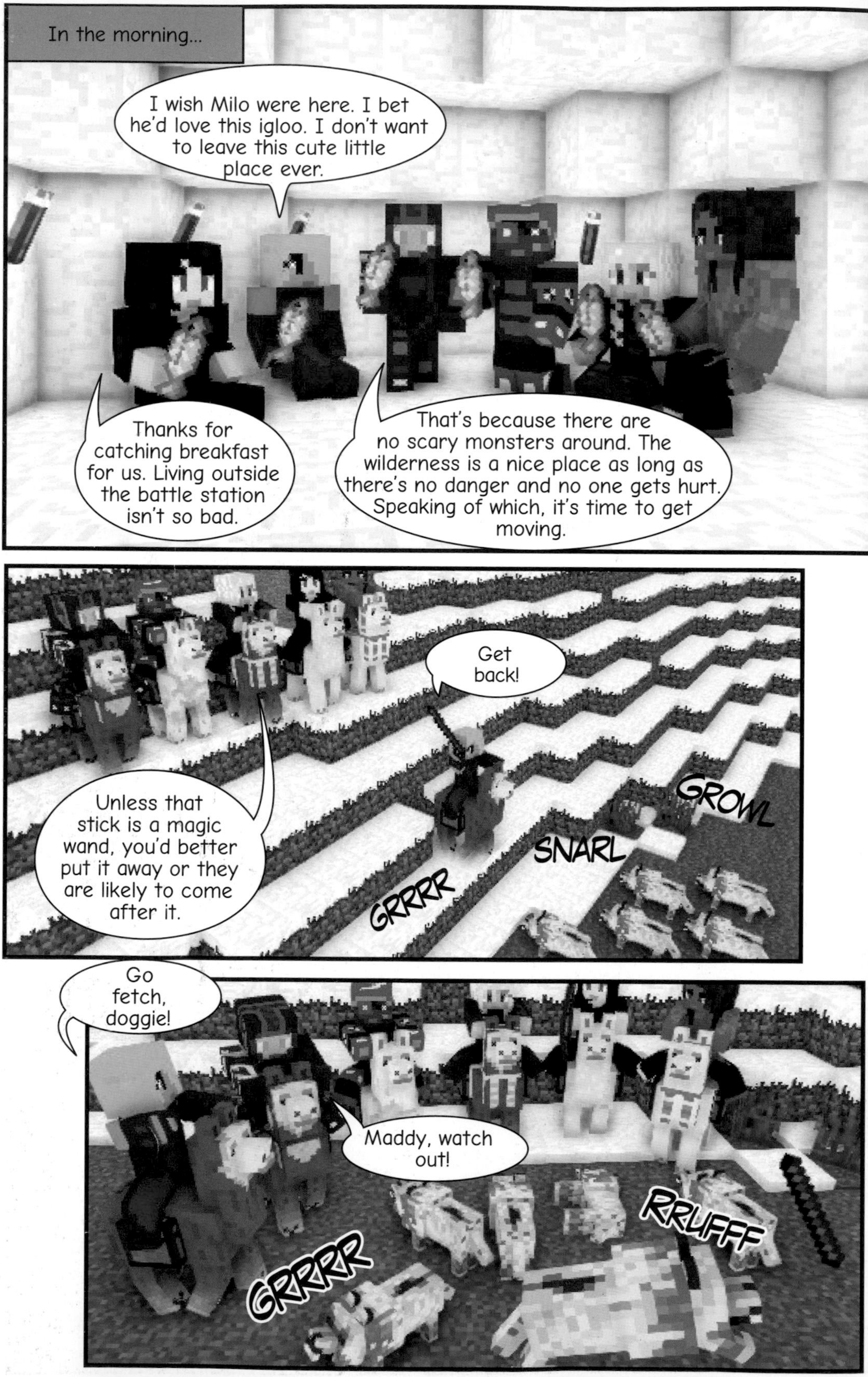
In the morning...
I wish Milo were here. I bet he'd love this igloo. I don't want to leave this cute little place ever.
Thanks for catching breakfast for us. Living outside the battle station isn't so bad.
That's because there are no scary monsters around. The wilderness is a nice place as long as there's no danger and no one gets hurt. Speaking of which, it's time to get moving.
Get back!
Unless that stick is a magic wand, you'd better put it away or they are likely to come after it.
GROWL
SNARL
GRRRR
Go fetch, doggie!
Maddy, watch out!
RRUFFF
GRRRR

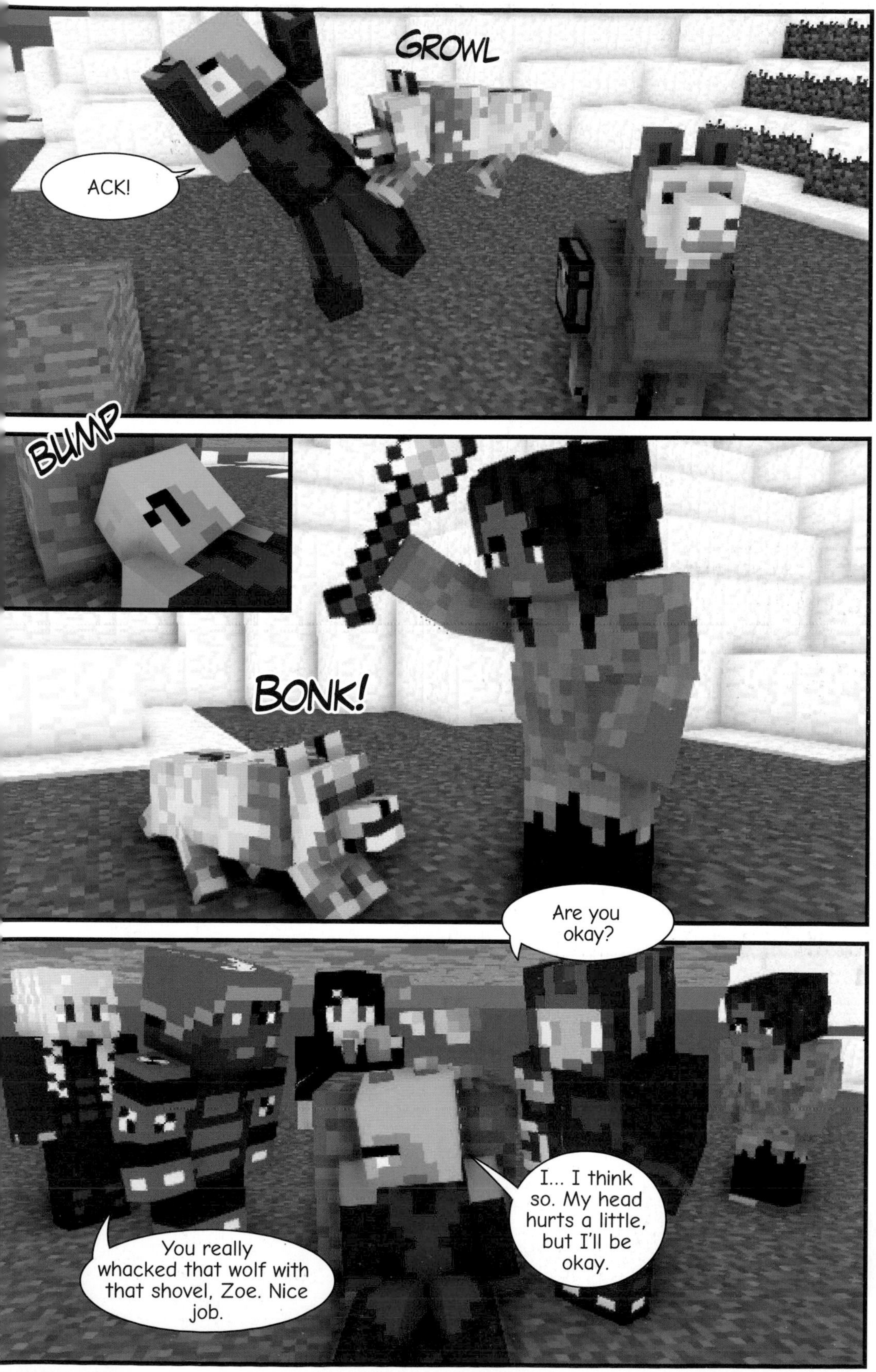
GROWL
ACK!
BUMP
BONK!
Are you okay?
I... I think so. My head hurts a little, but I'll be okay.
You really whacked that wolf with that shovel, Zoe. Nice job.

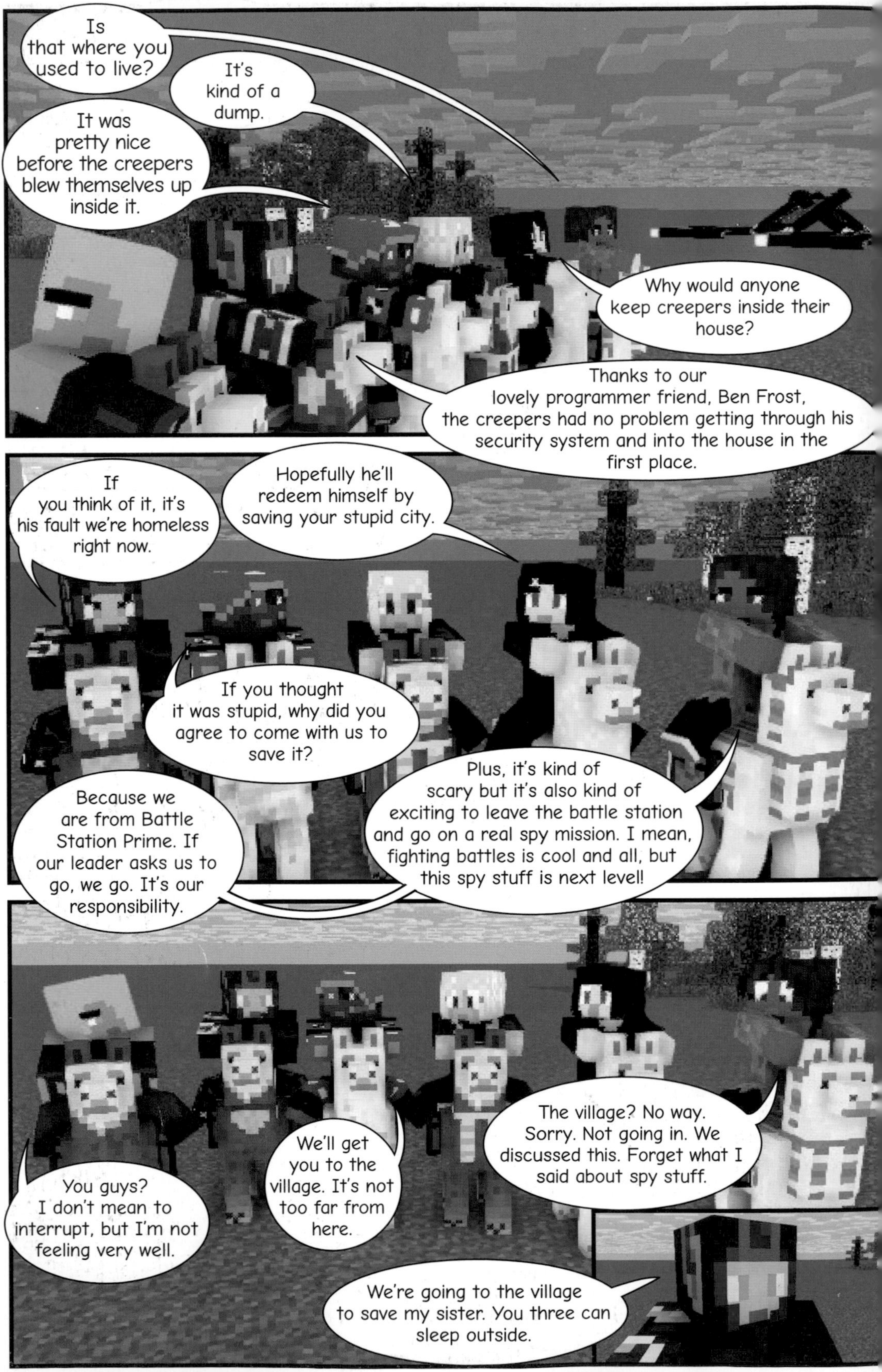
Is that where you used to live?
It's kind of a dump.
It was pretty nice before the creepers blew themselves up inside it.
Why would anyone keep creepers inside their house?
Thanks to our lovely programmer friend, Ben Frost, the creepers had no problem getting through his security system and into the house in the first place.
If you think of it, it's his fault we're homeless right now.
Hopefully he'll redeem himself by saving your stupid city.
If you thought it was stupid, why did you agree to come with us to save it?
Because we are from Battle Station Prime. If our leader asks us to go, we go. It's our responsibility.
Plus, it's kind of scary but it's also kind of exciting to leave the battle station and go on a real spy mission. I mean, fighting battles is cool and all, but this spy stuff is next level!
You guys? I don't mean to interrupt, but I'm not feeling very well.
We'll get you to the village. It's not too far from here.
The village? No way. Sorry. Not going in. We discussed this. Forget what I said about spy stuff.
We're going to the village to save my sister. You three can sleep outside.

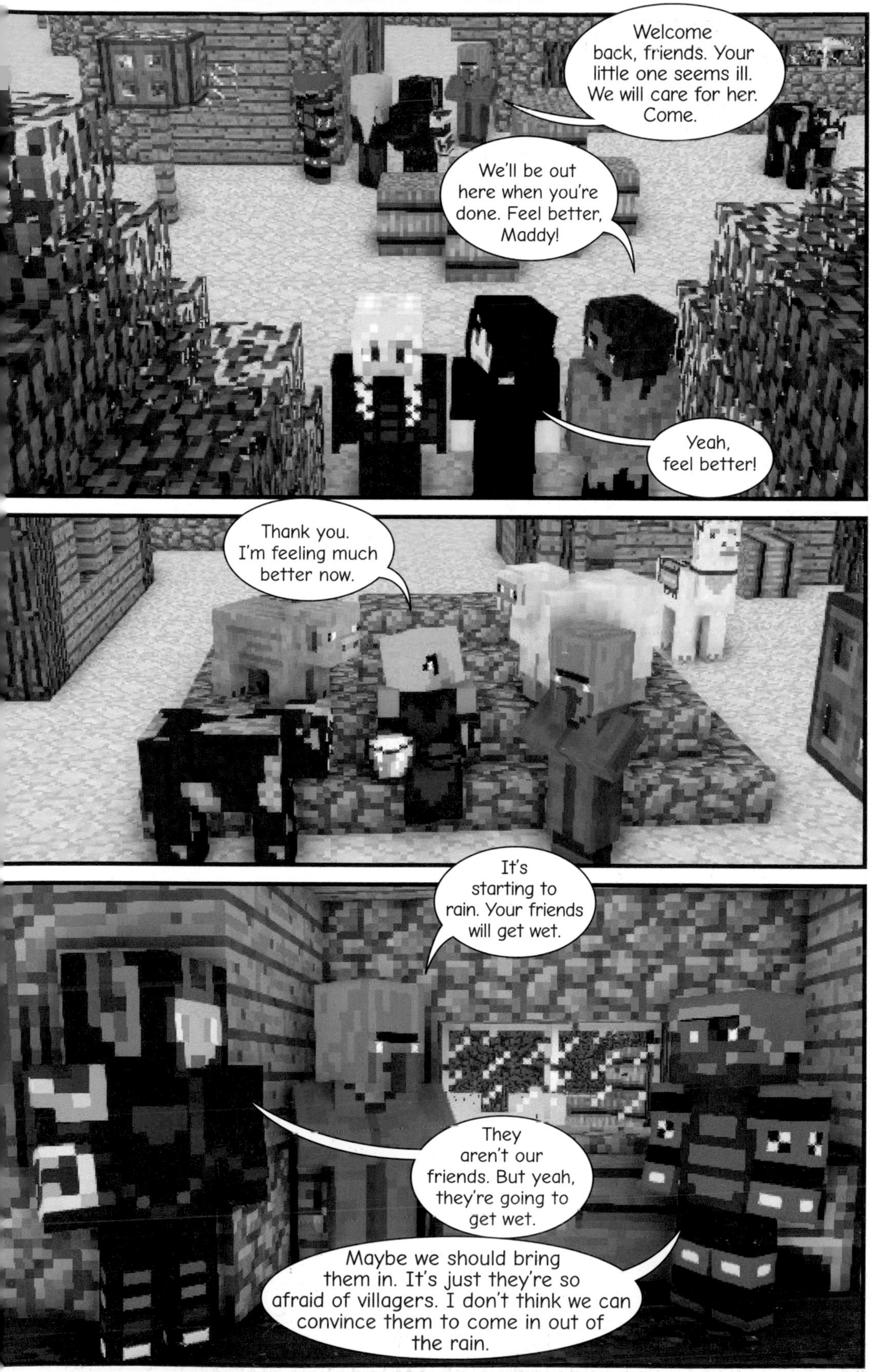
Welcome back, friends. Your little one seems ill. We will care for her. Come.
We'll be out here when you're done. Feel better, Maddy!
Yeah, feel better!
Thank you. I'm feeling much better now.
It's starting to rain. Your friends will get wet.
They aren't our friends. But yeah, they're going to get wet.
Maybe we should bring them in. It's just they're so afraid of villagers. I don't think we can convince them to come in out of the rain.

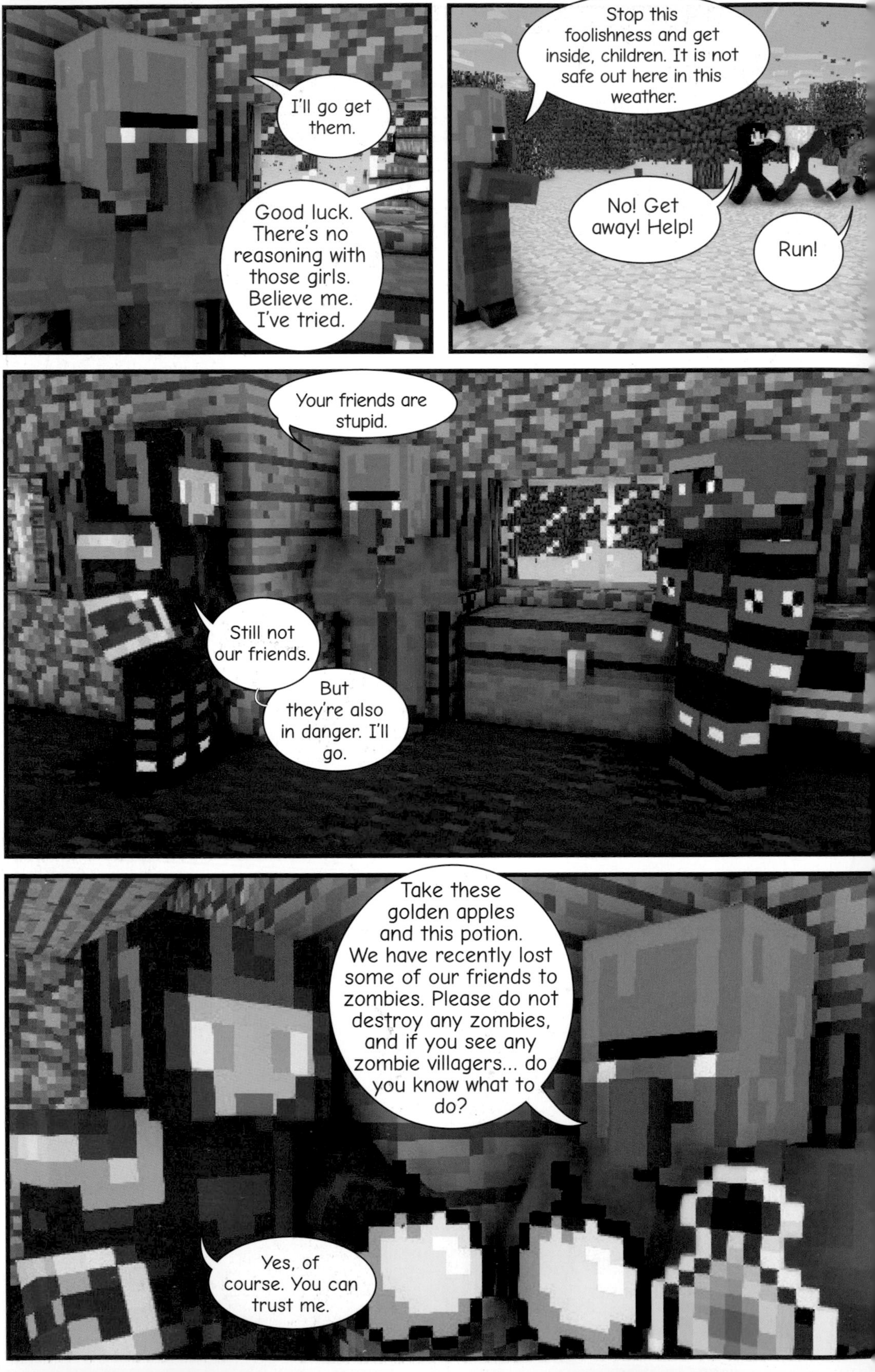
I'll go get them.
Good luck. There's no reasoning with those girls. Believe me. I've tried.
Stop this foolishness and get inside, children. It is not safe out here in this weather.
No! Get away! Help!
Run!
Your friends are stupid.
Still not our friends.
But they're also in danger. I'll go.
Take these golden apples and this potion. We have recently lost some of our friends to zombies. Please do not destroy any zombies, and if you see any zombie villagers... do you know what to do?
Yes, of course. You can trust me.

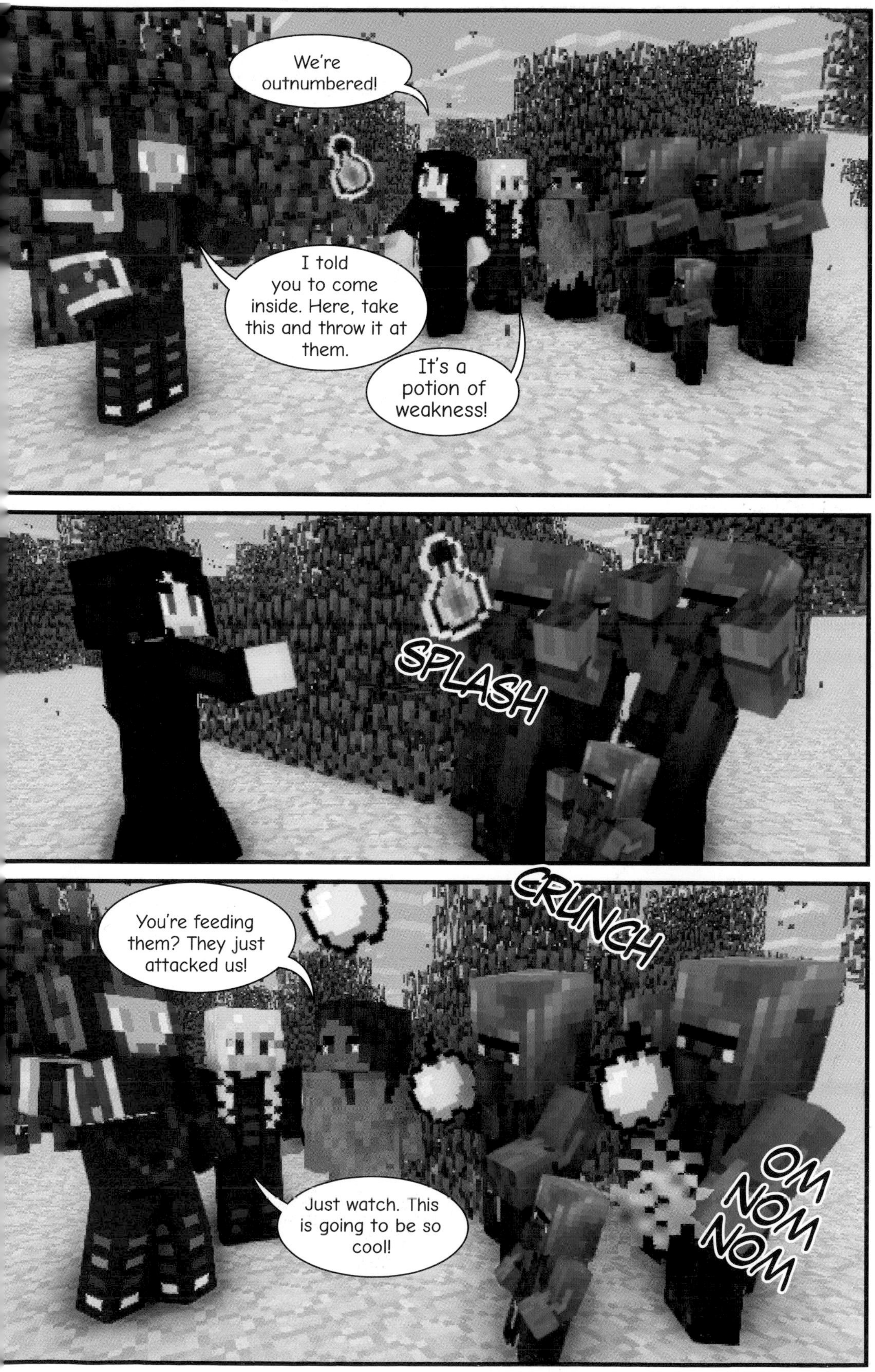
We're outnumbered!
I told you to come inside. Here, take this and throw it at them.
It's a potion of weakness!
SPLASH
You're feeding them? They just attacked us!
CRUNCH
Just watch. This is going to be so cool!
OM NOM NOM

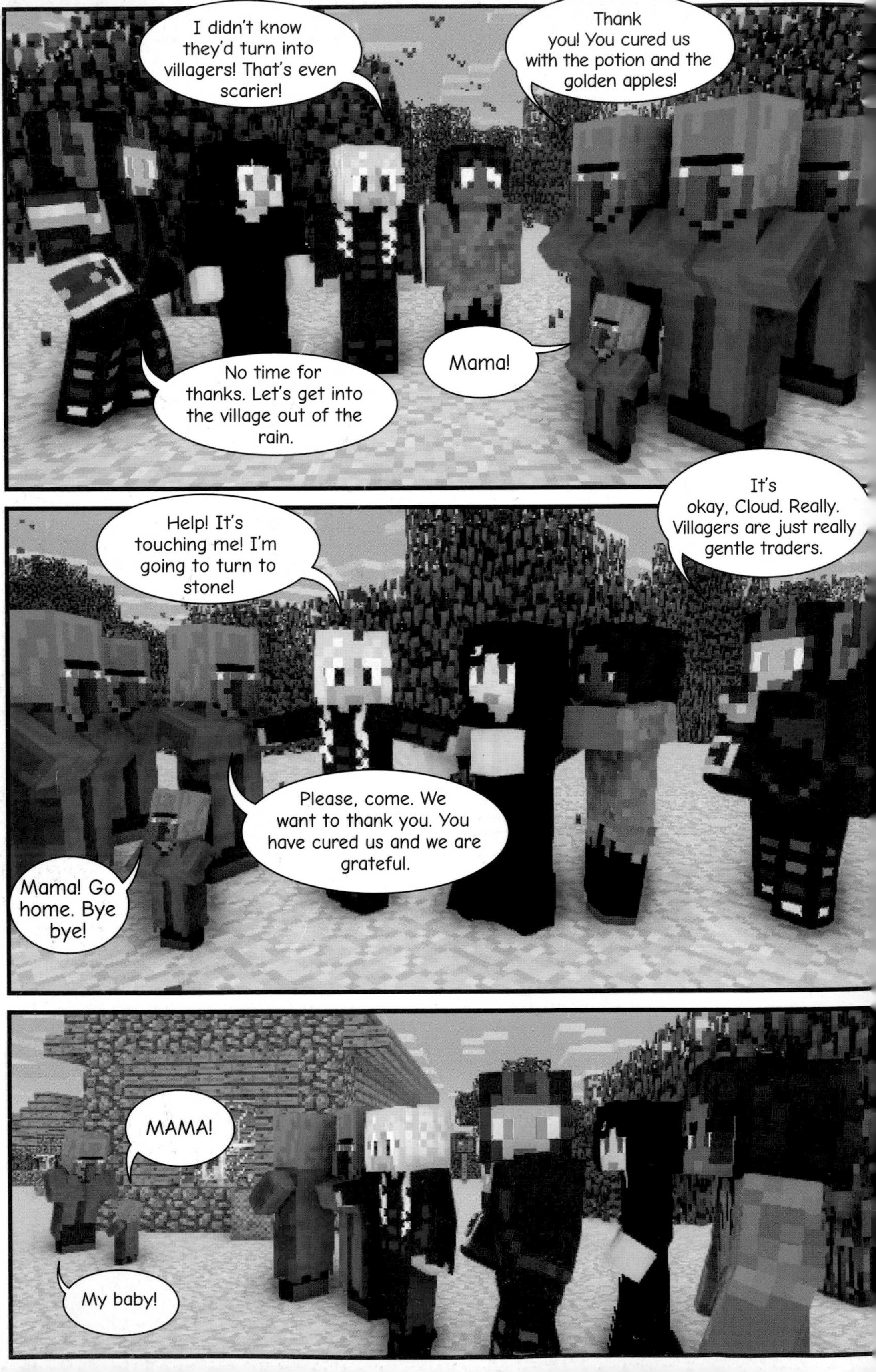
I didn't know they'd turn into villagers! That's even scarier!
Thank you! You cured us with the potion and the golden apples!
No time for thanks. Let's get into the village out of the rain.
Mama!
Help! It's touching me! I'm going to turn to stone!
It's okay, Cloud. Really. Villagers are just really gentle traders.
Please, come. We want to thank you. You have cured us and we are grateful.
Mama! Go home. Bye bye!
MAMA!
My baby!

CHAPTER 9

BACK IN TOWN

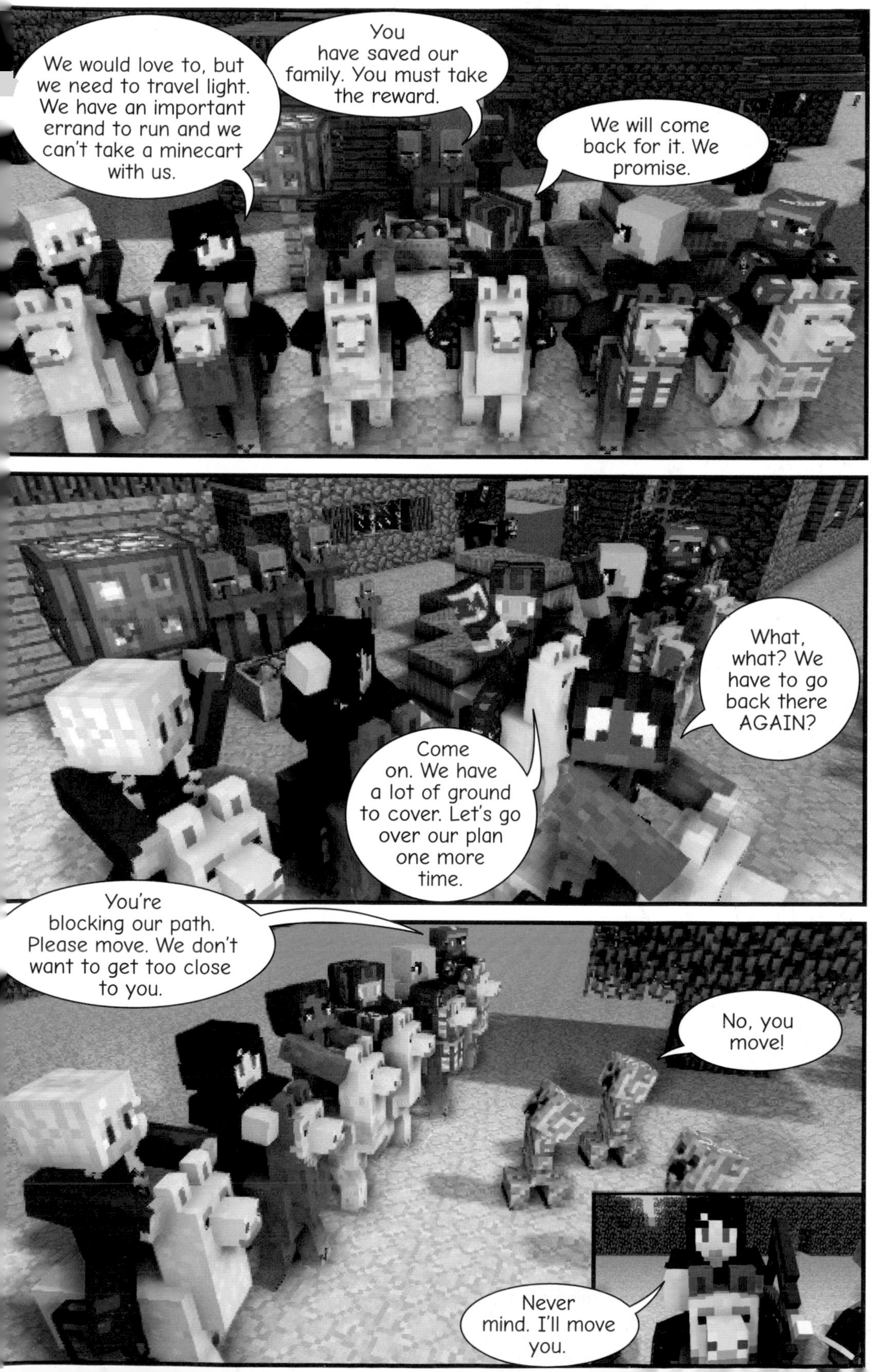

We would love to, but we need to travel light. We have an important errand to run and we can't take a minecart with us.
You have saved our family. You must take the reward.
We will come back for it. We promise.
What, what? We have to go back there AGAIN?
Come on. We have a lot of ground to cover. Let's go over our plan one more time.
You're blocking our path. Please move. We don't want to get too close to you.
No, you move!
Never mind. I'll move you.

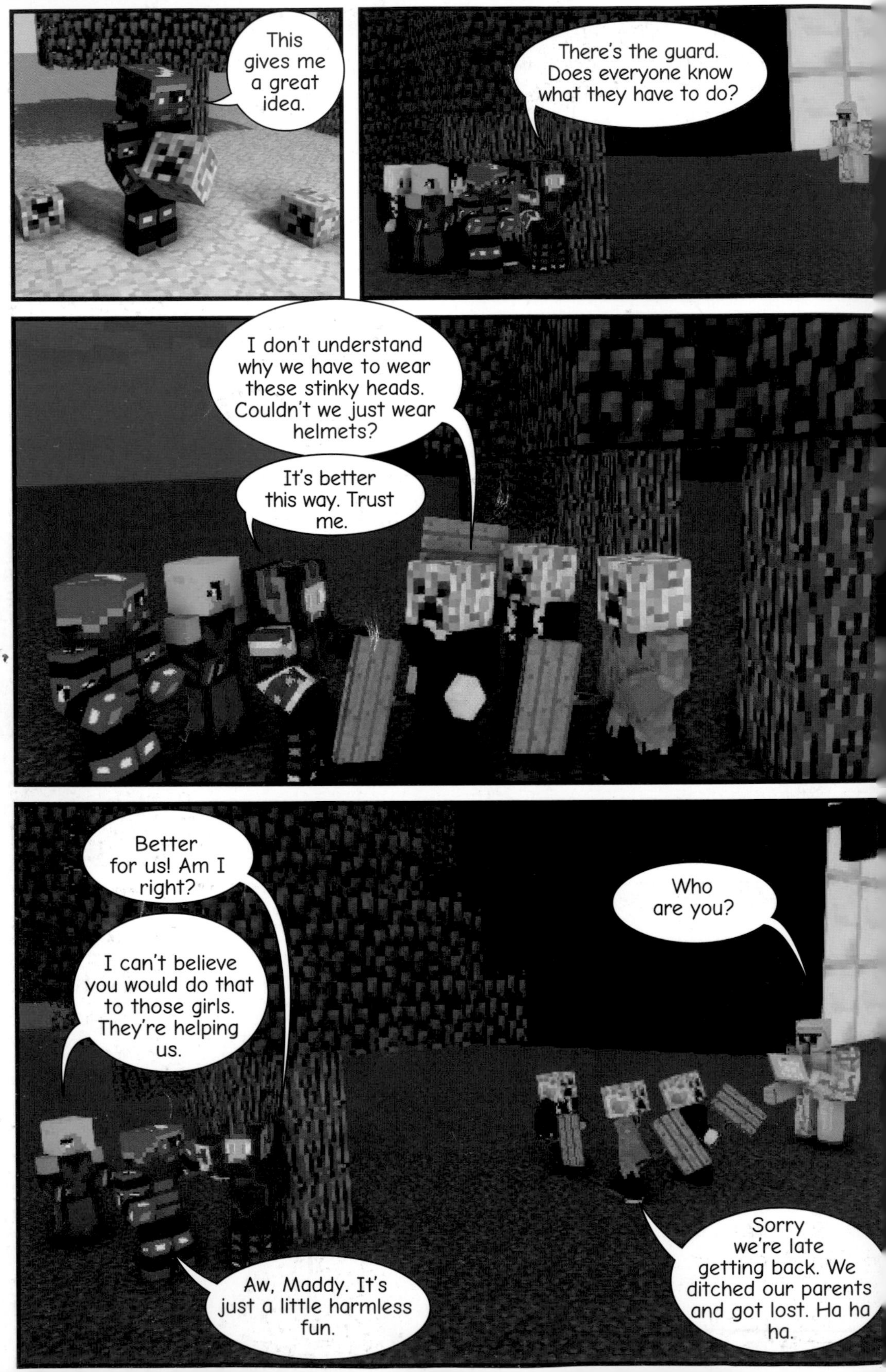
This gives me a great idea.
There's the guard. Does everyone know what they have to do?
I don't understand why we have to wear these stinky heads. Couldn't we just wear helmets?
It's better this way. Trust me.
Better for us! Am I right?
I can't believe you would do that to those girls. They're helping us.
Aw, Maddy. It's just a little harmless fun.
Who are you?
Sorry we're late getting back. We ditched our parents and got lost. Ha ha ha.

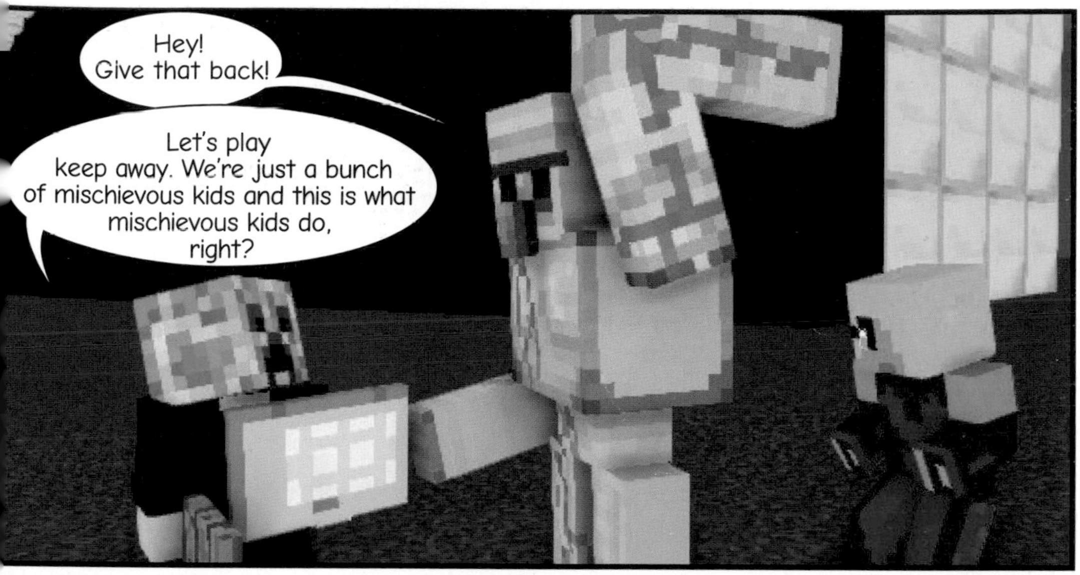
Hey!
Give that back!
Let's play keep away. We're just a bunch of mischievous kids and this is what mischievous kids do, right?

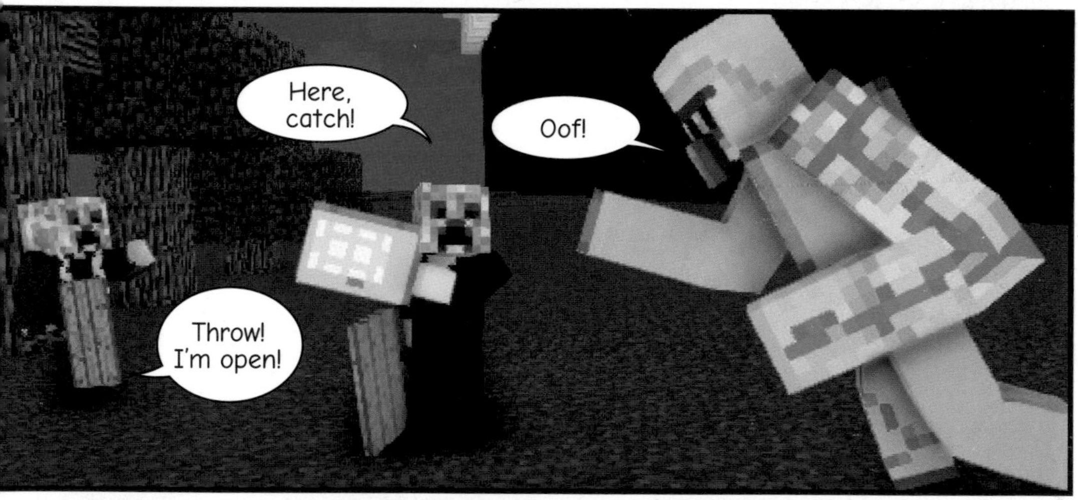
Here, catch!
Oof!
Throw! I'm open!

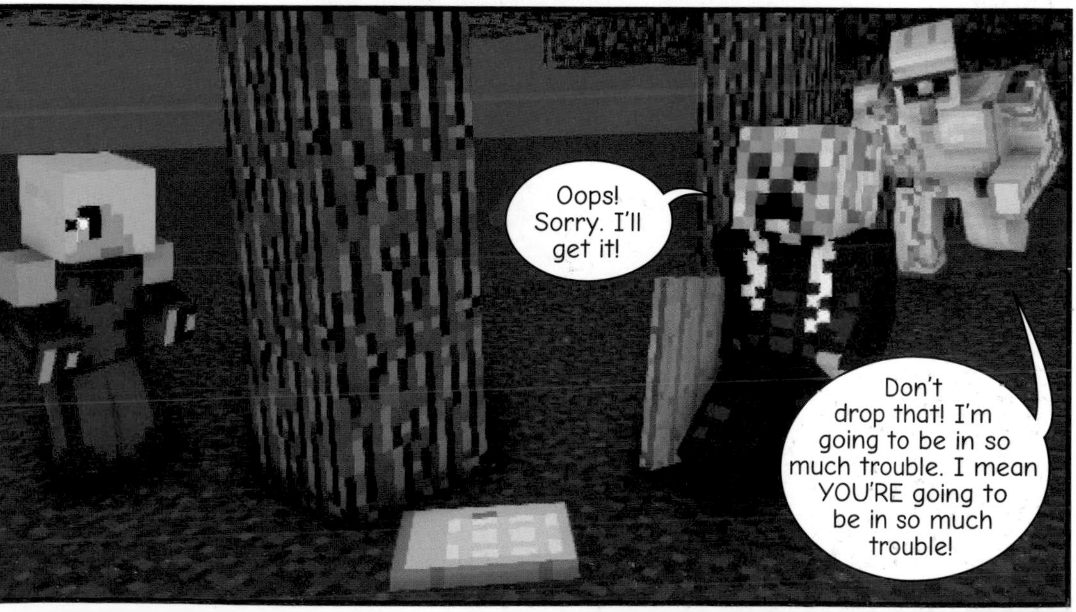
Oops! Sorry. I'll get it!
Don't drop that! I'm going to be in so much trouble. I mean YOU'RE going to be in so much trouble!

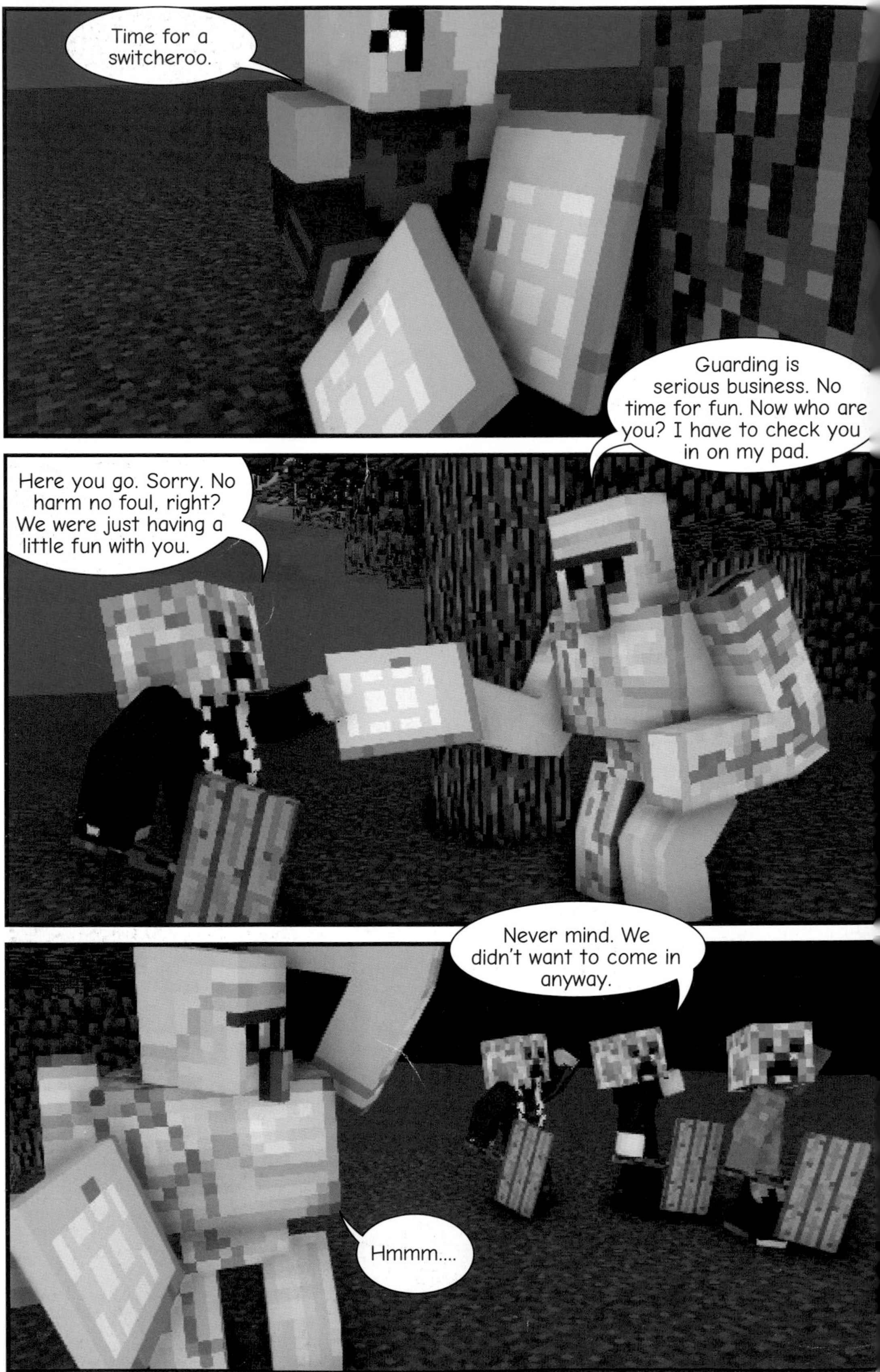

Time for a switcheroo.
Guarding is serious business. No time for fun. Now who are you? I have to check you in on my pad.
Here you go. Sorry. No harm no foul, right? We were just having a little fun with you.
Never mind. We didn't want to come in anyway.
Hmmm....

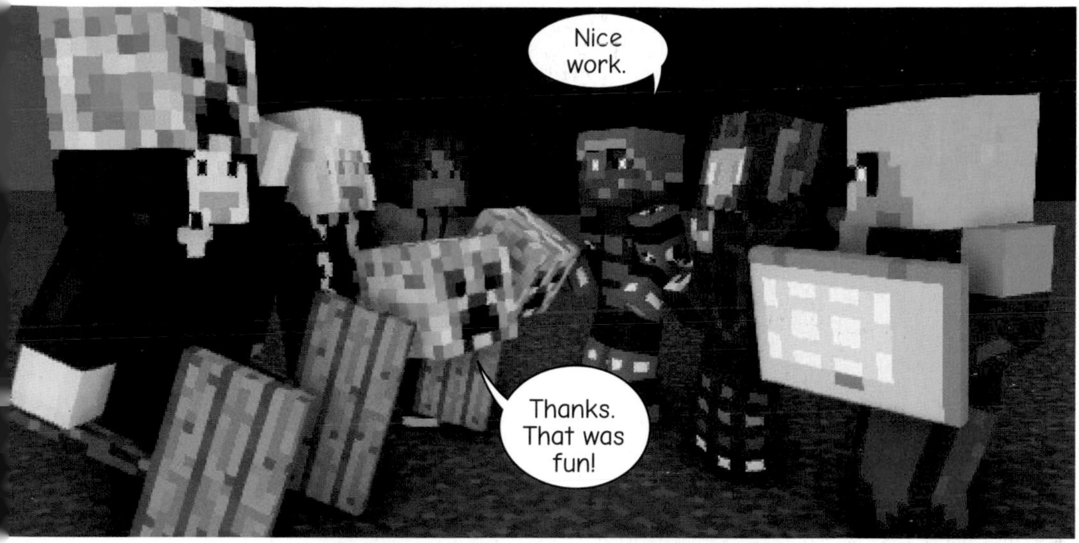
Nice work.
Thanks. That was fun!

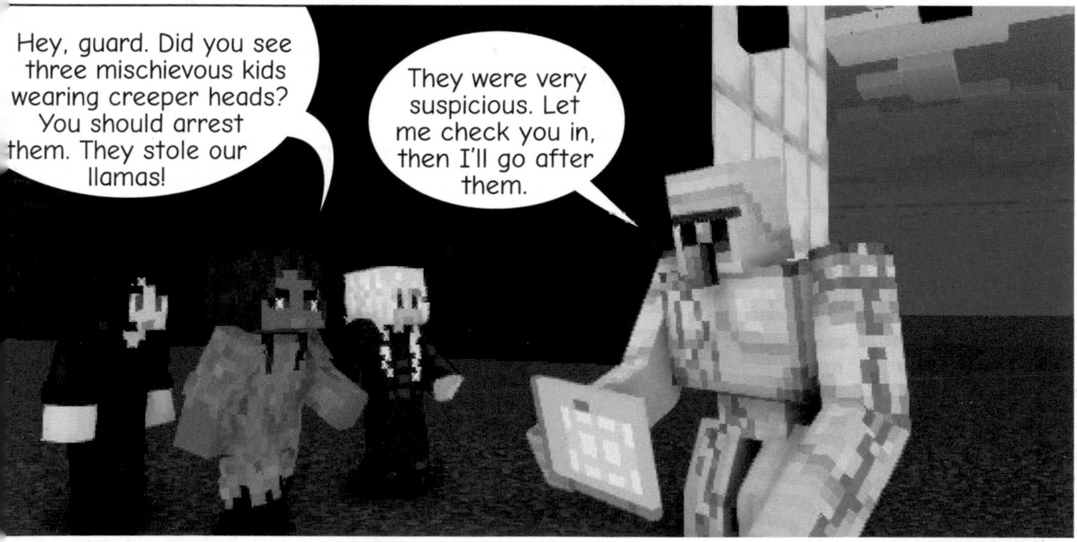
Hey, guard. Did you see three mischievous kids wearing creeper heads? You should arrest them. They stole our llamas!
They were very suspicious. Let me check you in, then I'll go after them.

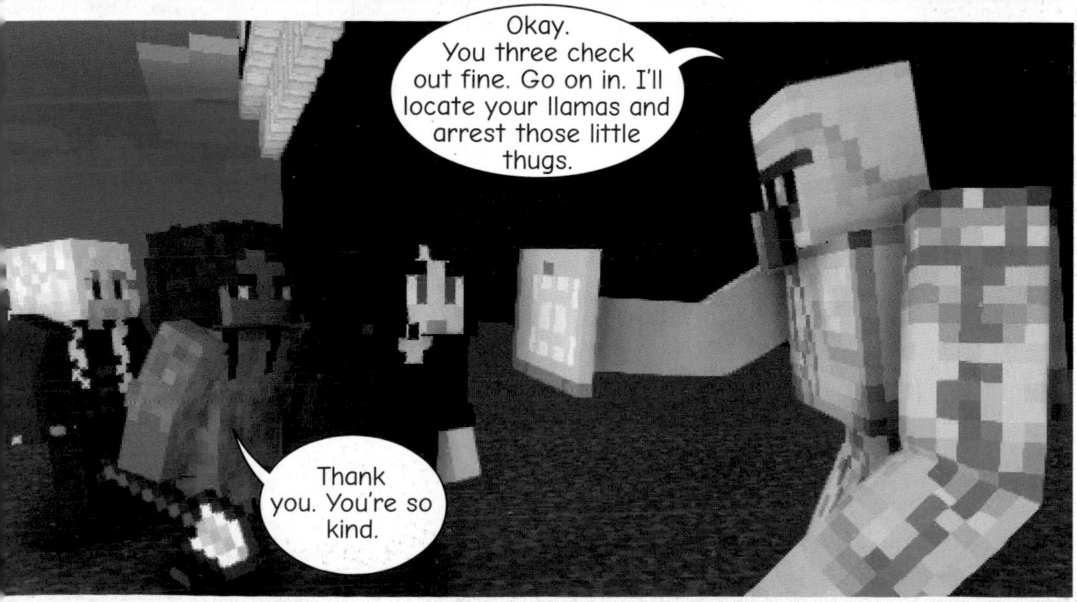
Okay. You three check out fine. Go on in. I'll locate your llamas and arrest those little thugs.
Thank you. You're so kind.

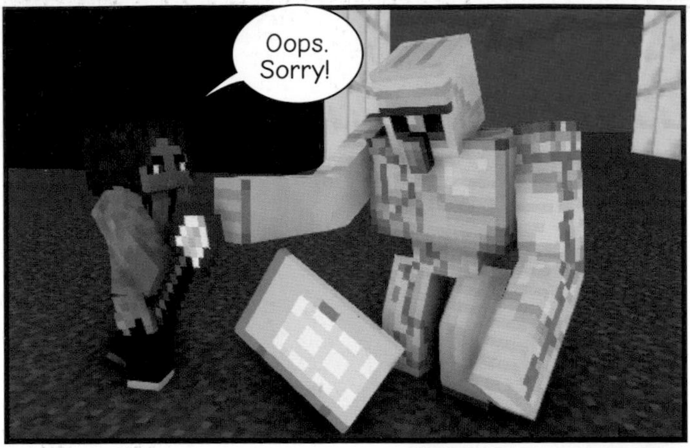
Oops. Sorry!

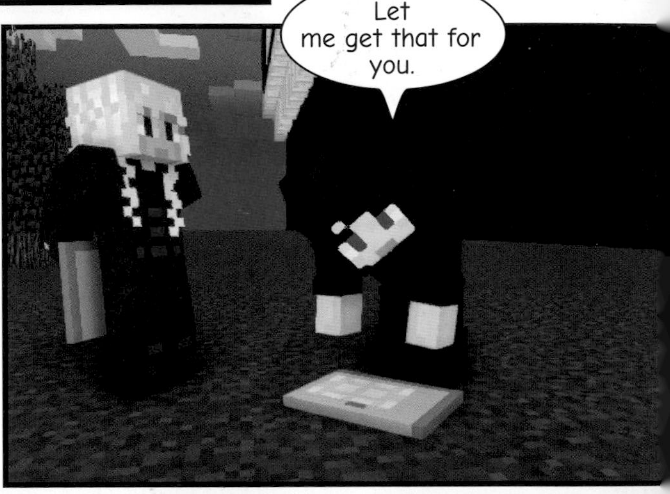
Let me get that for you.

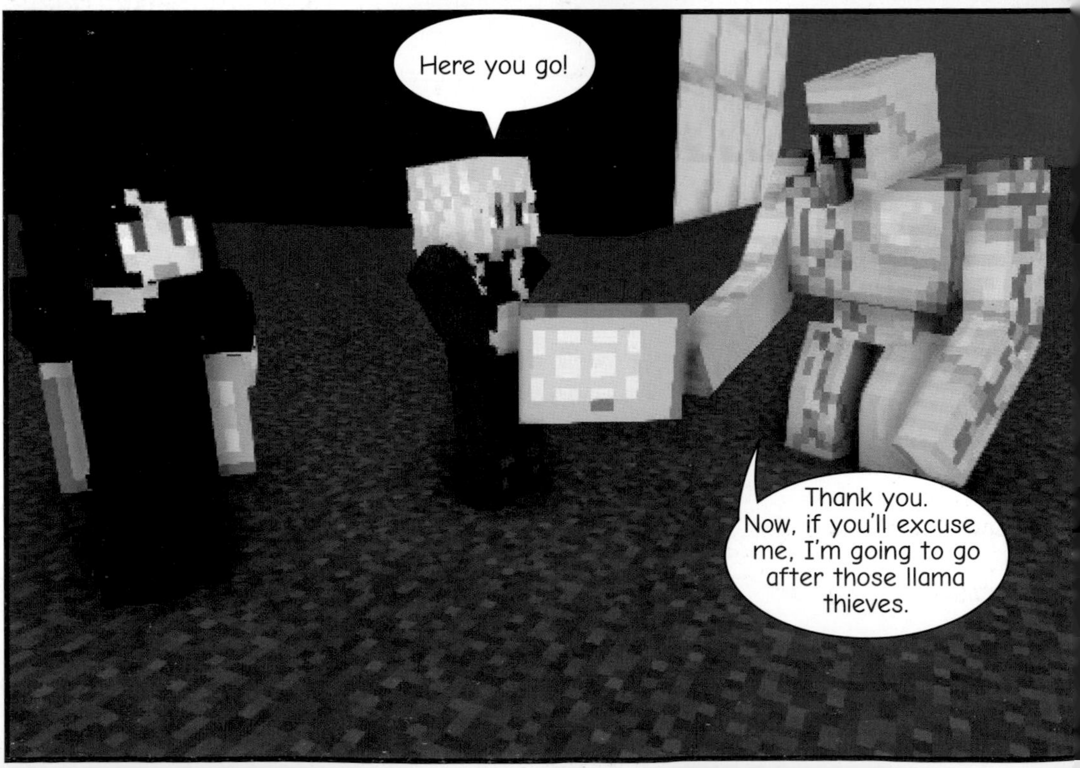
Here you go!
Thank you. Now, if you'll excuse me, I'm going to go after those llama thieves.

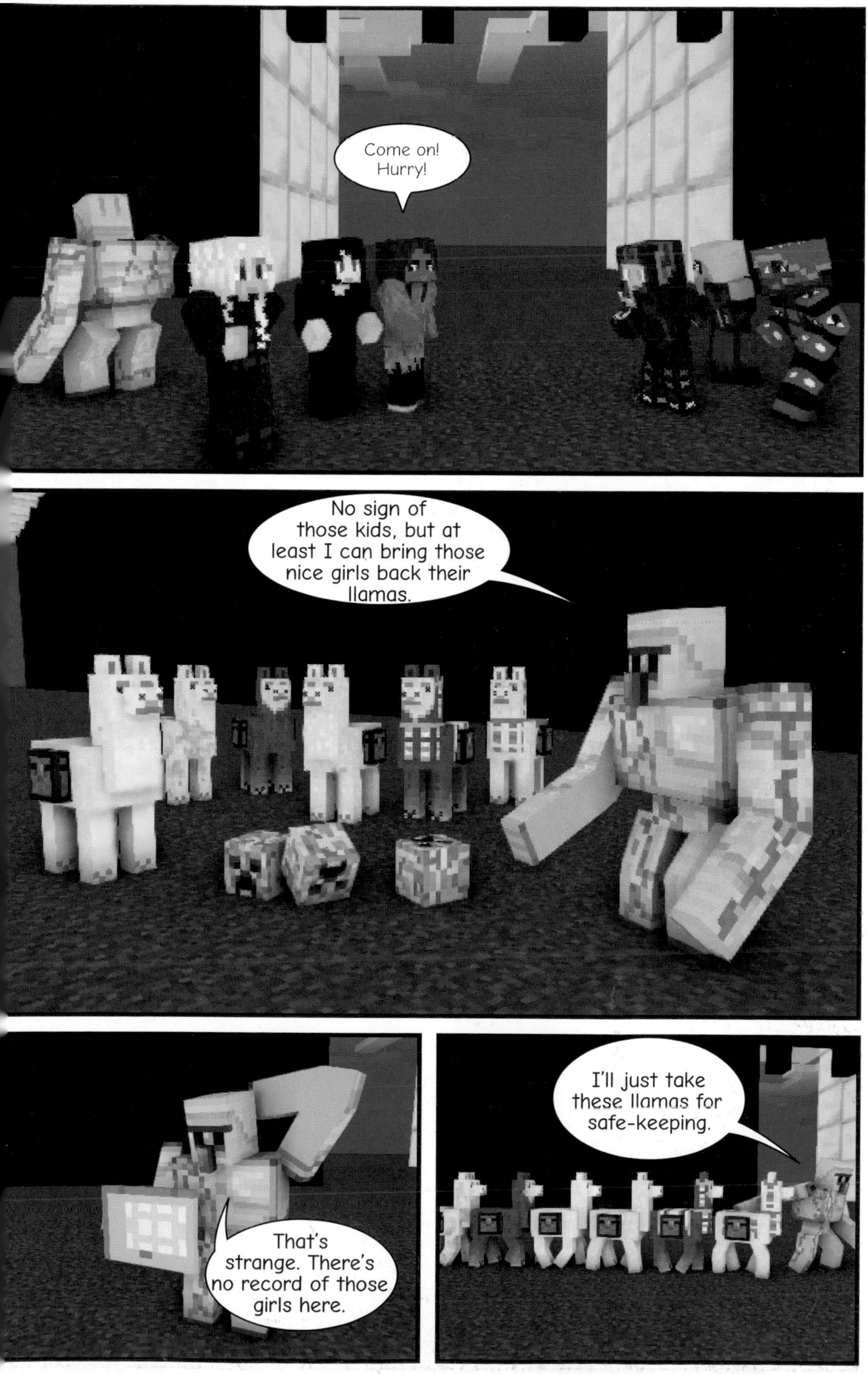
Come on! Hurry!
No sign of those kids, but at least I can bring those nice girls back their llamas.
That's strange. There's no record of those girls here.
I'll just take these llamas for safe-keeping.

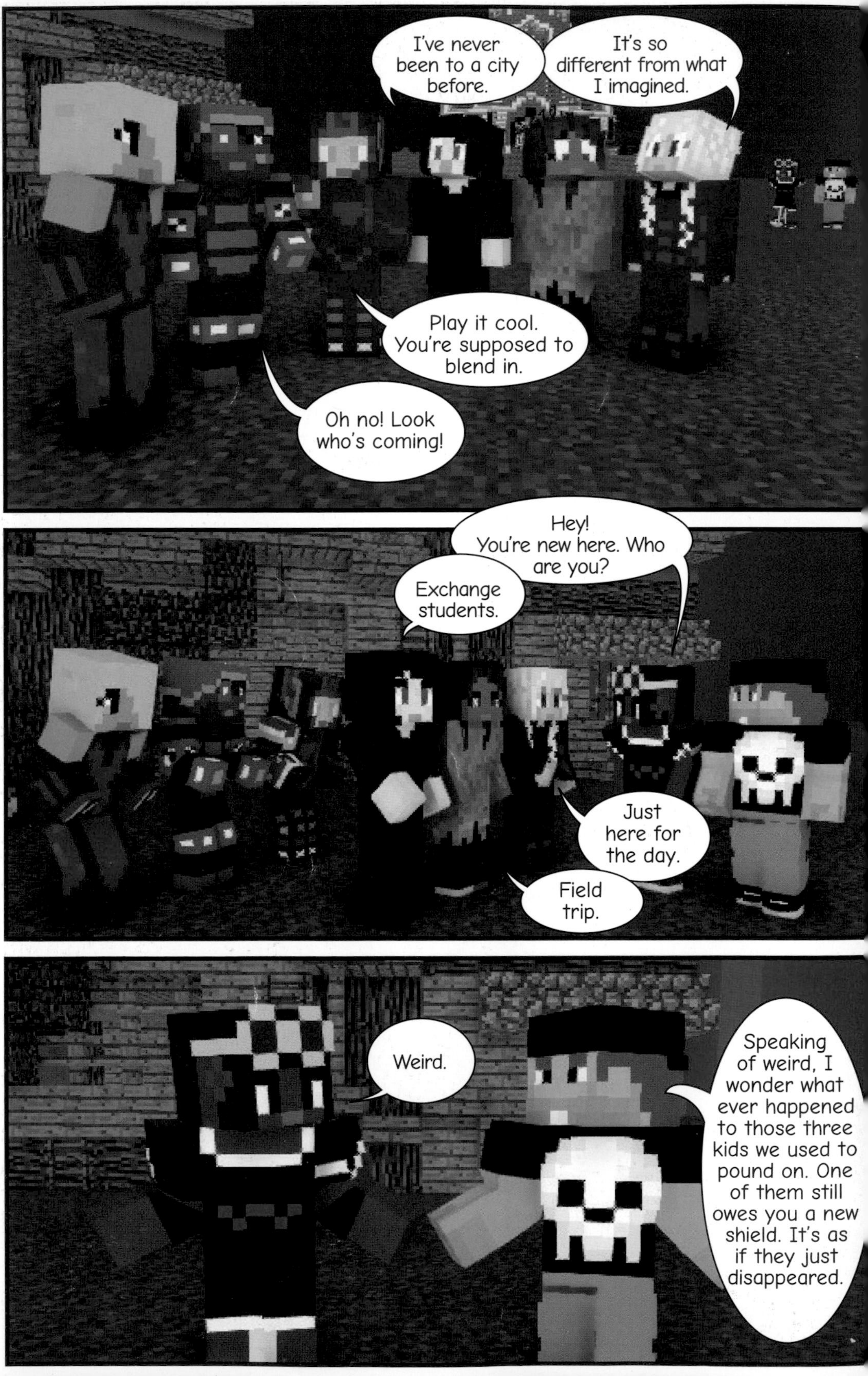
I've never been to a city before.
It's so different from what I imagined.
Play it cool. You're supposed to blend in.
Oh no! Look who's coming!
Hey! You're new here. Who are you?
Exchange students.
Just here for the day.
Field trip.
Weird.
Speaking of weird, I wonder what ever happened to those three kids we used to pound on. One of them still owes you a new shield. It's as if they just disappeared.

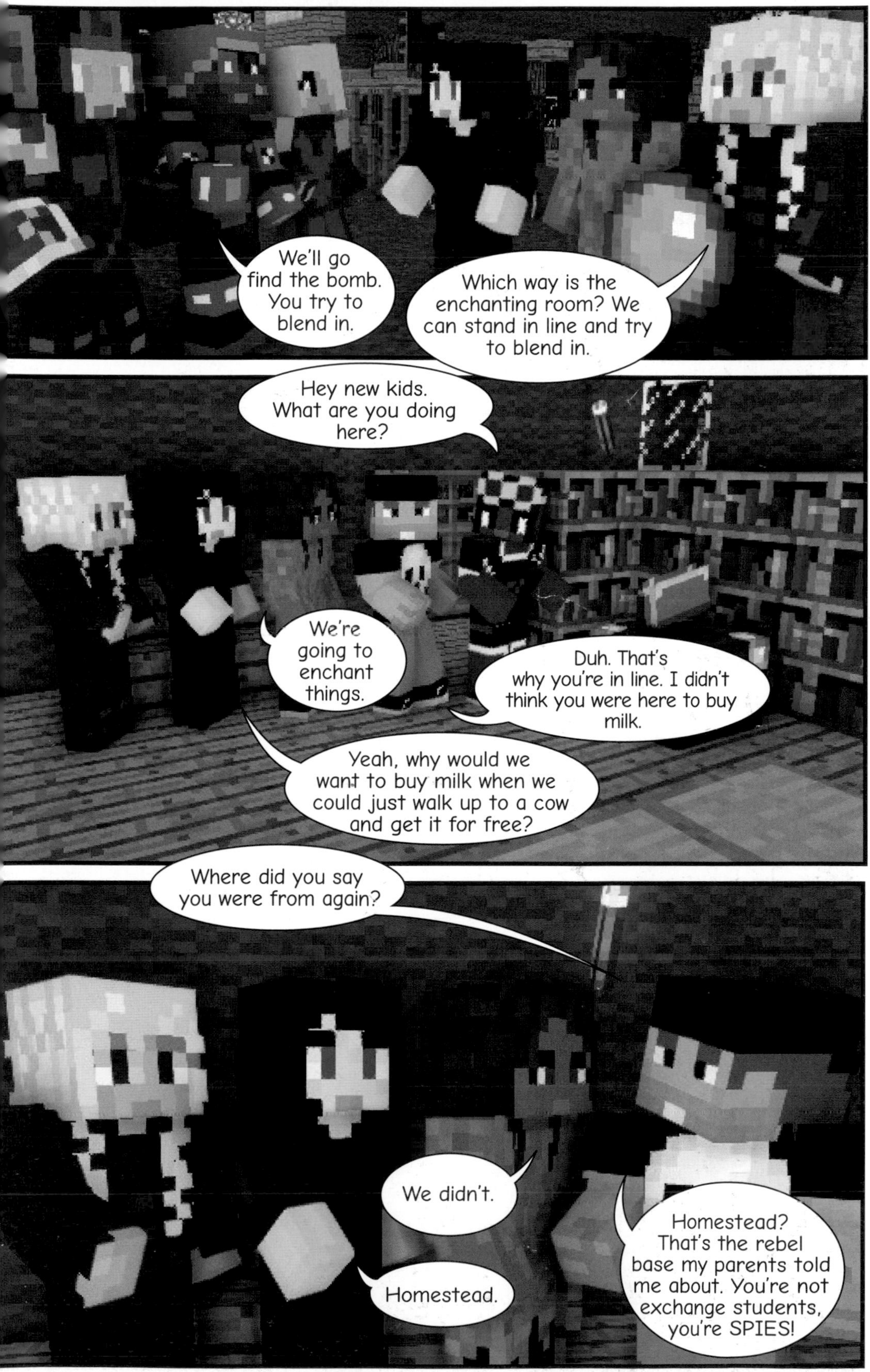
We'll go find the bomb. You try to blend in.
Which way is the enchanting room? We can stand in line and try to blend in.
Hey new kids. What are you doing here?
We're going to enchant things.
Duh. That's why you're in line. I didn't think you were here to buy milk.
Yeah, why would we want to buy milk when we could just walk up to a cow and get it for free?
Where did you say you were from again?
We didn't.
Homestead.
Homestead? That's the rebel base my parents told me about. You're not exchange students, you're SPIES!

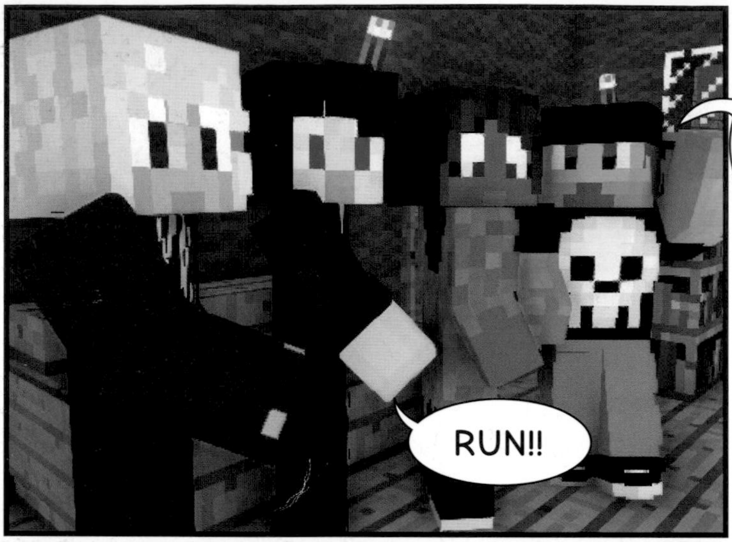
I need an ID check over here. I think we have some spies!
RUN!!

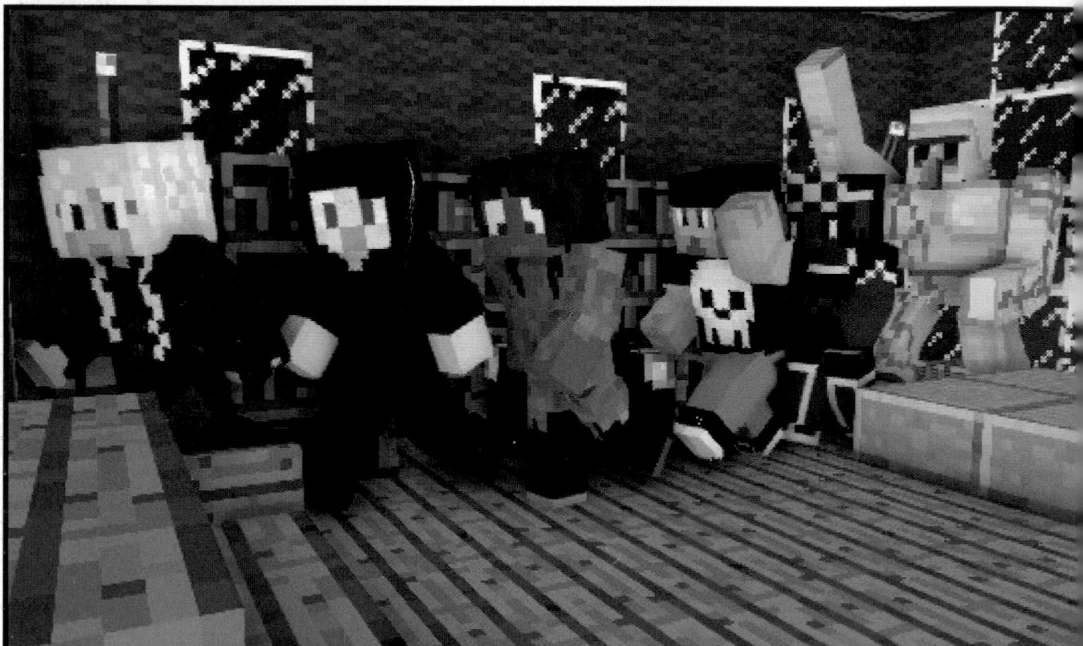

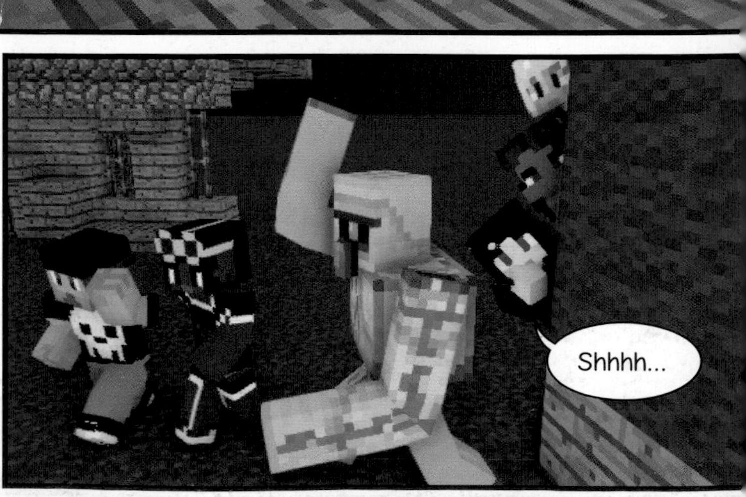
Shhhh...

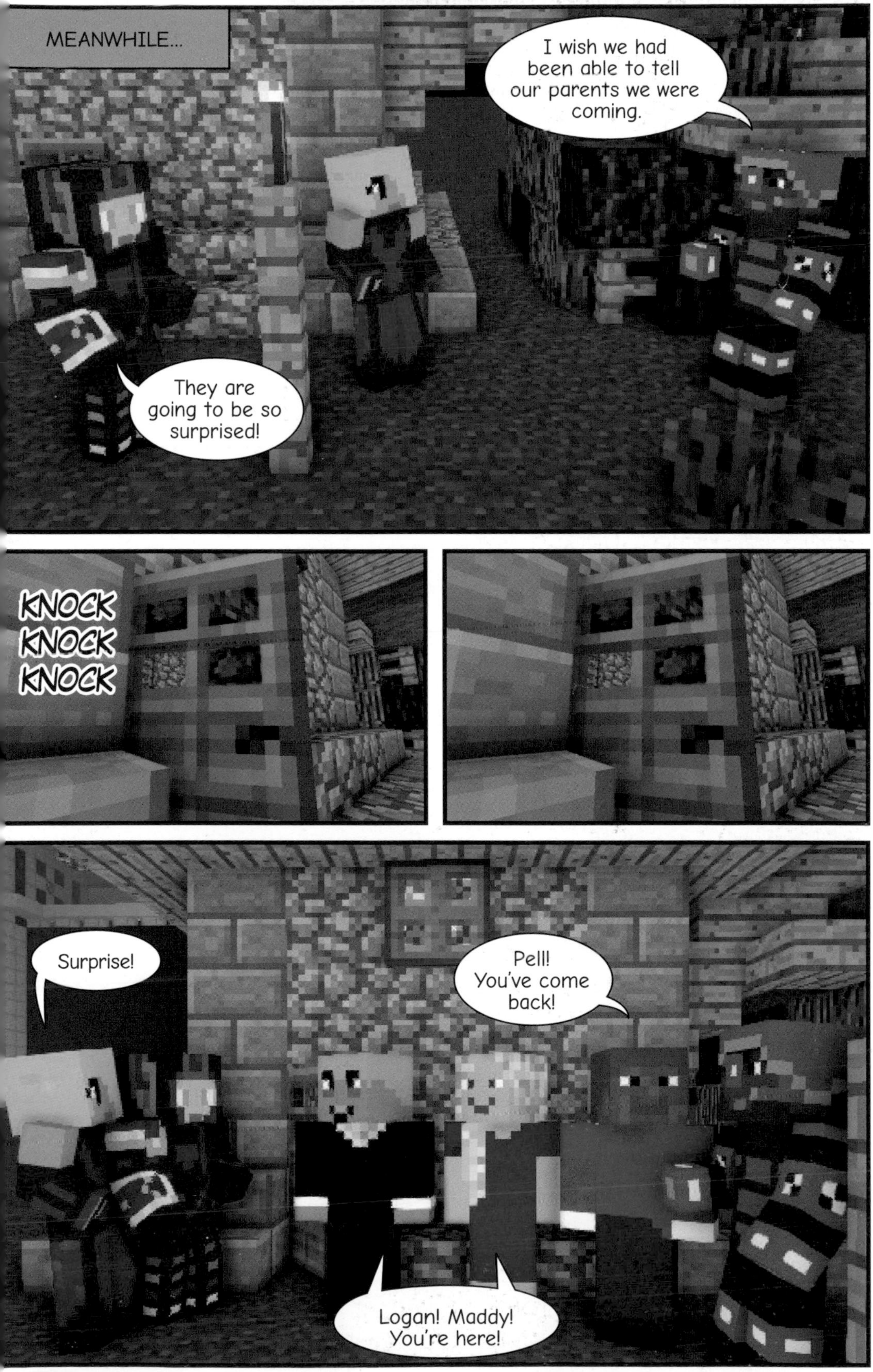
MEANWHILE...
I wish we had been able to tell our parents we were coming.
They are going to be so surprised!
KNOCK KNOCK KNOCK
Surprise!
Pell! You've come back!
Logan! Maddy! You're here!

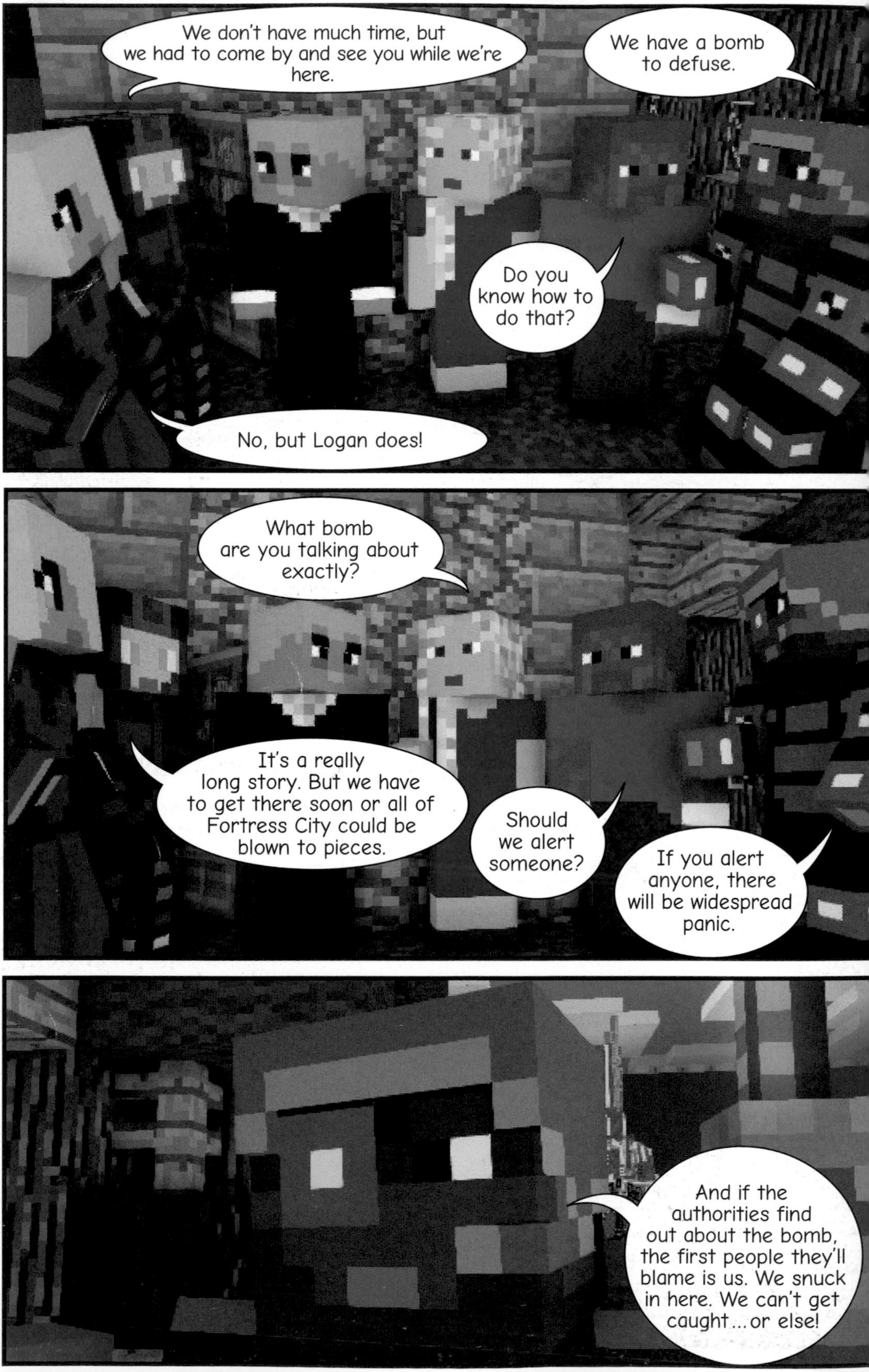
We don't have much time, but we had to come by and see you while we're here.
We have a bomb to defuse.
Do you know how to do that?
No, but Logan does!
What bomb are you talking about exactly?
It's a really long story. But we have to get there soon or all of Fortress City could be blown to pieces.
Should we alert someone?
If you alert anyone, there will be widespread panic.
And if the authorities find out about the bomb, the first people they'll blame is us. We snuck in here. We can't get caught... or else!

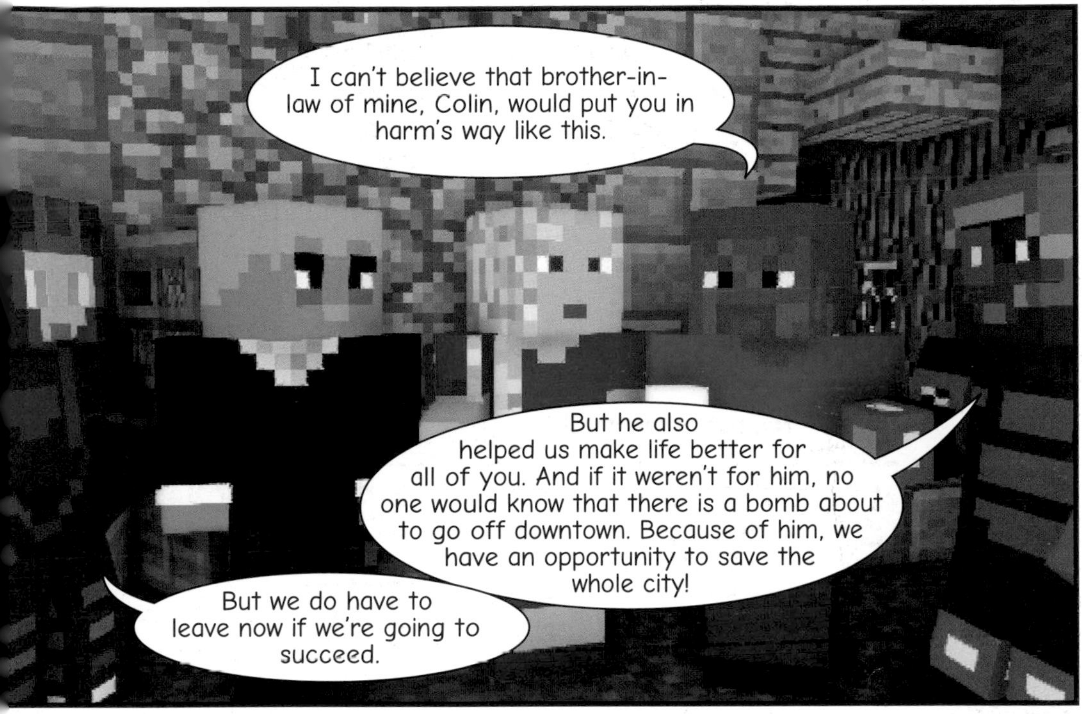
I can't believe that brother-in-law of mine, Colin, would put you in harm's way like this.
But he also helped us make life better for all of you. And if it weren't for him, no one would know that there is a bomb about to go off downtown. Because of him, we have an opportunity to save the whole city!
But we do have to leave now if we're going to succeed.

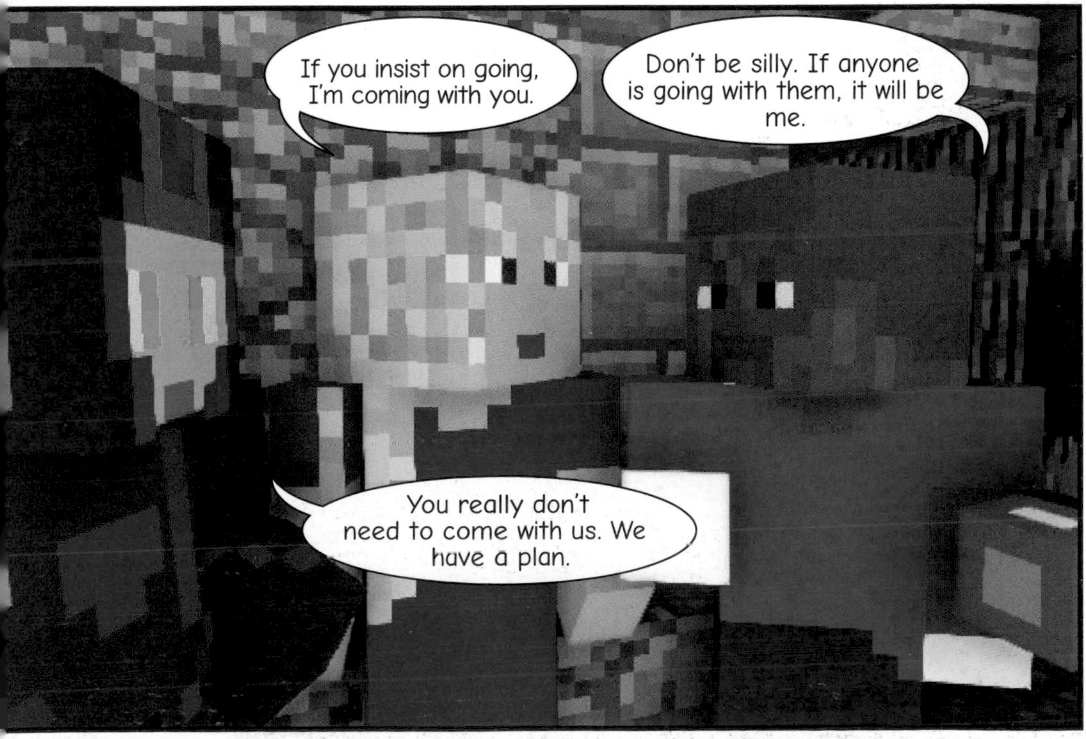
If you insist on going, I'm coming with you.
Don't be silly. If anyone is going with them, it will be me.
You really don't need to come with us. We have a plan.

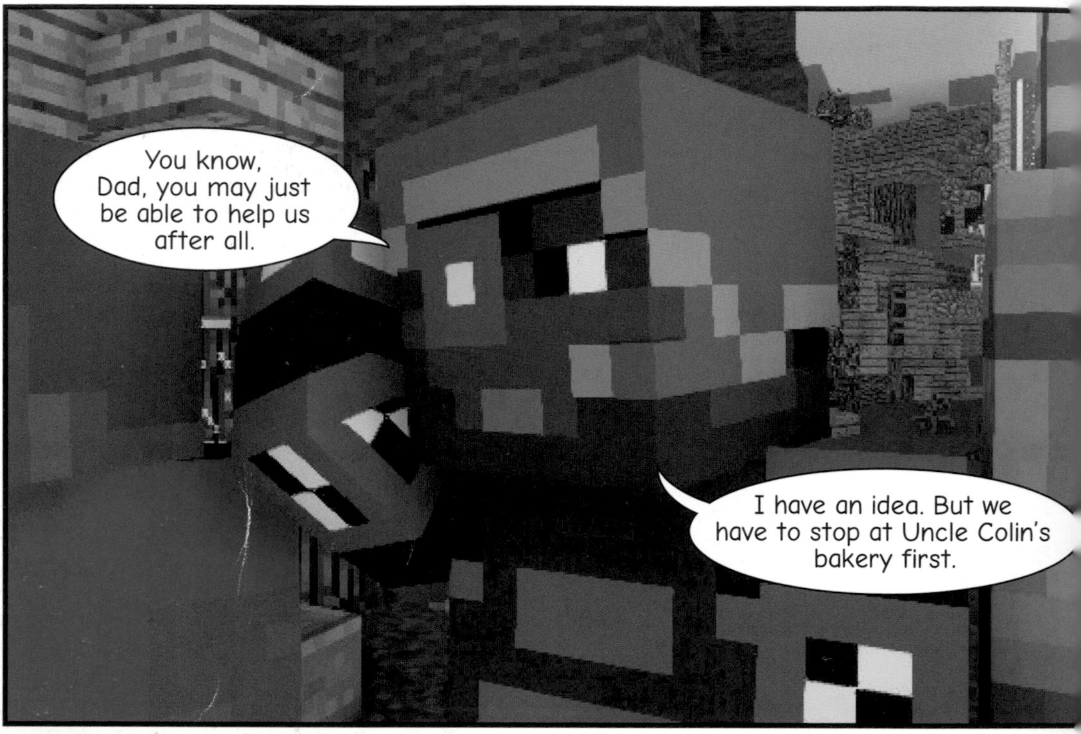
You know, Dad, you may just be able to help us after all.
I have an idea. But we have to stop at Uncle Colin's bakery first.

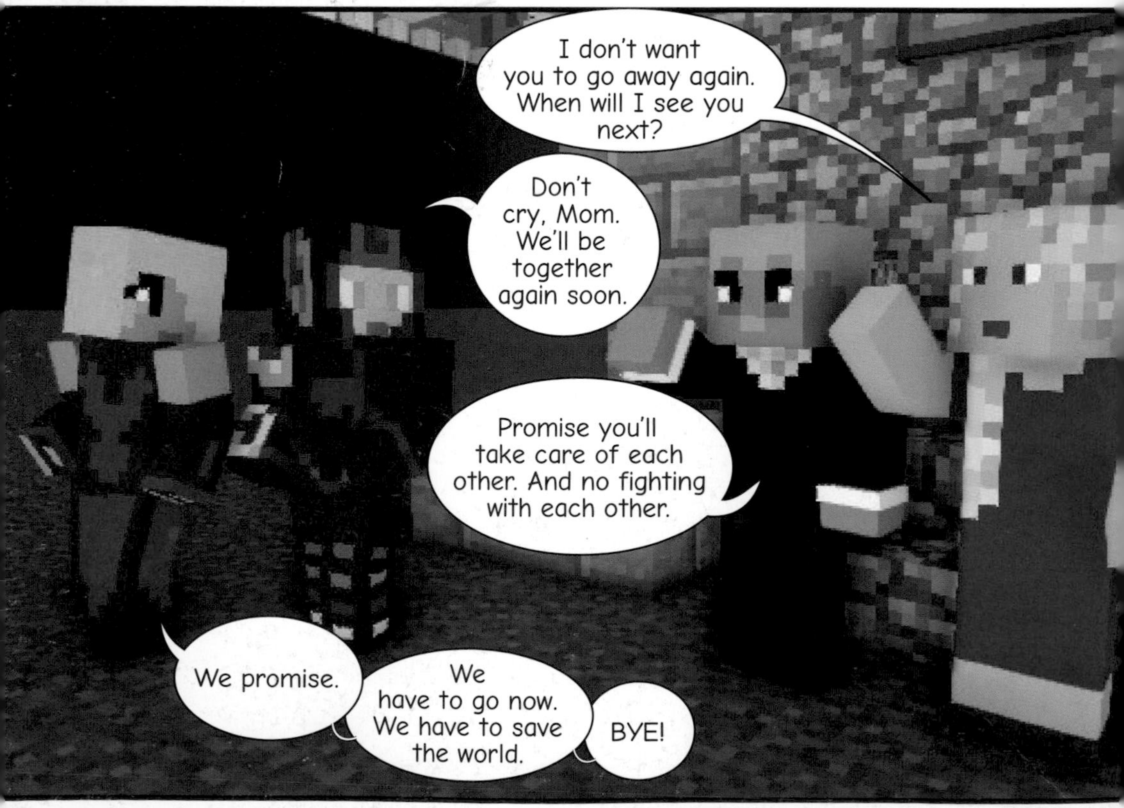
I don't want you to go away again. When will I see you next?
Don't cry, Mom. We'll be together again soon.
Promise you'll take care of each other. And no fighting with each other.
We promise.
We have to go now. We have to save the world.
BYE!

CHAPTER 10

BOMB SQUAD

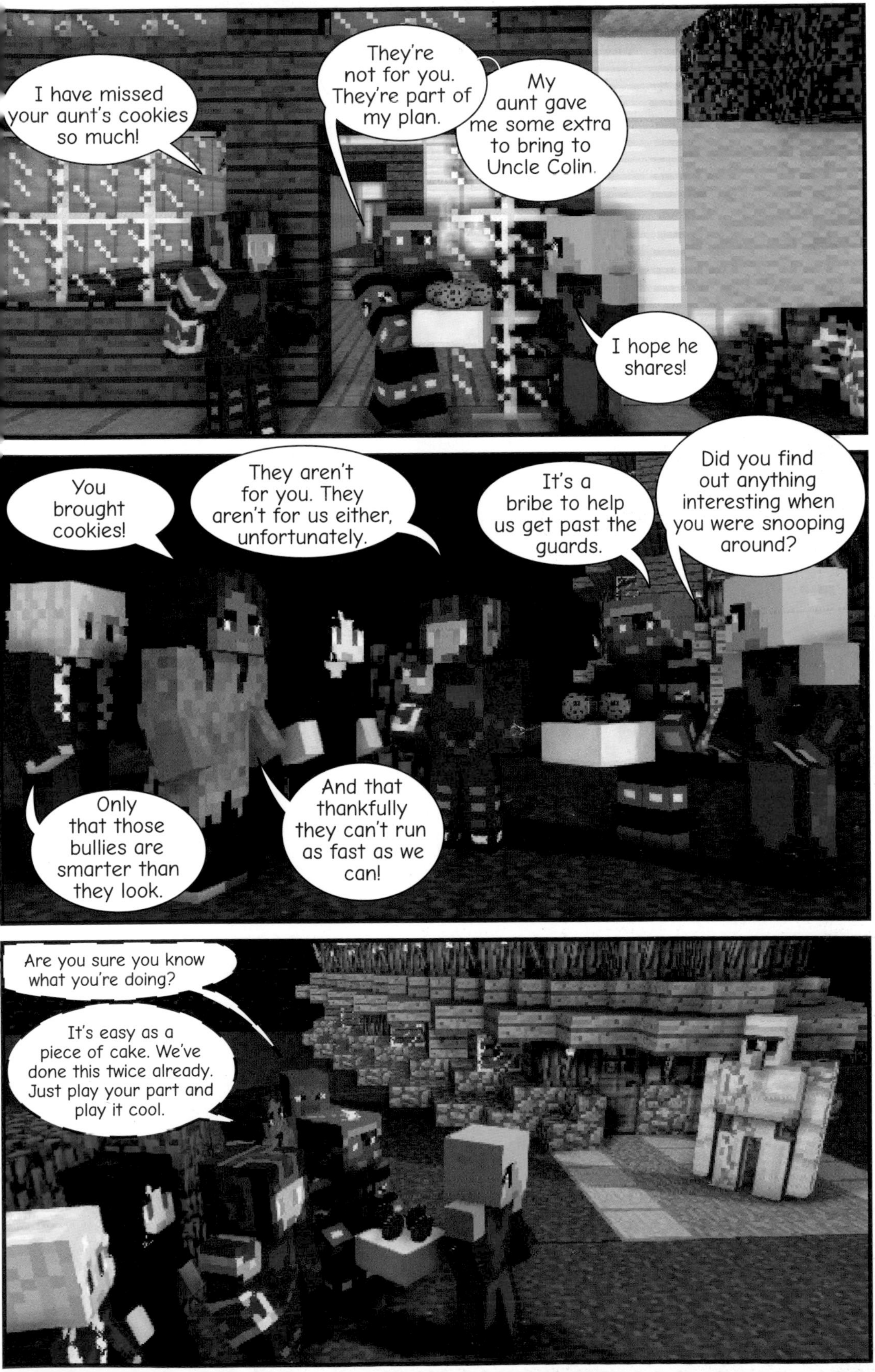
I have missed your aunt's cookies so much!
They're not for you. They're part of my plan.
My aunt gave me some extra to bring to Uncle Colin.
I hope he shares!
You brought cookies!
They aren't for you. They aren't for us either, unfortunately.
It's a bribe to help us get past the guards.
Did you find out anything interesting when you were snooping around?
Only that those bullies are smarter than they look.
And that thankfully they can't run as fast as we can!
Are you sure you know what you're doing?
It's easy as a piece of cake. We've done this twice already. Just play your part and play it cool.

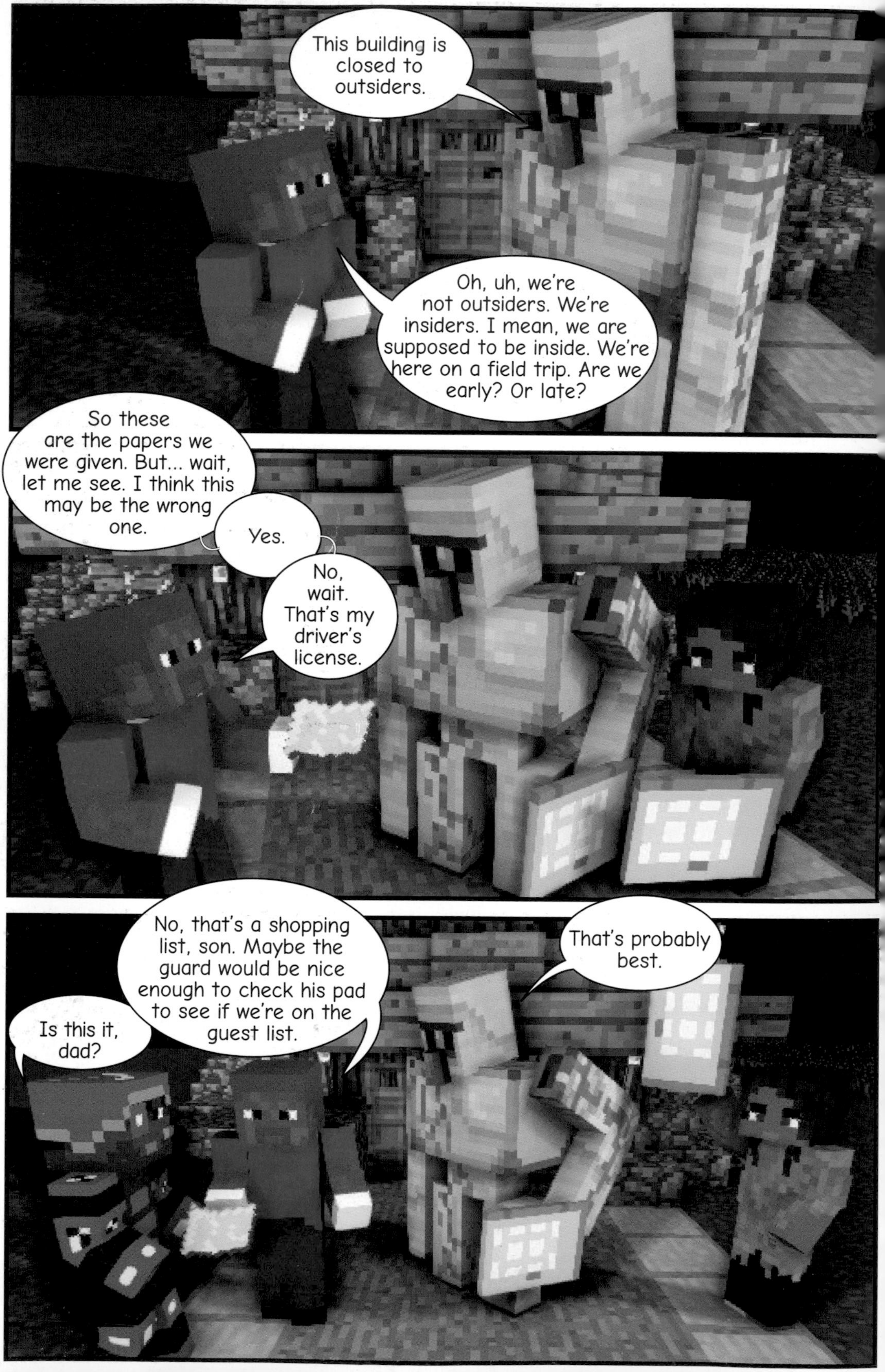
This building is closed to outsiders.
Oh, uh, we're not outsiders. We're insiders. I mean, we are supposed to be inside. We're here on a field trip. Are we early? Or late?
So these are the papers we were given. But... wait, let me see. I think this may be the wrong one.
Yes.
No, wait. That's my driver's license.
Is this it, dad?
No, that's a shopping list, son. Maybe the guard would be nice enough to check his pad to see if we're on the guest list.
That's probably best.

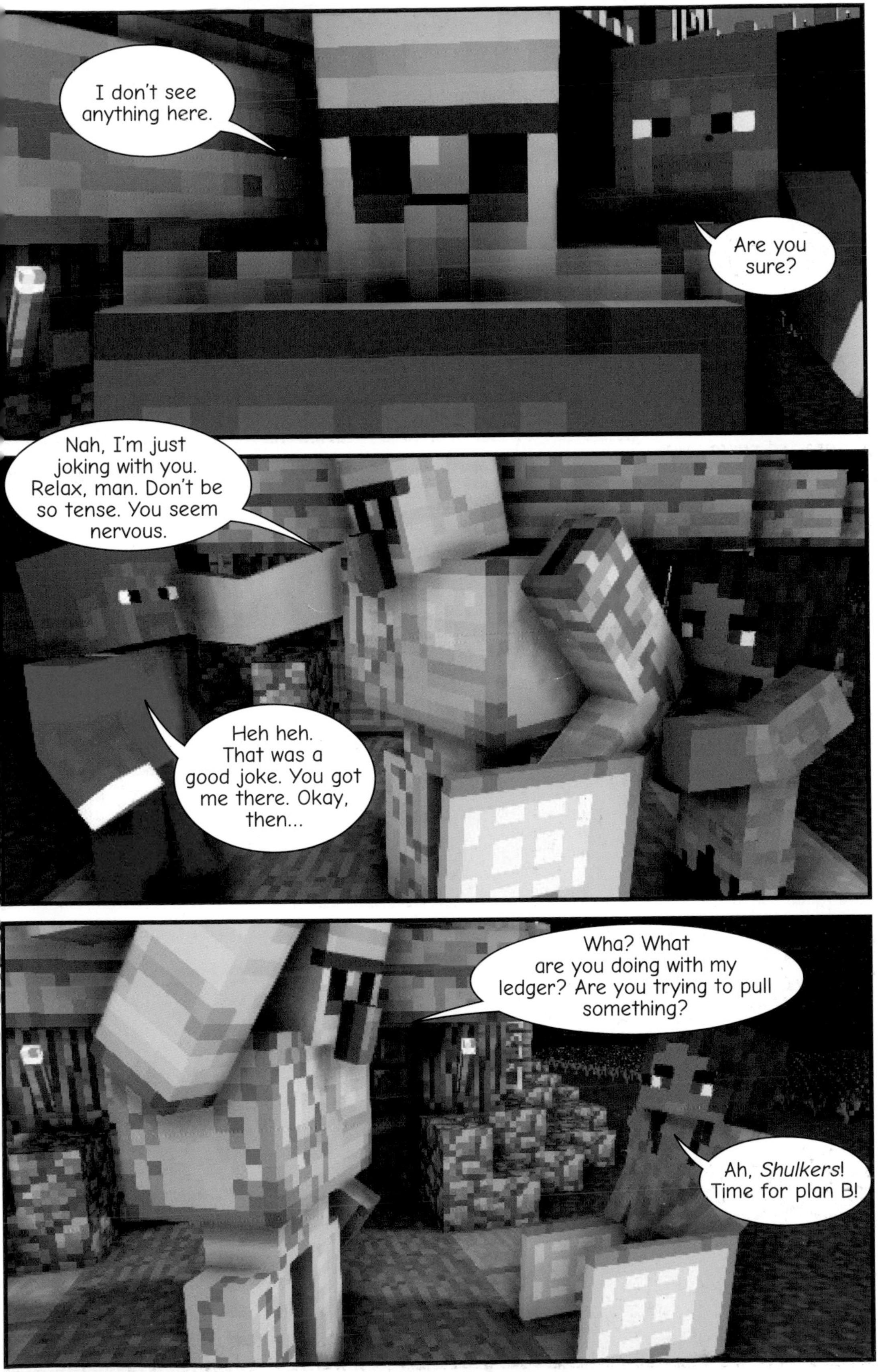
I don't see anything here.
Are you sure?
Nah, I'm just joking with you. Relax, man. Don't be so tense. You seem nervous.
Heh heh. That was a good joke. You got me there. Okay, then...
Wha? What are you doing with my ledger? Are you trying to pull something?
Ah, *Shulkers*! Time for plan B!

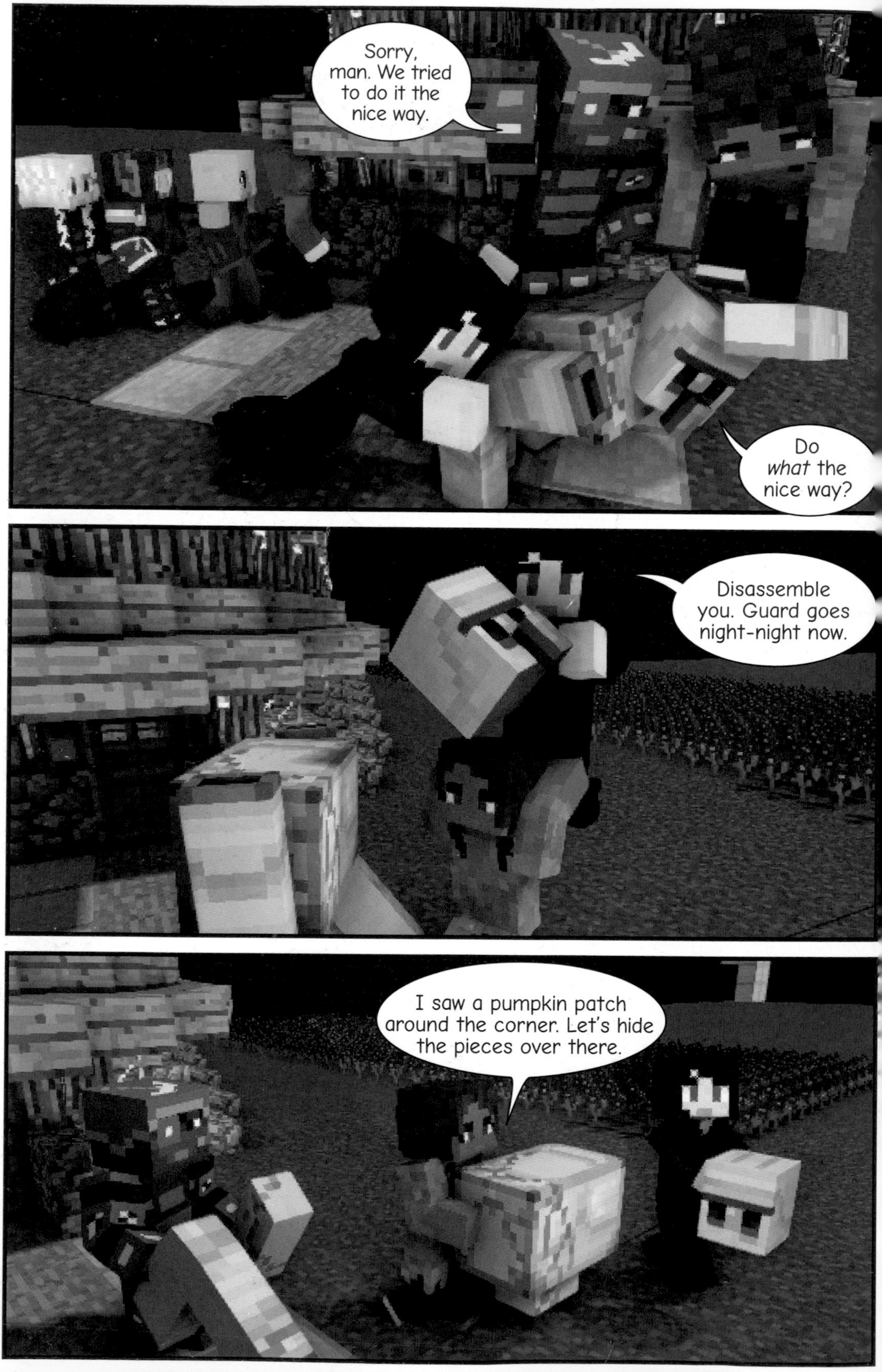
Sorry, man. We tried to do it the nice way.
Do *what* the nice way?
Disassemble you. Guard goes night-night now.
I saw a pumpkin patch around the corner. Let's hide the pieces over there.

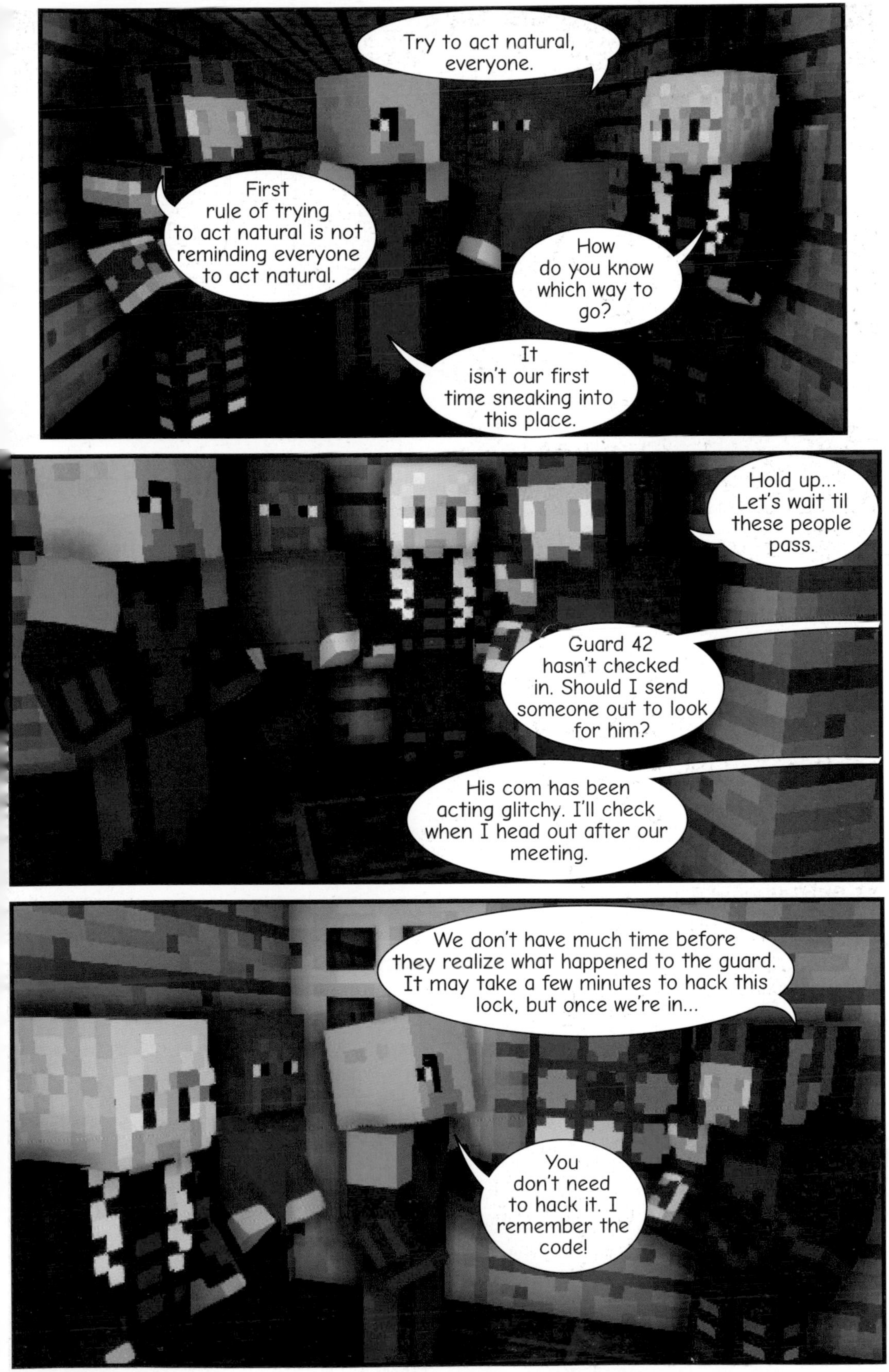
Try to act natural, everyone.
First rule of trying to act natural is not reminding everyone to act natural.
How do you know which way to go?
It isn't our first time sneaking into this place.
Hold up... Let's wait til these people pass.
Guard 42 hasn't checked in. Should I send someone out to look for him?
His com has been acting glitchy. I'll check when I head out after our meeting.
We don't have much time before they realize what happened to the guard. It may take a few minutes to hack this lock, but once we're in...
You don't need to hack it. I remember the code!

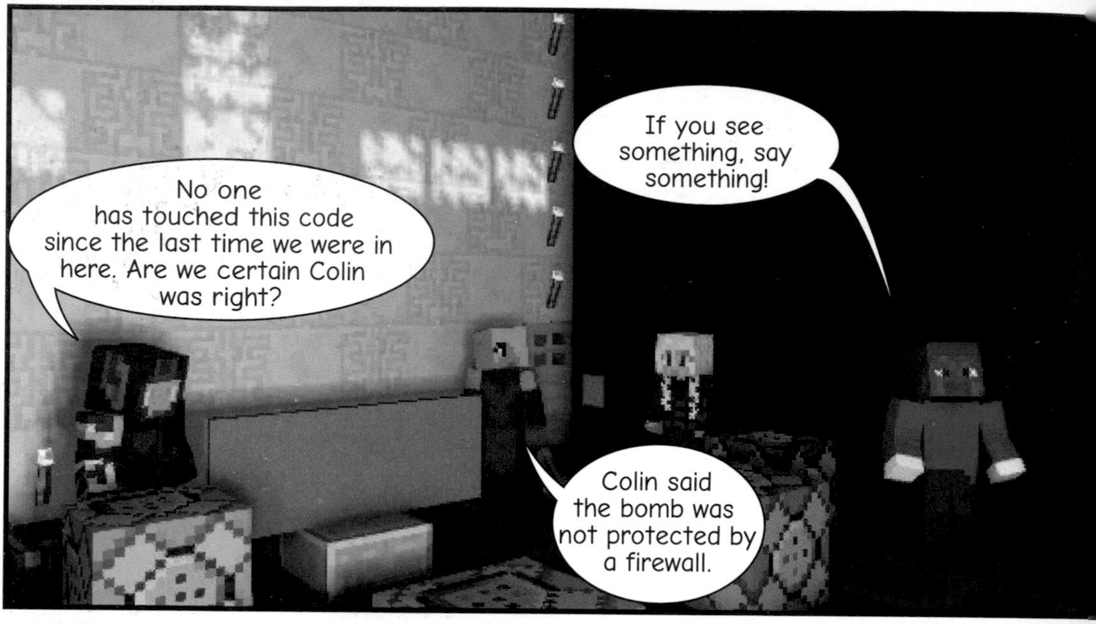
No one has touched this code since the last time we were in here. Are we certain Colin was right?
If you see something, say something!
Colin said the bomb was not protected by a firewall.

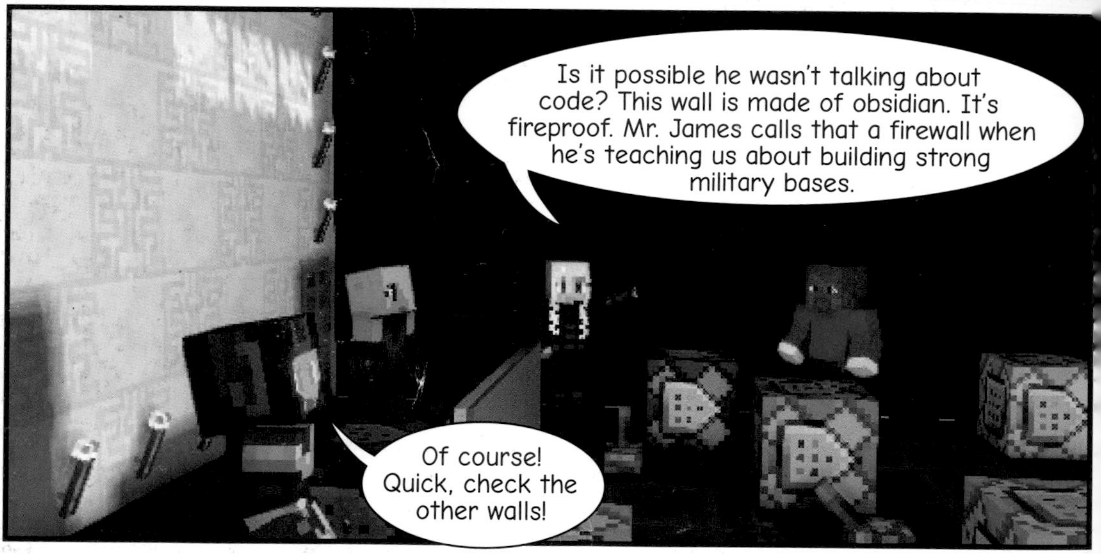
Is it possible he wasn't talking about code? This wall is made of obsidian. It's fireproof. Mr. James calls that a firewall when he's teaching us about building strong military bases.
Of course! Quick, check the other walls!

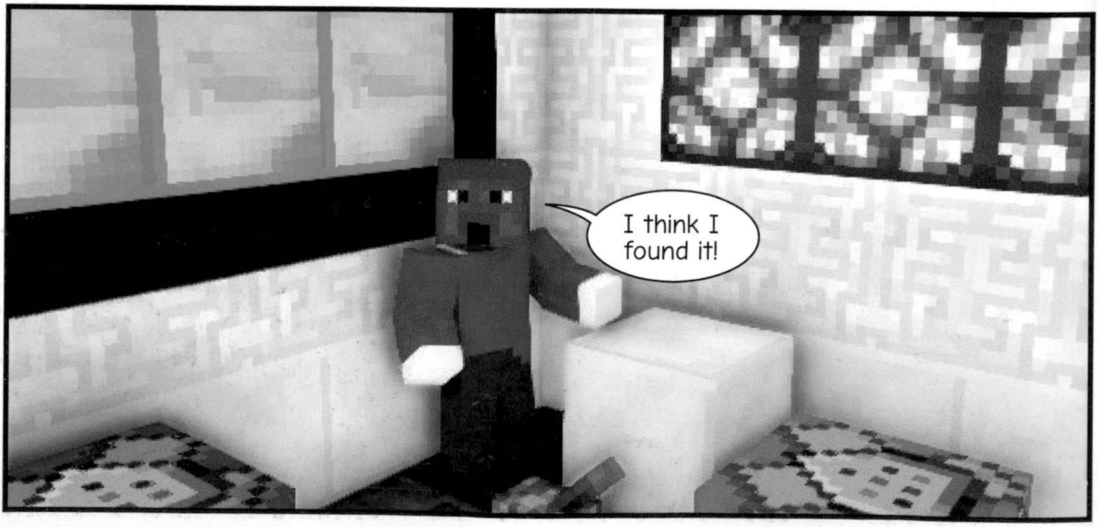
I think I found it!

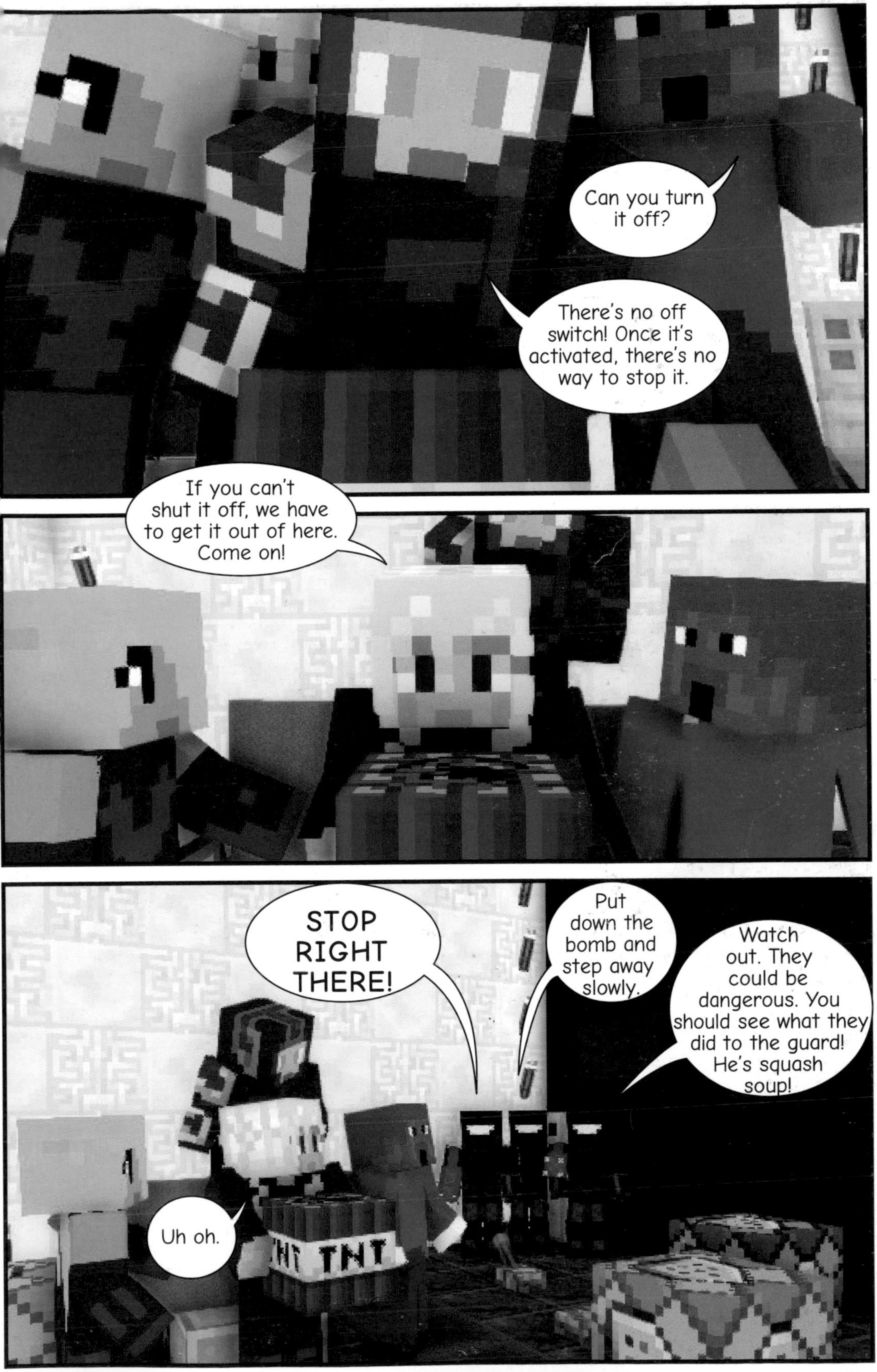

Can you turn it off?
There's no off switch! Once it's activated, there's no way to stop it.
If you can't shut it off, we have to get it out of here. Come on!
STOP RIGHT THERE!
Put down the bomb and step away slowly.
Watch out. They could be dangerous. You should see what they did to the guard! He's squash soup!
Uh oh.
TNT

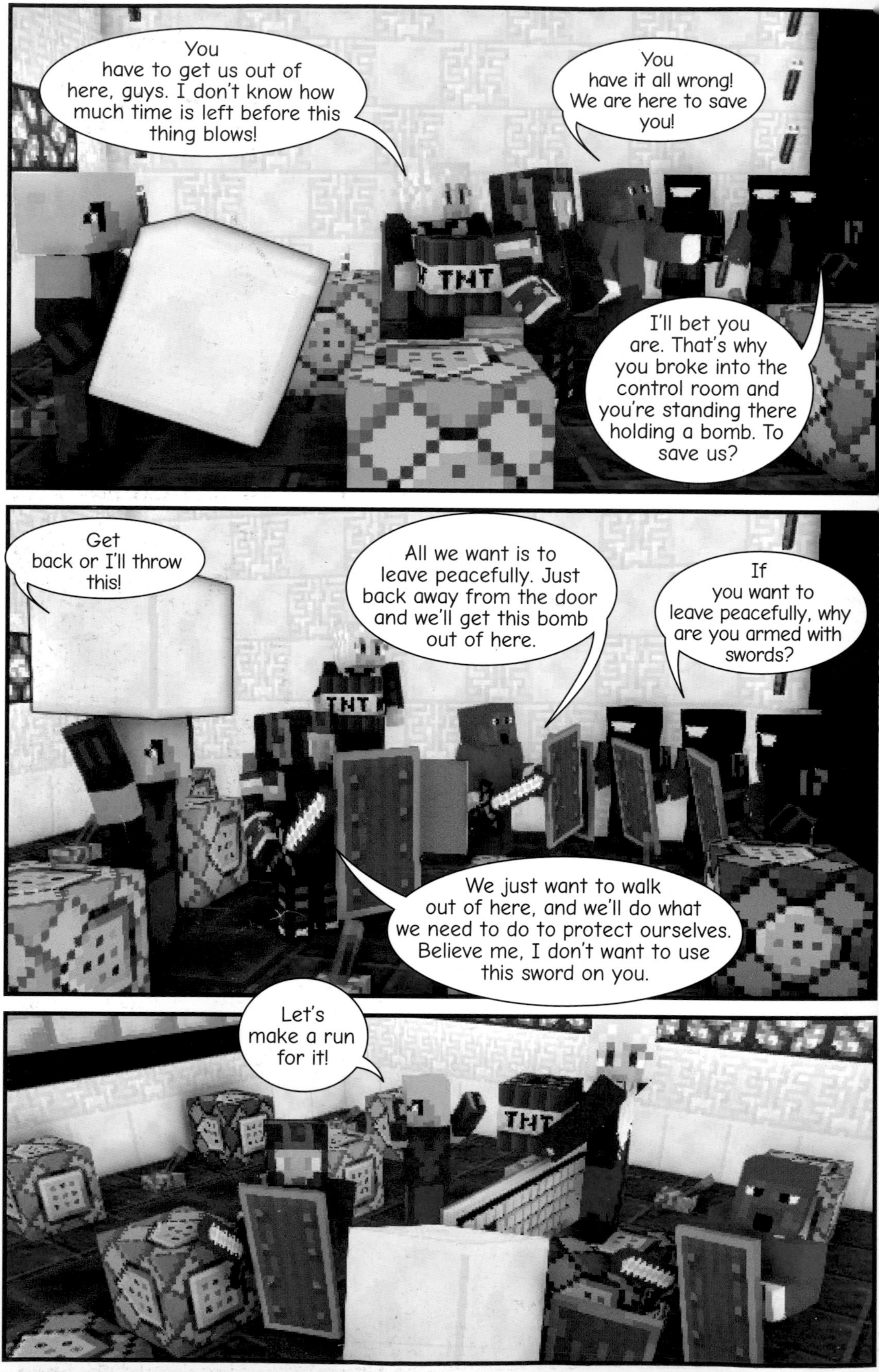
You have to get us out of here, guys. I don't know how much time is left before this thing blows!
You have it all wrong! We are here to save you!
I'll bet you are. That's why you broke into the control room and you're standing there holding a bomb. To save us?
Get back or I'll throw this!
All we want is to leave peacefully. Just back away from the door and we'll get this bomb out of here.
If you want to leave peacefully, why are you armed with swords?
We just want to walk out of here, and we'll do what we need to do to protect ourselves. Believe me, I don't want to use this sword on you.
Let's make a run for it!
TNT

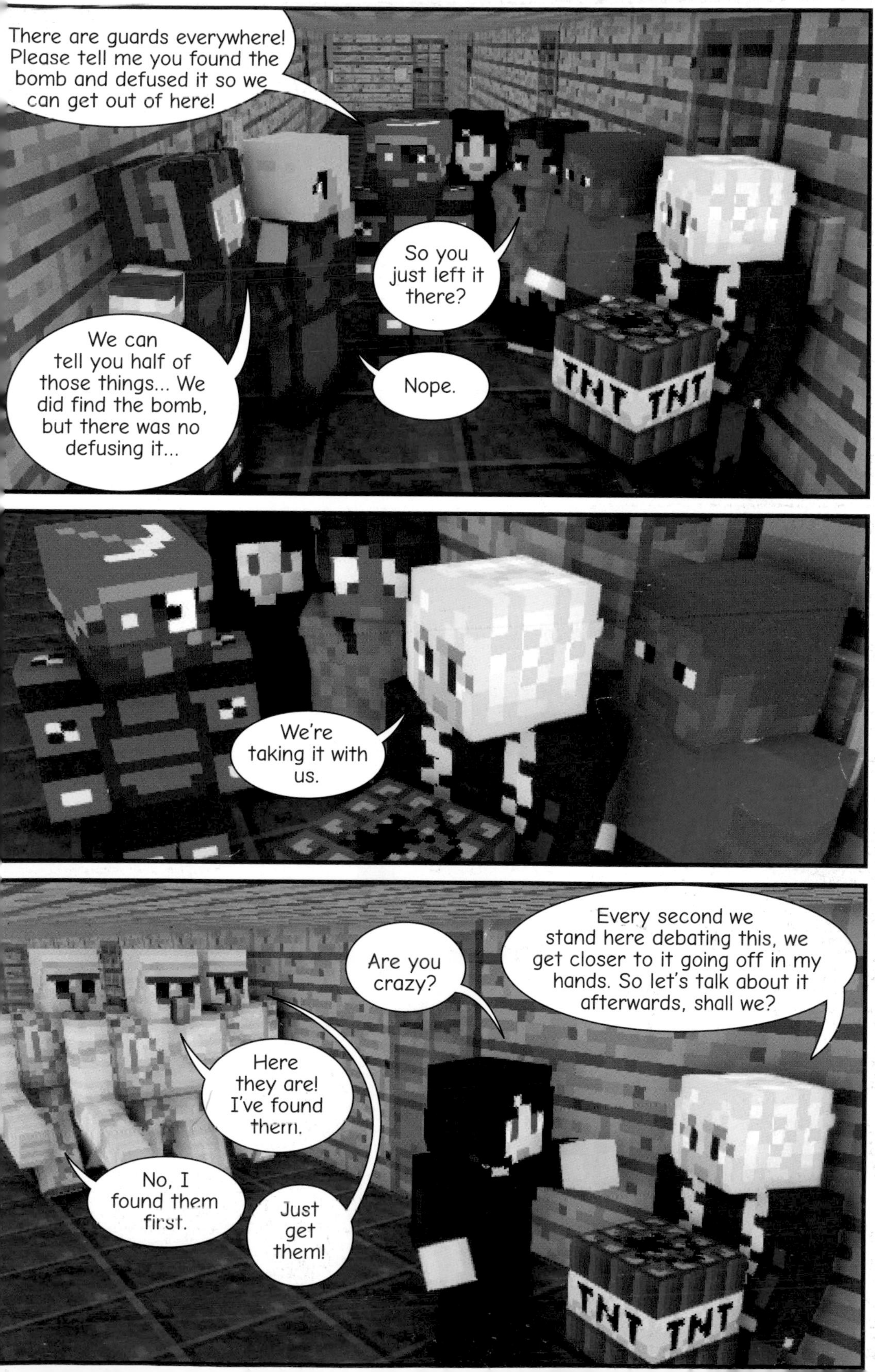
There are guards everywhere! Please tell me you found the bomb and defused it so we can get out of here!
We can tell you half of those things... We did find the bomb, but there was no defusing it...
So you just left it there?
Nope.
We're taking it with us.
Are you crazy?
Every second we stand here debating this, we get closer to it going off in my hands. So let's talk about it afterwards, shall we?
Here they are! I've found them.
No, I found them first.
Just get them!
TNT TNT
TNT TNT

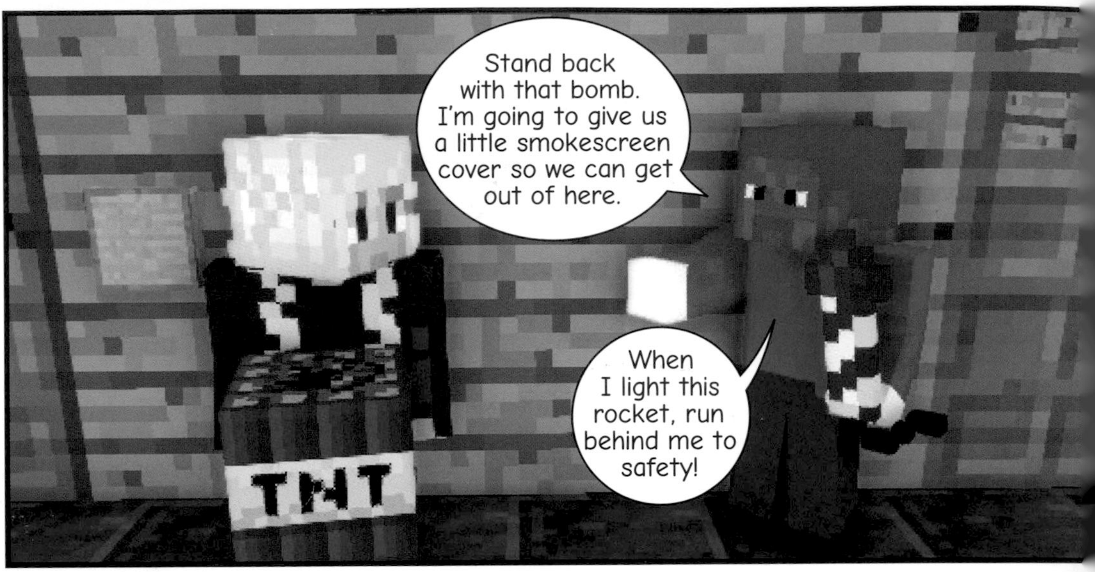
Stand back with that bomb. I'm going to give us a little smokescreen cover so we can get out of here.
When I light this rocket, run behind me to safety!
TNT

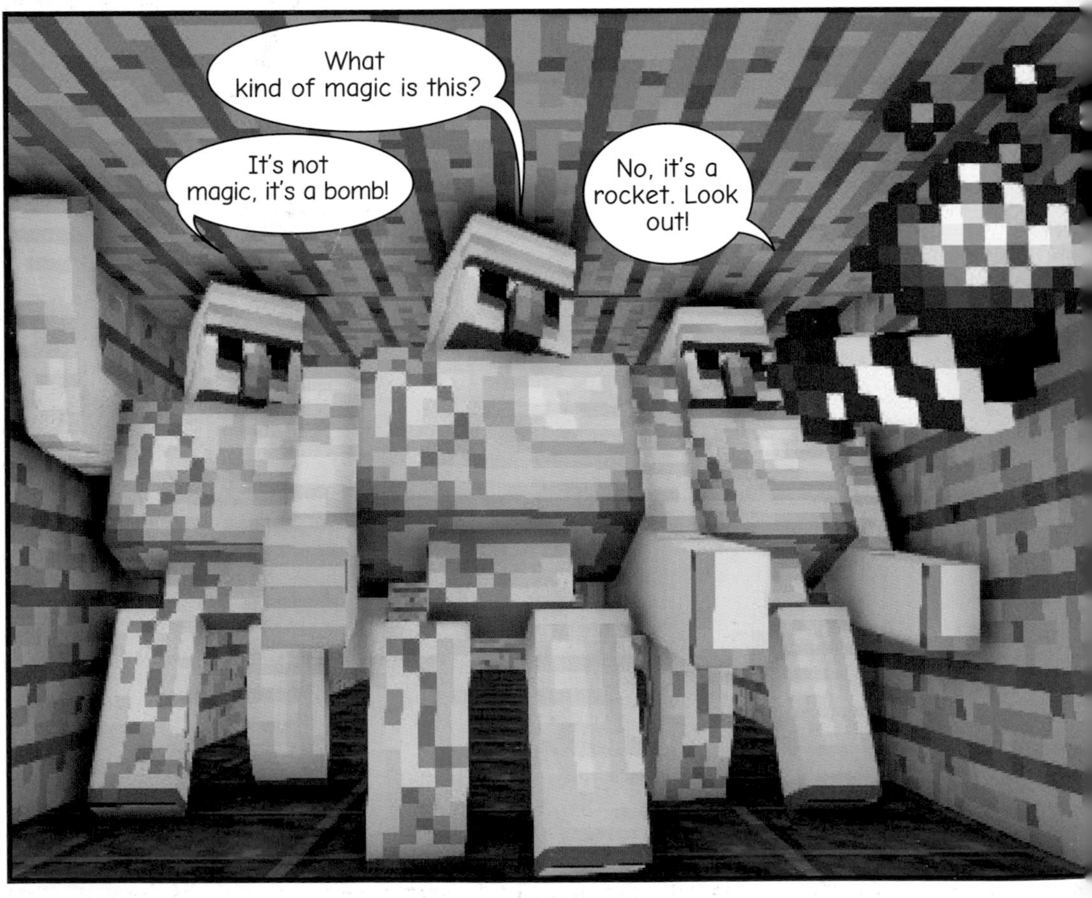
What kind of magic is this?
It's not magic, it's a bomb!
No, it's a rocket. Look out!

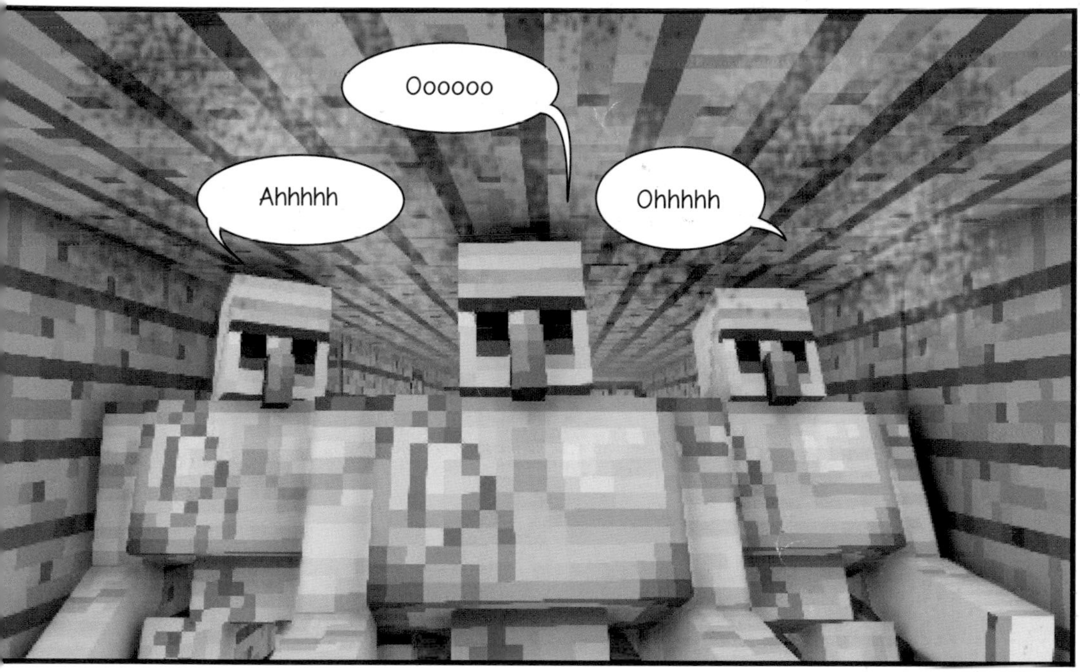
Ahhhhh
Oooooo
Ohhhhh

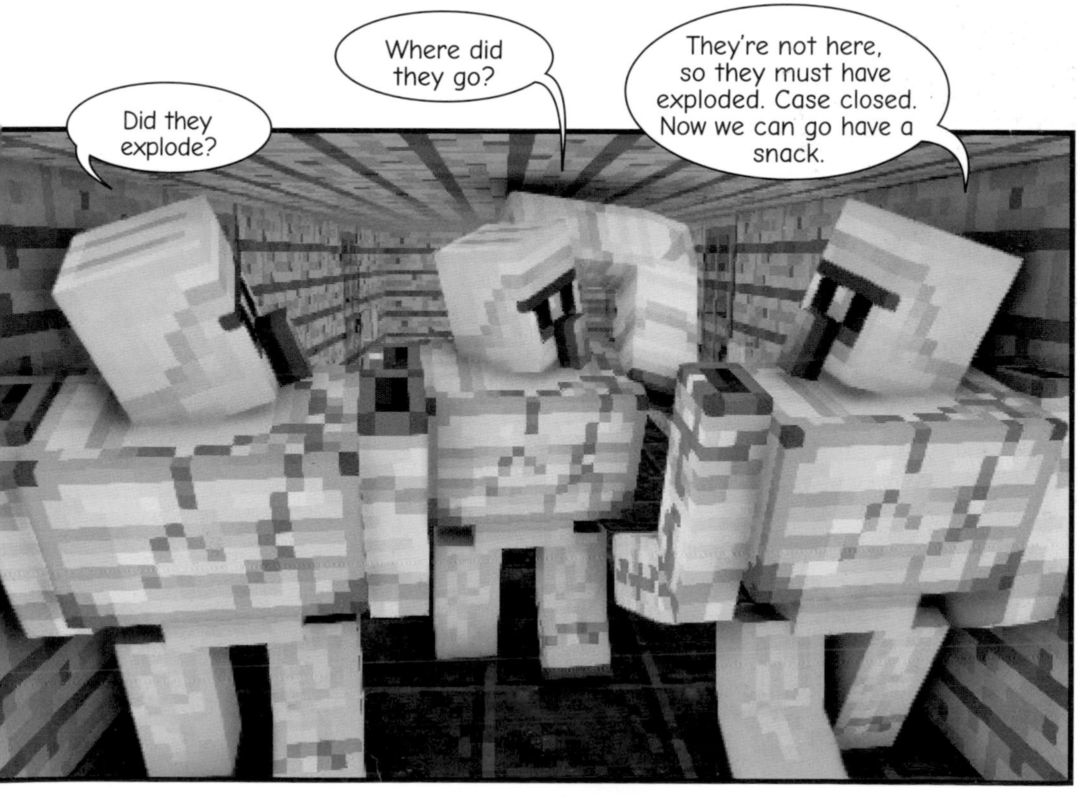
Did they explode?
Where did they go?
They're not here, so they must have exploded. Case closed. Now we can go have a snack.

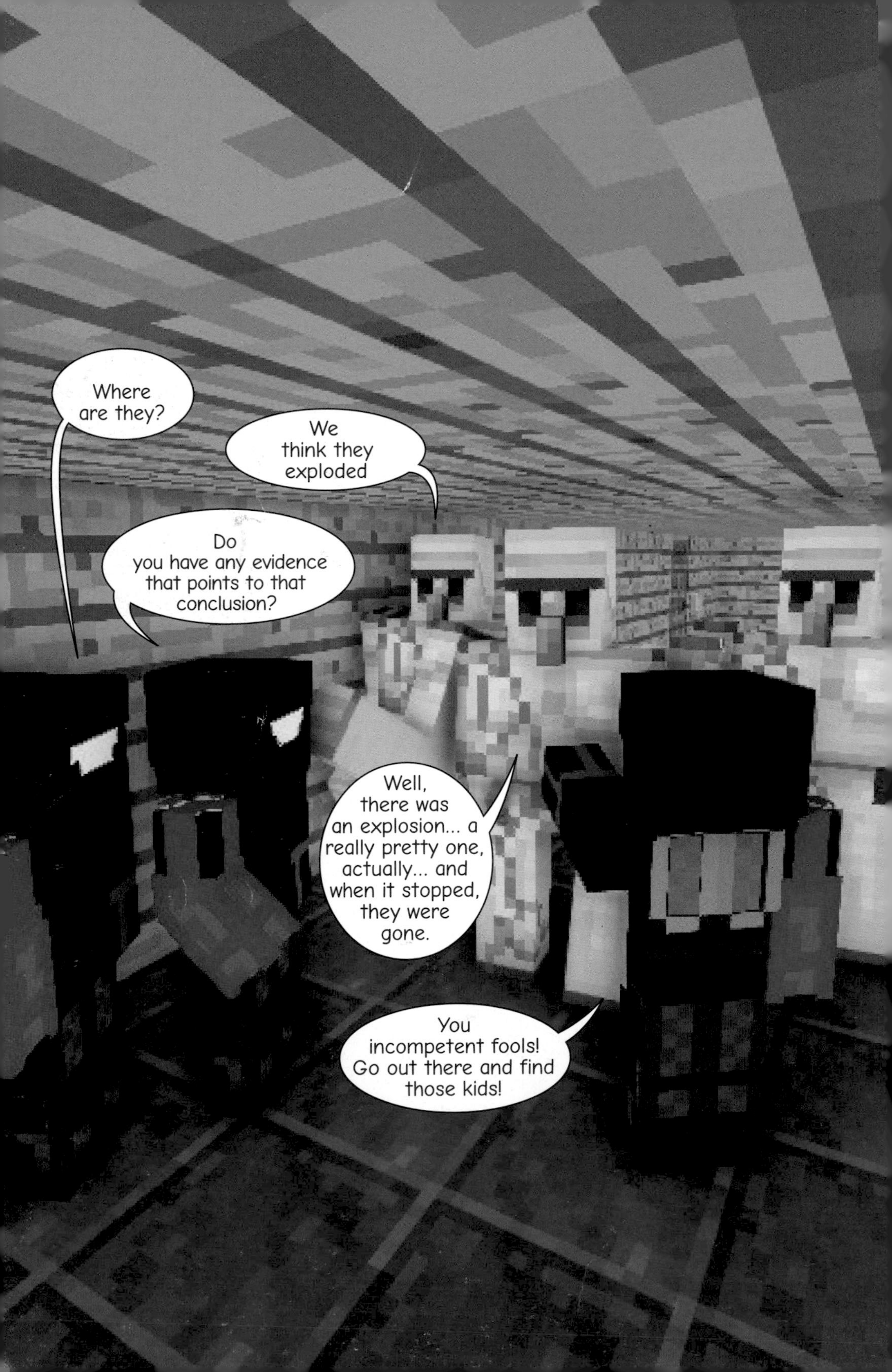
Where are they?
We think they exploded
Do you have any evidence that points to that conclusion?
Well, there was an explosion... a really pretty one, actually... and when it stopped, they were gone.
You incompetent fools! Go out there and find those kids!

CHAPTER 11

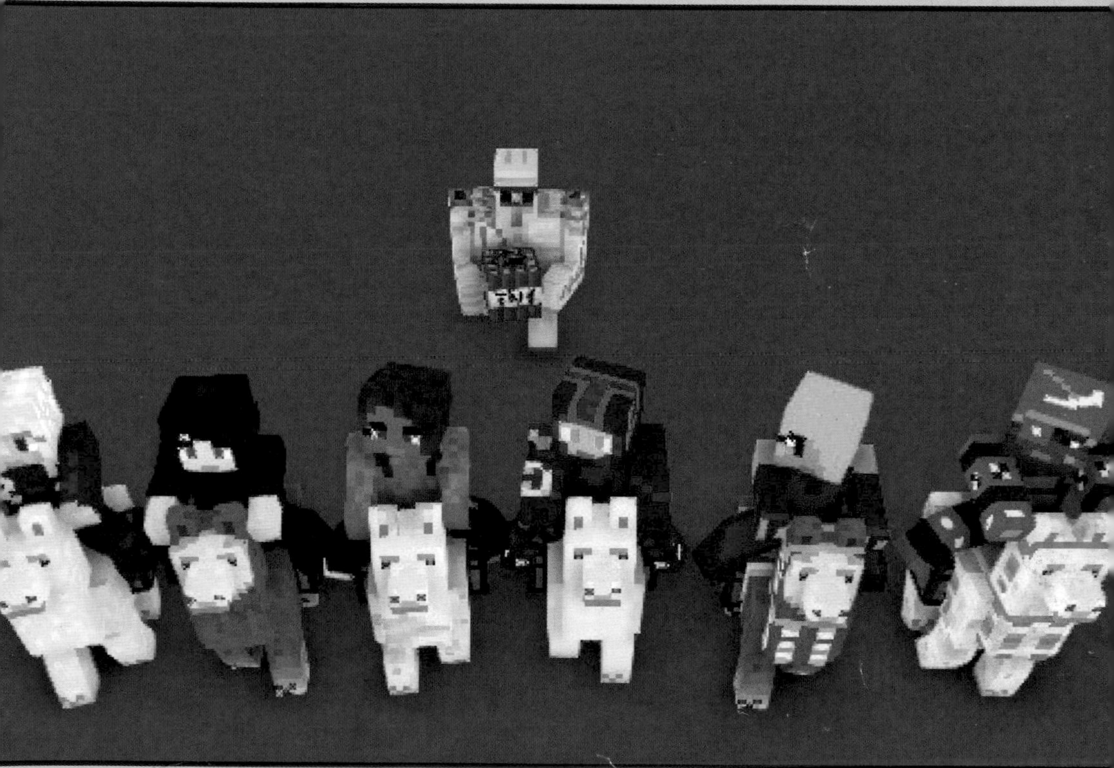

TNT

ESCAPE ROUTE

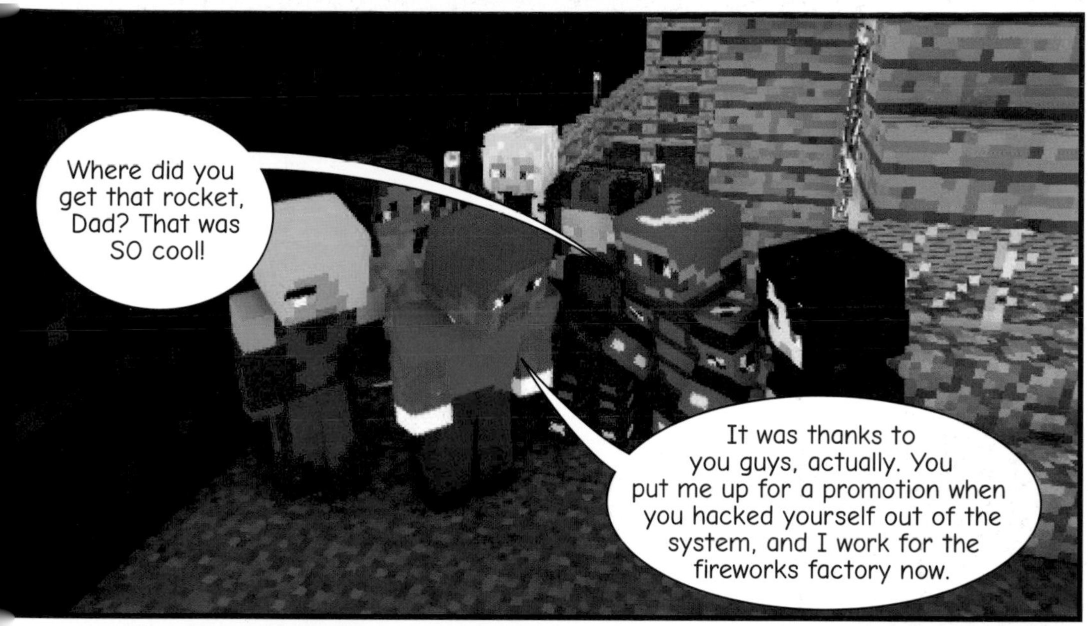
Where did you get that rocket, Dad? That was SO cool!
It was thanks to you guys, actually. You put me up for a promotion when you hacked yourself out of the system, and I work for the fireworks factory now.

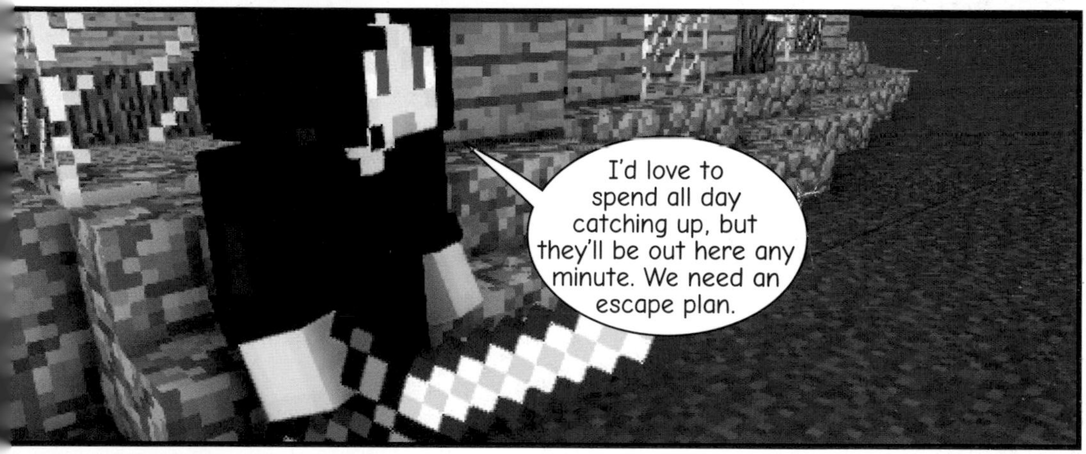
I'd love to spend all day catching up, but they'll be out here any minute. We need an escape plan.

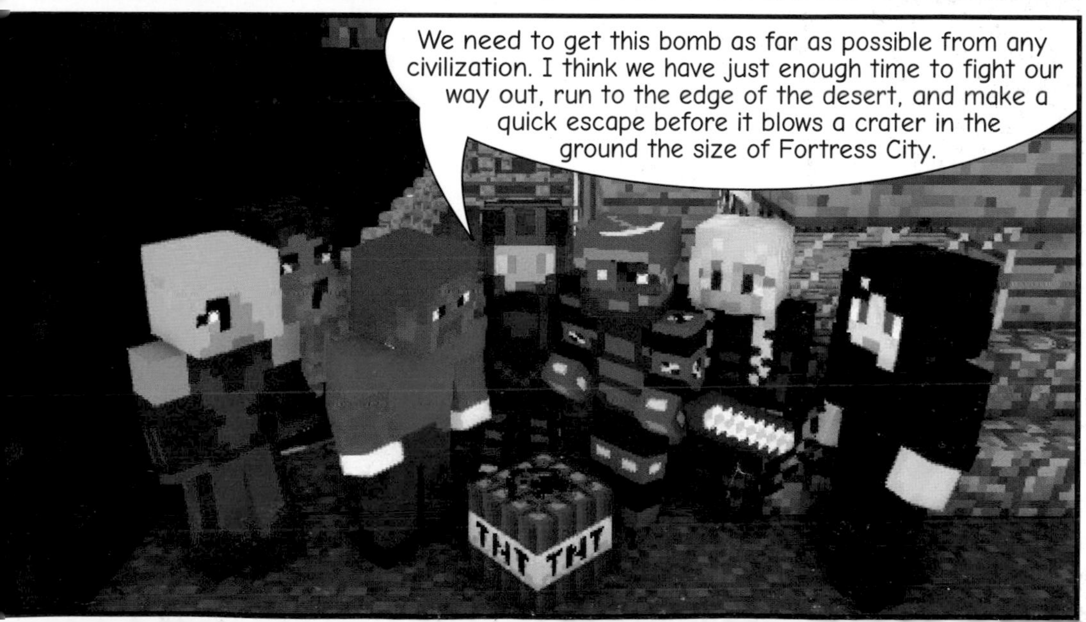
We need to get this bomb as far as possible from any civilization. I think we have just enough time to fight our way out, run to the edge of the desert, and make a quick escape before it blows a crater in the ground the size of Fortress City.
TNT TNT

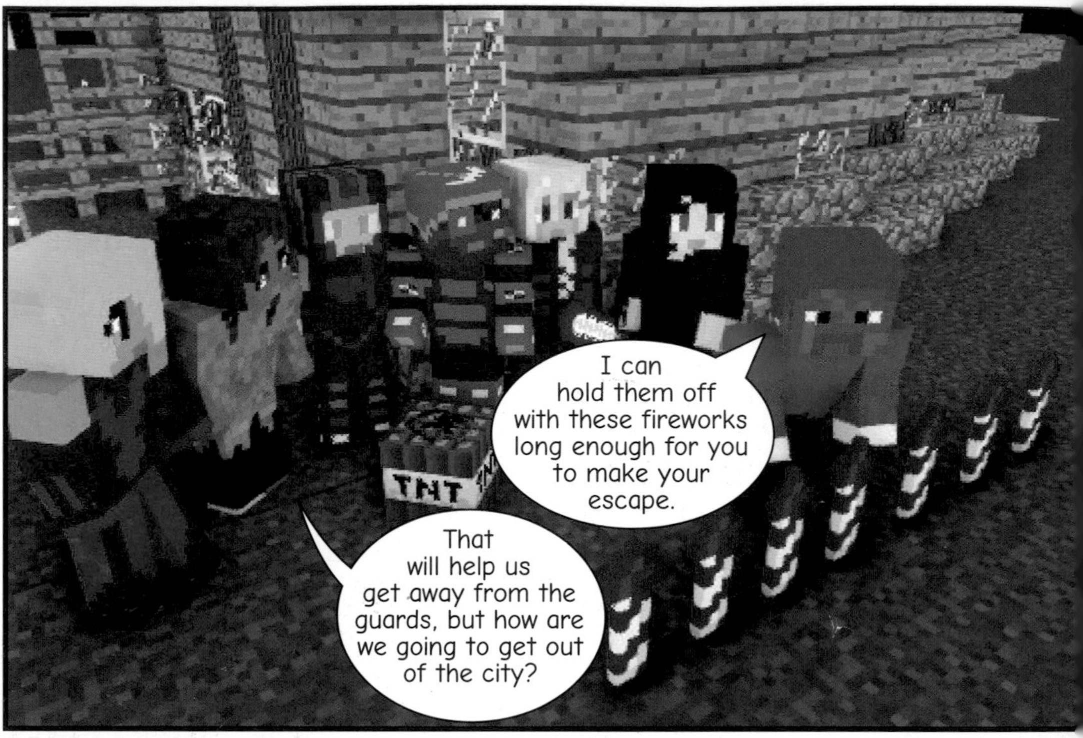
I can hold them off with these fireworks long enough for you to make your escape.
That will help us get away from the guards, but how are we going to get out of the city?

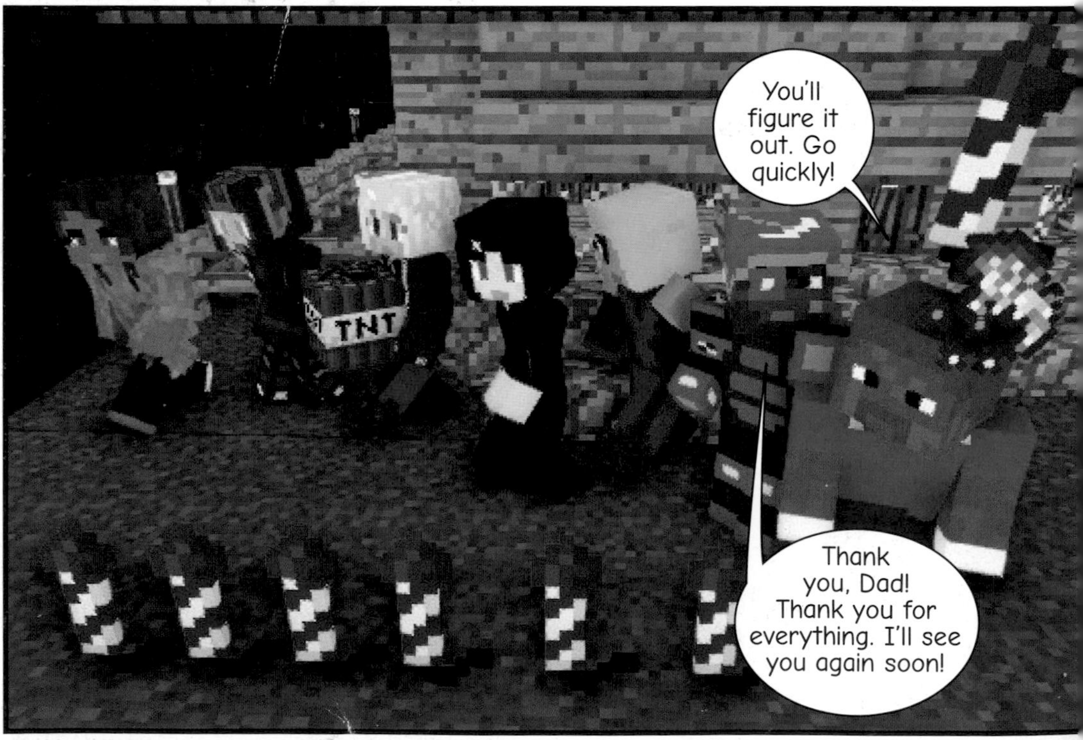
You'll figure it out. Go quickly!
Thank you, Dad! Thank you for everything. I'll see you again soon!
TNT

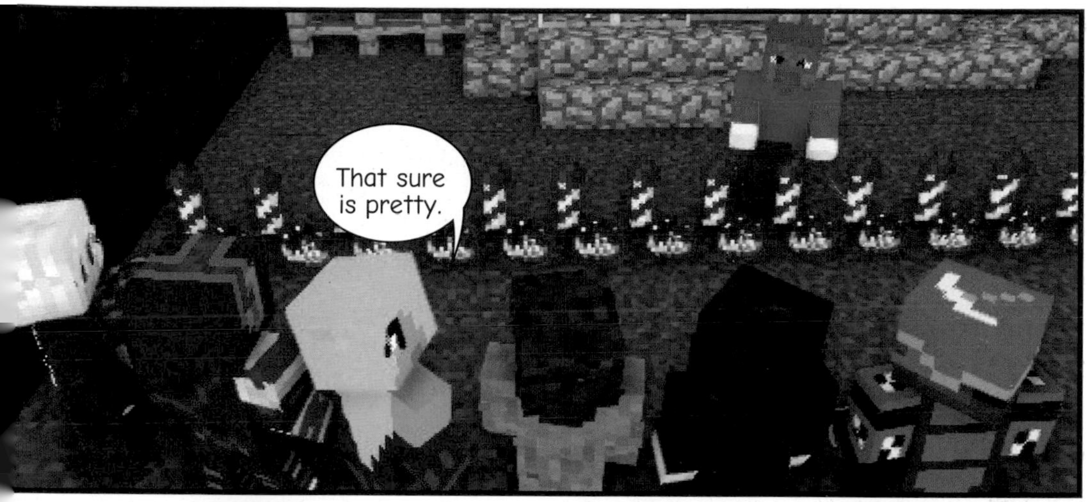
That sure is pretty.

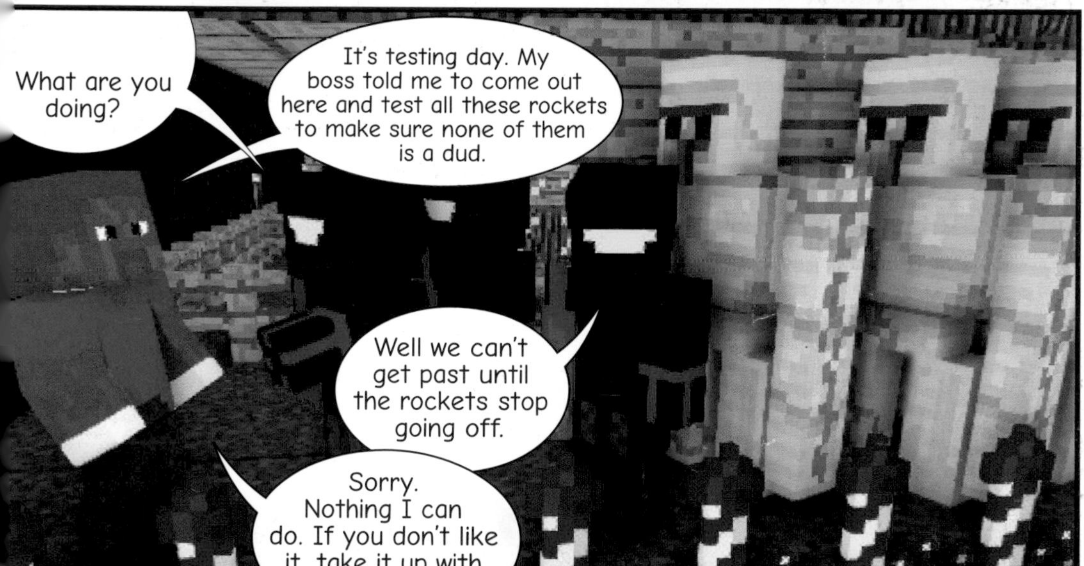
What are you doing?
It's testing day. My boss told me to come out here and test all these rockets to make sure none of them is a dud.
Well we can't get past until the rockets stop going off.
Sorry. Nothing I can do. If you don't like it, take it up with my boss.

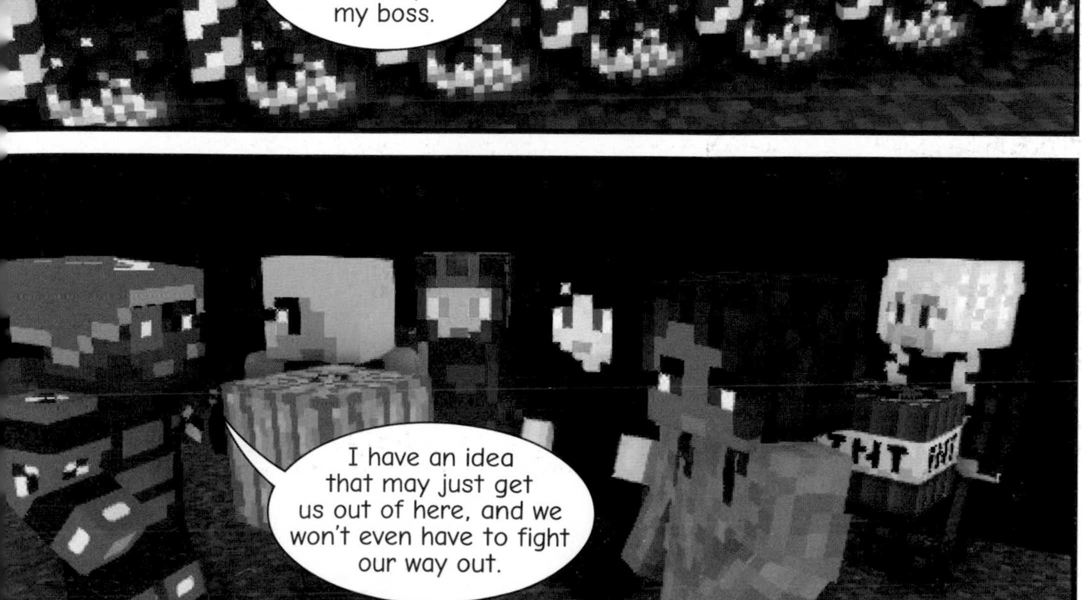
I have an idea that may just get us out of here, and we won't even have to fight our way out.

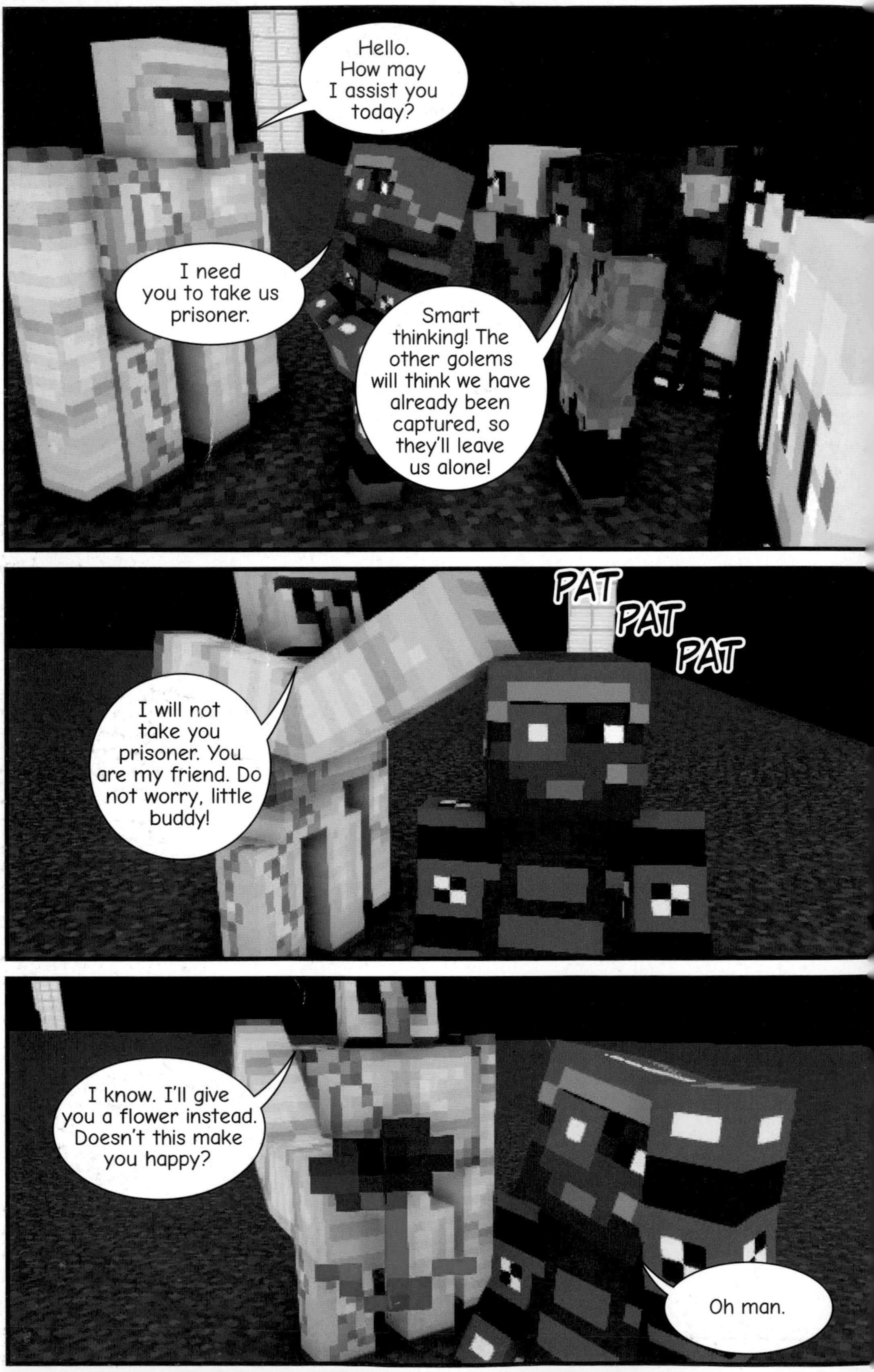
Hello. How may I assist you today?
I need you to take us prisoner.
Smart thinking! The other golems will think we have already been captured, so they'll leave us alone!
PAT PAT PAT
I will not take you prisoner. You are my friend. Do not worry, little buddy!
I know. I'll give you a flower instead. Doesn't this make you happy?
Oh man.

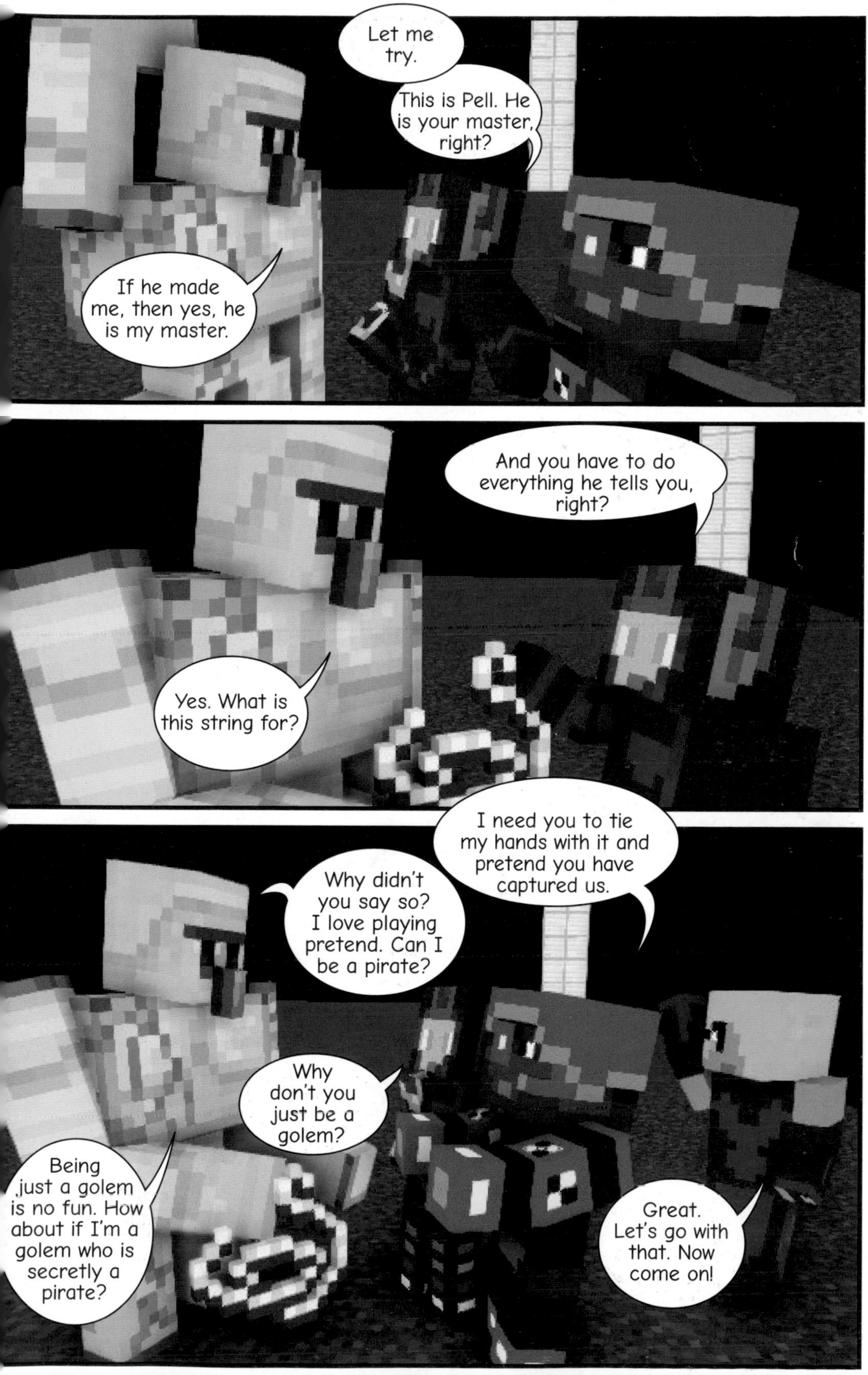
Let me try.
This is Pell. He is your master, right?
If he made me, then yes, he is my master.
And you have to do everything he tells you, right?
Yes. What is this string for?
I need you to tie my hands with it and pretend you have captured us.
Why didn't you say so? I love playing pretend. Can I be a pirate?
Why don't you just be a golem?
Being just a golem is no fun. How about if I'm a golem who is secretly a pirate?
Great. Let's go with that. Now come on!

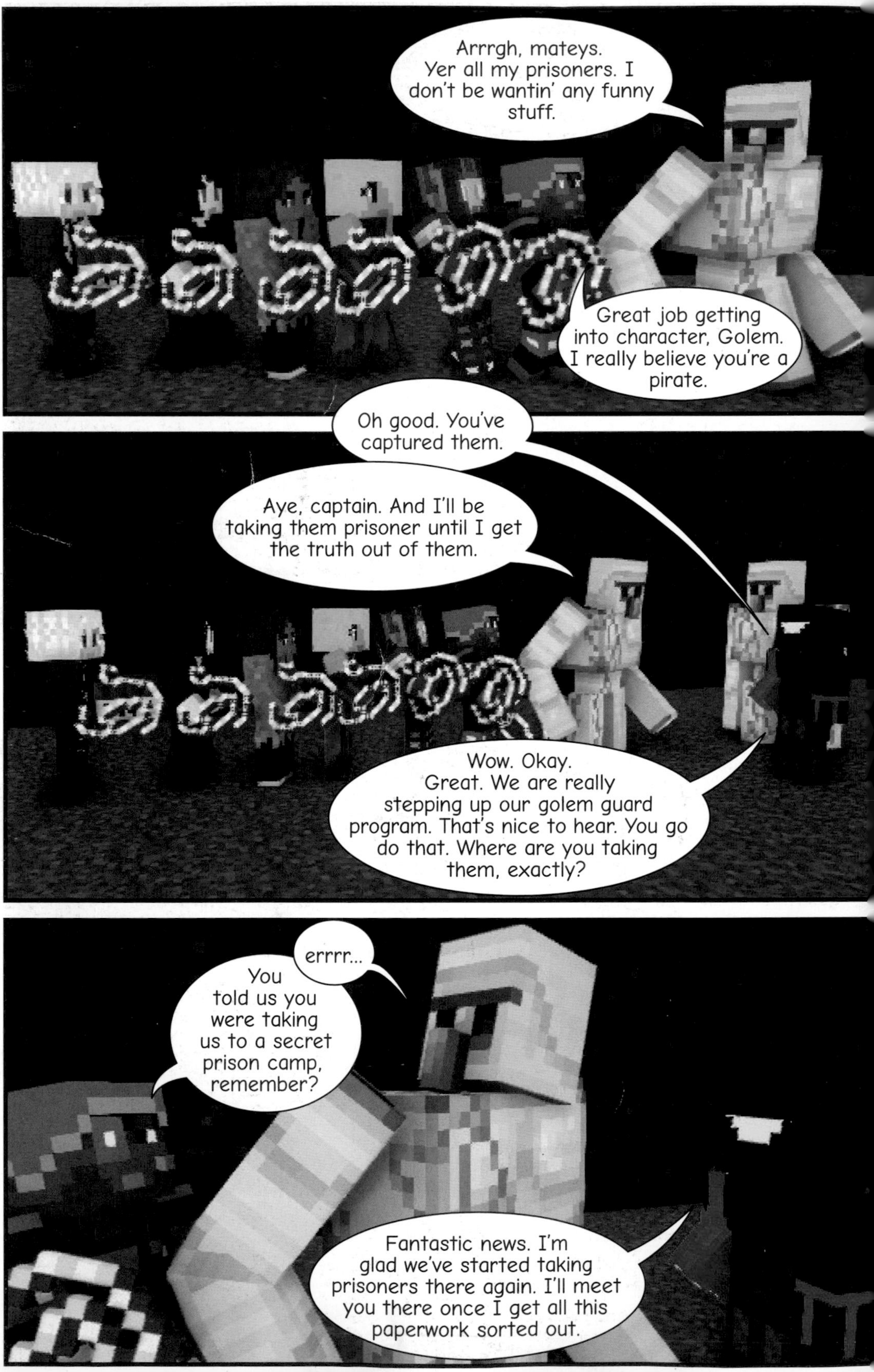
Arrrgh, mateys. Yer all my prisoners. I don't be wantin' any funny stuff.
Great job getting into character, Golem. I really believe you're a pirate.
Oh good. You've captured them.
Aye, captain. And I'll be taking them prisoner until I get the truth out of them.
Wow. Okay. Great. We are really stepping up our golem guard program. That's nice to hear. You go do that. Where are you taking them, exactly?
errrr...
You told us you were taking us to a secret prison camp, remember?
Fantastic news. I'm glad we've started taking prisoners there again. I'll meet you there once I get all this paperwork sorted out.

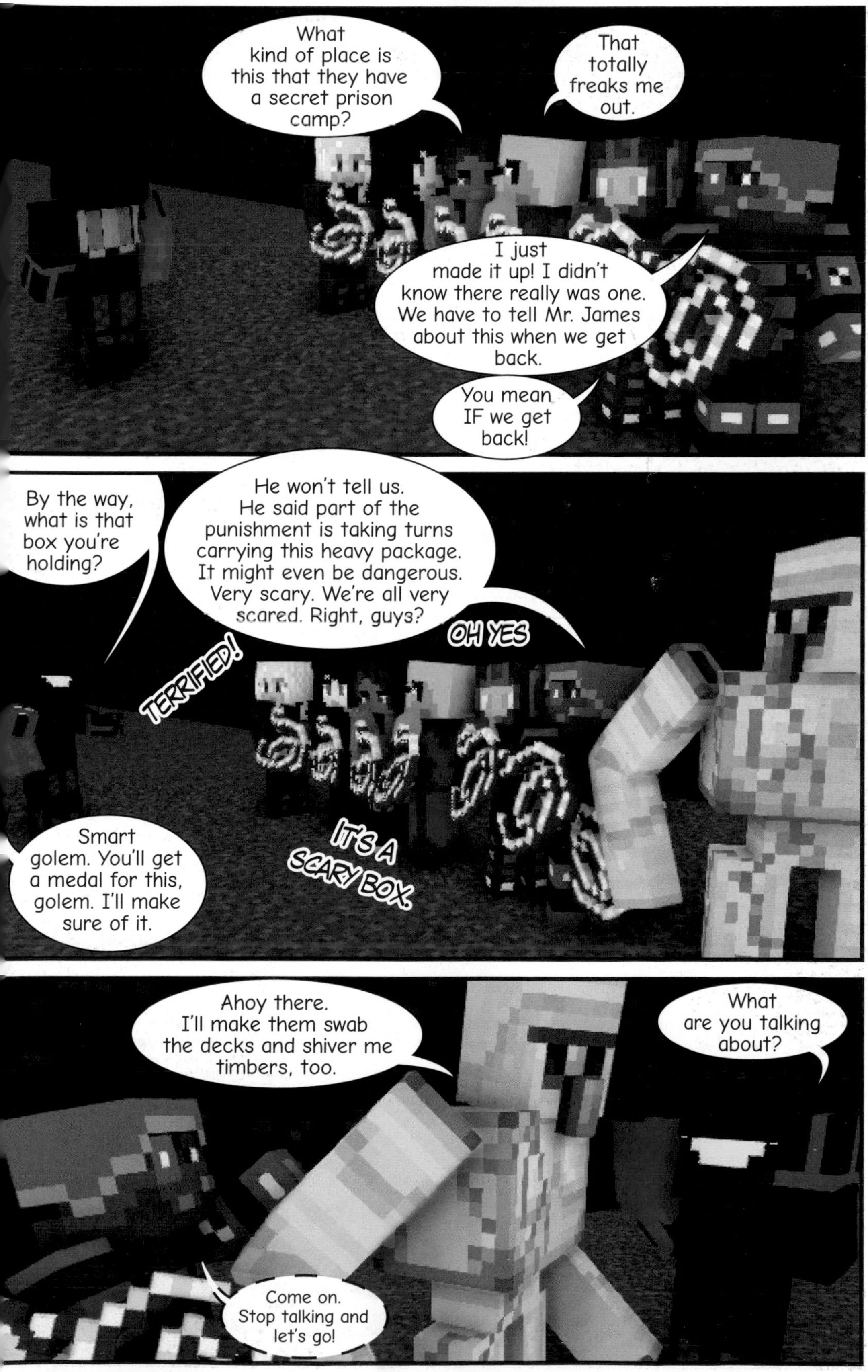
What kind of place is this that they have a secret prison camp?
That totally freaks me out.
I just made it up! I didn't know there really was one. We have to tell Mr. James about this when we get back.
You mean IF we get back!
By the way, what is that box you're holding?
He won't tell us. He said part of the punishment is taking turns carrying this heavy package. It might even be dangerous. Very scary. We're all very scared. Right, guys?
TERRIFIED!
OH YES
IT'S A SCARY BOX.
Smart golem. You'll get a medal for this, golem. I'll make sure of it.
Ahoy there. I'll make them swab the decks and shiver me timbers, too.
What are you talking about?
Come on. Stop talking and let's go!

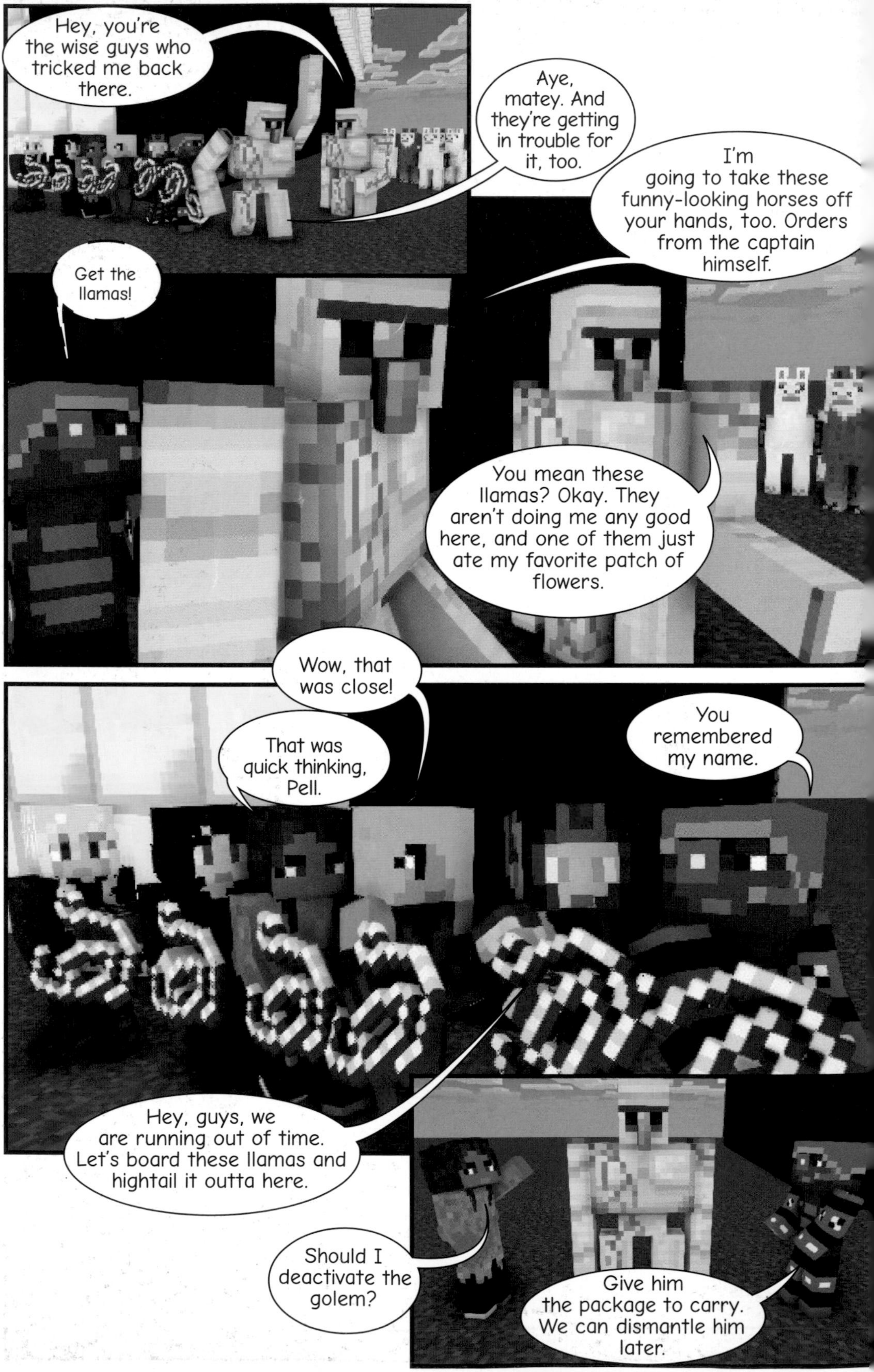
Hey, you're the wise guys who tricked me back there.
Aye, matey. And they're getting in trouble for it, too.
I'm going to take these funny-looking horses off your hands, too. Orders from the captain himself.
Get the llamas!
You mean these llamas? Okay. They aren't doing me any good here, and one of them just ate my favorite patch of flowers.
Wow, that was close!
That was quick thinking, Pell.
You remembered my name.
Hey, guys, we are running out of time. Let's board these llamas and hightail it outta here.
Should I deactivate the golem?
Give him the package to carry. We can dismantle him later.

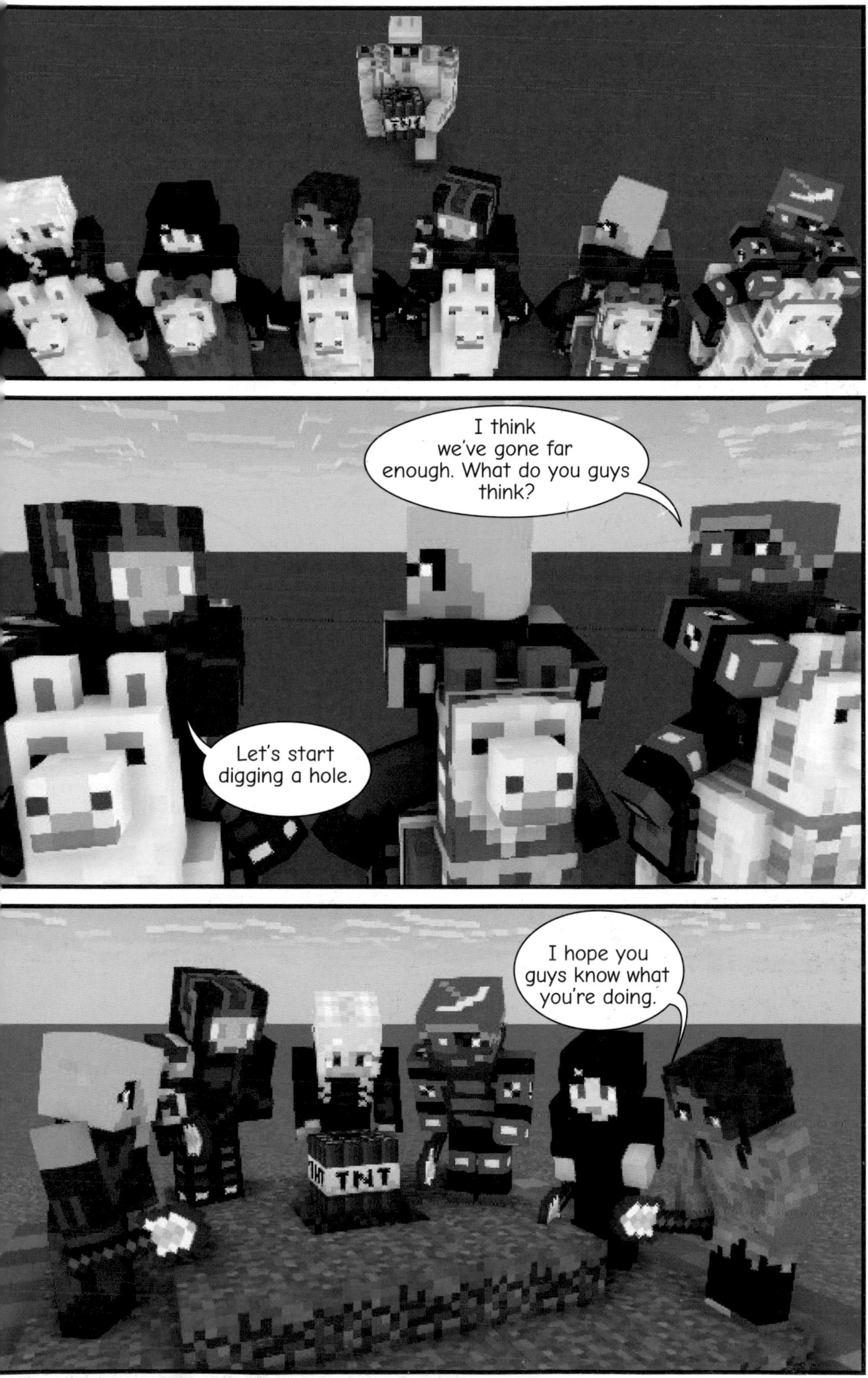
I think we've gone far enough. What do you guys think?
Let's start digging a hole.
TNT
I hope you guys know what you're doing.

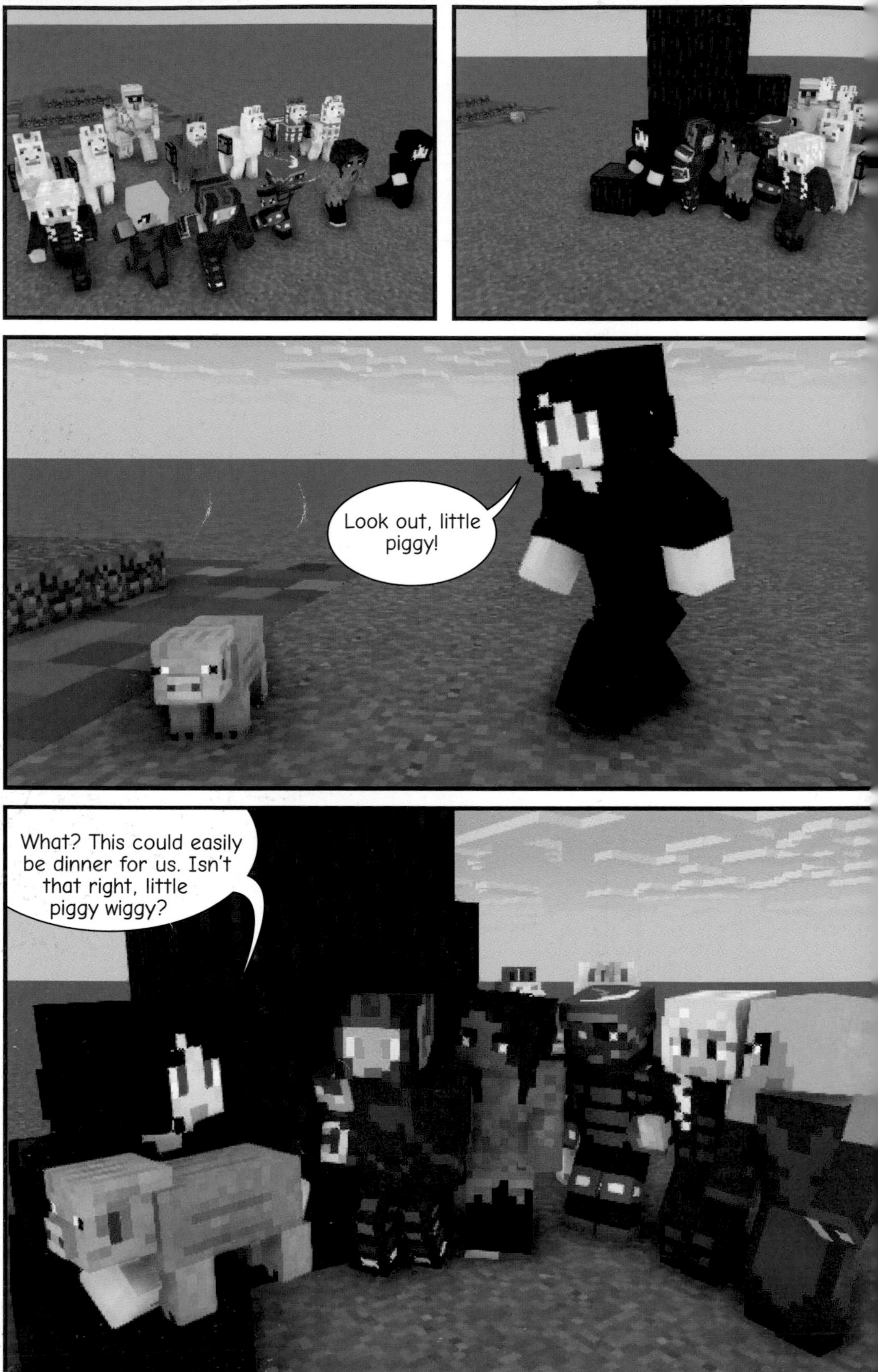
Look out, little piggy!
What? This could easily be dinner for us. Isn't that right, little piggy wiggy?

CHAPTER 12

TNT GOES "BOOM"

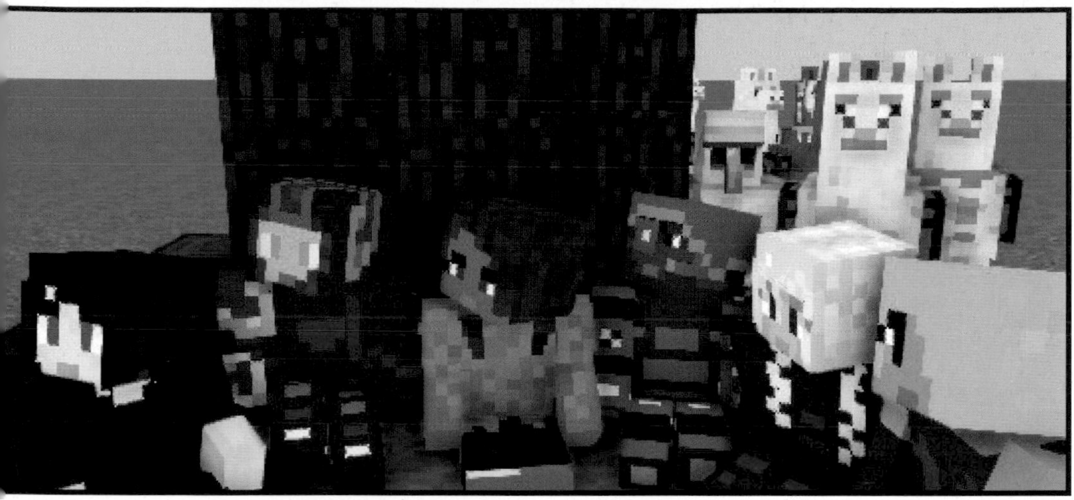

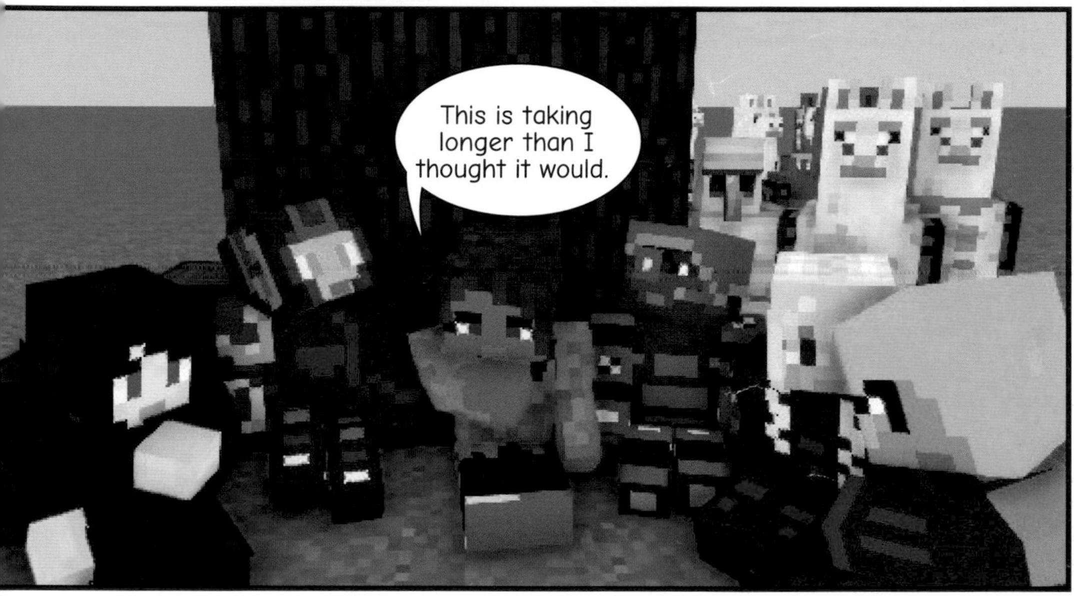
This is taking longer than I thought it would.

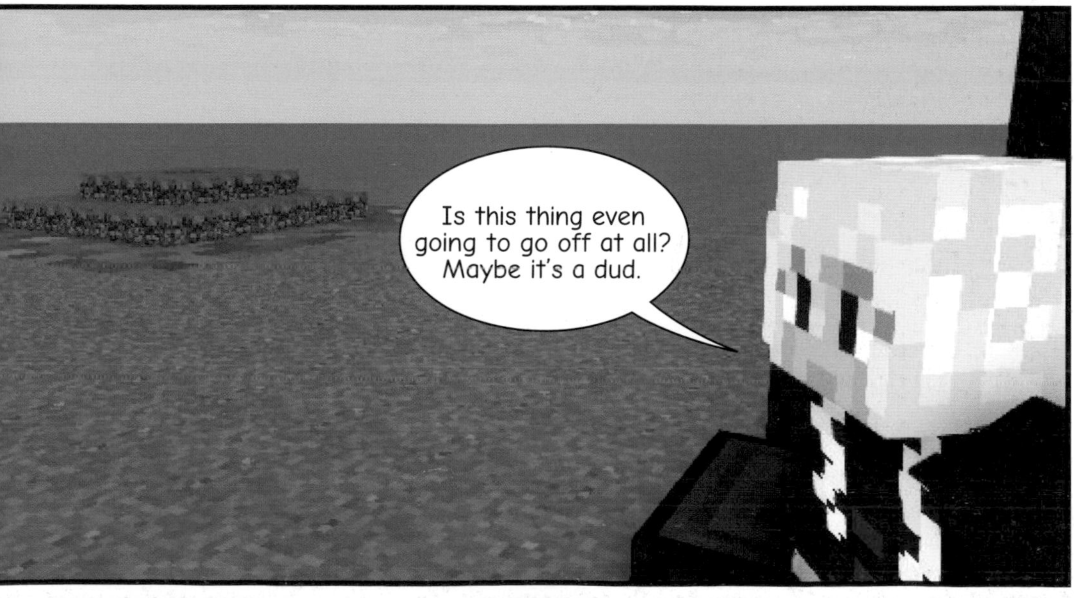
Is this thing even going to go off at all? Maybe it's a dud.

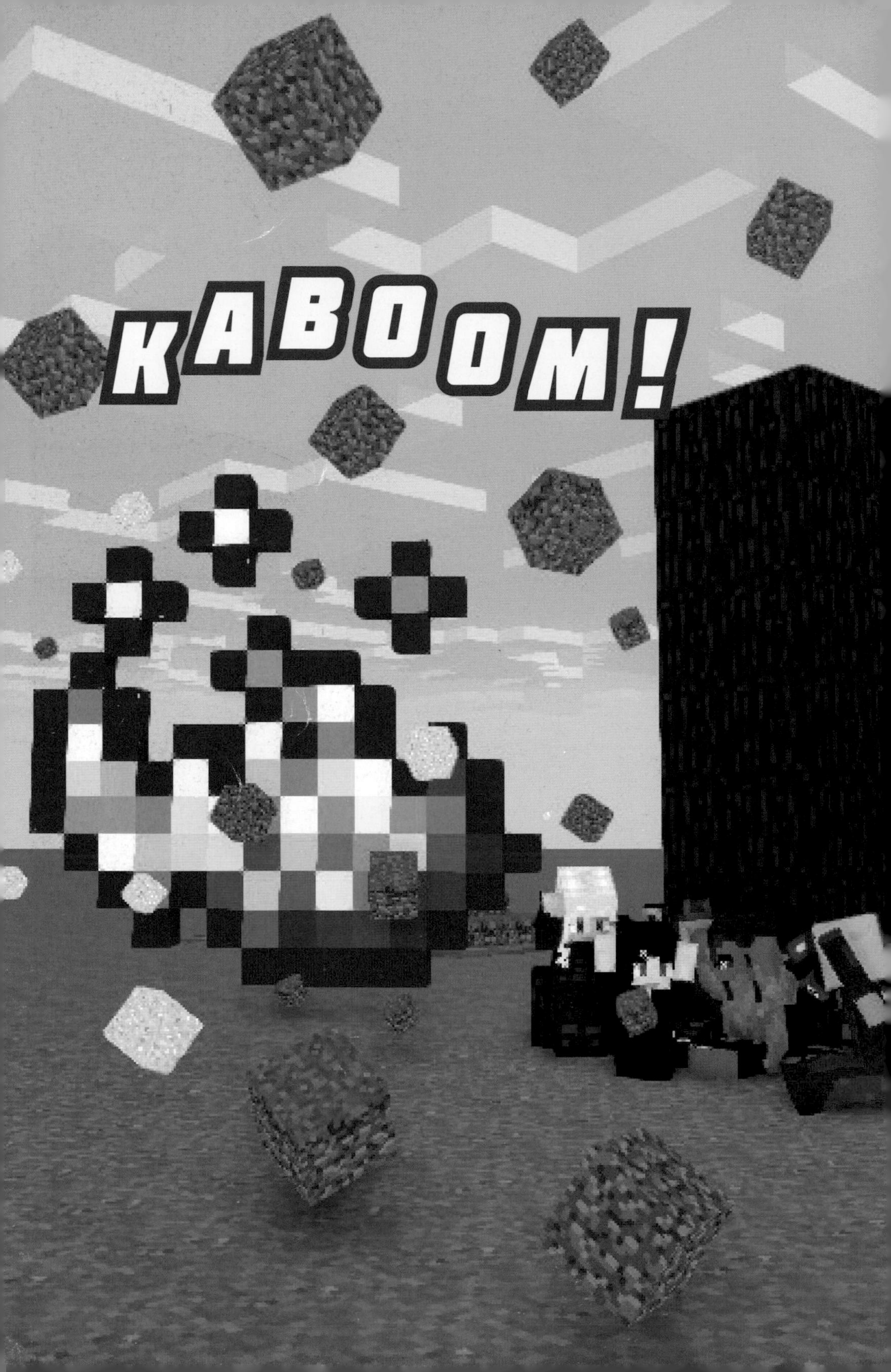
KABOOM!

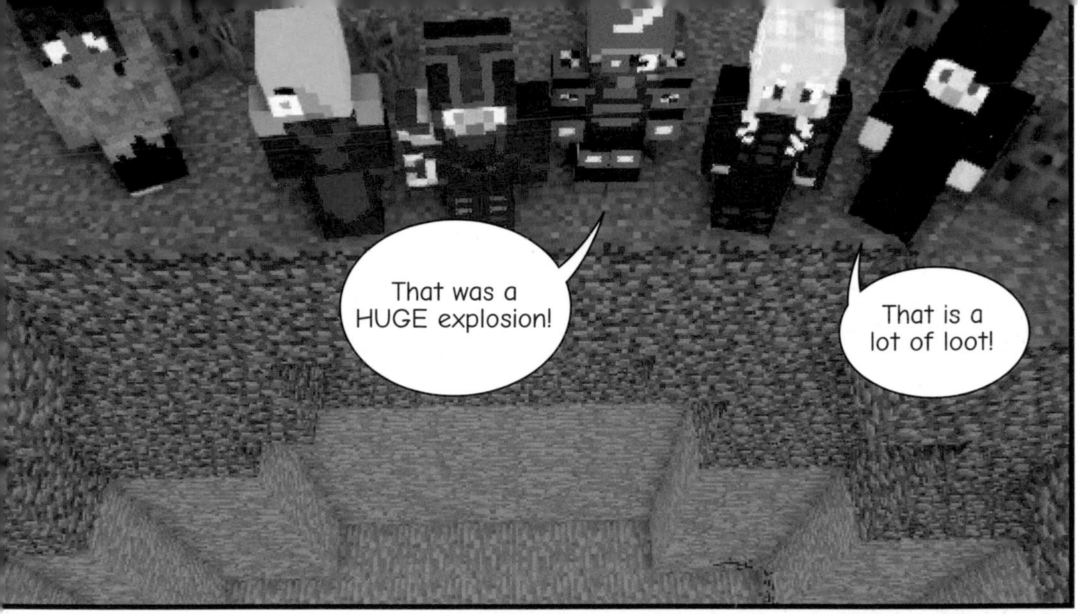
That was a HUGE explosion!
That is a lot of loot!

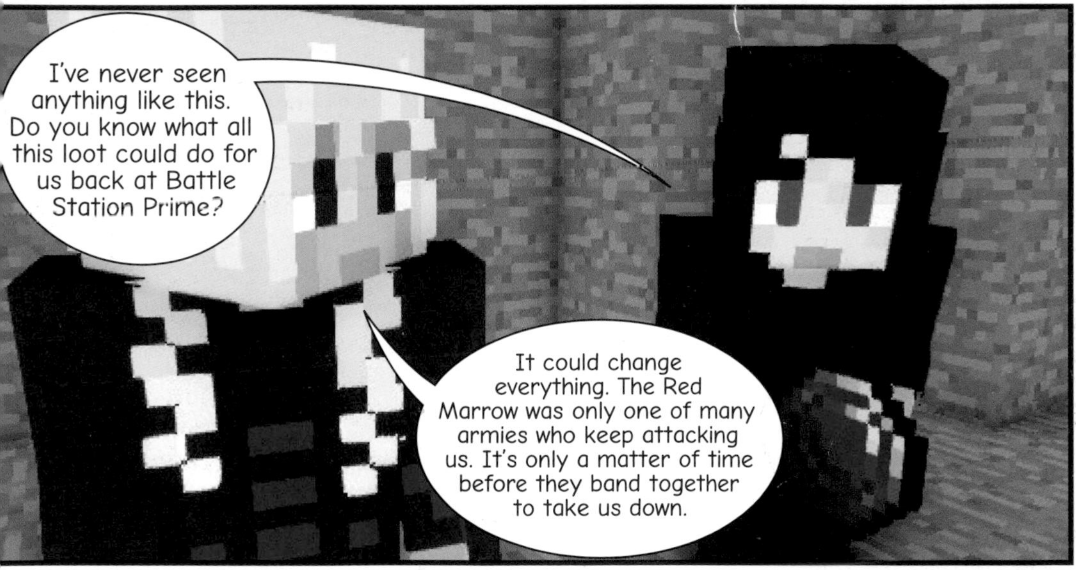
I've never seen anything like this. Do you know what all this loot could do for us back at Battle Station Prime?
It could change everything. The Red Marrow was only one of many armies who keep attacking us. It's only a matter of time before they band together to take us down.

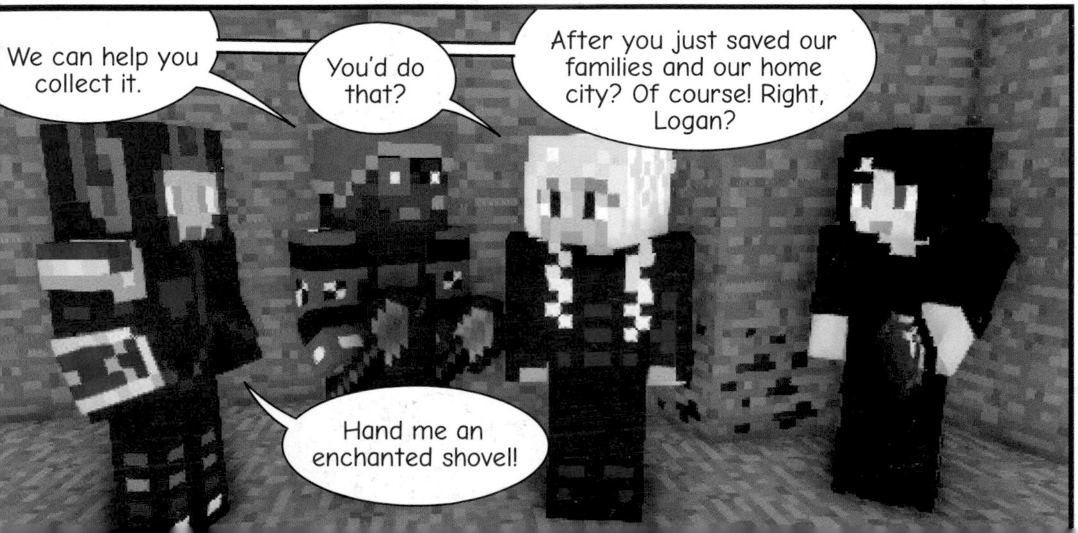
We can help you collect it.
You'd do that?
After you just saved our families and our home city? Of course! Right, Logan?
Hand me an enchanted shovel!

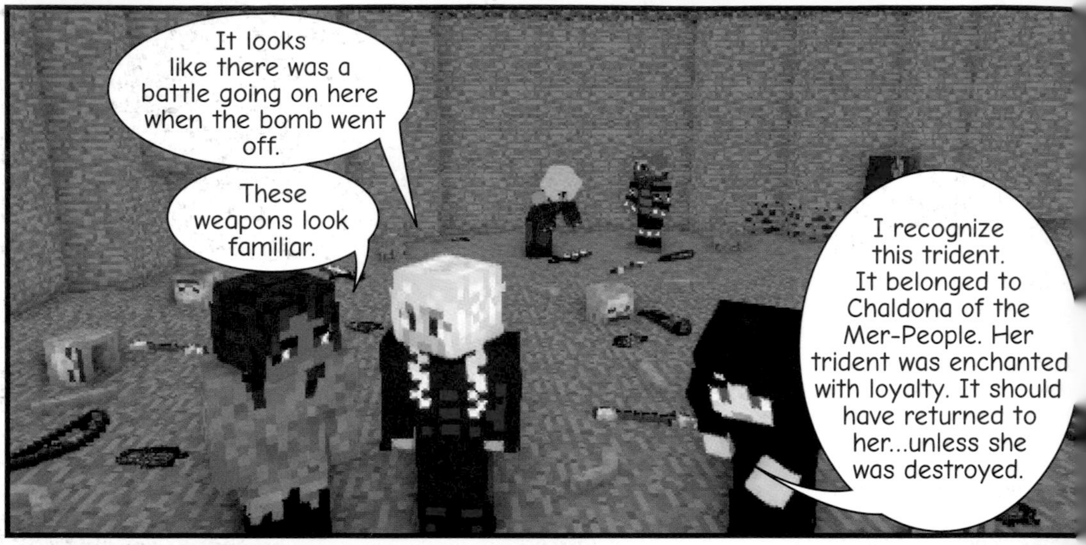
It looks like there was a battle going on here when the bomb went off.
These weapons look familiar.
I recognize this trident. It belonged to Chaldona of the Mer-People. Her trident was enchanted with loyalty. It should have returned to her...unless she was destroyed.

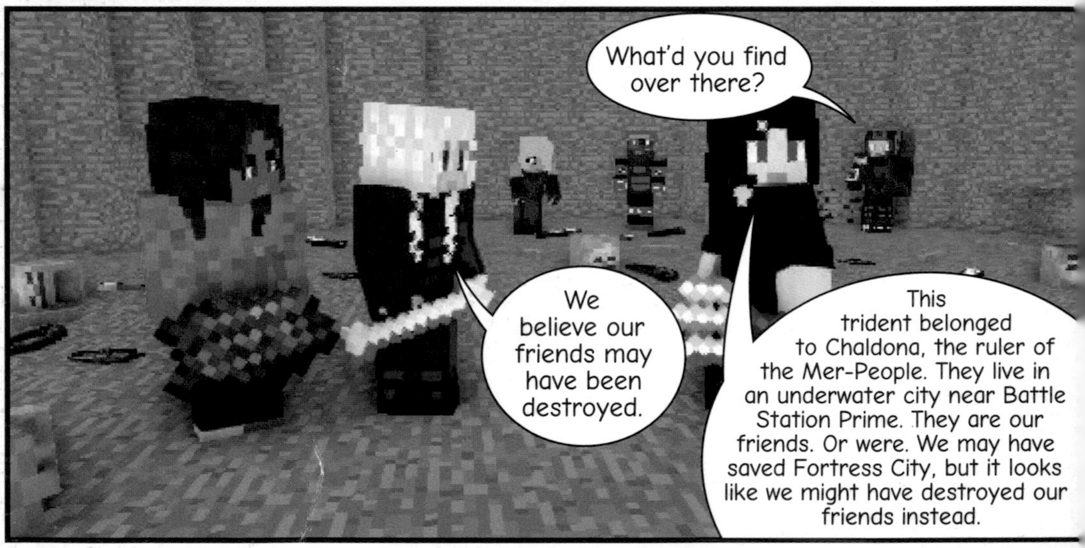
What'd you find over there?
We believe our friends may have been destroyed.
This trident belonged to Chaldona, the ruler of the Mer-People. They live in an underwater city near Battle Station Prime. They are our friends. Or were. We may have saved Fortress City, but it looks like we might have destroyed our friends instead.

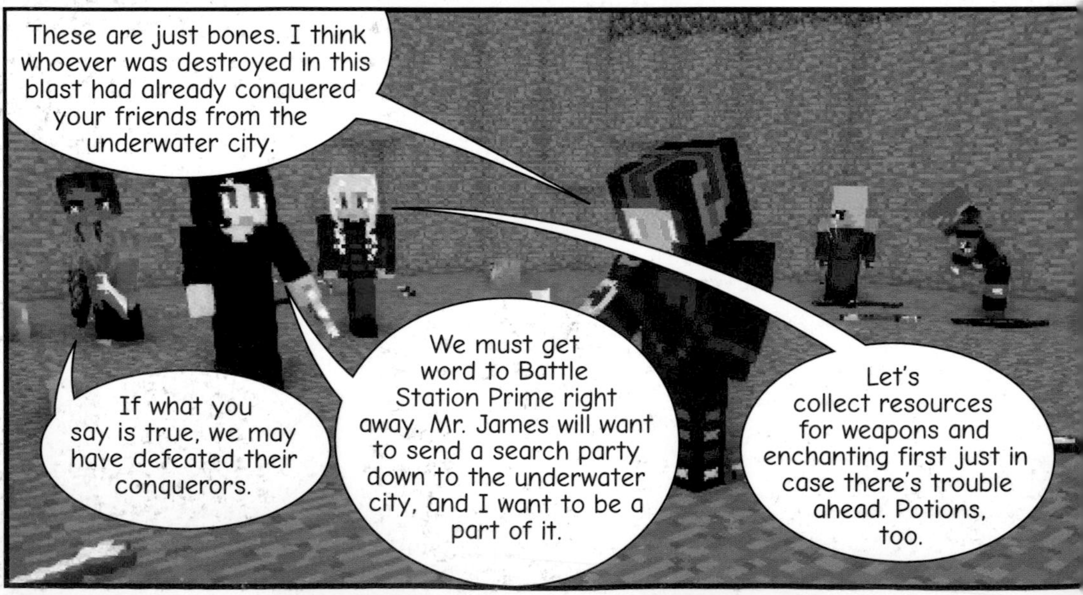
These are just bones. I think whoever was destroyed in this blast had already conquered your friends from the underwater city.
If what you say is true, we may have defeated their conquerors.
We must get word to Battle Station Prime right away. Mr. James will want to send a search party down to the underwater city, and I want to be a part of it.
Let's collect resources for weapons and enchanting first just in case there's trouble ahead. Potions, too.

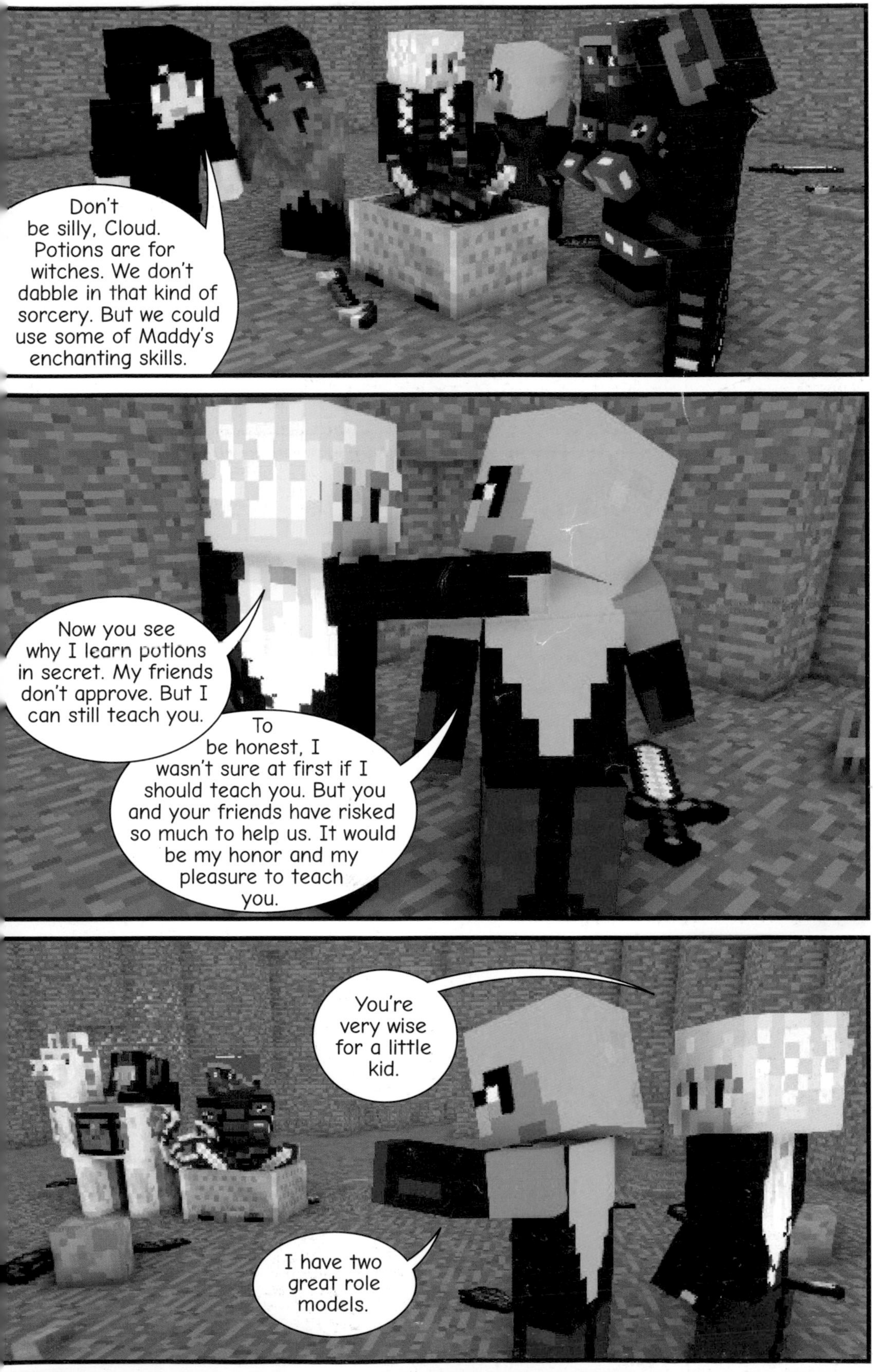
Don't be silly, Cloud. Potions are for witches. We don't dabble in that kind of sorcery. But we could use some of Maddy's enchanting skills.
Now you see why I learn potions in secret. My friends don't approve. But I can still teach you.
To be honest, I wasn't sure at first if I should teach you. But you and your friends have risked so much to help us. It would be my honor and my pleasure to teach you.
You're very wise for a little kid.
I have two great role models.

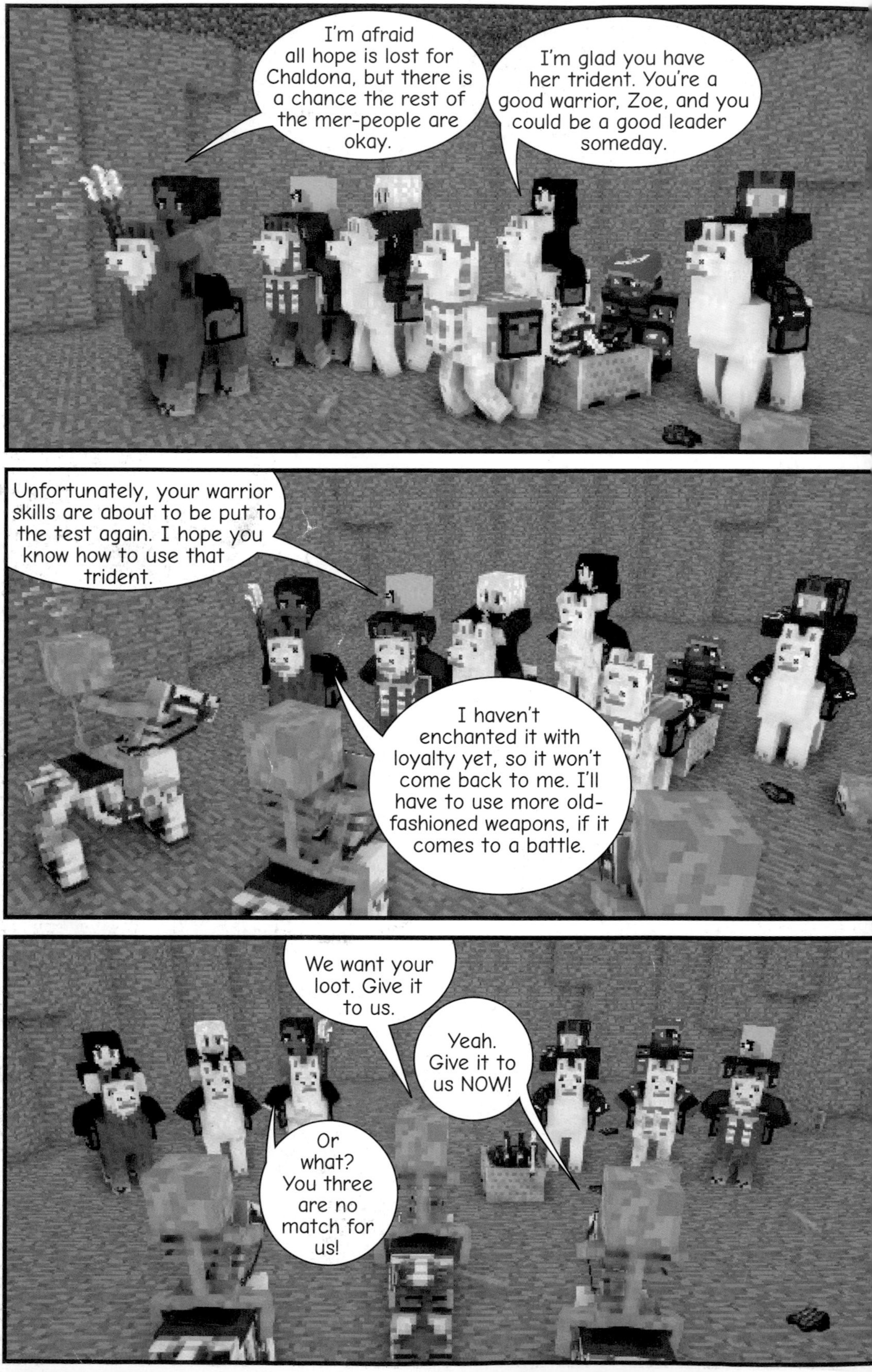
I'm afraid all hope is lost for Chaldona, but there is a chance the rest of the mer-people are okay.
I'm glad you have her trident. You're a good warrior, Zoe, and you could be a good leader someday.
Unfortunately, your warrior skills are about to be put to the test again. I hope you know how to use that trident.
I haven't enchanted it with loyalty yet, so it won't come back to me. I'll have to use more old-fashioned weapons, if it comes to a battle.
We want your loot. Give it to us.
Yeah. Give it to us NOW!
Or what? You three are no match for us!

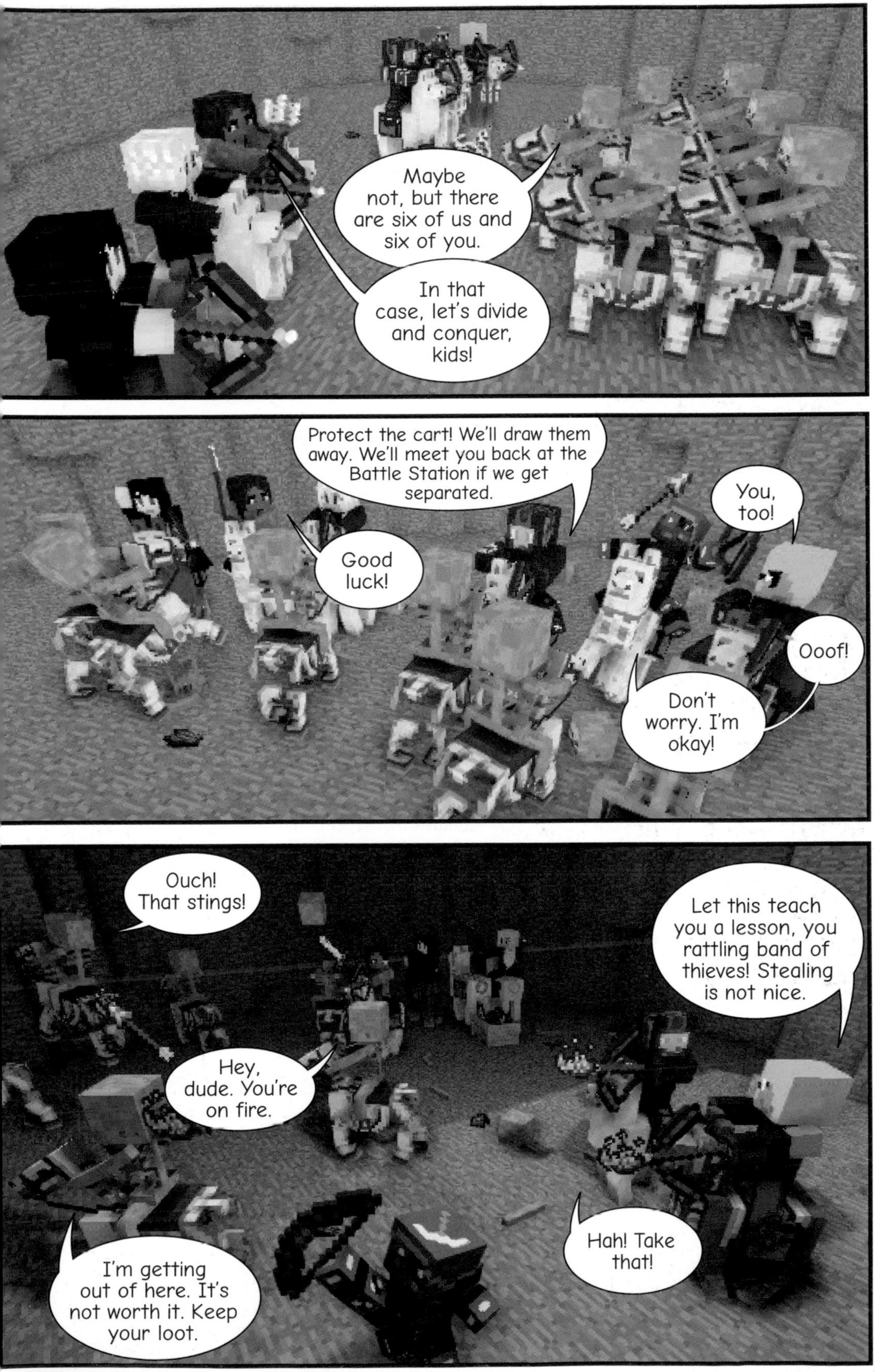
Maybe not, but there are six of us and six of you.
In that case, let's divide and conquer, kids!
Protect the cart! We'll draw them away. We'll meet you back at the Battle Station if we get separated.
Good luck!
You, too!
Ooof!
Don't worry. I'm okay!
Ouch! That stings!
Let this teach you a lesson, you rattling band of thieves! Stealing is not nice.
Hey, dude. You're on fire.
Hah! Take that!
I'm getting out of here. It's not worth it. Keep your loot.

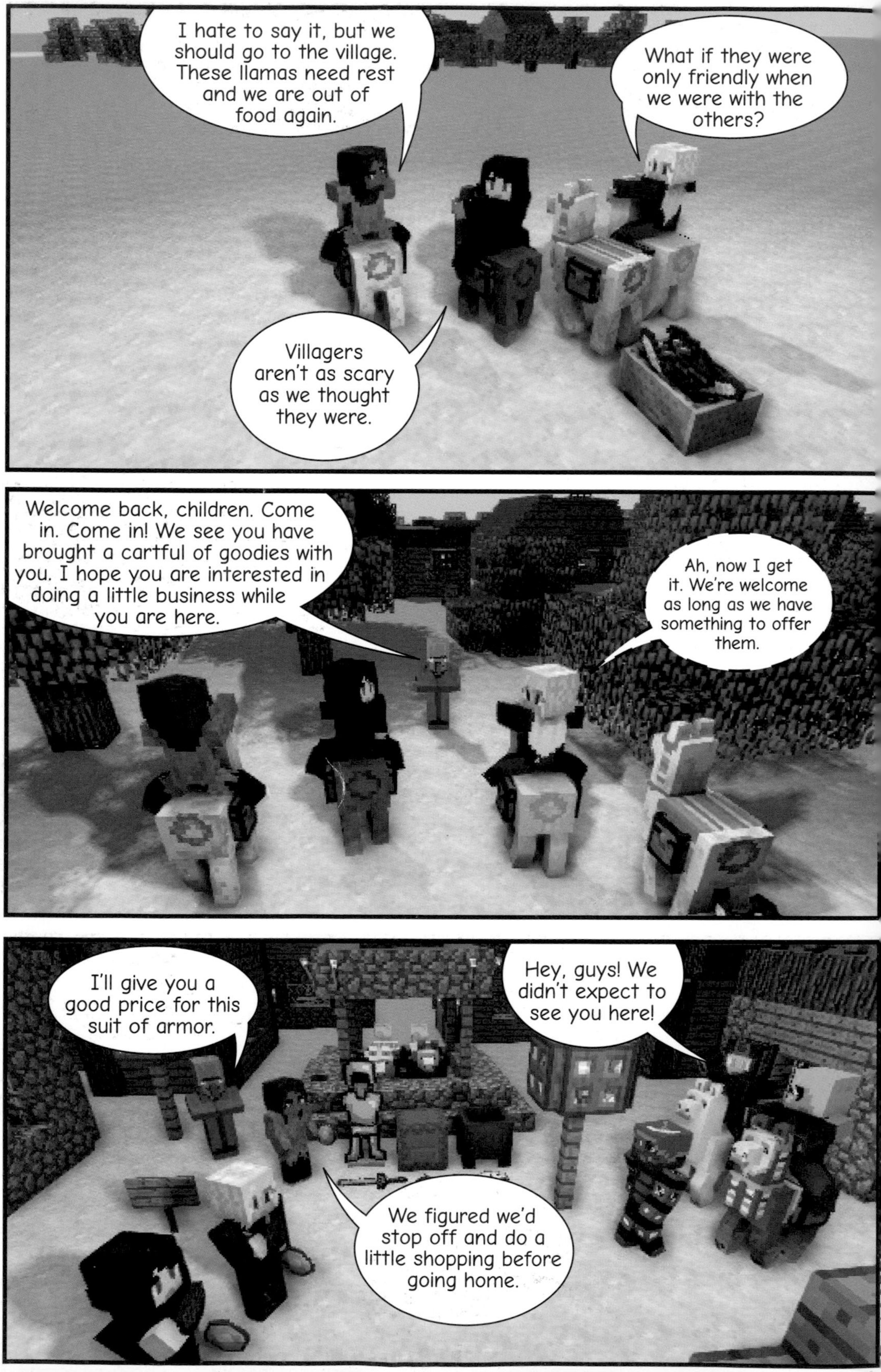
I hate to say it, but we should go to the village. These llamas need rest and we are out of food again.
What if they were only friendly when we were with the others?
Villagers aren't as scary as we thought they were.
Welcome back, children. Come in. Come in! We see you have brought a cartful of goodies with you. I hope you are interested in doing a little business while you are here.
Ah, now I get it. We're welcome as long as we have something to offer them.
I'll give you a good price for this suit of armor.
Hey, guys! We didn't expect to see you here!
We figured we'd stop off and do a little shopping before going home.

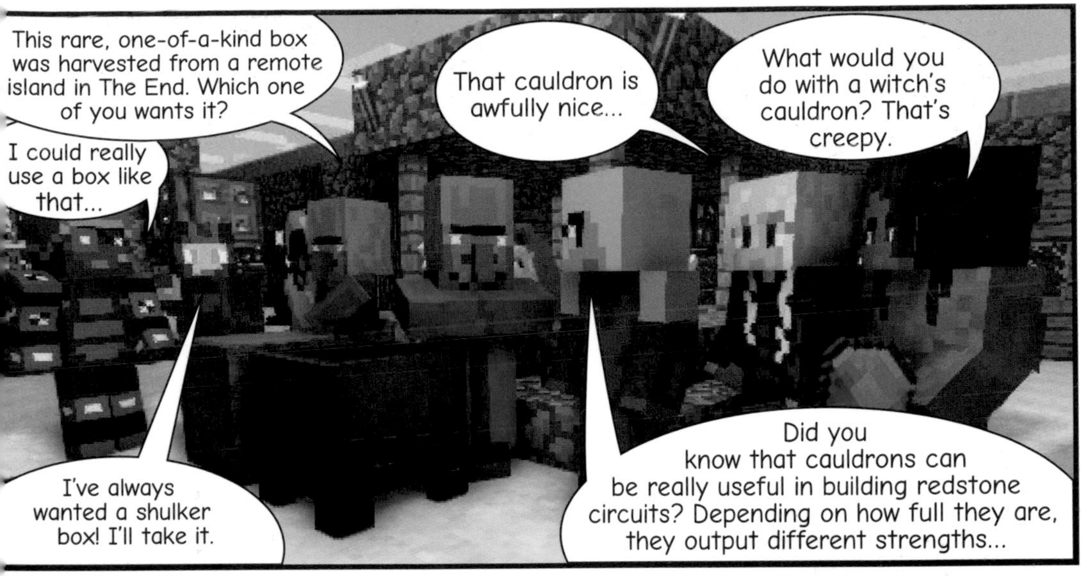
This rare, one-of-a-kind box was harvested from a remote island in The End. Which one of you wants it?
I could really use a box like that...
That cauldron is awfully nice...
What would you do with a witch's cauldron? That's creepy.
I've always wanted a shulker box! I'll take it.
Did you know that cauldrons can be really useful in building redstone circuits? Depending on how full they are, they output different strengths...
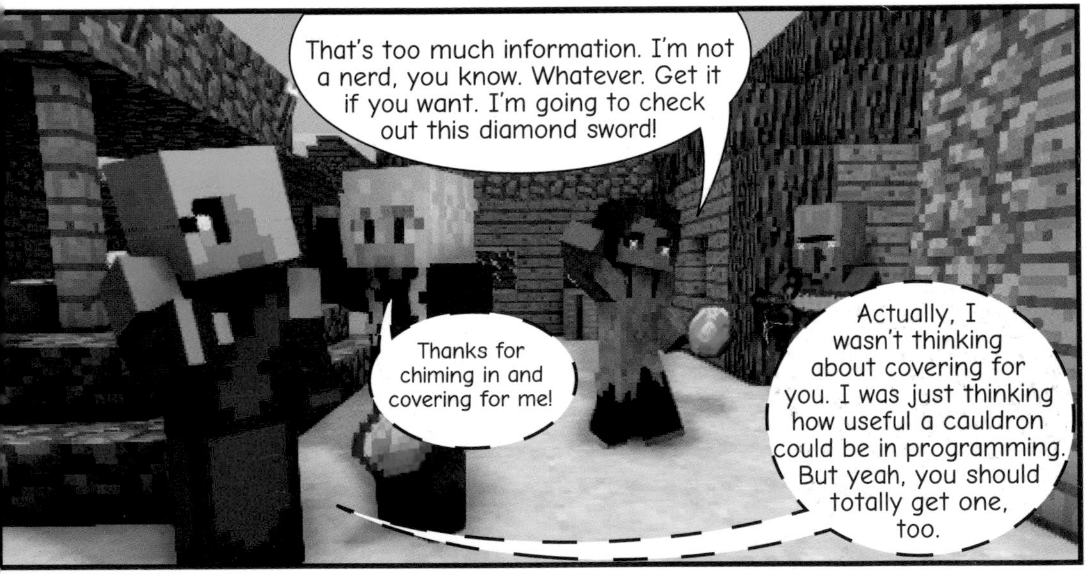
That's too much information. I'm not a nerd, you know. Whatever. Get it if you want. I'm going to check out this diamond sword!
Thanks for chiming in and covering for me!
Actually, I wasn't thinking about covering for you. I was just thinking how useful a cauldron could be in programming. But yeah, you should totally get one, too.
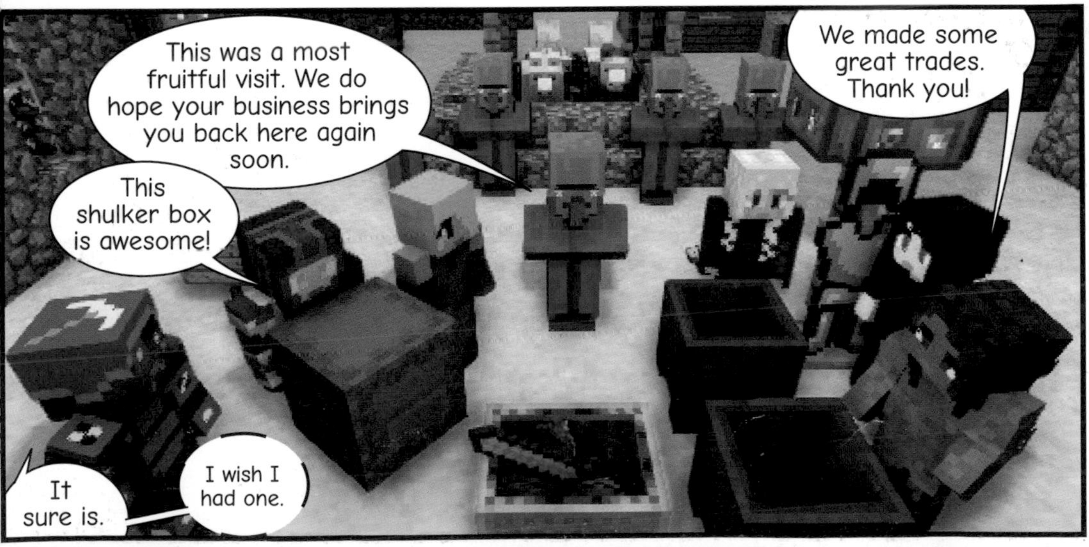
This was a most fruitful visit. We do hope your business brings you back here again soon.
We made some great trades. Thank you!
This shulker box is awesome!
It sure is.
I wish I had one.

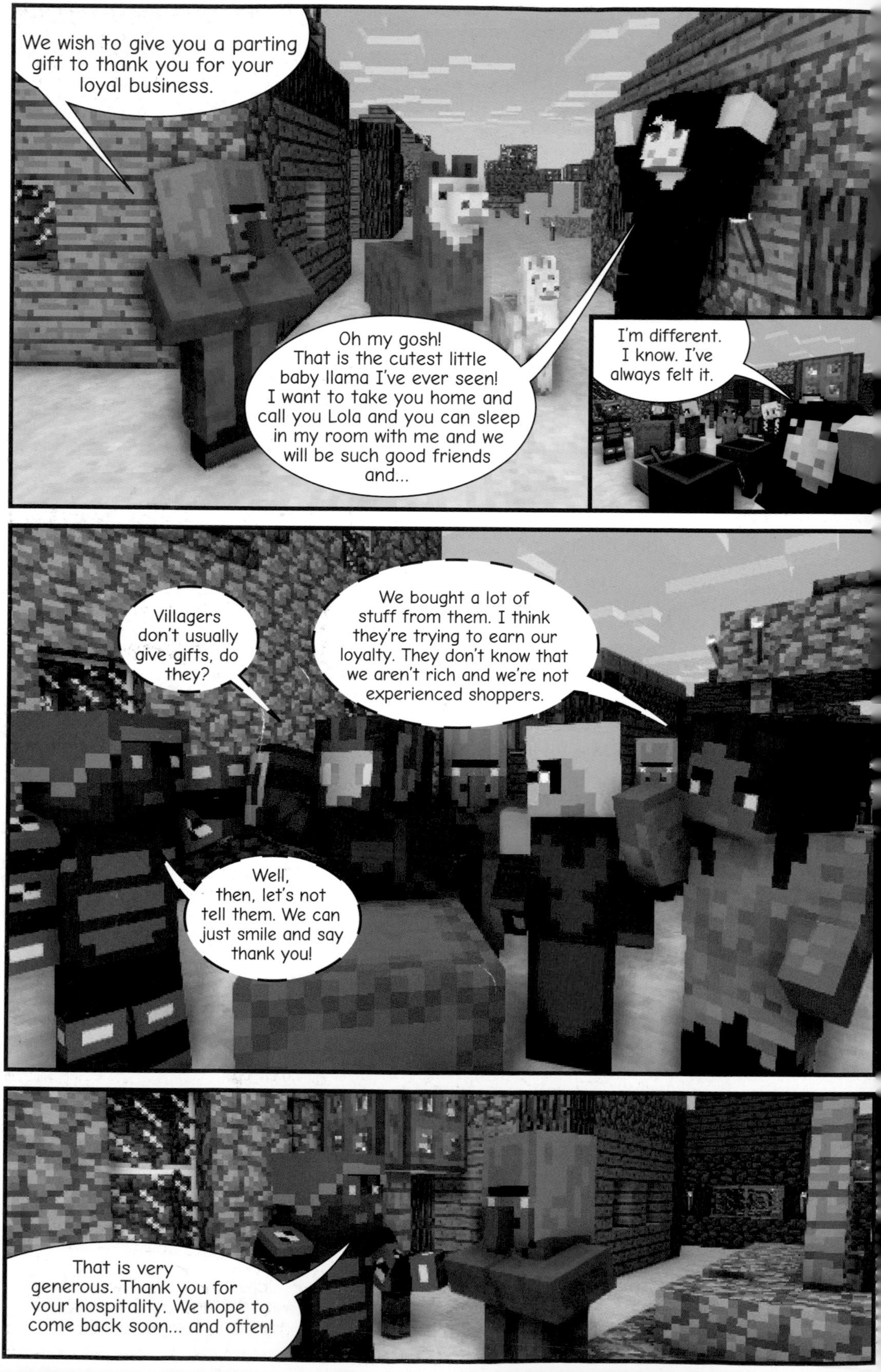
We wish to give you a parting gift to thank you for your loyal business.
Oh my gosh! That is the cutest little baby llama I've ever seen! I want to take you home and call you Lola and you can sleep in my room with me and we will be such good friends and...
I'm different. I know. I've always felt it.
Villagers don't usually give gifts, do they?
We bought a lot of stuff from them. I think they're trying to earn our loyalty. They don't know that we aren't rich and we're not experienced shoppers.
Well, then, let's not tell them. We can just smile and say thank you!
That is very generous. Thank you for your hospitality. We hope to come back soon... and often!

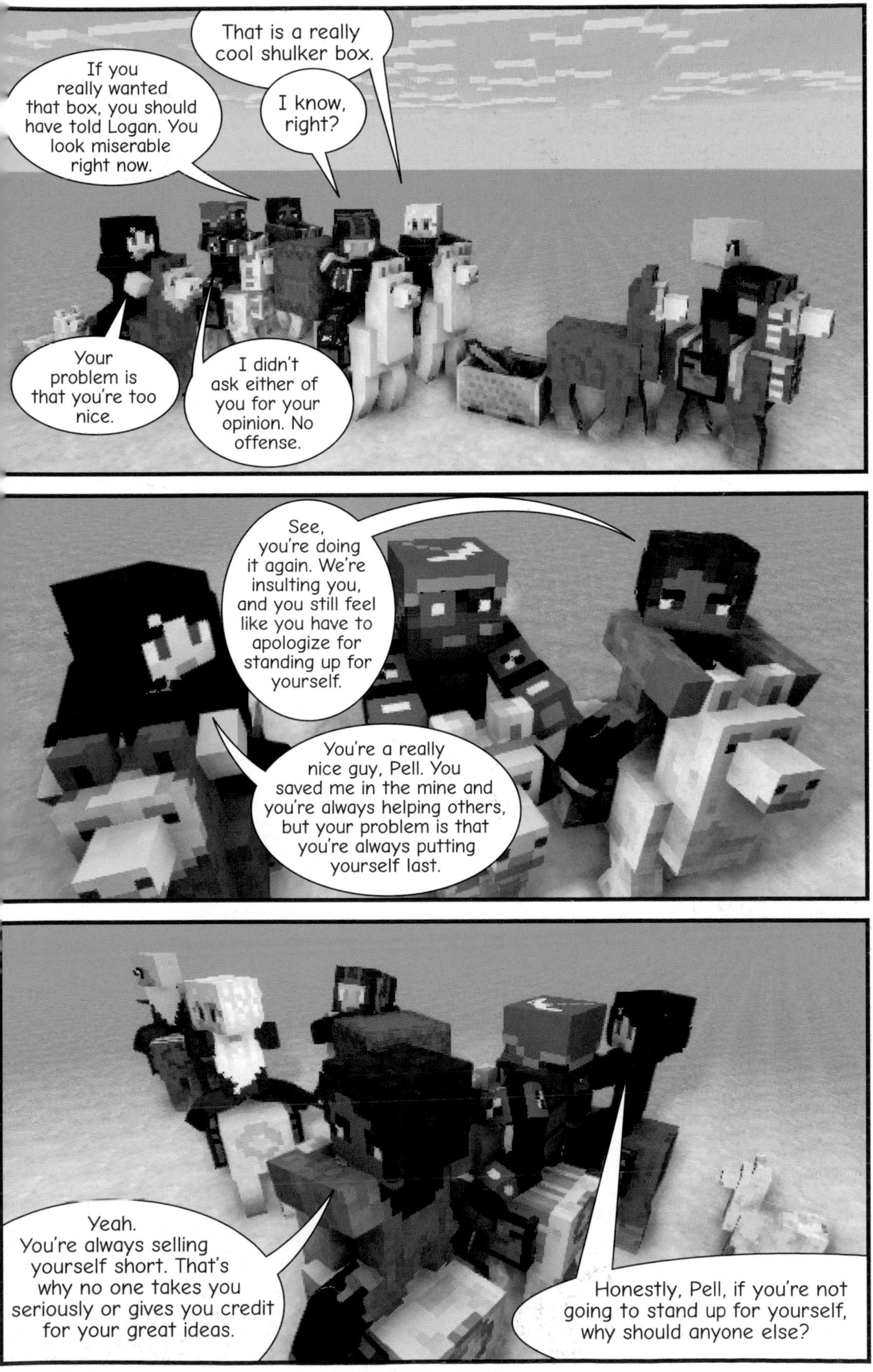
If you really wanted that box, you should have told Logan. You look miserable right now.
That is a really cool shulker box.
I know, right?
Your problem is that you're too nice.
I didn't ask either of you for your opinion. No offense.
See, you're doing it again. We're insulting you, and you still feel like you have to apologize for standing up for yourself.
You're a really nice guy, Pell. You saved me in the mine and you're always helping others, but your problem is that you're always putting yourself last.
Yeah. You're always selling yourself short. That's why no one takes you seriously or gives you credit for your great ideas.
Honestly, Pell, if you're not going to stand up for yourself, why should anyone else?

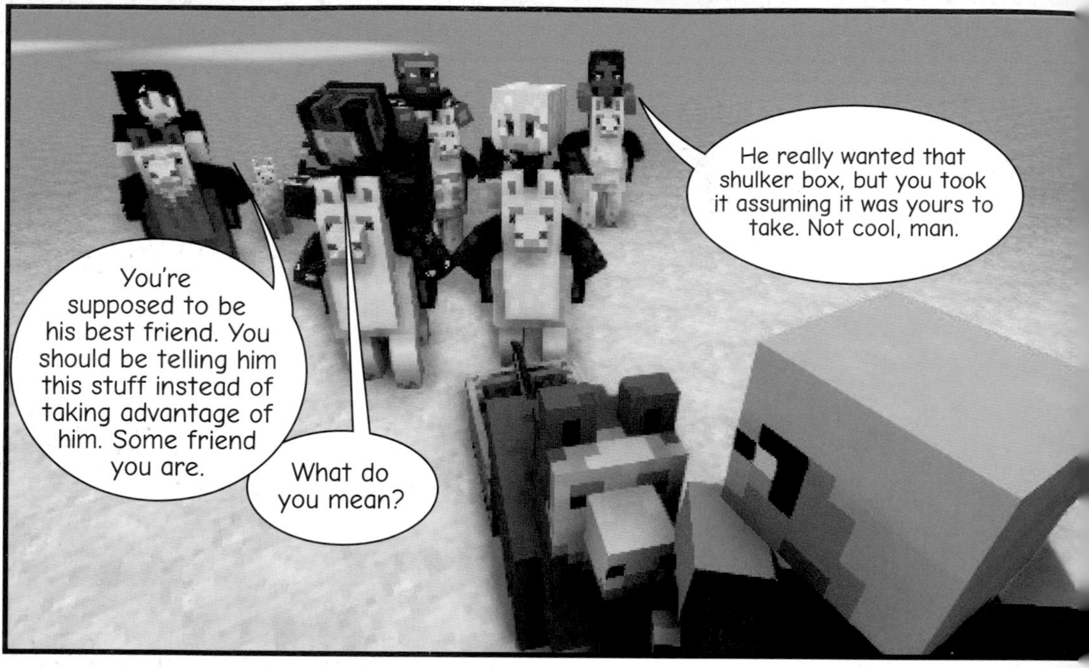
He really wanted that shulker box, but you took it assuming it was yours to take. Not cool, man.
You're supposed to be his best friend. You should be telling him this stuff instead of taking advantage of him. Some friend you are.
What do you mean?

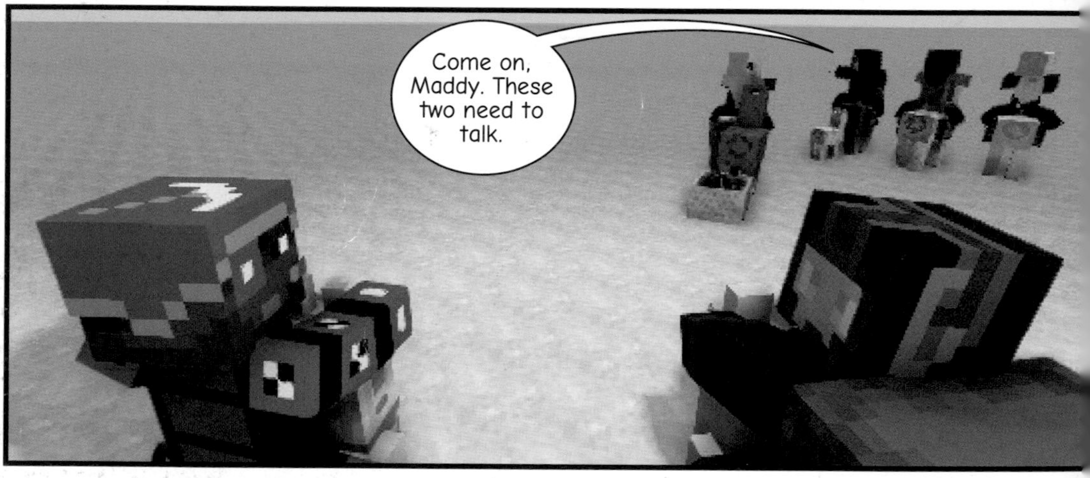
Come on, Maddy. These two need to talk.

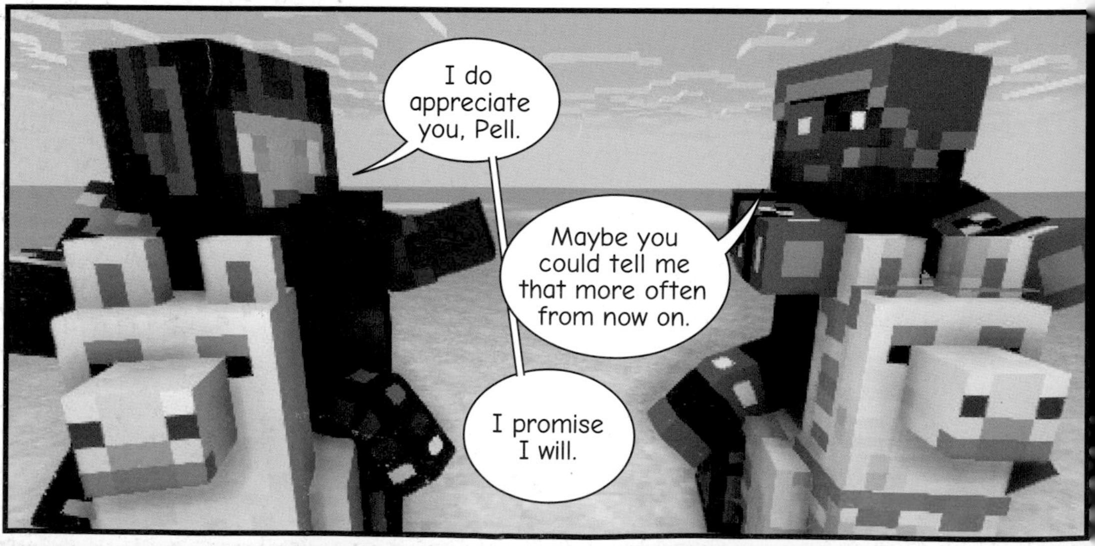
I do appreciate you, Pell.
Maybe you could tell me that more often from now on.
I promise I will.

CHAPTER 13

LOOK OUT!

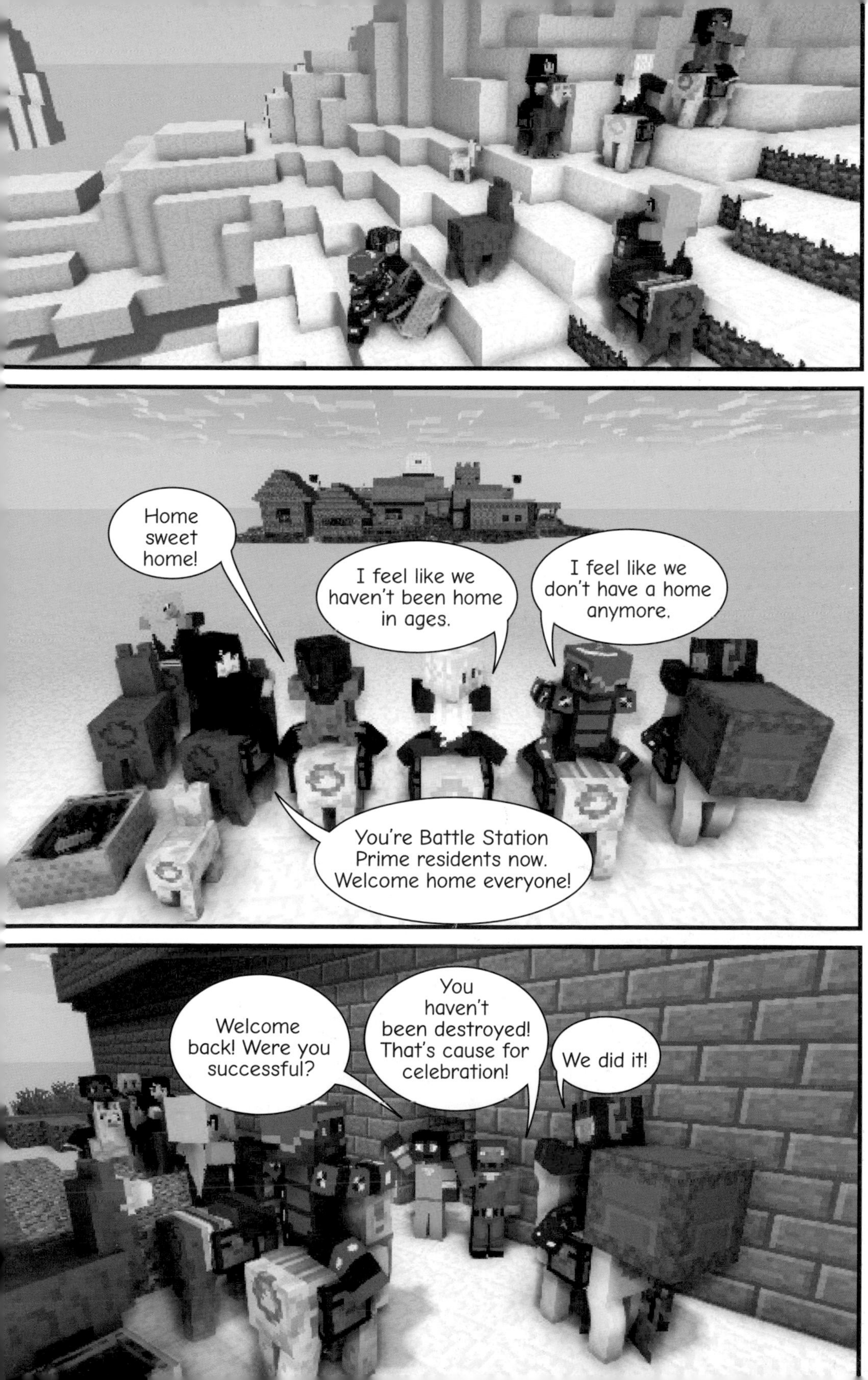
Home sweet home!
I feel like we haven't been home in ages.
I feel like we don't have a home anymore.
You're Battle Station Prime residents now. Welcome home everyone!
Welcome back! Were you successful?
You haven't been destroyed! That's cause for celebration!
We did it!

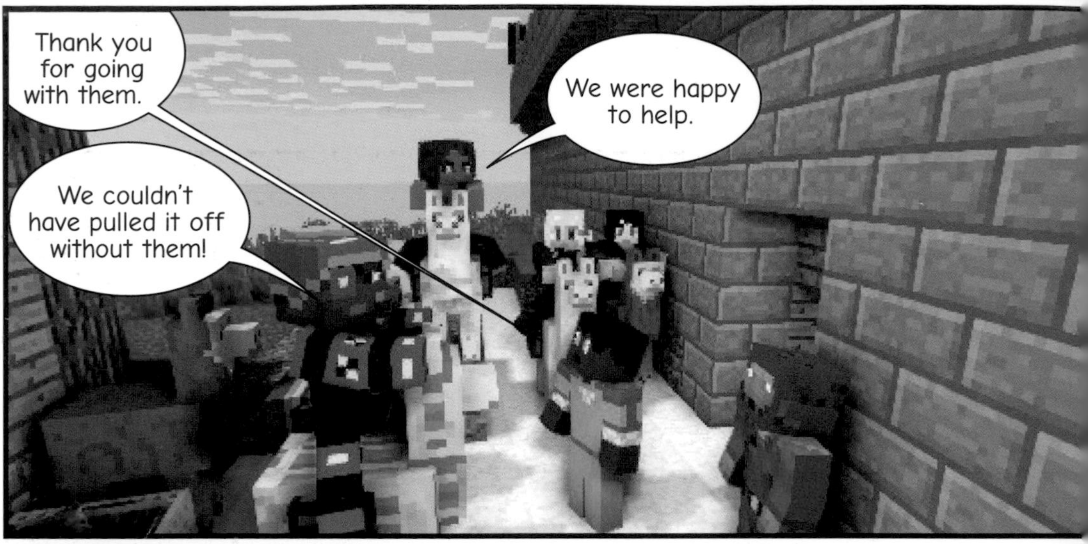
Thank you for going with them.
We were happy to help.
We couldn't have pulled it off without them!

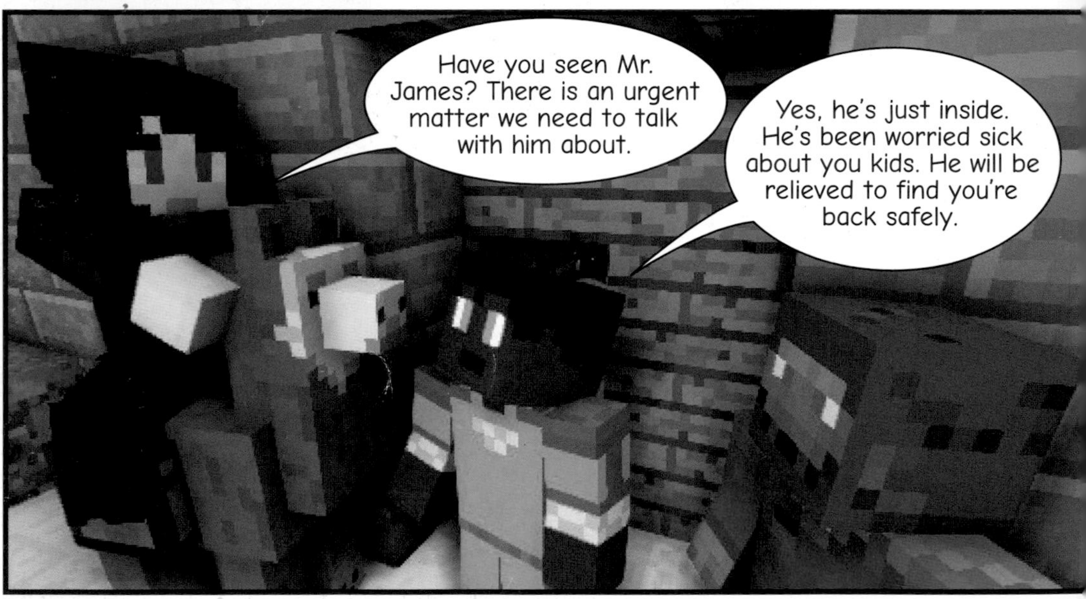
Have you seen Mr. James? There is an urgent matter we need to talk with him about.
Yes, he's just inside. He's been worried sick about you kids. He will be relieved to find you're back safely.

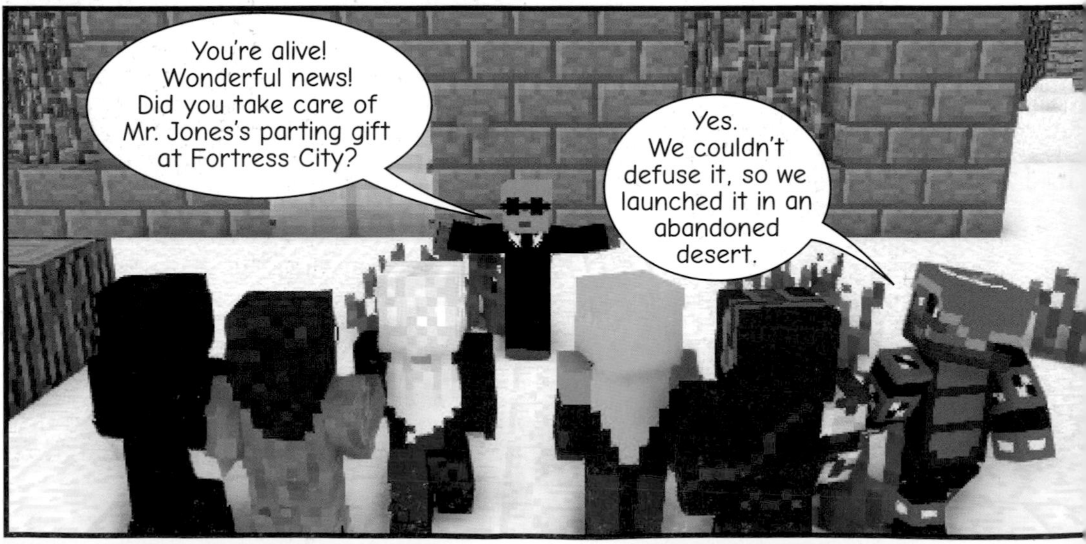
You're alive! Wonderful news! Did you take care of Mr. Jones's parting gift at Fortress City?
Yes. We couldn't defuse it, so we launched it in an abandoned desert.

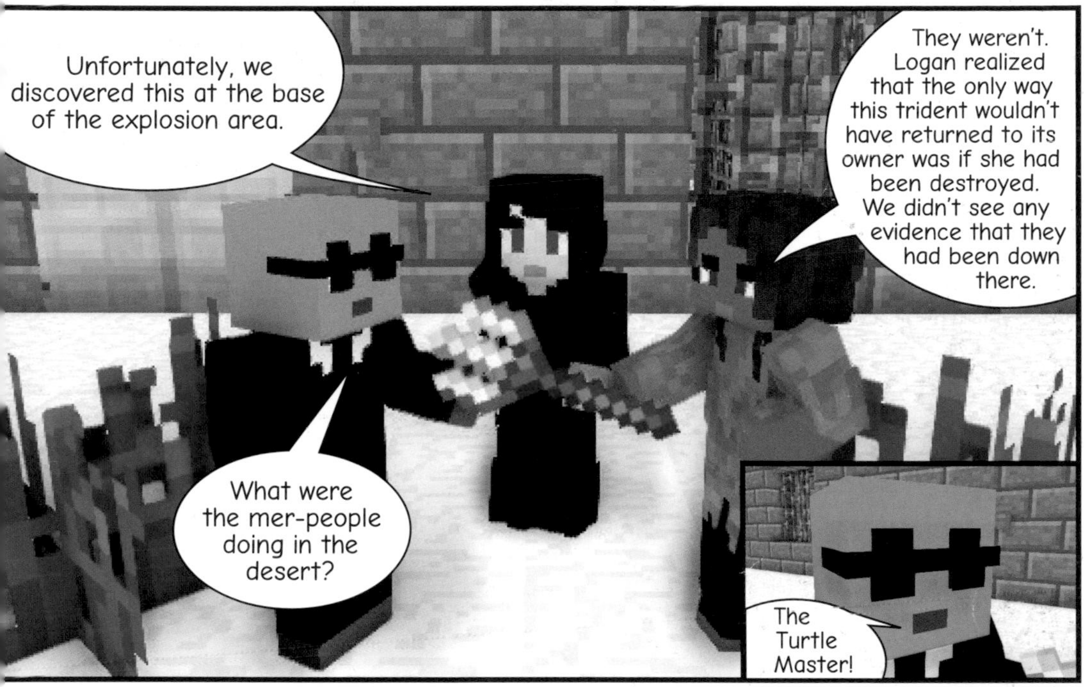
Unfortunately, we discovered this at the base of the explosion area.
They weren't. Logan realized that the only way this trident wouldn't have returned to its owner was if she had been destroyed. We didn't see any evidence that they had been down there.
What were the mer-people doing in the desert?
The Turtle Master!

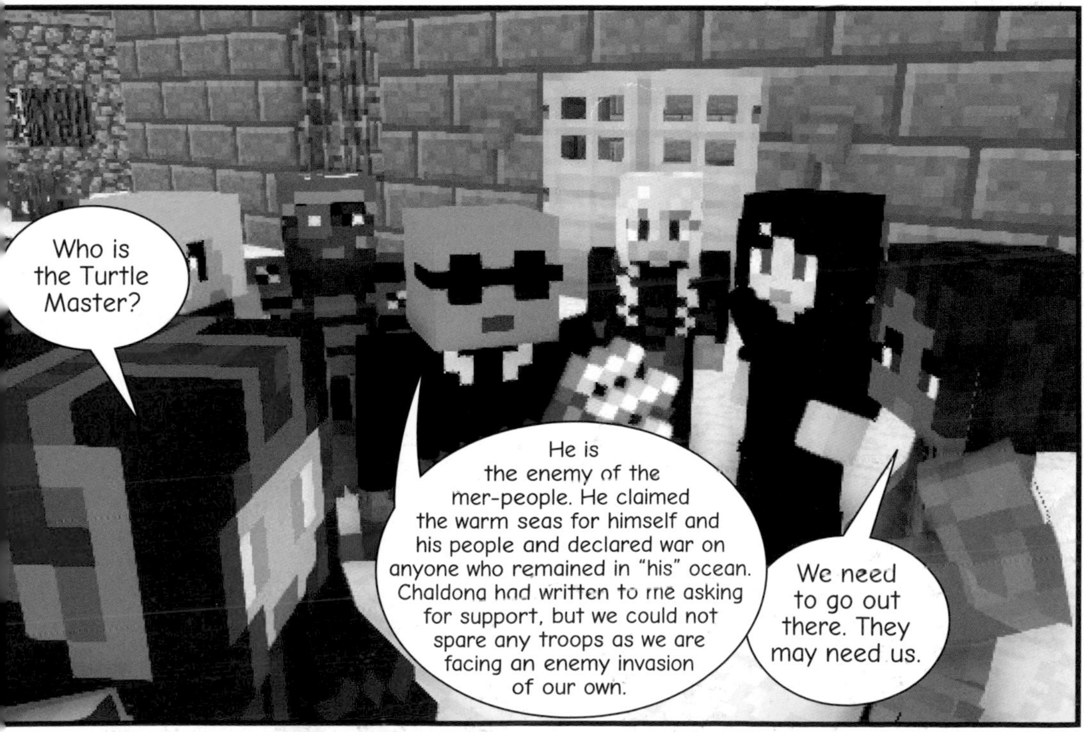
Who is the Turtle Master?
He is the enemy of the mer-people. He claimed the warm seas for himself and his people and declared war on anyone who remained in "his" ocean. Chaldona had written to me asking for support, but we could not spare any troops as we are facing an enemy invasion of our own.
We need to go out there. They may need us.

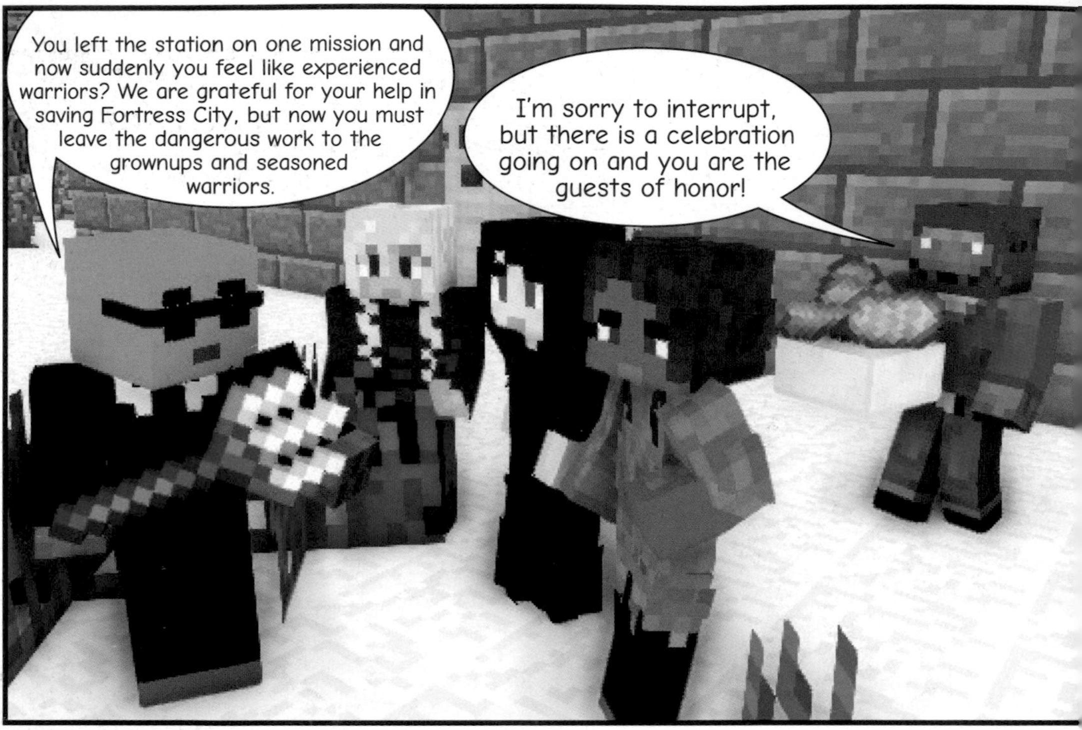
You left the station on one mission and now suddenly you feel like experienced warriors? We are grateful for your help in saving Fortress City, but now you must leave the dangerous work to the grownups and seasoned warriors.
I'm sorry to interrupt, but there is a celebration going on and you are the guests of honor!

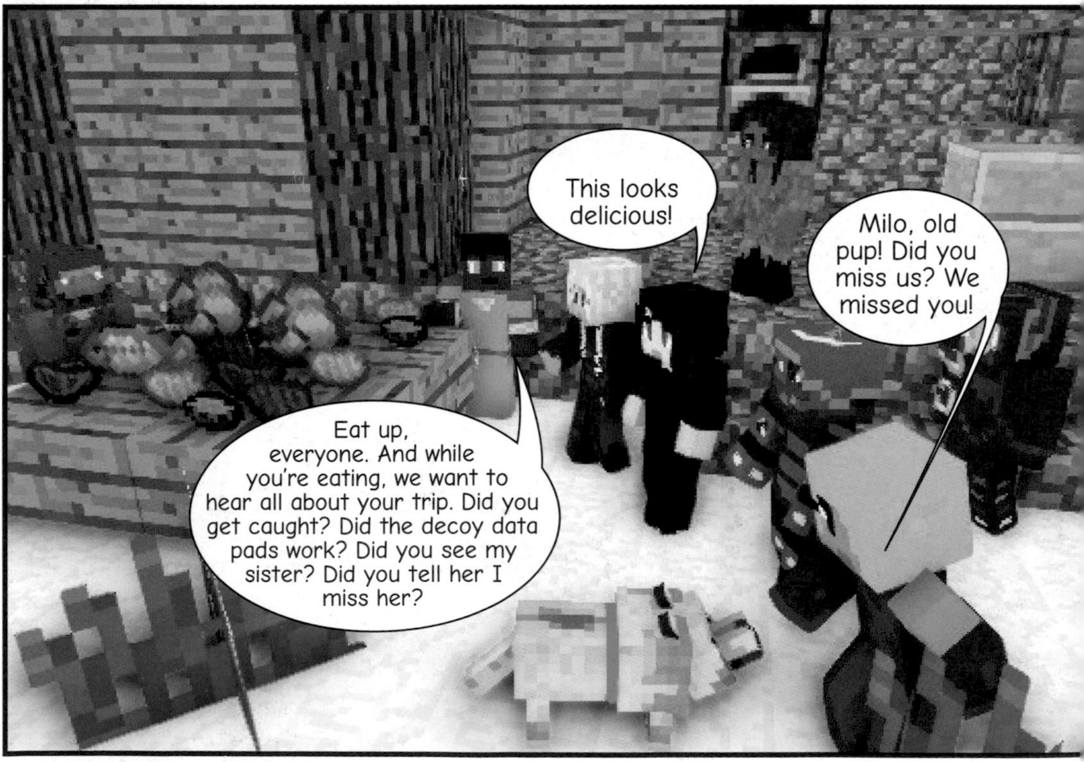
This looks delicious!
Milo, old pup! Did you miss us? We missed you!
Eat up, everyone. And while you're eating, we want to hear all about your trip. Did you get caught? Did the decoy data pads work? Did you see my sister? Did you tell her I miss her?

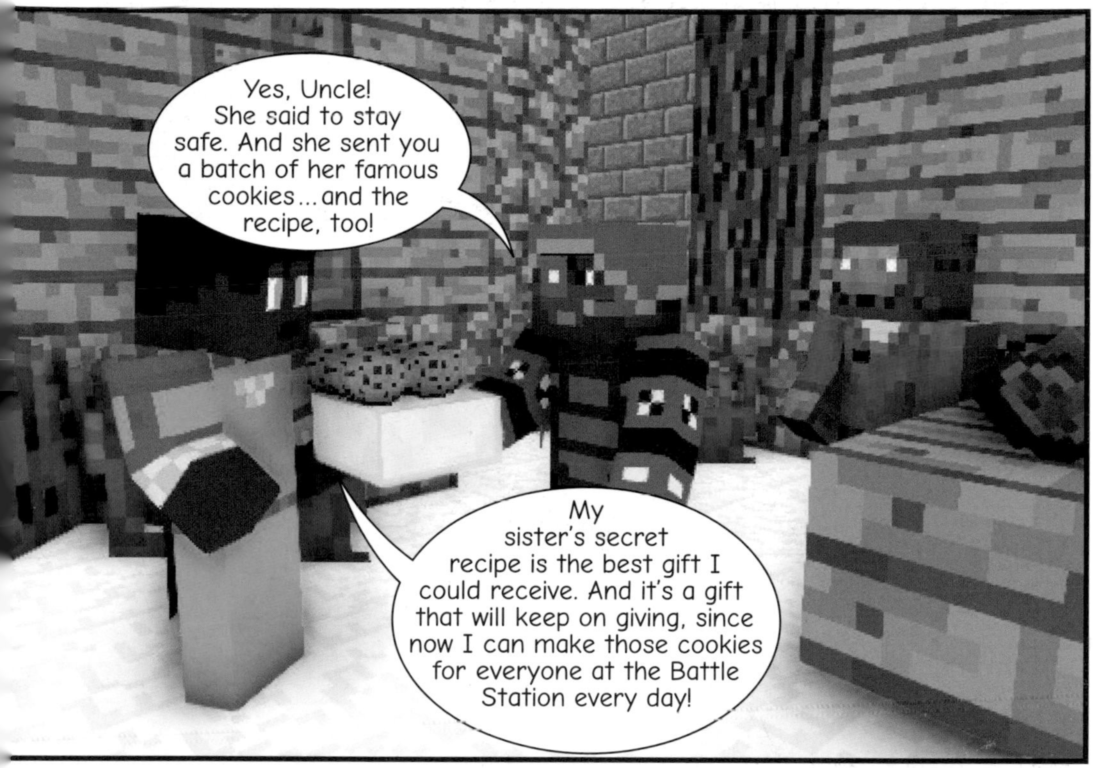
Yes, Uncle! She said to stay safe. And she sent you a batch of her famous cookies...and the recipe, too!
My sister's secret recipe is the best gift I could receive. And it's a gift that will keep on giving, since now I can make those cookies for everyone at the Battle Station every day!

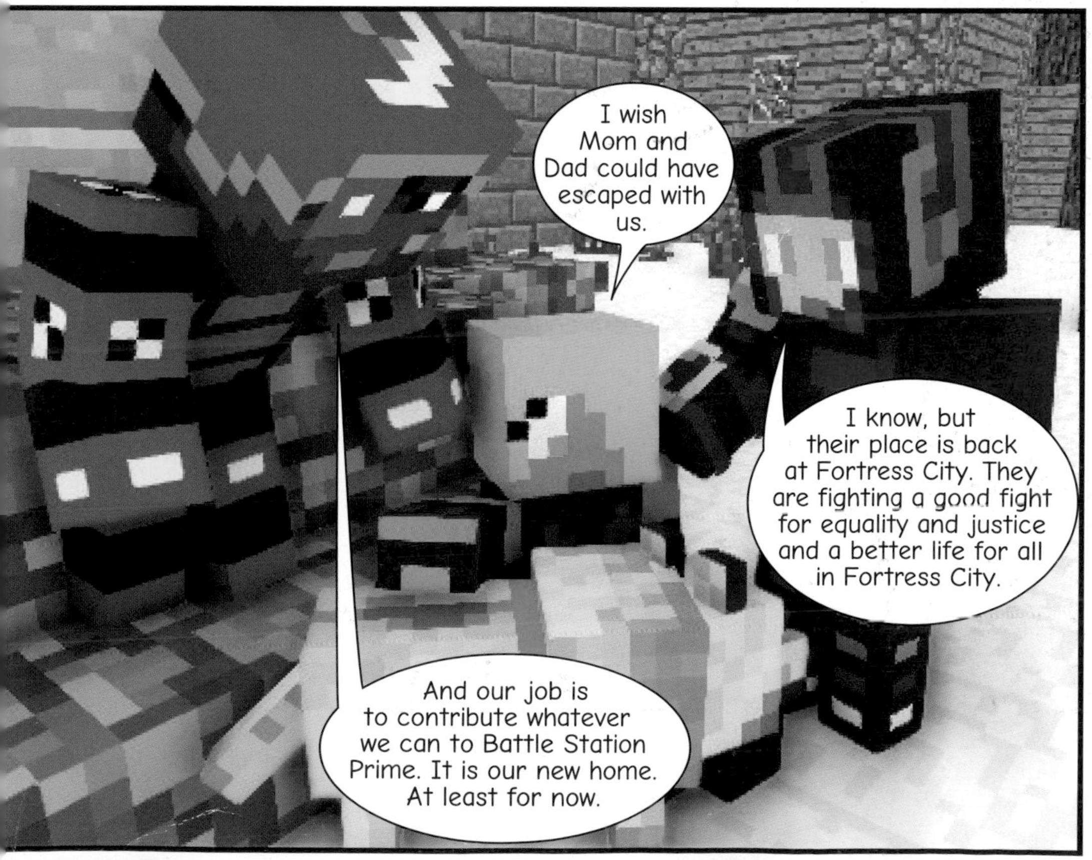
I wish Mom and Dad could have escaped with us.
I know, but their place is back at Fortress City. They are fighting a good fight for equality and justice and a better life for all in Fortress City.
And our job is to contribute whatever we can to Battle Station Prime. It is our new home. At least for now.

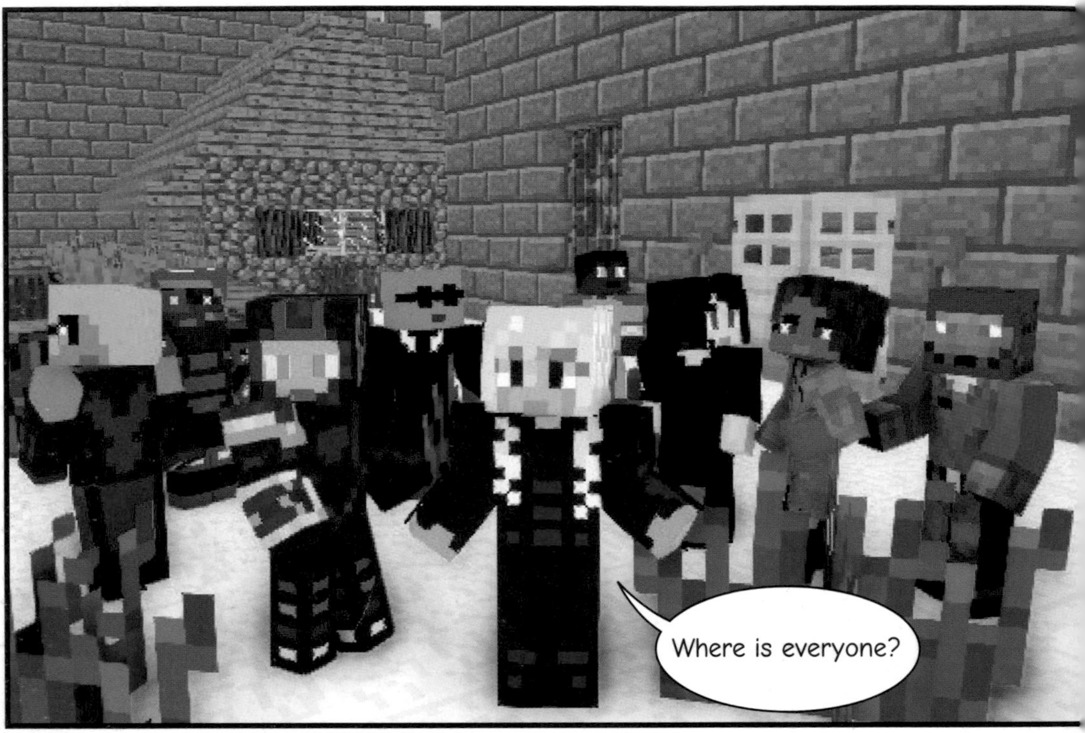
Where is everyone?

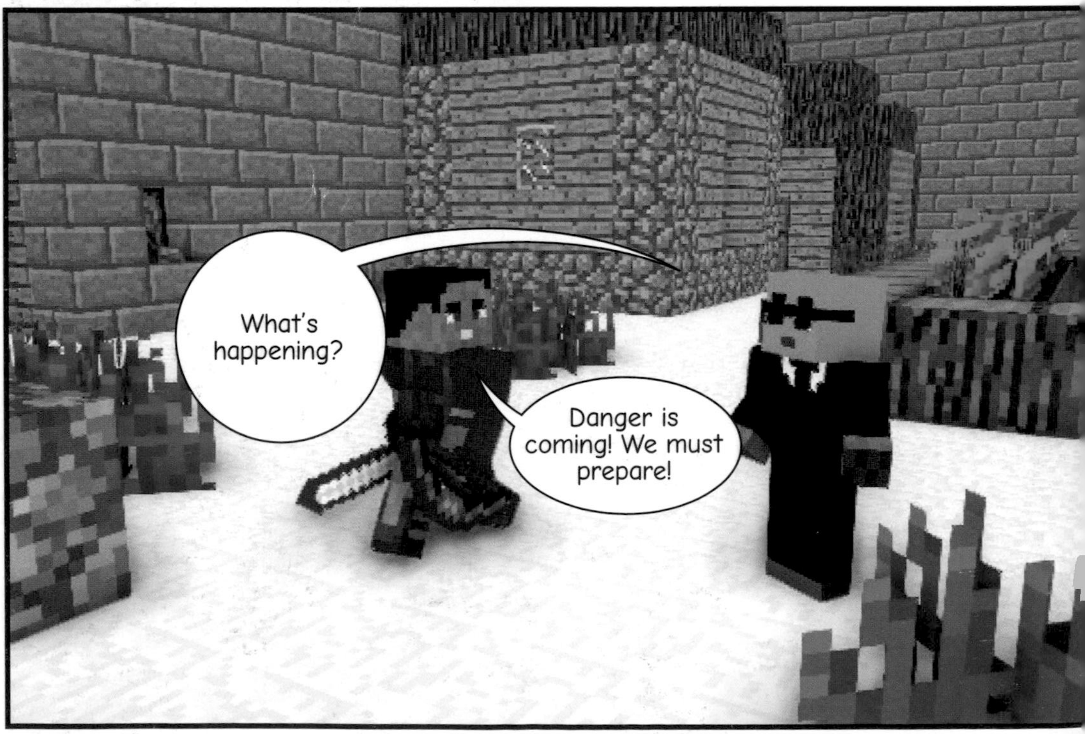
What's happening?
Danger is coming! We must prepare!

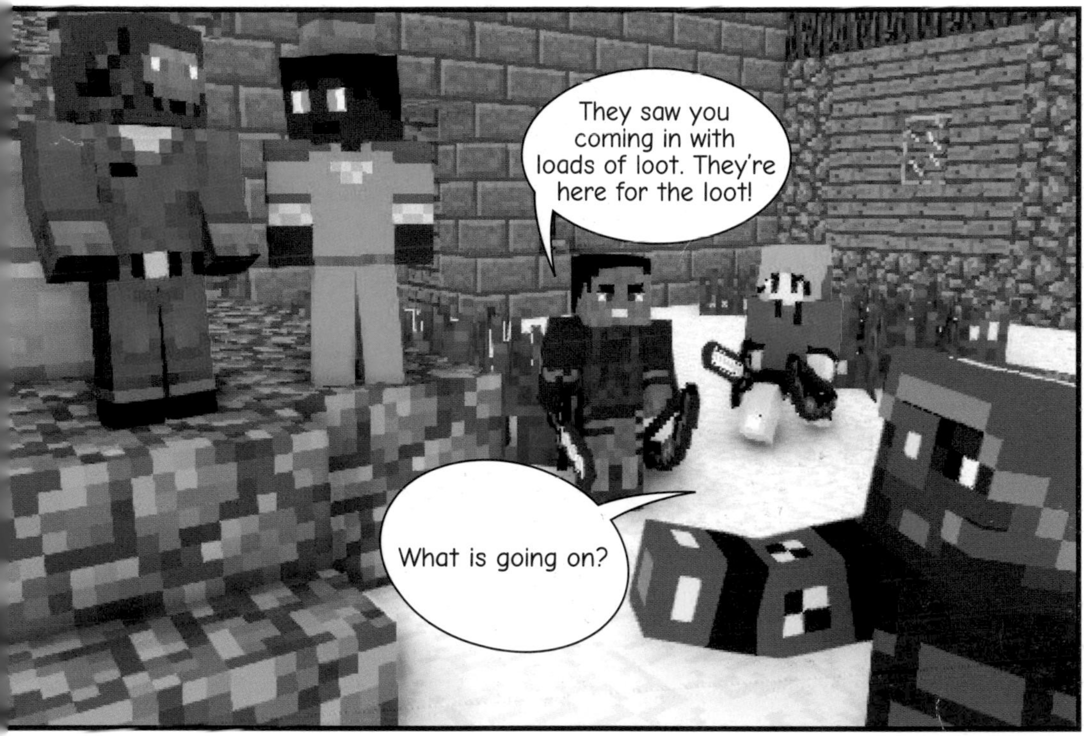
They saw you coming in with loads of loot. They're here for the loot!
What is going on?

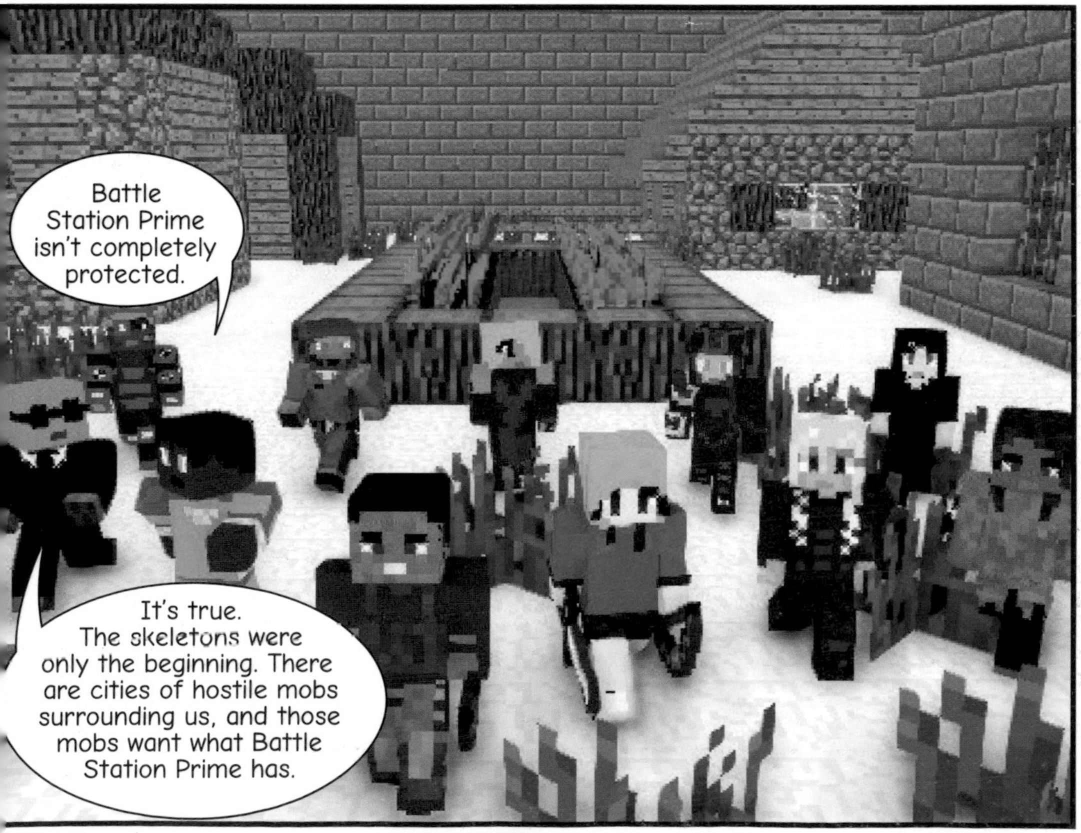
Battle Station Prime isn't completely protected.
It's true. The skeletons were only the beginning. There are cities of hostile mobs surrounding us, and those mobs want what Battle Station Prime has.

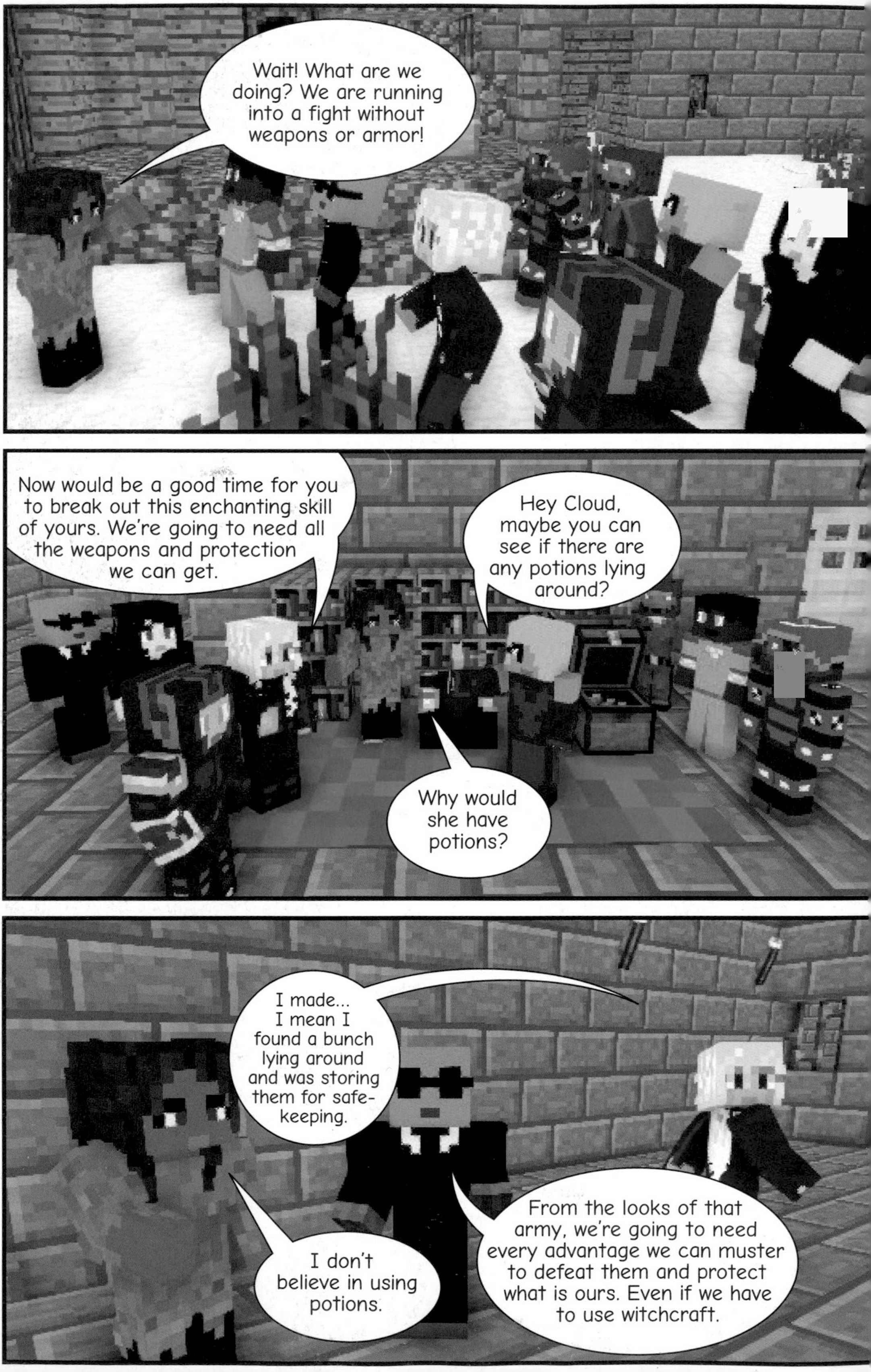
Wait! What are we doing? We are running into a fight without weapons or armor!
Now would be a good time for you to break out this enchanting skill of yours. We're going to need all the weapons and protection we can get.
Hey Cloud, maybe you can see if there are any potions lying around?
Why would she have potions?
I made... I mean I found a bunch lying around and was storing them for safe-keeping.
I don't believe in using potions.
From the looks of that army, we're going to need every advantage we can muster to defeat them and protect what is ours. Even if we have to use witchcraft.

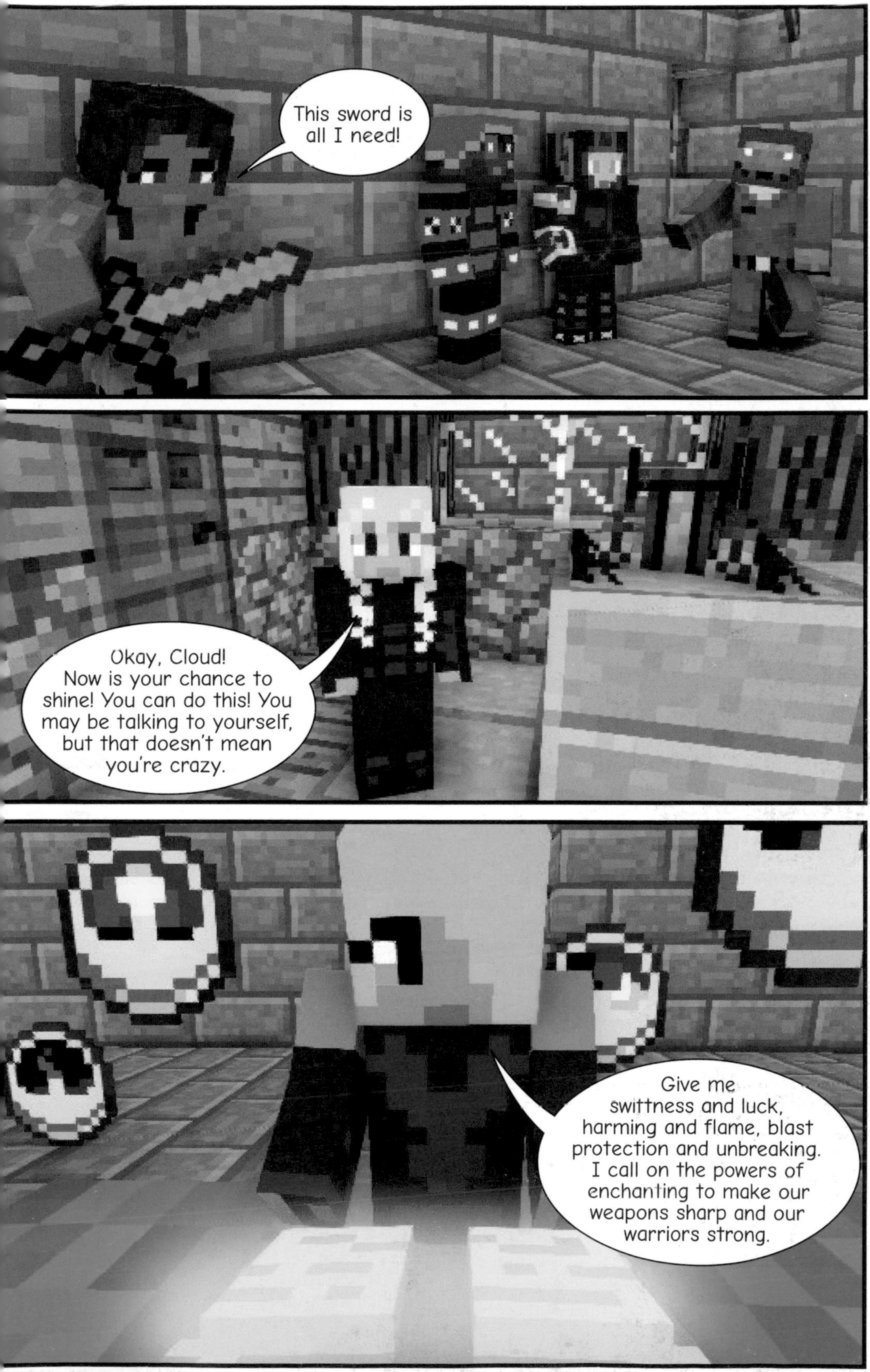
This sword is all I need!
Okay, Cloud! Now is your chance to shine! You can do this! You may be talking to yourself, but that doesn't mean you're crazy.
Give me swiftness and luck, harming and flame, blast protection and unbreaking. I call on the powers of enchanting to make our weapons sharp and our warriors strong.

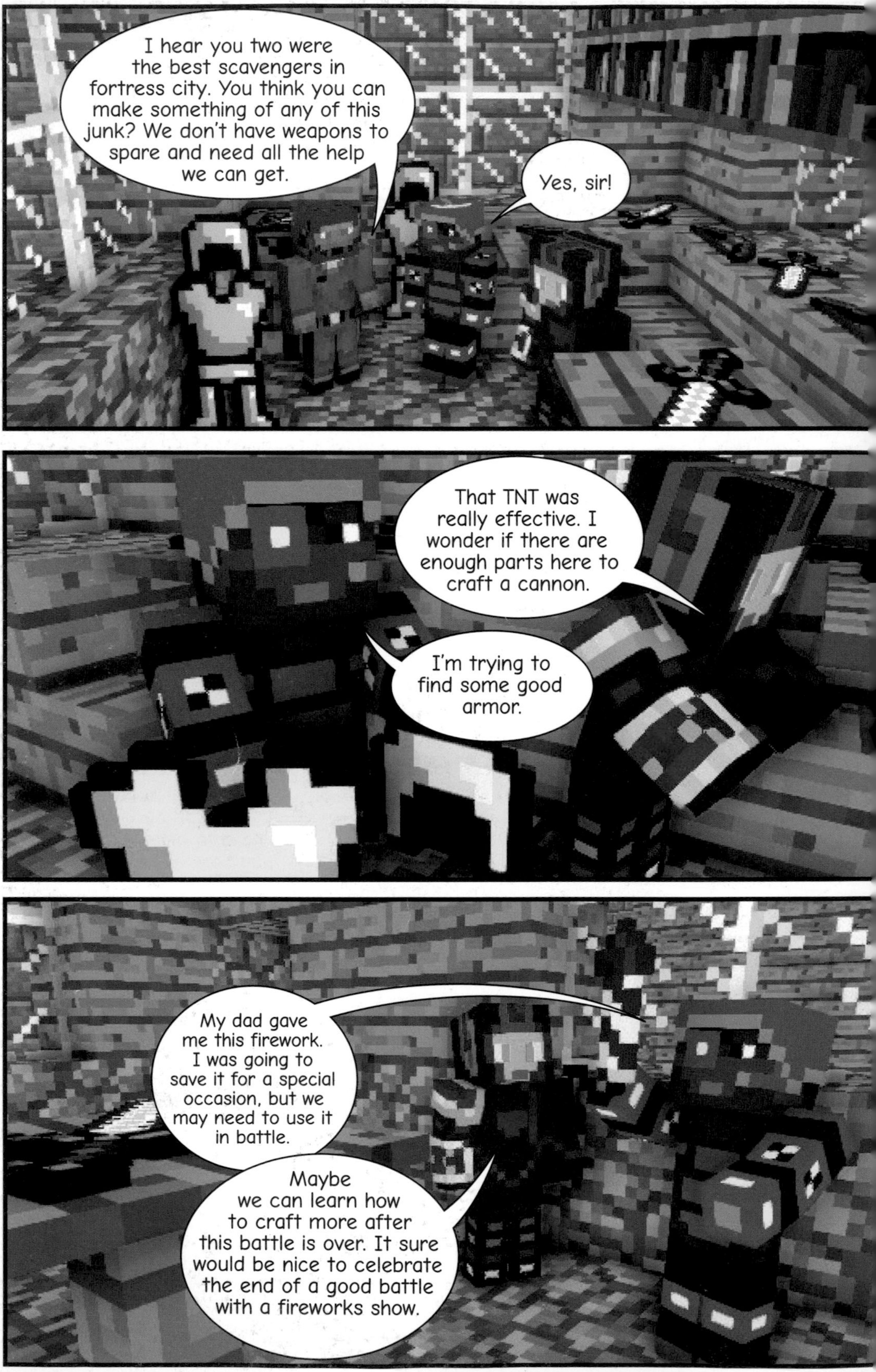
I hear you two were the best scavengers in fortress city. You think you can make something of any of this junk? We don't have weapons to spare and need all the help we can get.
Yes, sir!
That TNT was really effective. I wonder if there are enough parts here to craft a cannon.
I'm trying to find some good armor.
My dad gave me this firework. I was going to save it for a special occasion, but we may need to use it in battle.
Maybe we can learn how to craft more after this battle is over. It sure would be nice to celebrate the end of a good battle with a fireworks show.

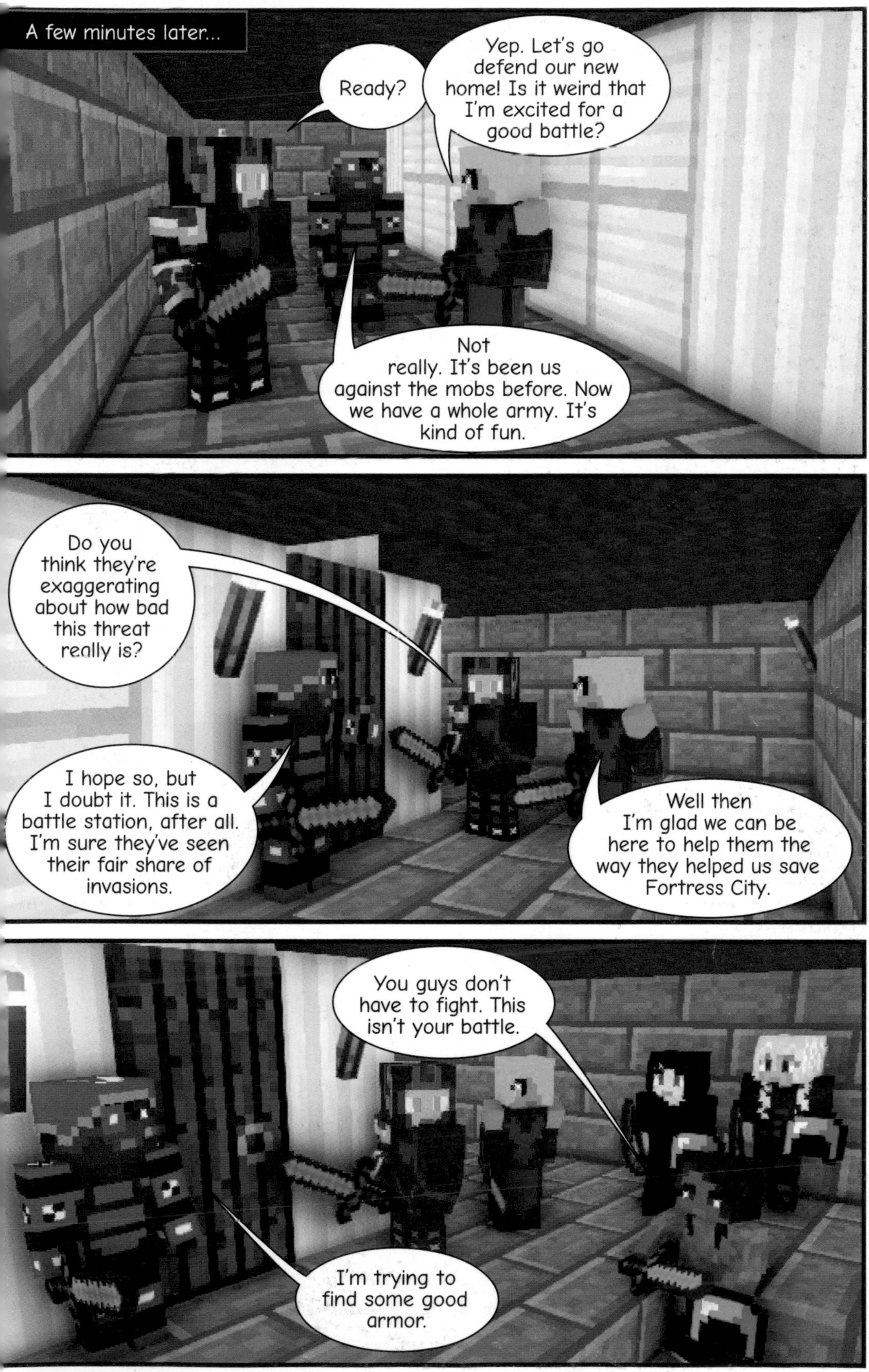
A few minutes later...
Ready?
Yep. Let's go defend our new home! Is it weird that I'm excited for a good battle?
Not really. It's been us against the mobs before. Now we have a whole army. It's kind of fun.
Do you think they're exaggerating about how bad this threat really is?
I hope so, but I doubt it. This is a battle station, after all. I'm sure they've seen their fair share of invasions.
Well then I'm glad we can be here to help them the way they helped us save Fortress City.
You guys don't have to fight. This isn't your battle.
I'm trying to find some good armor.

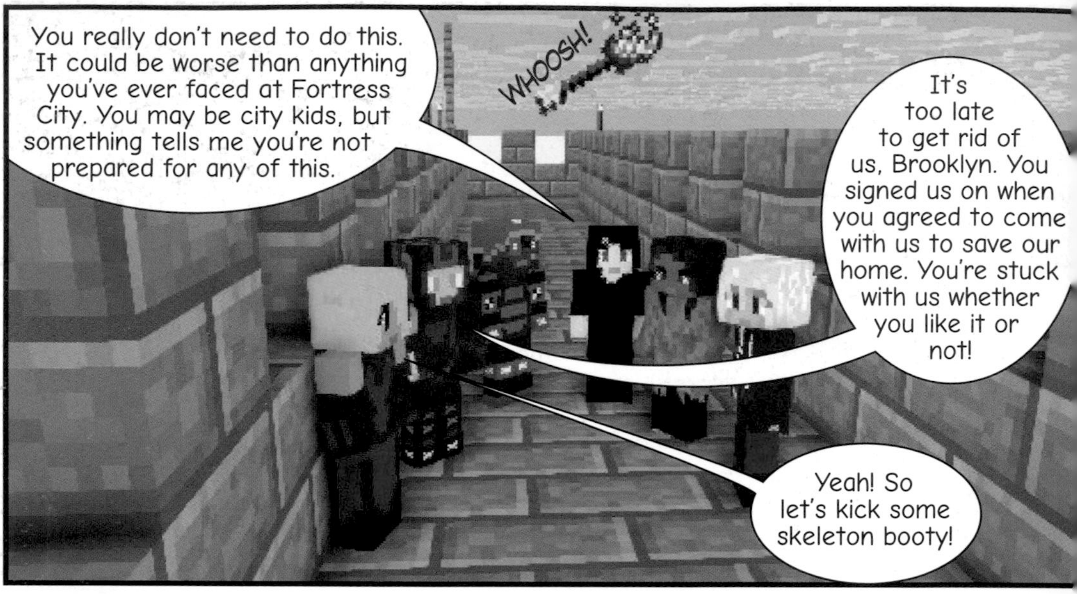
You really don't need to do this. It could be worse than anything you've ever faced at Fortress City. You may be city kids, but something tells me you're not prepared for any of this.
WHOOSH!
It's too late to get rid of us, Brooklyn. You signed us on when you agreed to come with us to save our home. You're stuck with us whether you like it or not!
Yeah! So let's kick some skeleton booty!

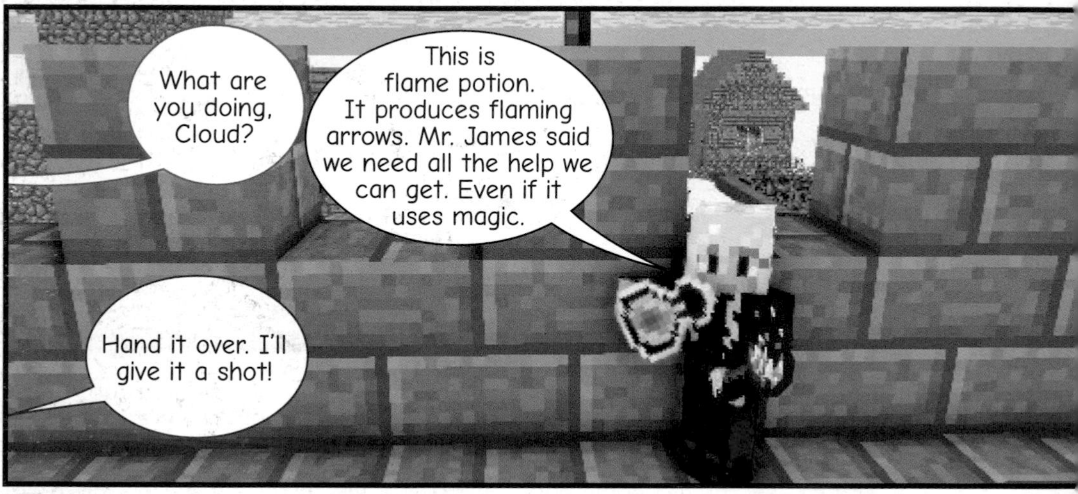
What are you doing, Cloud?
This is flame potion. It produces flaming arrows. Mr. James said we need all the help we can get. Even if it uses magic.
Hand it over. I'll give it a shot!

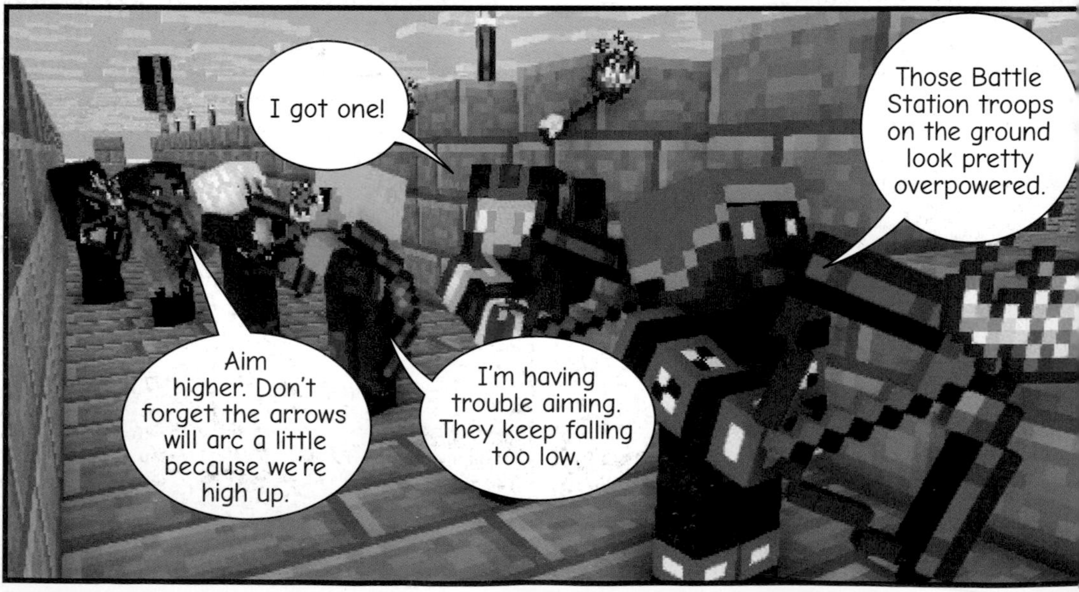
I got one!
Those Battle Station troops on the ground look pretty overpowered.
Aim higher. Don't forget the arrows will arc a little because we're high up.
I'm having trouble aiming. They keep falling too low.

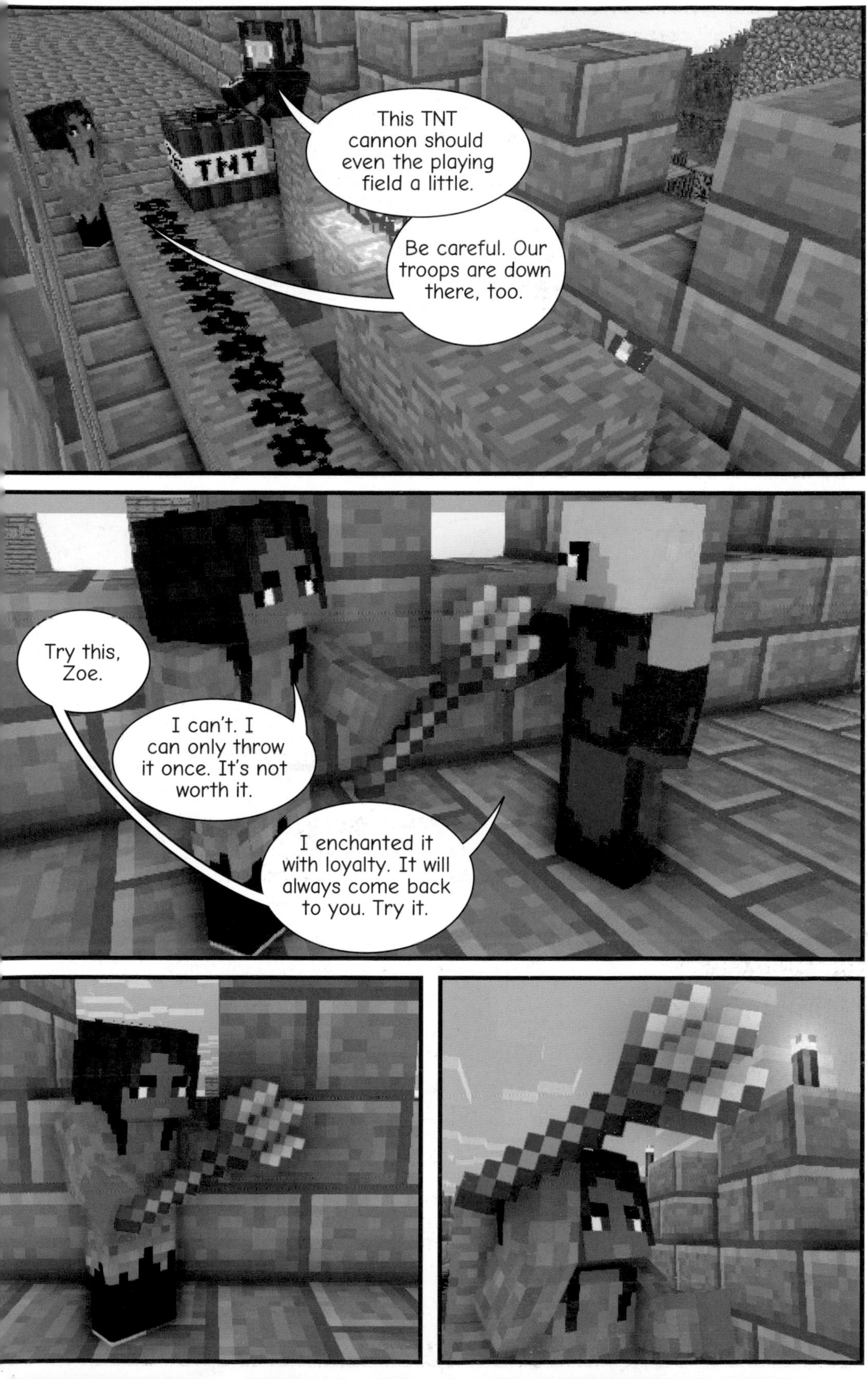
This TNT cannon should even the playing field a little.
Be careful. Our troops are down there, too.
Try this, Zoe.
I can't. I can only throw it once. It's not worth it.
I enchanted it with loyalty. It will always come back to you. Try it.

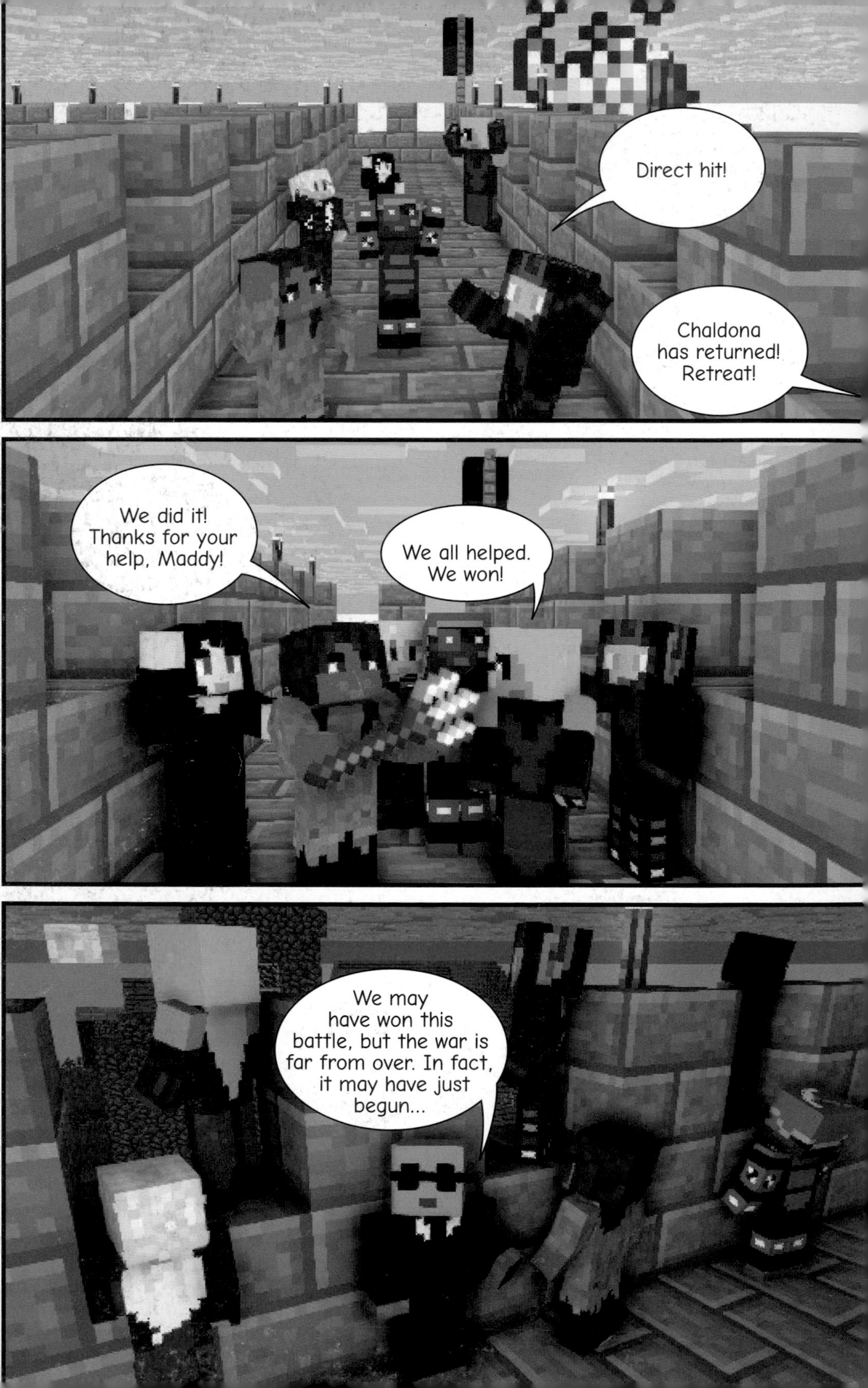
Direct hit!
Chaldona has returned! Retreat!
We did it! Thanks for your help, Maddy!
We all helped. We won!
We may have won this battle, but the war is far from over. In fact, it may have just begun...

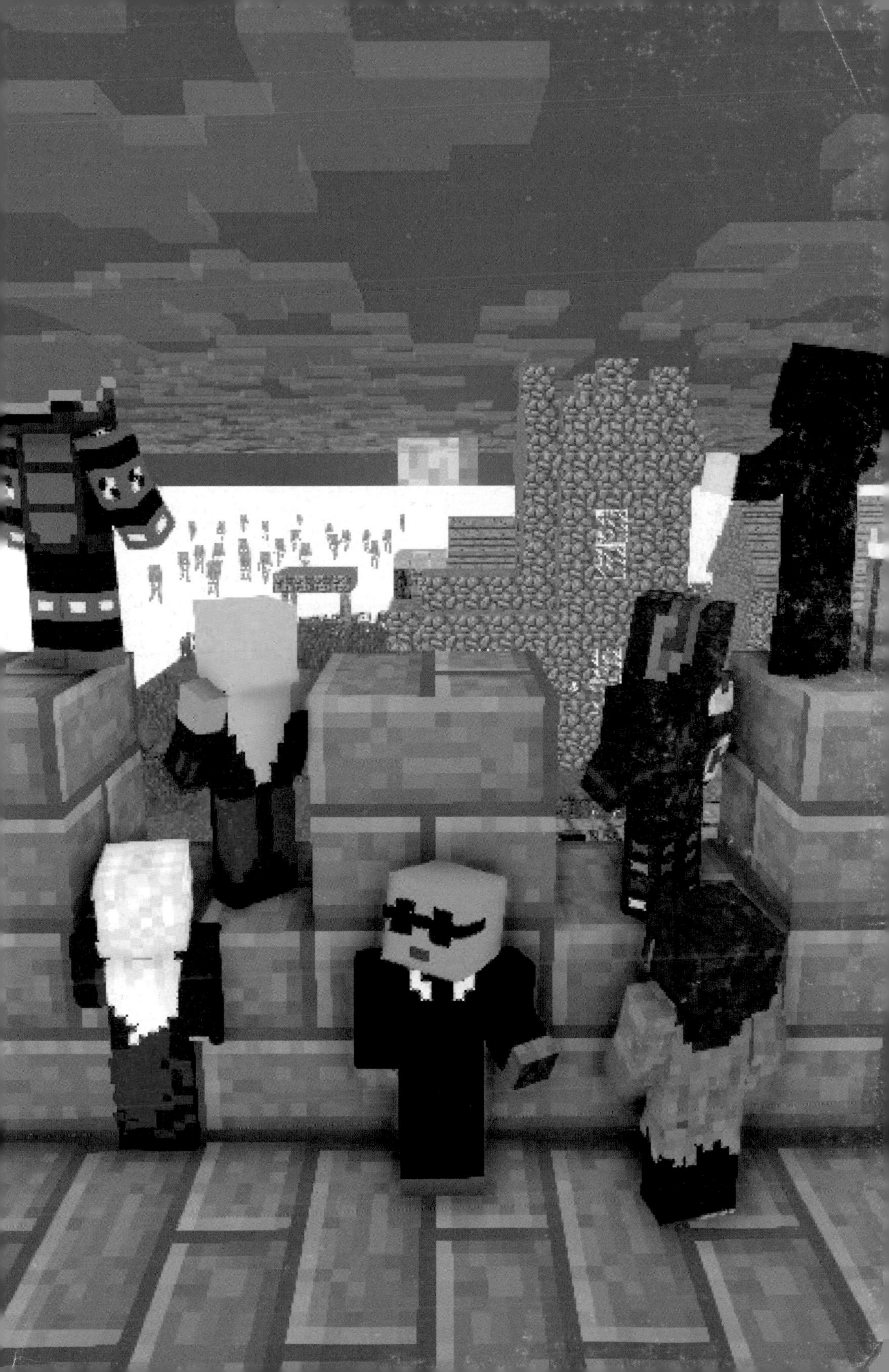